To

Bes

'KILL HIM, MARY!'

By R. J. ROBINSON

This is a work of fiction. Names, characters, businesses, places, events, locales, and incidents are either the products of the author's imagination or used in a fictitious manner. Any resemblance to actual persons, living or dead, or actual events is purely coincidental.

ISBN: 978-1-7392355-0-5

For Jake

PART ONE

CHAPTER ONE

John Stokes never saw himself as a hero. And yet, he would never turn a blind eye if someone were in distress – especially if that someone happened to be a damsel. He was perhaps a bit old-fashioned and chivalrous still in that way.

It was late one summer evening when he left the bar at the Dubai Palace Hotel where he was staying. By this time most of the other guests had retired to their rooms, and apart from the outdated atmospheric music playing in the background and the sound of a few late arrivals checking in at the reception desk, it was quiet.

Stokes was just about to enter one of the elevators in the lobby and make his way up to his room when he heard what sounded like a woman's muffled scream. It came from farther along one of the adjoining corridors where the function rooms were located. He hesitated at first, not quite sure if he was mistaken – which wasn't surprising after drinking half a bottle of scotch whisky! But then he heard it again. This time he didn't hesitate, he walked briskly down the long dimly lit corridor, passing one function suite after another, checking where the cry for help was coming from.

As he approached the last room at the end of the corridor, he could hear faint laughter coming from inside. Then, as clear as day, he heard the woman's voice repeatedly saying: 'Please, don't!' pleading with whoever was in there with her. Stokes immediately grabbed the door handle, pushed the door wide open, and entered.

Three or four metres in front of him, lying helplessly on the plush carpeted floor, with only half of her agonised face on view, was a young female Filipino hotel worker. That's because the other half of her face had a large, chubby hand over her mouth, stopping her from screaming; his other hand was busy trying to force her legs apart. The Arab's voluminous white thawb covered the rest of her petite, half-naked young body. At least some of her dignity was spared from the ogling onlooking eyes of his accomplices.

They were all standing together over to Stokes's right with their semi-erect dicks in their hands waiting for their turn. One of them was also Arabic-looking and dressed in the traditional costume; another man was dressed in a smart suit and tie and looked European, while another was wearing a high-ranking UAE police officer's uniform and seemed more interested in the other guy's dicks than he did in the girl.

'Get off her!' shouted Stokes angrily as he went to pull the huge beast off the terrified girl, stepping over her discarded panties as he did.

The fat, goatee-bearded Arab twisted his ugly sweat-drenched face around and spat out the words, 'Fuck off!'

'This is a private party,' then said a posh English voice – whose shiny gold badge read, 'Hotel Manager' – as he started to approach Stokes threateningly, 'and you're not invited!'

'Yeah, well the parties over, fuck-face!' said Stokes as he landed the back of his right fist smack-bang on his hooter, causing his head to jolt sharply backwards. The sound of breaking bone was palpable. Then as the poshly-spoken English guy impulsively reached up to check his blooded nose, Stokes swept his left leg from under him with the inside of his right foot and, with a slight push from his right palm, caused him to lose balance and go flying backwards, landing with a thud on the floor.

The Arab – the slimmer one that was standing, that is – just stood there in disbelief with his now withered dick still held firmly in his hand (probably now for protection more than anything else). A snarl from Stokes was then all it took to send him scurrying away cowering in a corner.

The floored Englishman then started to lean his head up. Stokes turned his head sharply towards him and raised his tightly clenched fist, saying: 'Don't even think about it!' to which the guy immediately lowered his head again and closed his eyes.

As for the police officer, he just stood there watching with no intention of getting his hands bloodied.

By this time, the fat Arab had given on with the attempted rape and was trying to pull himself off the poor, squashed motionless girl.

'Hey, let me give you a hand!' said Stokes as he grabbed hold of the back of the Arab's collar and yanked him off her. The Arab made a choking sound as he did, gurgling something in Arabic. Then, before the Arab was fully upright, Stokes punched him hard in the stomach, losing his fist in the folds of his flesh, and only winding him slightly. The Arab quickly responded by placing both his sweaty hands around Stokes's neck in a vice-like grip. But thanks to his martial arts training, Stokes soon freed himself and threw a right hook to his face, causing the Arab to stumble backwards and create a little distance between them.

Now, there's something most disturbing and just plain weird about facing a male opponent in a dress with a huge stiffy. Yet despite Stokes's macho-man instincts telling him not to go there, he grabbed hold of the man's Burj Khalifa and, with a vice-like grip, swung the wincing fat Arab around in a dizzying circle before releasing him and sending him tumbling backwards on top of the Englishman. Whose scream of pain now suggested his nose wasn't the only body part that was broken! The fat Arab wasn't much better off either (Stokes would admit, it was an unusual self-defence technique)!

Stokes then quickly went and knelt beside the young girl's body, placing his two outstretched fingers upon her neck, hoping to find a pulse. But there was no pulse - she was dead! She had suffocated by the Arab guy's sheer weight or his large and chubby hand covering her airways.

Stokes looked over at the fat Arab. 'She's dead!' he called out to him, horrified. 'You've *killed* her!'

No sooner had he said that he felt an intense pain at the back of his head. Then he blacked out.

Now there were two motionless bodies piled up on the floor - one was dead and the other unconscious. Standing over them with a revolver held the other way around was another man Stokes hadn't seen hidden behind the door.

When Stokes regained consciousness, he got the shock of his life - even more shocking than what he remembered happened earlier. He immediately sat bolt upright. He was sat in a pool of blood that even the luxurious shag-pile carpet couldn't soak up. The girl's throat had been slit and he was holding a bloodied knife, which he immediately dropped in despair.

His first reaction was to panic - well who wouldn't in this dire situation? But he took some deep breaths and pulled himself together as best he could. Panicking right now was not going to help him. His tours of duty in Afghanistan had at least taught him that.

His head still hurt, and he could feel it was swollen but couldn't tell whether any of the blood on his hands was his or all from the girl. But having a sore head was the least of his problems right now!

A glance around the room convinced him that the perpetrators had all since left - which was at least some relief. But it didn't take him long to figure out that he was being framed for her murder. His DNA was all over the place. And when the authorities finally got round to checking the security video footage, any evidence of the real perpetrators being present would've been edited out, and the footage showing his unmistakable European features entering the room shortly before the murder took place would remain. John also had a very distinctive tattoo of a Royal Marine Commando dagger on his inner right forearm.

The court prosecutor would claim that he got blind drunk (partially true) and then attempted to rape a female hotel member of staff before murdering her! And no one was going to believe his side of the story. Basically, he was fucked!

Thinking quickly, Stokes stood up, being careful not to step in the blood. Then promptly wiped the blood from his hands onto the back of his trousers which, if he got the chance, would burn along with his blood-stained shirt later.

The blood hadn't yet congealed, so he couldn't have been unconscious for very long (the steel plate in the back of his head because of a war injury had no doubt helped!). The perpetrators clearly hadn't taken this into consideration, otherwise he would have probably been cuffed and arrested by now. Which could buy him some precious time to make his escape he thought. But he knew that as soon as they had covered their tracks and worked out their alibis together, a member of staff would be sent unwittingly along to discover the crime scene. It made Stokes wonder how many other poor young girls had fallen victim to their wicked ways.

He had tried to help a damsel in distress, but who was now going to help him? He needed a change of clothes, as he couldn't very well just step out into the corridor and make his way back to his room covered in blood. He was bound to be seen. He quickly reached into his hip pocket and pulled out his tiny, now considered unfashionable, mobile phone and phoned his friend and boss, Steve Reynolds, who lived nearby. When he looked at the time, it was approaching 02:00 AM.

He hadn't known Steve all that long, but in the twelve or so months he had worked out there as a petroleum engineer, they got on very well together and had built up a good trustful friendship with one another. They also had a lot in common: both ex-military; both 37 years of age; both 6′6, and well-built; both had once lived in Royal Tunbridge Wells, Kent; both liked a drink; both mad football supporters; and both tough as fuck! Though, Steve was the better looking out of the two and the one with the most charm and charisma – especially when it came to the ladies. And didn't he know it (you know the type: smooth-talking, even features, square jawline, full head of hair, and someone you just want to punch in the face! Though, you'd think twice about it with this guy).

The phone just kept ringing for a while. 'Pick up, pick up,' Stokes kept saying into the mouthpiece. He then changed it to: 'Come on, come on!'

'John, what the fuck are ya ringing me at this ungodly hour about – I was getting my beauty sleep before you woke me up! And unless you've got a damn good excuse like going out partying, I'm not fuckin' interes—' babbled on John's friend before being interrupted.

'Steve, just shut the fuck up and listen!' said John with understandable urgency in his voice. 'Something awful has happened, and I need your help!' There was a moment's silence. 'I'm being framed for murder!'

'Murder!' exclaimed his friend in shocked surprise.

'It's a long story and I don't have time to explain it now.'

'Where are you now?' asked Steve.

'I'm at my hotel,' John quickly answered. 'I'm in the Princess something or other function suite, I think. It's the one down at the far end of the corridor. I'm covered in blood, and I need you to bring me a change of clothes and something to put my stained clothes and the murder weapon in!'

'A bag?' suggested Steve.

'Yeah!'

'Oh, my days! *Fuck!* Okay, hang tight, mate. I'll be there as soon as I can!'

'Hurry, the cops will be here any moment!'

Steve promptly ended the call and quickly got dressed. Then grabbed his sports bag, chucked it on the bed, fetched a pair of slacks and a polo shirt from his wardrobe and shoved them inside.

'Where are you going?' said a woken broken-English female voice from under the satin sheets of his Queen-size bed.

'I've gotta go out, babe,' answered Steve, still half asleep.

'Out? Where?' she said, surprised.

'Don't cha worry your pretty little head, Suzie,' he

said as he hurriedly grabbed his set of keys and mobile phone from his bedside table before necking the remainder of his glass of JD left from earlier on. 'Go back to sleep.'

Suzie was his latest girlfriend from Singapore. Beautiful and petite, with long black hair reaching all the way down to the small of her back. She worked as a cocktail waitress by day and a pole dancer by night. Then Steve met her, and she became a lady of leisure.

She switched her bedside light on and sat up in bed revealing she wasn't petite in all areas. 'I'm wide awake now that you've woken me up!'

'Sorry babe, but I have to go!'

Suzie then shook her voluptuous tits from side to side. 'I'll give you a titty-fuck!'

Now Steve, being the sort of hot-blooded fellow he was, would not normally have turned an offer like that down. But as they say: 'A friend in need is a pain in the ass!'. And so, he thought, *fuck it,* and let her give him a quick blowjob instead. Well, he didn't want to upset her. He was goodhearted like that.

Half an hour or so later, Steve was driving his FF Porsche through the brightly lit streets of Dubai. Constantly reminding himself not to drive too fast in case he gets stopped by the traffic cops. They also had Super Cars!

Since leaving the Marines ten years ago, Sergeant Steve Reynolds had done very well for himself. He retrained as a petroleum engineer and started up his own management company in Dubai. And thanks to the booming oil industry out there, his business had grown and grown, turning over millions in revenue each year. Plus a few other sidelines helped.

In the meanwhile, John was pacing up and down, wondering what the hell was taking his friend so long while at the same time trying not to look at the corpse in the centre of the room. You'd think that as an ex-soldier, he'd have got used to seeing dead bodies by now. But seeing her lying there like that brought back painful memories from his time on the front line.

It was 02:45 AM when Steve finally pulled into the Dubai Palace Hotel car park in Downtown Dubai. Which was not as nice as it sounds, as the three-star rating indicated. And was often used as a knocking shop, where rich Arabs and wealthy international businessmen would take their bit on the side for some rumpy-pumpy and where hookers and drug dealers would hang out.

He parked up and had a quick look round. Then reached into his secret hiding place - his glove compartment. Pulled out a small packet of snow, stuck his wet finger inside, and promptly gave his teeth a good brush with it. Now feeling much more refreshed and alert, got out the car and shut the door. Then promptly opened it again and reached over and grabbed the sports bag he'd forgotten from the passenger seat. Then headed for the hotel entrance.

Once inside, Steve casually walked past the reception desk, trying not to draw too much attention to himself, offering a smile and the greeting *As-salamu alaikum* to the attractive female receptionist, which she returned. And resisting the temptation to stop and give her his phone number, he continued as if he were going to the elevators. The receptionist wouldn't know he wasn't a hotel guest. Then as soon as he was around the corner and out of sight, lowered his baseball cap so his face wouldn't be recognized by the security cameras, and headed quickly down the corridor until he reached the Princess Suite. He then knocked quietly on the door and, keeping his voice down, acknowledged who he was. 'Thank fuck!' he heard his mate say through the door.

The door partly opened, and John's blood-stained hand grabbed his arm and pulled him sharply inside, promptly shutting the door behind him.

'You took ya bleedin' time, didn't cha, mate?' said John, slightly peeved while at the same time relieved to see him.

'Sorry mate. Something came up!' said Steve unconvincingly.

Yeah, I bet it did, ya randy bastard! thought John. John had gotten to know his impetuous and undisciplined ways by now. And if the Marines couldn't sort him out then nothing would. Oh, I forgot to mention, Steve was discharged from the military on medical grounds – he couldn't stand up straight because he was pissed most of the time. Anyway, that's another story.

John then moved to one side.

'FUCK!' suddenly exclaimed Steve upon seeing the horrific sight now on view. Having completely forgotten for a moment the reason he was there in the first place.

'Keep your voice down!' warned John.

'Yeah, sorry. *Shit!* Poor girl!' He, too, had never become unaffected by the sight of mutilated dead bodies – especially those not in military uniform. And any soldier who tells you otherwise is either lying or a psychopath.

'I didn't do it, Steve!' proclaimed John, soberly. 'Honest I didn't!'

'I believe you, mate!' replied Steve. 'You don't need to say that to me.'

'Did ya bring the change of clothes?' then quickly asked John.

'Yeah, yeah – they're in the bag,' Steve replied, handing it over to him. Still in shock as to the magnitude of what he was getting himself involved in. 'So, what happened?'

John quickly swapped his blood-stained clothes for fresh clean ones while briefly explaining what went on.

'… Bastards!' said Steve, still shaking his head in disbelief.

'I need to go up to my room and collect a few things,' said John as he shoved his bloodied clothes into the bag.

'There's no time for that!' said his mate. 'You can hide out at my place while things quieten down a bit and while we work out the best plan to get you safely out of the UAE – if you get caught, you're a dead man!'

John nodded.

Steve was right about that: If John were captured by the authorities, he would face the death penalty – which in this part of the world was either death by firing squad, hanging, or stoning – and if the real criminals caught him, they would kill him because he was a witness. Either way, he was a dead man!

'Oh mate, I don't know how to thank you enough!' expressed John, starting to tear up slightly.

'Save all that for later. Right now, let's get the fuck outta here while we still can!'

Steve then glanced back towards the semi-naked corpse. 'Don't forget the murder weapon!'

'Oh, yeah! *Fuck!* I'm not thinking straight!'

'Well, lucky I'm here to think for ya!'

John went straight over and gingerly picked up the sticky knife and dropped it into the bag and zipped it up. He spotted the victim's waistcoat under a table nearby. It looked like it had just been carelessly tossed away and left abandoned, as was he and the girl. So, he went and fetched it and used it to cover her bare breasts, face, and dignity. It was then he noticed her name badge for the first time. It read: *Sunshine.*

'I'll go ahead and distract the receptionist while you discreetly slip out the main entrance. And I'll meet cha in the car park round the back,' then advised Steve.

'Forget that - you'll be chatting her up all night!' responded John.

'Morning!'

'What?'

'Technically, it's the morning!'

'Look, nevermind the pedanticism - just go and start the bleedin' car and I'll follow shortly behind you.'

'No, it's best if I go and distract the hotel manager, in case he sees you!' argued Steve. He could be very annoying and stubborn at times.

'You said the *receptionist!'* John argued back.

'Bollocks did I!'

'Yeah, ya did!' John insisted.

'... Oh, did I? Well, I meant the manager. *Okay!'*

'Look, why are you now wasting time arguing with me?' argued John, starting to get annoyed. 'You're the one who just said about hurrying up and getting the fuck outta here!' He then added sarcastically, 'Why don't we just stay here and continue arguing and wait for the cops to turn up?'

'You're the one who's arguing, mate!'

'No, I'm not!'

'Yes, you are!'

Anyway, after squabbling like little children and wasting precious time, Steve reluctantly agreed to do what John said and, lowering his cap again, headed out the door carrying the bag of evidence with him. But not without saying once more that his idea was better.

John gave Steve a chance to get ahead of him. Then nervously with his heart beating ten to the dozen, ventured out of the room himself and started walking back down the long corridor. Part of him wished he hadn't walked up it in the first place. It wouldn't have made any difference if John covered his face or not – it had already been seen by multiple cameras in the corridor.

When he got about halfway along, he saw a night porter heading towards him from the other end. Things were beginning to play out just as he'd imagined it.

'Can I help you, sir?' asked the Indian porter as he approached him.

Most of the staff working at the hotel weren't the locals. The rich Emiratis wouldn't get their hands dirty. In fact, eighty per cent of people living in Dubai were foreigners.

John forced a smile, replying, 'I must've got lost!' and continued walking, ignoring the porter's attempt to give him directions. John quickened his pace without trying to make his escape look too suspicious. Almost there, he thought to himself as he crossed the concourse, heading for the entrance. Out of the corner of his eye, he could see that wanker, the hotel manager, now with a large plaster over his nose, standing behind the reception desk. Luckily, he was busy talking to some guests and hadn't spotted him - or at least he hoped not. He figured he would know if he had.

Relief! He was outside the building. But there was no time to waste. Stokes knew that it was only a matter of time - minutes - before the cops were alerted and would be arriving in force.

Stokes made haste, walking quickly at first, heading for the rear of the building. Then thought, *fuck it!* and started running. His heart was beating even faster now. *I'm getting too old for this shit,* he said to himself.

When he reached the car park, he discovered it was chock-a-block. Including about six red Ferrari's that looked identical to Steve's. And none of them had their engines running or their lights on to indicate where he was. Then after searching for a while and wasting even more precious time, one of the Ferrari's headlights came on. John ran over to it, and there was his mate, leaning over the dashboard doing a line of coke.

Oh, for fucks sake! thought John, shaking his head in disbelief. He quickly got into the passenger side. What the *fuck* d'ya think ya doin'?!' said John, annoyed.

'What does it look like?' answered Steve. 'D'ya want some?'

'No, I *bleedin'* don't' snapped John. 'Come on! Let's go! Let's go!'

'Alright, alright. Keep ya hair on!'

'Anyway, I thought you'd given that shit up?'

Steve didn't answer, just started the engine, which roared as he pulled away.

The glove compartment was still open, and John couldn't help but notice that lying, ominously, inside was a Glock 17 Gen4 and several loose 9x19mm cartridges. Recently issued to the British armed forces as their new weapon of choice. He was beginning to think that there were a lot of things about his friend he didn't know!

John didn't say anything about the weapon but couldn't help wondering how Steve managed to get his hands on one. And indeed, why he would need one in the first place? These were questions that would have to wait. Right now, he needed to focus on getting the fuck away from this shithole of a hotel and get to the safehouse. However, it also crossed his mind, how safe would staying at Steve's place be?

Steve erratically steered his beast of a car out of the hotel complex and onto the E11, otherwise known as the Sheikh Zayed Road.

'Will you try driving in a fucking straight line!' sharply said John to his mate, concerned. 'The cops will pull us over if they see you driving like that!'

'Alright, alright, calm down, calm down,' replied his mate.

As they headed south, they suddenly became aware of a convoy of police vehicles travelling at high speed, lights flashing, coming towards them in the opposite direction.

'Quick get ya head down!' quickly warned Steve.

John instinctively followed orders and tried to slide his body downwards to avoid being seen. But when you are 6'6 tall and long-legged like John, that doesn't work in a sports car.

'Put ya head on my lap then!' next suggested Steve.

John looked at his mate horrified. *'Fuck off!* I'd rather be caught than put my head on your sweaty groin!' He then quickly grabbed Steve's baseball cap off his head and put it on, shielding his face from view.

'What? I was only trying to be helpful!'

'Just fucking drive!'

The fancy cop cars whizzed past them one by one. The rear-view mirror soon revealed the convoy turning into the hotel complex the pair of them had only just come out of a short while ago.

'That was close!' commented Steve, whose adrenalin was racing as fast as the cop's supercars, as was John's.

'Yeah, no thanks to you!'

'Now, now,' said Steve, smiling widely. 'I got ya outta there, didn't I?'

'Yeah, ya did,' admitted John, smiling wearily. 'Thanks a million, Steve. I owe you big time!'

'Well, you never know, one day I might call you up on that.'

'Hey, listen, you just saved my skin, so just name it!'

'Well, don't speak too soon. You're not out of the UAE yet!' Steve then firmly put his foot down on the accelerator.

John had got a bit carried away with himself – he was just so relieved to have escaped and not been caught back then.

A little farther on, Steve took a right onto Hessa Street, heading down to the waterfront. He kept looking at his rear-view mirror, trying to make up his mind if they were being tailed. The same black S-Class Mercedes-Benz was still behind them since they left the hotel grounds. He could have been mistaken but he wasn't taking any chances.

'We need to take a slight detour!' said Steve. 'I think we might be being followed!'

He then sped up again. But so did the Merc. So he took a sharp right into a built-up industrial area to try and lose whoever the fuck they were. But they remained hot on their tail. *'Fuck!'* exclaimed Steve, punching his fist against the ceiling. And it was all going so perfectly.

The next thing they knew, gunshots were heard, and Steve's pride and joy was being sprayed with bullets. John didn't hesitate this time, he put his head straight on Steve's lap.

'Ouch!' came the sound out of Steve's mouth. 'What the fuck are doin'!'

'Well, you said I could put my head on your lap!' John quickly responded.

'That was then! Get my gun out of the glove compartment and start shooting the bastard's back!'

'Oh, *shit!'* mumbled John, thinking, *as if I'm not in enough bleedin' trouble already!*

Keeping as low as he could, he reached into the glove compartment and pulled out the Glock.

'Somebody at the hotel must have spotted you leaving,' said Steve.

John immediately knew what was coming next.

'I told you I should have distracted the hotel *bleedin'* manager!'

John ignored him, lowered his window and,

leaning out of it as far as he dared, began firing back. It was a long time since he'd fired a gun, but to a military veteran like Stokes, it was second nature. Leaning out of the window of the Merc was the same Arab he recognised earlier. The one who went and cowered in the corner of the room with his dick between his hands – though he appeared a lot more confident now that he had an MP5 submachine gun in his hands!

Suddenly the Ferrari's rear window shattered to pieces. 'Look don't *piss* about!' screamed Steve. 'Hurry up and kill the fuckers!'

'Well, if you stopped swerving about all over the fuckin' place, I might stand a bleedin' chance!' John called back before pumping several more bullets at their attackers. *Fuck this for a game of soldiers!* he thought, immediately seeing the funny side. Though, this was no laughing matter.

To both ex-soldiers, it felt like being back on the front line. It was either kill or be killed!

Steve then started moaning, 'This is gonna cost me a fortune to fix!'

The high-speed chase continued for a little while around the otherwise quiet streets of the industrial area. Then suddenly the gunfire stopped and there was an enormous explosion: the driver of the Merc had been hit and the car swerved off the road and smashed into a building.

'Well done!' said Steve, matter-of-factly, slowing

down slightly. John sat back down, shoving the still smoking-hot gun back into the glove compartment and closing it. Steve then continued driving around the block, until they eventually came back onto the same road leading up to the junction where they entered. He then turned right and headed in the same direction he had originally intended. Both remained quiet for a little while.

Then Steve broke the silence by saying: 'Seems like, whoever these shit-bags are, have now decided to take the law into their own hands and want you dead ASAP!

'No shit!' said John sarcastically.

But if Steve was being completely honest with himself, he couldn't be sure whether it was John or him they wanted dead! He had plenty of unsavoury acquaintances in the UAE who would not be too disappointed to see him disappear – far from it!

They reached the end of the street and Steve turned left onto the Shari' al-Malik Salman Bin Abd al-'Azeez Al Su'oud road (try saying that to a taxi driver when you're legless from a night out!). Then to the sounds of the emergency services sirens blaring out in the distance, they made their way to the affluent area of Palm Jumeirah, where Steve lived.

Before reaching there, Steve pulled over and got out of the car.

'Where are you goin'?' asked John bewildered, thinking, *now's not the time to go for a slash!*

'Give us ya phone!' demanded Steve.

'What?'

'Give us ya phone!' repeated Steve more emphatically.

John leaned over and handed Steve his precious mobile phone wondering what for. Steve then suddenly chucked it down onto the pavement and slammed the heel of his shoe onto it for good measure, smashing it to pieces before booting it away somewhere.

John looked on, speechless and horrified.

Steve then got calmly back into the car.

'What the hell did ya do that for?' asked John, annoyed.

'It was no good to you anymore – the cops would be able to trace the signal right back to my place, so we had no choice but to get rid of it, mate!' explained Steve as he pulled away.

John flopped back in his seat, shaking his head slightly. He knew that Steve was right, of course. But after everything that had happened, he wasn't thinking straight. It was the disappointment of losing his most personal possession containing all his cherished photos – none more so than of his beloved mum. As for most people, his phone was like another limb to him.

One thing he did know for sure was that he didn't

know what he'd have done without his friend's help.

CHAPTER TWO

Palm Jumeirah is a large man-made waterfront area designed as the name implies in the shape of a palm tree. As well as grand, lavish hotels - including the magnificent Atlantis The Palm situated at the apex - there are exclusive residential areas of luxury villas and apartments - all with a private beach - with a large ex-pat community living there.

Steve's beaten-up Ferrari limped up his drive into his spacious double garage, parking next to his girlfriend Suzie's pristine Jeep Renegade. Steve's mind was already thinking, *I'm gonna need to borrow that!*

The vehicle's clock read: 03:55 AM. 'Here we are!' said Steve. 'You can kip in the spare bedroom for the time being.'

'Thanks, mate,' John replied sleepily, now feeling exhausted.

'You'd better get some ice on your bonce!' said

Steve, hurrying him up.

John just nodded.

They got out of the vehicle and briskly made their way into the villa via an internal door.

Up against the far side wall, John noticed the shape of a motorbike covered over with tarpaulin material. And at the bottom end, also covered up, were various box-like shapes - probably containing bottles of spirit knowing Steve, thought John.

'Don't worry about the evidence,' said Steve reassuringly as he locked the door, referring to John's blood-stained clothes and the murder weapon. 'I will get rid of that for ya!'

By now John was so tired and confused that he had completely forgotten about that.

Steve led John through the large, open-plan kitchen/lounge area, advising him to be quiet in case his girlfriend woke up, then showed him where his bedroom and the bathroom were.

'D'ya wanna a stiff one before goin' to bed?' asked Steve.

'No thanks, mate,' he replied. He'd seen enough 'stiff ones' for one night - and I'm not talking about the alcoholic type.

Steve took some painkillers instead. And then went and just flopped himself on the bed and crashed out.

It was now the weekend, and sometime during

mid-morning, Stokes was awakened by the sounds of moaning and groaning and the occasional scream. But these weren't the sounds of misery and pain: these were pleasurable sounds.

'FUCK ME HARDER!' he then heard a lady's voice scream repeatedly from the adjacent master bedroom across the hall.

John pulled the pillow over his head to try and block out the noise so he could get back to sleep. But it was no good, now he was awake and would have to endure listening to Steve and his girlfriend fucking their brains out, tormented by the fact that he wasn't getting any – and hadn't for quite a while.

His sex life was almost non-existent. And he hadn't been in a long-term relationship for a long time. Ever since he left the military, he struggled to hold on to relationships: his partners always blamed it on his mood swings – sometimes aggressive. As with many soldiers involved in conflicts, he suffered from complex PTSD, which his partners never fully understood. And he often didn't take his medication, which can't have helped – taking it would be an admission that he had mental issues. But he'd also suffered trauma long before he joined the armed forces.

After what seemed like an eternity, the ever-increasing wet and squishy slapping sounds and screams of ecstasy coming from the other room finally reached an orgasmic climax.

Thank God for that! thought John.

A little while later, as John lay there still trying desperately to get the picture of them going at it out of his head, he heard their door open. And through the gap in his doorway, he caught a glimpse of the sex goddess' voluptuous naked body as she slithered out from hers on her way to the bathroom - her hard erect nipples leading the way. He thought he must be dreaming.

John did manage to doze off to sleep again for about an hour. Then he woke up to hear the same female's voice singing to herself alone in the kitchen. Some modern song he'd never heard of before. She was busy cooking scrambled eggs and sausages.

John got up and, after visiting the bathroom, wandered into the spacious kitchen. She had her back to him. This time dressed in a sexy oriental-style silk dressing gown, leaving nothing to the imagination - the flimsy material was caught between the cheeks of her ripe peachy arse.

'Morning!' said John.

She looked over her shoulder at him and smiled. 'Morning! John, is it?'

'Yeah,' he replied, smiling, too. 'And you must be Helga!'

'Helga?! No, I'm Suzie!' she replied, suddenly sounding a bit put out.

Oops! Suzie must be his latest bird! John suddenly thought. Quickly changing the subject, he said, 'You have a lovely voice!' thinking, arse – he thought her voice sounded crap!

'Oh, thank you, darling. I want to be a pop star!' Suzie said excitedly while she continued to cook.

'Really!'

'Yeah, Steve said I sound like Beyonce, and one day I will be famous!'

John just smiled widely.

'He told me he will pay for me to go to a recording studio!'

'Did he now!' replied John, while thinking, *and Steve's also full of shit!*

'Yeah – he's a real sweetie!'

'Where is Steve?' he then asked her.

'Oh, he's still in bed – he's exhausted!' Suzie answered sympathetically.

I bet he is! thought John, trying to hide a big grin.

Then, after a short pause. 'Steve told me all about what happened last night,' she said as she leaned against the kitchen unit, arms folded. 'How awful – that poor young girl!'

John nodded, just saying, 'Yeah!' Immediately getting horrendously vivid flashbacks.

There was a moment's silence again. Then Suzie told John that he was welcome to stay for as long as he needed to, which was reassuring to hear.

There was no point in lying to Suzie about what

happened at his hotel as, no doubt, the story would break out across the media very soon anyway - albeit he would maintain total fabrication.

She then turned on the extractor fan and began singing again.

'... What's that song you're singing?' he asked just to be polite. But due to the noisy extractor fan and her even nosier singing, she didn't hear him, suddenly calling out 'Scrambled eggs and sausages?' which John found highly amusing but managed to restrain his laughter, answering, 'Yes, please!'

'Take a seat - I'll bring it over to you when it's ready!'

He watched in awe - almost mesmerised - as her ample tits and ass wobbled unrestrained while she whisked the eggs and continued singing.

After a little while, she stopped singing, much to the relief of John's ears, and slinked over to where he was sitting, looking more sizzlingly hot than the sausages, carrying a mountainous plate of food in one hand and a mug of strong black coffee in the other. 'I hope you're hungry!' she said. Then as the sex goddess leaned over from John's right-hand side to place his breakfast down on the table in front of him, her dressing gown gapped wide open revealing her magnificent right boob - her left boob was equally magnificent! To say he got an eyeful is an understatement. But a commanding sergeant-major-like voice in his head made the order, *Eye's front!* and he immediately averted them away and stood firmly to attention if you know what I mean!

Before she left to go back to the stove, she firmly squeezed his huge right bicep, saying with a wink, 'A big boy like you needs a big breakfast!' He smiled and started tucking into his breakfast, blushing ever-so-slightly.

'Oh, by the way,' she then called out to him. 'Has the swelling gone down?'

He nearly choked on his sausage. And had to think twice about what she meant. Slightly embarrassed, he answered: 'Oh, you mean my *head!* Yeah, the swelling's gone down, and it feels much less painful now, thanks!'

'Well, what else did you think I meant?' she then asked him flirtingly. 'Cheeky!'

John then went even redder and just continued eating without answering.

She then took Steve's breakfast to him on a tray.

From where John sat, he could see her walking along the corridor, teasing him even more as she swayed her sexy hips exaggeratingly from side to side – clearly for his benefit. *Lucky so and so,* John then said to himself, *he even gets breakfast in bed!*

Then, no sooner had she entered their bedroom, John could hear the pair of them arguing with one another. The couple's irate voices became louder and louder. And, before long, he heard crockery and glassware smashing against the wall.

I need to get out of this madhouse ASAP! John instantly thought to himself.

The next thing he knew was Steve hurrying out the door and slamming it behind him, stark-bollock-naked, and calling out to her from the safety of the other side: 'BUT I DON'T EVEN KNOW A HELGA, BABE!'

He then started strutting down the corridor towards the kitchen.

'Oh, for fucks sake!' John said to him. 'Cover yourself up man – I'm trying to eat my breakfast!'

'Well, you're fucking lucky, mate – mine's all over the bleedin' wall!' Steve quickly responded, totally pissed off.

Steve then doubled back on himself and fetched his matching His and Hers silk, dressing gown from the bathroom. Then continuing to talk: 'You've really gone and landed me in it – what d'ya have to bleedin' go and mention Helga for?'

'Well, I didn't know that you'd split up with her – you could have bloody well told me!'

'Shh!' went Steve, putting his forefinger to his lips. 'I haven't – I'm still seeing her,' he then said quietly. 'So, keep ya voice down.'

Helga Hellström was a tall, fit, long-legged blonde in her late twenties from Sweden, and like Suzie also had huge bazookas (Steve had a thing for women with big tits). She charters her luxury yacht, docked at a nearby marina, to wealthy tourists – which Steve often frequents behind Suzie's back for more than just sailing.

John just shook his head in bewilderment, losing count of the number of girlfriends Steve's had over the last year since knowing him. He felt sorry for Steve's wife back in England, whom Steve had mentioned very little about – other than what a cow she was, and they couldn't stand the sight of each other. He would happily divorce her, but since he was living the high life in sunny Dubai, he was not in a rush to do so. And besides, he knew his wife would refuse him because she wouldn't want to sell their luxury six-bedroom house in Royal Tunbridge Wells, and it would mean a messy court battle, which he couldn't be arsed to fight.

'Suzie gets very jealous, you see,' then added Steve.

John nodded.

They could hear Suzie sobbing in the bedroom.

'She'll be alright in a minute,' said Steve. 'She always puts on the amateur dramatics and turns on the waterworks straight after we've had a row. We then make love and everything's rosy again!'

Oh, for fucks sake, not again! thought John.

'She could win an Oscar!' then claimed Steve.

John then started laughing.

'What ya laughing at?' said Steve, puzzled.

John then pointed to Steve's hair, which still had a large lump of scrabbled egg stuck in it (at least, that's what he was hoping it was?!), prompting Steve to laugh also.

Steve then asked if he could nick John's last sausage.

'You can have it, mate. Seeing your red shrivelled-up dick has put me right off it!' Both laughed again.

The sobbing then suddenly stopped, and shortly after, out from the bedroom strutted sexy Suzie, dressed in high heels, and wearing the skimpiest bikini you ever saw!

Fuck me! thought John as she sizzled past them. She looked like a million dollars!

'I'm going for a swim – you two can clean up!' she ordered as she lowered her Gucci shades over her eyes, opened the patio doors and ventured outside to their private swimming pool and the soaring heat.

'Sure, babe! Anything you say!' Steve called out, grovelling to her.

John had to smile.

'You need to watch her, mate' then commented Steve, 'she's a right prick-tease!'

Steve and John then went and plonked themselves down on the comfy white leather sofa facing out to the pool area. John, suddenly appearing serious, asked: 'Did ya get rid of the evidence?'

'Yeah, yeah,' answered Steve, 'it's all taken care of! I got rid of it all last night after you'd gone to sleep.' John didn't need to ask for more details, his concerned-looking expression was enough. After all, it was in his best interest to ensure that no trace of the incriminating evidence was ever found. So, Steve carried on. '… I burnt your clothes in the incinerator and ditched the knife over by the marina – don't worry, the sea's very deep there, and the luxury motor yachts will churn up the sand on the seabed and bury it!

'Good!' said John, very relieved. 'I can't thank you enough!'

'Well, you can start by doin' the washing-up!' said Steve, grinning.

'Sure!' John replied, grinning back.

John's heart started racing again as he watched the sex goddess remove her bikini top and fling it to one side before bending over in her thong and diving effortlessly into the pool. He forced himself up from the sofa and turned his gaze away from Suzie's pert little bottom bobbing up and down in the water, and headed over to the kitchen sink, chuckling to himself, thinking, *she'll never drown with the size of her built-in buoyancy aides!*

'Oh, and make us a cup of tea, would ya, mate!' called out Steve.

'Now ya pushing it!' John replied. Both laughed.

While John was waiting for the washing-up bowl to fill up with water, he would sometimes catch himself looking out to the pool at Suzie, then quickly turn his head back the other way and castigate himself for his lack of self-discipline. Suzie was a no-go zone, and he already had enough people trying to kill him and didn't want his mate, Steve, to join them! He had to admit though, she was a pleasant diversion from the shitstorm he had now found himself in.

And while Suzie was outside doing her laps, and John was still trying to squeeze the tiny rubber washing-up gloves on, Steve switched on his large 75-inch plasma TV screen and flicked around the channels until he came to the UAE news. And it wasn't long before the very serious-looking news presenter reported on the sexual assault and murder of the young Filipino girl at the Dubai Palace Hotel. John stopped what he was doing immediately and went over and joined his friend again - both listening intently. A large blown-up image of John Stokes's face then appeared on screen with an urgent message from a high-ranking UAE senior police officer, Colonel Ahmad Fayed, warning the public to be on their utmost guard and alert against this man, who he then named before adding, that if they see him, not to approach him as he could be armed and dangerous, but instead call the police and advise them of his whereabouts as he is wanted for questioning in connection with the heinous crime.

John was convinced it was the same corrupt police officer he'd seen that tragic and fateful night in the hotel conference suite.

'Now that everyone knows who you are, it's gonna be a lot more difficult for you to hide. And it won't be long before the cops come sniffing around my business premises, asking questions about you and your whereabouts.'

John just listened.

'So, we need to get you out of here before they start knocking on my front door!' continued Steve, now sounding concerned for the first time.

Coincidently, the doorbell then rang. Both men just looked at one another a bit startled. Both, thinking, *Fuck, that was quick!* But in no mood to joke about it. Then Steve said: 'Just stay down, behind the sofa and I'll check who the bleedin' hell it is!' Tensions now heightened, he promptly went over to a bookshelf in the lounge, reached behind the top row of books and pulled out an Uzi, submachine gun. Which John thought was a tad OTT. Leading him to immediately speculate why the owner of a petroleum engineering firm living in purportedly the safest country in the world would need one of those bad boys, a revolver, and God knows what other military hardware he has hidden around the place.

Now armed, soldier 20143281, then checked the CCTV security surveillance monitor nearby to see who was at the front door. John thought if it had been him, he would've probably checked the monitor first before going to the extreme of arming himself with a weapon – but then, under the current circumstances, any such paranoia was understandable.

'False alarm!' John called out to Steve. 'It's just the spotty-faced bleedin' pool attendant.' Then sounding suddenly surprised. 'What the *fuck's* he doin' here! – I'm sure I fired him for ogling at Suzie's tits!'

They're hard to miss! John thought to himself, smiling inwardly.

'Suzie must've re-hired him!' continued Steve.

The handsome, eighteen-year-old, French pool attendant's name was Andre – and he wasn't spotty-faced. And yes, him and Suzie were shagging each other. Truth be known, Steve and Suzie were both as bad as each other.

The doorbell rang again.

Steve then started to head towards the front door, continuing to moan. 'If the spotty-faced wanker, does it again, I'll bleedin' kill 'im!'

John's eyebrows raised slightly. He then quickly called out Steve's name to get his attention. Steve stopped and turned round to see John gesticulating towards the Uzi still held in his hand.

'Oh, yeah – force of habit!' He then tossed it towards John, saying: 'Catch!'

'No, I was referring to your other weapon!' John pointed again, grinning. 'Your todger's showing!'

Steve looked in a right state! He secured his dressing gown on his way to the door, and John quickly disposed of the weapon and then returned to his chores.

Andre persistently rang the bell again.

'Alright, alright, give me a bleedin' chance!' called out Steve as he reached for the door latch.

'… Bonjour, Monsieur Reynolds!' said Andre smiling confidently as the door opened. *'Ca va?'* he then asked while he stood there looking very tanned in his tight-fitting white shorts, with his short-sleeved pale-blue shirt completely unbuttoned, showing off his chiselled six-pack.

I'll give you, 'Ca va', you, snail-munching-garlic-breathing-tosspot! thought Steve as he looked at him unwelcomely. 'Use the side gate!' Then pointing his finger at him, he added, 'And no looking at my girlfriend's tits!' thinking, *no wonder he's always fuckin' smiling whenever he comes round here!*

'Pardon?' said the Frenchman, looking confused.

'You heard me, Frenchy. Now fuck off and do what I pay ya for! Or I'll re-fire you – got it!'

The Frenchman nodded nervously, and Steve abruptly shut the door.

And as the pool attendant went about his job –

being very careful not to stare at Suzie's magnificent tits - Steve eventually calmed down and got dressed, John finally finished doing his chores - though, forgot about making Steve a cup of tea, and Suzie continued sunning herself while doing a good job at looking gorgeous.

CHAPTER THREE

It was now late in the afternoon. Andre had left by now, disappointed that he hadn't got his end away. John and Steve were sitting outside under a sunshade just finishing their lunch, which Steve had cooked on the barbecue. And Suzie was on a sun lounger, busy chatting with her friend over the phone while sucking her ice-cold popsicle – wishing it was Andre's big French cock instead.

'That was delicious, mate!' John said to Steve as he finished the last bite of his hot dog.

'Yeah, it wasn't bad if I do say so myself!'

Noticing that there was still some tension in the air between Steve and Suzie, John leaned forward and, speaking quietly and confidentially, said: 'Aren't you two gonna try and make up then?' To which Steve replied: 'No, I'm too knackered, mate!' Which, John was quite relieved to hear, because reading between the lines, he now knew what that usually involved, and didn't want to have to put up with all those weird sex noises again so soon. Steve then added: 'I think this one's a nymphomaniac!'

John smiled, thinking, *some people have all the luck!*

'Hey, d'ya wanna hear a dirty joke?' asked Steve with a cheeky grin.

'Go on then,' answered John hesitantly with scepticism in his voice – he'd had to endure his bad jokes many times this past year.

'A pig in mud!' said Steve with an even broader grin as he delivered the punchline.

John laughed cynically, shaking his head. 'That's got to be the worst joke I've ever heard! That was awful!'

'It wasn't that bad.'

'Yes, it was!'

'D'ya wanna hear another one?'

'No, I bleedin' don't!'

Steve laughed.

'... Listen, I've gotta go out soon!' then suddenly announced Steve. And after a slight pause, he looked John straight in the eye and, with his poker face on, casually said: 'But *you* can fuck Suzie if you like! I've seen the way you both look at each other.' John didn't respond – he didn't know how to. He just sat there for a moment in shocked surprise, finishing his beer and pretending not to have heard. Was his mate just testing him? Or did he really mean it? Steve then broke the strained silence by laughing. John just smiled uncomfortably, still unsure whether Steve was joking or not.

Desperate to change the subject, John asked his mate if he would spot him for ten thousand dirhams (the equivalent of about two thousand pounds sterling). 'Just to tide me over,' John said. 'I'll pay ya back as soon as I can.'

Steve just looked at him blankly for a moment, then chuckled. 'I'll tell what, stick ya hand up my arse – I've got piles!'

'Oh, go on, mate – you're loaded!' quickly responded John, failing to see the funny side.

Steve scoffed. 'You're 'aving a laugh, aren't cha?!' he finally replied, shaking his head a little. 'My money is all tied up in the business.' He wasn't lying.

Yeah, right! thought John, looking disappointed.

'I can lend ya a couple of thousand dirhams, but that's it.'

John smiled, uttering only, 'Thanks,' but thinking, *Tight bastard!*

Then, after an uncomfortable couple of minutes, Steve suggested that they go inside and watch some sport, which they did. It was a relief to get out of the intense heat and come back inside into the cool air-conditioned villa – in more ways than one.

'Another beer?' asked Steve.

'No, thanks!' replied John. 'I'm still recovering from drinking too much booze last night.' Then after a short pause, he added, 'I expect the whack on the head didn't help!'

'Well, I'm gonna have another one – are ya sure you don't want another?' persisted Steve as he pulled a cold beer out of the fridge for himself.

'Yeah, no, I'm fine, mate, honestly!'

'You're becoming a bit of a lightweight in your old age, you are!' joked Steve.

John chuckled.

On his way over to join John relaxing on the sofa, Steve noticed his new house guest staring at the topless Suzie, now lying spread-eagled on her back with her feet dangling in the water atop a pink inflatable Lilo.

'Life is like a Lilo …' suddenly said Steve randomly, '… one minute you're up and the next, you're down!'

John immediately turned his gaze towards John and smiled without comment. Was it just a generalization, or was Steve trying to tell him something? *Maybe he's depressed about something?* he thought. John knew the feeling well. He then got annoyed inside. *What's a man born with a silver spoon in his mouth got to worry about?!* He then surmised Steve could have large gambling debts, knowing how much he likes to gamble.

Steve then picked up the remote and switched on the TV to watch the Dubai World Cup, which is one of the most famous and prestigious horse racing events in the world, held at the Meydan racecourse in Nad Al Sheba. The epic nine-race card attracts more than 60,000 spectators with an epic top prize of $12,000,000.

'Do you like horse racing, John?' asked Steve as he removed a cigarette from his pack of Marlborough's. He didn't offer John one because he didn't smoke anymore. A bad habit he picked up in the Marines – along with drinking and swearing, which he was yet to give up.

'Yeah, I watch it occasionally and make the odd bet.'

'I'm going to the racecourse shortly to have a little flutter myself,' said Steve, jokingly adding, 'I would've already been there by now if I hadn't been up half the night saving your ass!'

Now in truth, Steve never has a 'little flutter', and had already lost a lot of money gambling.

John started to thank him again but was cut off.

'Best if you don't mention it to Suzie – she doesn't approve of my gambling habits.'

Suzie had since come out of the pool and now sat sideways on her sun lounger, hunched over a small poolside table doing a line of coke.

'Don't worry, I shan't mention it!' quickly answered John, reassuring him.

'... Plus, I'm meeting Helga there,' he confided to John with a grin and a wink. Then more seriously added, 'I'll find out if she will charter her luxury motor yacht for you to escape.' Which, John was pleased to hear. 'It's called Slow Motion and moored at the nearby Palm Jumeirah West Marina. Your best chance of escape would be to travel by sea to Pakistan or India.'

'Yeah, I've already thought about going to Karachi!'

One of the races had finished and, through a cloud of smoke from Steve's cigarette, John immediately recognised the elated, largely built owner of the winning thoroughbred - he was stroking its luxurious mane while being interviewed along with the equally happy, much more diminutive Irish jokey. The pair of them looked comical standing together, and the Arab even joked about their size difference. But John didn't find it amusing!

Dressed in a white thawb, headdress, and sunglasses, the enormous Arab smiled broadly at the cheering crowds. But even with sunglasses on, how could John not recognise him: he had his sweaty, chubby hands around his neck the night before! There was no question in John's mind that he was the same monster who had killed the poor innocent Filipino girl.

John's whole demeanour quickly changed. His face curled up, his body became tense, and he found himself clenching his fists tightly. He was as angry as hell!

By comparison, Steve looked happy that the Arab's horse had won, saying well done to the screen.

'That's the Arab *bastard* that killed the girl!' angrily called out John, pointing at him.

Steve was taken aback. He turned his head sharply towards John looking flabbergasted. 'Do what?'

'That's him! That's the killer!'

'Are you sure?'

John nodded as he continued staring at the TV.

Steve shook his head. 'No, you must be mistaken – d'ya know who that is?' he then asked, still surprised by John's wild claim.

'I don't give a *shit* who the fuck he is! That's him, I'm telling ya. Lend me your fuckin' gun, and I'll go and pop a bullet through the sick *bastard's* brain!'

'You can't just go and do that!'

'You bleedin' watch me.'

'Use your common dog,' advised Steve (Bootneck jargon for common sense). 'You'll get arrested before you can even get close to him. I think that knock on your head has sent you a bit doolally!'

There was a pause. 'Go on, who the fuck is he then?'

'That's Abdullah Hussein! He's the UAE's government minister of state for happiness and related to the ruling royal family!' explained Steve (believe it or not this ministerial position does exist in Dubai). John thought he certainly hadn't made the murdered Filipino girl feel happy!

John obviously couldn't go with Steve for fear of detection. But if he did go, he certainly would've liked to wipe the cheesy smile off the vile minister's face!

The mood had turned sour, and Steve could see that John didn't want to watch the programme anymore, so he switched it off.

'I'm gonna head off now, mate,' said Steve. 'I'll tell ya about the outcome of the conversation with Helga when I get back late tonight. Fingers crossed she'll agree!'

'Yeah! Thanks again, Steve. Have a good time! See ya later!'

'No problem! See ya!' Then as an afterthought, 'Help yourself to anything, wontcha.'

John smiled and nodded.

A short while afterwards, John heard the garage door open, shortly followed by the Renegade's engine starting up. Steve figured Suzie wouldn't mind him borrowing it, since he bought it for her. But he was wrong, she was furious, and came running in, bare boobs bouncing in every direction, swearing at the top of her voice. 'You, fucking pig!' she screamed amongst other profanities. But it was too late, Steve had driven away before she got there – probably just as well!

John just sat there minding his own business, not

uttering a word, and trying unsuccessfully to avert his gaze.

Before being interrupted, he had been studying a pocket map of the local area. Suzie was so busy trying to prevent her boyfriend from taking her car that she hadn't even noticed him.

'Oh, *hi!* I didn't see you sat there!' she said more calmly, somewhat surprised, quickly covering herself up with her sarong she still held in her hand but hadn't had time to put on.

'Hi!' John just replied, not knowing quite what to say – or where to look.

'I can't believe he's just taken my car without even asking me! The *pig!*' moaned Suzie, still full of rage inside.

Well, at least that's an improvement on *'fucking pig',* thought John.

She then continued ranting at high speed. 'He must think I'm stupid or something! But I bet I know where he's gone! He's gone to see that floozy of his – Helga!'

John just shrugged his shoulders, suggesting he didn't know.

'The *bitch!*' Suzie blurted out. She then paused to take a breath. 'Did he say where he was going?'

John quickly shook his head, this time answering verbally: 'No, he didn't,' knowing full well that she wouldn't believe him anyway.

Suzie frowned, looking unconvinced as John

expected, then turned and walked over to the kitchen to make a cocktail to try and cheer herself up, leaving him convinced *they'll be sparks flying later – as well as a few more plates and glasses!*

'… Would you like a Sloe Screw?' she suddenly called over to him with a sexy grin and flirtatious eyes as if she had already forgotten about the car.

John chuckled. 'No, I'll pass, thanks!'

'Pity!' she replied, pouting (in both senses of the word). 'You'd find it very satisfying and pleasurable!' She licked her lips as if to emphasise it.

John promptly looked back down at the map. He was looking for the best sea route out of there. He had already ascertained that travelling by land was a no-go because there were now too many security checkpoints and heightened border controls. And, by now, all airports would have been notified about him, making it virtually impossible to travel by air. So, his best bet to evade capture would be to travel by boat through the Gulf of Oman to the Arabian Sea and try and reach the port of Karachi, Pakistan. And from there, hopefully, get a flight to the UK. Anywhere that was safe!

Sexy Suzie had finished shaking her cocktail shaker - amongst other things - and poured herself a Sloe Screw, concocted of 1.5 ounces of Gordon's Sloe Gin, 1.5 ounces of Smirnoff Red Vodka, and 3 ounces of freshly squeezed orange juice into a highball glass filled with ice and garnished with a slice of orange. The colour of the drink matched nicely with the orange of her sarong.

She took a quick sip of her cocktail. Then seductively licked her lips again, making an exaggerated sound reminiscent of the pleasurable one John had heard her make while making out in the bedroom earlier, hoping to get his undivided attention, which failed, as he continued intensively studying the map. Slightly disappointed, she lowered her shades and glided towards the patio doors, trying hard not to spill her lethal concoction.

'Why don't you come and join me by the pool and look at that boring map later!' she told him in her 'come to bed' voice – or rather, 'come to pool' voice.

He looked up at her, hesitated for a moment; then, smiling, said: 'Yeah, sure, why not – I could do with some vitamin D!' Then tossed the map aside, got up and opened the patio door for her and followed her outside. Well, he didn't want to appear unsocial.

Fortunately, the large pool area was secluded and kept private by tall palm trees and other vegetation.

She continued to glide over to her sun lounger and, before lying down, untied the knot on her sarong, allowing it to slip off her and reveal her goddess-like body. John's hypnotised eyes followed its descent to the ground as if under the seductress's spell. She immediately pulled the adjacent sun lounger nearer to hers, saying: 'Come and relax next to me.'

John kept his polo shirt on and lay down next to her, trying desperately not to look at her bare breasts to avoid any temptation of forbidden fruit.

She next reached down by the side of her sun lounger and picked up a bottle of suntan lotion, tossing it to him, saying forwardly, 'Smear this over my back, please, sweetie!'

John caught the bottle, looking like a rabbit caught in the headlights for a moment, then smiled and said: 'Sure!' immediately questioning himself as to whether this was a good idea.

Expectantly, sexy Suzie had already rolled over onto her front and moved her long locks of hair out of the way without waiting for an answer. His undisciplined eyes immediately became drawn to her perfectly formed arse cheeks. But his military training soon kicked in, and he managed to avert his eyes away from the danger zone, quickly shifting his gaze towards her upper back. But just when he thought it was safe, he now faced two even greater danger zones: her boobs were so big that they billowed outwards on either side, squashed against the sun lounger.

Pull yourself together – there's no need to panic, he said to himself. He was on a mission and would have to just soldier on! So, he swung round on his sun lounger and squirted a large dollop of lotion onto the palm of his hand; then leaned over her and began smearing it first onto her upper back. The coldness of the creamy lotion against her warm skin made her shudder a little.

'*Mmm,* that's nice!' she expressed to her pleasant satisfaction. 'You have such big strong hands!'

John didn't respond, just carried on with the task at hand.

Once he'd smeared her upper back in lotion, he manoeuvred his hands down towards her lower back. Then, squeezing more onto his oily palm, he accidentally spilt a big blob of it onto her right buttock cheek, which quickly ran down into her crutch area, tickling her and causing her to giggle. She spontaneously parted her legs slightly, and reaching behind herself, adjusted the elasticated string of her thong, briefly exposing the *Clitoria* flower in her overgrown Garden of Venus. Then in a continuous movement, she reached up and grabbed his free hand, forcibly moved it down onto her right buttock cheek and began using it to rub the lotion into her skin.

John couldn't control himself anymore, and his garden hose began to harden. He felt the searing urge to bang her right there and then. It was clear to him that she would be up for it. Why should Steve have all the luck? But that would be wrong – especially after everything Steve has done for him. And although he was no saint, one of his redeeming qualities was that he was loyal. So, after battling with his conscience for a little while, he quickly released his hand from hers, breaking the spell, lamely saying, 'All done!' Then he promptly sat back down on his sun lounger, raising his right knee to conceal the embarrassing lump in his shorts.

But the sex goddess wasn't going to give up that easily. 'You must be *boiling* in that shirt!' she commented, adding, 'Why don't you take it off?' quickly followed by, 'Here, let me do it for you!' as she leaned over towards him and brazenly began removing it for him without waiting for an answer again.

He immediately grabbed both her wrists in his big strong hands, slightly agitated, saying firmly, 'Let go!'

Her smile instantly dropped, and she let go in a state of shocked surprise, saying, *'Ouch, that hurts!'* but not before she had caught a glimpse of his badly scarred back, which looked horrific!

He let go of her, saying, 'Sorry, I didn't mean to hurt you.'

'I was only having a bit of *fun!*' she replied, miffed. *'My God!'*

Suzie got straight up in a huff without commenting about his injuries and dived into the pool. It was hard to tell whether she was more shocked by his horrific injuries or by his rejection of her sexual advances. She was so used to getting her way with men that when she didn’t, she hated it.

John lay back down and closed his eyes – he was back in Sangin, Helmand Province, Afghanistan, amidst a ferocious firefight with the Taliban.

CHAPTER FOUR

'AMBUSH!' screamed the commanding officer of the eight-man unit of 3 Commando Brigade, Captain Todd Richards, as bullets rained down from higher up the mountainside.

They were on a reconnaissance mission, driving in two MWMIK Jackals along a low ridge in the Taliban stronghold of Sangin, and had stopped to check for IEDs about twenty metres ahead. What drew their suspicions was a dead goat blocking the narrow road, which was a well-known tactic used by the enemy to entice the infidels out of the relative safety of their armoured vehicles.

Four of the brigade's personnel had gotten out of the vehicles, including Corporal John Stokes, to search and secure the area in case their worst fears were correct. And, no sooner had the captain shouted the word 'ambush' when a bullet hit the soldier sweeping for IEDs up ahead in the chest.

'MAN DOWN! MAN DOWN!' shouted Corporal Stokes at once as he bravely ran to his fellow soldier's aid. Followed by shouts of 'MEDIC!'

By now, the gunners of both vehicles had swivelled their powerful mounted .50 cal. machine guns around and returned fire, while others used the armoured vehicles as shields and fired their SA80 Individual Assault Weapons, L129A1 Sharpshooter Rifles, and mortars at the enemy.

Amid a tirade of oncoming enemy fire, including RPGs, Corporal Stokes picked the young fallen soldier up in his arms as blood poured out of his gaping-open chest and began carrying him back towards the protection of armour-plated front Jackal, determined to save the poor souls life!

It was as Corporal Stokes was carrying the wounded soldier back towards the vehicles when he suddenly felt immense heat all over his back and his uniform ripping to shreds from the blast. One of the enemy's bullets must have set off an IED close by!

The blast had sent him falling to his knees, but he still managed to get up and carry the soldier to safety before passing out. The next thing Corporal Stokes remembered was waking up in a field hospital bed in Camp Bastion and being told that the soldier he had tried to save sadly died from his injuries. He had suffered severe injuries to his back and head himself and was lucky to be alive.

Witnesses say his back was still on fire as he staggered back to the rest of his unit.

Fortunately, due to the sheer firepower from the Jackal's machine guns and the steely determination of the men not to be another statistic in this seemingly hopeless and never-ending war, they were able to defeat the enemy that day.

For his bravery in the face of the enemy, John Stokes received the Military Cross. Though, whenever the subject came up, he would always play it down and point out that his fellow soldiers would have done the same.

As John Stokes lay on the sun lounger with his eyes closed, reliving the nightmare of what happened that day in Sangin, he suddenly felt the sensation of something wet dripping down his face: it was Suzie playfully splashing him with water from the pool.

John suddenly sat bolt upright and let out a terrified scream, mistaking the water for blood. And upon opening his eyes, he saw her leaning seductively over her pink inflatable Lilo, now with bright pink lipstick to match, and with her huge bare boobs propped up on full display close to the edge of the pool where he lay.

Giggling, she mouthed the word 'sorry', oblivious of the trauma he was going through, then smiled and blew a kiss.

John faintly smiled back.

She then stood up waist-high in water, her cold, wet nipples hard as bullets – and just as deadly. 'Why don't you come for a swim?' she called out. 'It's lovely!'

'Another time,' he called back as he got up from his sweat-drenched sun lounger. 'I've got stuff I need to sort out.'

Upon saying that, Suzie continued doing her laps and John went inside, glad to get out of the heat in more ways than one.

He figured that Suzie was just one of those insecure types that always needed attention. She was probably bored out of her brains: Steve was out working most of the time – and whatever shenanigans he was up to. And let's face it, Emirati women do not enjoy the same kind of freedoms as they do in the West. He felt sorry for her in a way.

Anyway, he had himself to worry about now – getting the fuck outta Dodge!

Once inside, John headed for the sofa to take another look at the map but then changed his mind: he thought while Suzie was still outside, he would take the opportunity to have a scout around the property. He was curious to know if there were any more British Armed Forces standard issue firearms lurking about the place.

He started his search in the double garage. The key was still in the internal door – no doubt inadvertently left there in Steve's rush to leave.

And Suzie was so enraged chasing after him that she hadn't noticed it.

His eyes were immediately drawn to the covered-up box-like shapes at the far end. So, without hesitation, he moved swiftly over there and pulled the dusty tarpaulin off. Stacked on top of each other were many various-sized and shaped wooden crates. And staring him in the face, stamped onto the top of each of them, was the abbreviation for the Ministry of Defence!

John's eyes widened as he stood there flabbergasted. Was his newfound friend a gun runner - selling stolen MOD firearms to the Arabs? He strode over to the wall of hanging tools, searching for a crowbar. Then, having found it, went back to the suspect crates and, wedging the sharp end of the implement under one of the nailed-down lids, prised it open. Inside, as he suspected, were half a dozen BAF standard-issue SA80a2 rifles. Then, quickly opening another, smaller crate, discovered one dozen Glock 17 Gen4 pistols - the same make of pistol he had fired the night before. The magazines for these, containing 9x19mm bullets, he located in a wooden box nearby, already opened. A much longer crate revealed an RPG inside.

'Fuck me!' he mouthed. Then he hurriedly put the lids back on, but not before helping himself to one of the Glocks and a few magazines. *This might come in handy!* he thought. *It can't be classed as stealing if it's already been stolen,* he reasoned, *and Steve did say to help myself to anything.* He shoved the firearm quickly down the back of his shorts and covered it over with his polo shirt. Next, covered the crates again before making his way back to the door.

He wasn't sure what surprised him the most: Steve dealing in the illegal arms trade or his pathetic attempt to hide his large cache of firearms? The latter of which immediately started alarm bells ringing. Because if Steve wasn't all that concerned about hiding it from the authorities, it probably meant they were involved!

He knew that Steve still had connections with active members of the Royal Logistic Corps, who may be involved in the theft of MOD firearms and supplying him. And putting two and two together, maybe Helga was also involved, ferrying firearms from place to place in her yacht with somewhat impunity? What if those same firearms ended up in the hands of Islamic terrorists? The very same enemy he'd been fighting against and nearly lost his life. But this was all just conjecture.

As he began to open the door, he suddenly spotted Suzie leading the French pool attendant by the hand along the corridor to her bedroom. John stopped abruptly in his tracks, pulling the door towards him so as not to be seen.

That's not the way to the pool, thought John. *Which*

can only mean one thing. Fuck! More annoying sex noises! She must have called him and told him that Steve was out! They'd better not let Steve catch them at it!'

He waited for the lustful pair to enter the room and close the door behind them, then came through the internal garage door, back into the villa, wondering what the hell he was going to say to Steve about the shitload of military hardware he'd just discovered (let alone what Suzie and the Frenchman get up to when he's out!). If indeed, it would be wise to say anything about it at all.

No wonder he can afford this lavish lifestyle, John thought as he made himself a chicken mayo sandwich, slapping the slices of chicken down onto the bread, peeved at Steve for betraying His Majesty's Armed Forces. It was treason and he certainly didn't want any part of it. He couldn't believe how quickly his life seemed to be spiralling out of control. Talk about 'out of the frying pan and into the fire'!

Before the moaning and groaning intensified, John moved out onto the sun terrace, shutting the patio doors firmly behind him as a lame attempt at protest.

He hadn't even finished his sandwich when the happy smiling couple came bounding past him. *Blimey, that was quick!* he thought, referring to their sexual exploits. *Those Frenchie's don't hang about!*

He then watched as they raced to the pool and

dived in, thinking, *Ah, the carefree innocence of youth!* He immediately corrected himself. *They're not that innocent!* Quickly shutting any further such thoughts out of his head as it brought back painful memories of his only true romance that went sour: while he was away on a tour of duty, he found out that his bride-to-be was cheating on him. And he's had a mistrust for women ever since! Which probably explains why he's not been in a long-term meaningful relationship in a long while.

John finished his sarnie and went back inside to make himself a refreshing cup of tea and leave the two lovebirds at it. Even at seven in the evening, the sun's powerful rays were still blazing hot upon the sun terrace.

Meanwhile, at the racecourse, tempers were also blazing hot. Steve had just lost a ton of money on the previous race. He stood watching the races from one of the grandstand's private boxes, along with several UAE dignitaries. He also felt annoyed because Helga hadn't turned up yet. But they weren't the only reasons he was pissed off.

'… But we had a deal!' exclaimed Steve, showing his outrage.

'Now, now, calm down, Steve,' said the UAE Minister of State for Happiness in a much quieter and calmer voice as he caressed his goatee beard. 'Getting all worked up won't solve anything! As you must know by now, one of your employees is now a fugitive and wanted in connection with the attempted rape and murder of a young female hotel worker here in Dubai. And the authorities here take a very dim view of anyone aiding and abetting any such criminals. Now, my associates and I have already discussed it – *and* if you are willing to shed some light on the whereabouts of Mr John Stokes,' – Steve started shaking his head but let him continue without interruption – 'then we would be willing to overlook this rather … awkward matter and continue doing business with you. Perhaps even increase our order of firearms the next time!'

'I honestly don't know where he is – I've not heard from him.'

'Come, come, now, Steve, you know that is not true. And unless you tell us, this deal and any future deals are off! Not to mention the amount of trouble you could be in!' threatened the huge Arab, whose smile was beginning to fade.

Steve continued shaking his head.

'We could make things *very* difficult for you living in the UAE. I should think twice if I were you!' he continued less patiently. Steve remained silent. 'Well, you leave us no choice then! We will start our search at your villa and confiscate any weapons found there. I was trying to save you the embarrassment this would cause by asking you nicely first, but –'

'FUCK!' screamed Steve in his head before

reluctantly interrupting with, 'Okay! Okay! He's at my villa!'

The minister smiled widely, saying, 'At last!' He then clapped his hands loudly. 'Bring us another bottle of the finest Champagne!' he ordered one of the stewards. He then stepped away from Steve and removed his mobile phone from his pocket. '… He's at Steve Reynolds villa in Palm Jumeirah – you know what to do!'

Helga eventually turned up about an hour later, looking glamorous and sexy but also troubled and worried, blaming the heavy traffic for her tardiness. Surprisingly, Steve didn't get upset with her – he had far more important things on his mind.

Back at Steve's villa, Suzie and Andre were by now drying themselves off on sun loungers, holding hands and staring romantically into each other's eyes, and John was once again sat on the sofa arduously studying the map of the marina area.

Previously, while the two lovers had been frolicking in the pool, after quickly finishing his cup of tea, John continued his search of the villa. And in Steve and Suzie's bedroom, inside Steve's bedside table drawer, he found a security pass to the marina and a large bundle of cash – mainly dirhams and some dollars. Both of which he would need if he had to make a quick get-away – which was fast becoming his favoured option. He made a mental note of where the items were and then left, pleased to be away from the pungent lingering smells of sex.

John knew the longer he waited at the villa, the more chance there was of him getting caught. Suzie and Andre were preoccupied merrily chatting by the poolside, and Steve and Helga were a fair distance away at the racetrack, so why not get off the hamster wheel and make his escape now? And with a pass to the marina, nothing was stopping him from taking Steve's motorbike, boarding Helga's yacht, and sailing off into the sunset. Even without a key, being a trained marine engineer, he would have no trouble starting the vessel. But that would mean betraying the person who had helped him escape in the first place!

He now had a dilemma: should he grab what necessities there were and make his escape now while he still could? Or should he wait for Steve's return to find out if Helga is willing to help a wanted man escape or not and risk further delay?

His mind was soon made up for him when he heard loud terrified screams and gunshots coming from the pool area. Shortly followed by the sound of shattering glass as the patio doors became sprayed with bullets.

John immediately dived into action - quite literally over the back of the sofa, where he instinctively withdrew his loaded pistol, pointing it in the direction of the pool terrace and the three hooded assassins closing in on him.

Sadly, it was too late to save poor Suzie and Andre. They were swiftly taken out the moment the gunmen entered the premises via the side gate and the beach. First, the Frenchman, shot in the head as he lay on his sun lounger, and then Suzie as she got up to run, falling dramatically into the pool before she had even gotten a metre away! Even as she fell, she looked graceful and balletic!

John watched in horror as the pool water turned red to match the sunset. Then as soon as the attackers came into sight, he opened fire, unleashing about half his magazine of 9x19mm bullets in quick succession, wishing now that he'd have taken the L7A2 machine gun instead. Then it would've been game over in no time! One of the bullets hit its target, though, nullifying one of them. John watched him fall spectacularly onto the terrace about ten metres away before diving flat onto his belly as bullets punctured the sofa cushions, sending small pieces of stuffing material high into the air, which fell incongruously like snow. He crawled to the end of the sofa, waiting patiently for one of the fearless attackers to enter, then opened fire, hitting his opponent's ankle, causing him to fall conveniently to the floor for John to pop a bullet into his brain.

There was no time to think, only to act, and hope

that all his military training and experience would be enough!

By John's reckoning, that was two down and one more to go. But while he had been busy dealing with the last attacker he killed, he hadn't seen the other one come running in behind him. John looked up, and there he was, now standing on the arm of the sofa brandishing a dagger and about to pounce on him. He took of his balaclava and smirked as if he was going to enjoy killing his opponent. He was a European-looking, ugly motherfucker with a face full of tattoos and body piercings. John quickly rolled over onto his back and raised his gun, but before he had a chance to shoot, his opponent kicked the gun out of his hand like Jackie fucking Chan and then jumped on top of him screaming, pinning him down.

John gripped his opponent's wrist, preventing the tip of the eight-inch razor-sharp blade from piercing his chest, only an inch or so away. Then, quickly swinging his right leg up and over the guy's head, he hooked it around his neck and pulled him sharply backwards. This did two things: 1. Disoriented his opponent. And 2. Brought the dagger safely away from the kill zone. John immediately sat up (this is where a hundred sit-ups a day help), and then while he kept him in a tight headlock, worked on removing the dagger from his hand in the best way he knew - biting his hand as hard as he bleedin' could!

It worked! John's adversary soon relinquished his grip on the dagger, enabling John to take it from him; and in a continuous motion, while the guy fumbled desperately with both hands for it, stabbed all eight inches of the blade right through the guy's mouth and out through the top of his skull, killing him instantly. 'How's *that* for a body piercing!' said John full of rage.

If it wasn't clear to John before, he certainly knew that the authorities wanted him dead now. Including no witnesses!

It was now time to bite the bullet and leave! John quickly shoved the limp, still hot and sweaty, lifeless body off him. And, feeling exhausted, stood up, saying to himself, *Shit! That was close!* Then after taking a quick breather, he located his newly acquired pistol and quickly went to fetch it in case any more assassins were lurking about the place, stepping over the two dead bodies as he did. He then bolted out of the open-plan living area (or maybe that should be 'dying area') and down the corridor to Steve's bedroom to quickly change his blood-splattered polo shirt for a clean one and grab the marina pass and cash from the bedside drawer, wishing he'd have done that in the first bleedin' place.

Needing something to write on to leave Steve a note explaining what had happened, John quickly pulled the map out of his pocket – he'd already memorised what he needed to know – then hastily began scribbling.

He needed to get out of this place ASA-fucking-P! After writing the note, he shoved the map inside the drawer, then swiftly left the room and ran back down the corridor. Then just as he was about to open the internal garage door to make his exit, there was suddenly an almighty explosion, and the front door blew in. And amidst the thick choking acrid smoke and chaos, more armed men came charging in with guns at the ready. The blast knocked John to the ground and caused him temporary hearing and sight loss, but he knew the whereabouts of the front door and pumped several shots in that direction, instantly taking out at least two of them at the front before they had a chance to spot him. *Fuckin' hell!* he thought, *they've brought the whole fucking Dubai SWAT Team!*

What had been a quiet and peaceful residential area was now more like a war zone. The whole area became quickly cordoned off, with residents given strict orders to remain inside their properties, and roadblocks to all main escape routes were set up and secured.

Then without hesitation, John disappeared into the garage like a magician in a puff of smoke. He slid over the bonnet of the beaten-up FF Ferrari and quickly pulled the cover off Steve's motorbike, revealing it was a Kawasaki Ninja ZX-14R, which has an enormous 1,441cc engine with a top speed of 186 miles per hour!

Pretty damn impressive! immediately thought John.

In his younger days, John used to own a motor racing bike and competed in many races – and often won and had an impressive collection of silverware. He also loved performing stunts. So, he was now in his element!

Fortunately, just as Steve was careless about leaving crates of firearms lying around in the garage, so was he with the key to his superbike, which John found conveniently hanging from a hook on the wall, saving him some valuable time not having to hotwire it. He figured that only a fool would try to break into Steve's property with all the CCTV cameras and military hardware he had in place.

Stokes shoved on one of a choice of three snazzy helmets lying neatly on a shelf above. Then hopped onto the bike and manoeuvred it to where the door release button was located on the wall nearby, thumped it with his fist, and as the garage door began to swing open, he started the powerful engine. Now leaning his upper body as flat against the bike as he could, he revved the engine until it roared, and when the door wasn't even halfway open, he zoomed out of the garage and onto the road.

And so, another chase on the streets of Dubai began!

CHAPTER FIVE

As Stokes exited the garage door, SWAT team members entered through the internal door firing their assault rifles at random and causing even more damage to Steve's prized Ferrari.

He had just got out in the nick of time. But his troubles weren't over yet! He now had to somehow shake off the four police patrol cars and three motorcyclists that were now on his tail, having seen him just flash past them outside on the street.

'He won't get very far with all the roadblocks we have in place!' declared the officer in charge, Ahmad Fayed, confidently smiling at his deputy standing next to him outside Steve Reynolds's villa.

The local and national TV crews were also there by now filming what they could. It was due to this massive media presence that orders were made not to fire at the fugitive. Unless, of course, it was necessary to prevent further loss of life. And the authorities certainly didn't want innocent bystanders getting caught in the crossfire.

'Remember! Do not discharge your weapons unless he fires first! I want him captured alive!' said the officer in charge over the radio.

By now, few cars remained on the main road in and out of Palm Jumeirah.

70 - 80 - 90 - 100 - 110 - 120 - 130 - 140 - 150 - 160 - 170 miles per hour Stokes had now reached. It was like he was on a racetrack again. But in this high-octane race, there was no shiny trophy for the winner. Only his pride and freedom on offer - and John would be happy with just that right now!

As he left the area, he could hear the call to evening prayer, known as Isha, in the distance. It was strangely calming.

He was well ahead of the cops still chasing him, but he could see roadblocks on both sides of the carriageway up ahead. 'FUCK!' he screamed into his helmet. Any calmness he felt quickly disappeared! He now had a separate race in his head: it was a race against time to think of a quick escape route to evade capture. Having studied the map of the area, he knew the turn-off to the marina was just a few hundred metres past the roadblocks. If he could get past them, then it would be easier to lose the cops once he was in the busy marina area. He had already figured that since the cops were not shooting at him, they probably wanted him captured alive. And that had more to do with the kudos the Dubai authorities would receive than his welfare. Not to mention the humiliation it would cause the British Government if an ex-British soldier were captured and tried for a crime on their soil.

But as his bike thundered ever closer towards the blockade, he could now see that there was little chance of him getting through: it was as tight as a straight man's arsehole after suddenly realising he was in a gay bar.

John couldn't go forward, and he couldn't turn round and go backwards either. He was trapped – or screwed as John would put it. He slowed the thoroughbred motorbike down and drove around the deserted carriageway in circles, pondering what to do.

'Give yourself up! You cannot escape! We have you surrounded!' said a commanding broken English voice through a megaphone.

No shit! thought Stokes.

The police vehicles chasing behind him were now almost upon him. John revved his engine to full throttle twice, then sped towards the roadblock, leaving skid marks on the hot tarmac (and his underpants). Then within only several metres away, amid car horns blaring, he suddenly diverted towards the central crash barrier. As he approached it, he did a wheelie onto a tapered end section and continued driving at speed, skilfully balancing along it like Evel Knievel.

The cops, positioned behind their vehicles with their weapons poised outstretched in front of them, couldn't believe their eyes as the escapee casually rode past them. Nor could all those stuck in the traffic jam on the other side of the carriageway: they, too, watched in sheer disbelief – and awe – as the spectacle unfolded. Some had even gotten out of their vehicles for a better look. It was like watching a Hollywood action movie – only this was real!

Now safely past, John whizzed through the air as he jumped back down off the crash barrier and onto the carriageway, giving the cops the finger as he made his escape.

As it turned out, the roadblock meant to stop John Stokes had worked in his favour, as it had now stopped the oncoming cops chasing after him from getting past. One of the cop motorcyclists tried to copy Stokes by mounting the crash barrier but embarrassingly fell off and crashed. And, by the time the cops had unblocked the carriageway, the Houdini motorbiker had already reached the junction and headed west towards the bustling marina area.

Now on the smaller roads, Stokes greatly reduced his speed to comply with the national speed limits and joined the busy traffic flow. The last thing he wanted now was to get stopped by a traffic cop.

Stokes could hear a couple of police choppers circling above him, but by the time they got there, the daylight was quickly fading, and he had blended in with the traffic unseen.

John couldn't quite believe that he had made it that far, and as he slowly approached the barrier to the marina entrance, he felt a growing sense of relief. Though, he didn't allow himself to become too complacent as he still had to get past the guard.

Meanwhile, the Dubai World Cup had ended, and Steve and Helga were now on their way back to Palm Jumeirah, oblivious to the carnage that had taken place at his villa.

Steve hadn't had the chance to speak to Helga about chartering her yacht. But it all seemed pointless to him now that John would've been captured and taken into custody – or so he expected. So, he didn't bother to mention it. Instead, he continued moaning about losing a shitload of money as Helga bobbed her head rapidly up and down giving him a blowjob.

'FUUUCK!' he hollered with delight as cum mixed with saliva oozed out of the yachtswoman's mouth and ran down his main mast. 'Quick! Swallow it! Don't let it get on my Dolce and Gabbana suit!' he quickly exclaimed, panicking as he continued to drive well over the speed limit, high on alcohol and cocaine.

Back at the marina, John raised his helmet visor and handed his security pass to the guard, hoping he would pass as his mate Steve. He spoke with the same accent, and had the same skin complexion and eye colouring as Steve, not to mention he was wearing his clothes and riding his bike, so why not?

Good evening Mr Reynolds! I thought that was you!' said the friendly, smiling Indian guard. Adding, 'I recognised your bike.' John smiled with his eyes. The guard then remarked nonchalantly: 'No Helga with you this evening then?'

'No, I'm planning on surprising her when she arrives later!' answered John, winking.

The guard's smile grew wider, coming to a salacious conclusion as to what John meant by 'surprising her', politely saying, 'Have an enjoyable evening, sir!' The chatty guard then looked up towards the sky as he started to raise the barrier, remarking, 'Those police choppers must be keen to find whoever they're searching for!'

John just nodded his head in agreement. Then as soon as the barrier was clear, drove slowly forward, keeping within the 5-mph speed limit.

Suddenly, the guard came running after him shouting his name followed by something else, which he couldn't quite make out. Stokes's immediate reaction was to grasp the handle of his pistol tucked under his shirt. Then as the guard got nearer, John heard him repeat: 'You forgot your pass!'

John stopped and thanked him as he took the pass back from him, relieved that was all it was, and drove on. His impersonation of Steve had worked!

Stokes drove past one gleaming luxury yacht after another, looking for Helga's, named 'Slow Motion', hoping it was a lot faster than the name implied.

Then towards the far end of the long jetty, there she was, dwarfed by the two 200ft plus luxury superyachts on either side. It was one of those hybrid types of yachts with sails and a motor called a Motor Sailer.

'Oh, man! You've got to be fucking kidding me!' mumbled John to himself. Helga's yacht was only a fraction of the size of all the others. And by John's estimation, it was only about 14 m in length.

His immediate thoughts were that he'd never be able to sail a vessel of that size through the Gulf of Oman – it would be far too dangerous in those turbulent waters. It was immediately apparent that Helga's boat was probably only used for short sailing trips along the coast. But what choice did he have? He couldn't just commandeer one of the other nearby yachts like a bleedin' pirate – he could see lights on inside and out and that there were multiple occupants onboard them. That would cause far too much commotion – which was the last thing he needed right now. So, reluctantly, he wheeled the bike along the gangplank, making as little sound as possible, and parked it on the aft deck. He managed to find a large sheet of tarpaulin and rope in one of the storage bins and quickly covered and secured it to a railing so it would be out of view.

Then without hesitation, he headed below deck to the small engine room to hotwire the engine (there wasn't a key left carelessly lying about there). He located a toolbox and some electrical wires. Then before working his engineering magic, he set about removing the large engine cover to access the Cummins 245 hp diesel engine. Cover removed, he quickly located the battery and identified the ignition wire and the starter wire. Then began rewiring the ignition system to bypass the switch and complete the electrical circuit. Once complete, he held his breath and cranked the engine. Fortunately, it started the first time!

Leaving the engine running, he put the cover back on, dashed back to the cockpit, flicked a few switches to turn on the GPS navigational system - among other things, and then pressed a button that automatically pulled up the anchor. Which he was pleased about as it saved him precious time not having to do it manually. He then hurried back onto the aft deck, across the gangway, and quickly released the mooring ropes from the quayside bollards. Then, it was back onto the vessel to slide the gangway on board and hurl in the mooring ropes before darting back to the bridge to take the helm.

Usually, other crew members would help with these shipboard tasks, but he didn't have this luxury and just had to get on with it.

Stokes had already checked, and there was a full tank of fuel with spare onboard and enough food and drink supplies to last him for a few days. *I expect Helga had a charter booked for tomorrow,* thought the new captain of the 'Slow Motion' as he steered away from her berth and out of the shadows of the two superyachts on either side and then out of the marina.

It was then that John suddenly realised he still had his helmet on – he wondered why the other yachtsmen were giving him funny looks! He would laugh at this every so often as he ventured out into the open sea and the unknown.

Steve's flies now zipped back up; on the approach to the Palm Jumeirah turnoff, they came upon a massive traffic jam with a tailback several miles long.

'Oh, *shit* it!' expressed Steve as he abruptly slowed down before coming to a complete halt.

'I told you the traffic was bad! Maybe there's been an accident?' commented Helga, equally pissed-off, hoping to have got back to her yacht without any hold-ups so she could get an early night and be fresh for an early morning charter booked.

''ere, put my gun in your handbag just in case we get stopped by the traffic cops!' he said as he reached into his glove compartment and handed it to her. 'They're less likely to search you.'

She reluctantly dropped the large pistol into her handbag where there was an audible metal upon metal clinking sound.

'What was that I heard?' asked Steve, curious as he leaned over and peered inside her bag not waiting for an answer. *'Fuck me!* Where d'ya get that Glock from?' There was another identical pistol inside.

'You gave it to me a while back, in case I needed to protect myself, remember?' answered Helga, coolly.

Steve frowned as if he couldn't remember, grunting a little.

'You were probably too high on coke to remember, sweetheart,' she commented, grinning nervously.

'GOD DAMN IT!' he suddenly shouted in frustration, slamming the steering wheel hard with the palms of his hands, his attention once again focusing on the traffic jam. 'I can't believe the tailback is this fucking far!'

'I bet there's been a pile-up!' she repeated before tutting loudly. 'There are often accidents on this busy road. I was driving along here only last' – she paused to think – 'Oh, when was it?' she asked herself. '... On Thursday, that's right, and there was an accident then, as well! Too many vehicles on the roads, that's the problem ...'

Steve had a good idea why there was a hold-up but didn't mention it to Helga. Instead, he just sat there, arms folded, oblivious to car horns honking and Helga ranting in his ear, wondering if John had got away.

I bet he's outfoxed the bastards! Slipped out of their slimy grasp! Steve thought, smiling inwardly. *He's probably taken my superbike – that's what I would've done.'* Then, *'Shit, I hope not!* he suddenly thought, less cheery. *And I expect he's nicked a yacht and is sailing on the high seas by now! Oh, fuck! Not Helga's yacht!*

He then turned and smiled gingerly towards Helga.

It would be two years before John and Steve's paths would cross again.

CHAPTER SIX

Once John was far enough out at sea, he charted a course to Karachi (24°54′20.16″N, 67°4′55.92″E. 746 nautical miles), clinging on to the UAE coastline for as long as he could - or dare. Through a pair of binoculars, he could see police patrol boats speeding back and forth nearer land, but in the busy shipping lanes, he could hide behind the many other much larger vessels.

He spotted the unmistakable iconic contours of the world-famous QE2 cruise liner. Now permanently docked at Port Rashid and used as a floating hotel - like him, now decommissioned from service. He remembered his father telling him that he travelled aboard her when she set sail for the Falklands War on the 12th of May 1982. He regretted not visiting her while he was staying in Dubai, taking it for granted that he would at some point. Now that was not likely to ever happen.

His thoughts then turned to Steve Reynolds. He hoped that Steve and his girlfriend Helga would not report the yacht missing for a while – at least until he had a chance to reach Karachi. Part of him now regretted telling Steve his plans – just in case he spilt the beans. What if he had? He may have done. And for all John knew, there could be a massive police presence waiting to arrest him at the port. No doubt Interpol would be involved by now. Any such troubling thoughts he quickly shut out of his mind – at least for the time being.

Fortunately, the Persian Gulf was relatively calm that evening – except when huge tanker ships would pass by and create waves, causing his yacht to sway uncontrollably from side to side. And as the daylight faded into darkness, he cautiously switched on the wheelhouse lights for the first time. Then with the autopilot switched on, set about preparing himself some food in the small galley below. He was starving! Scouting around, he soon found some bread, cheese and pate, and a bottle of Merlot to wash it all down. Indeed, there was a whole wine rack of the stuff, which cheered him up slightly.

Sitting under the stars on the aft deck, it didn't take him long to polish it all off. It was the first time in 24 hours that he felt safe. And, as he relaxed, taking frequent swigs out of the bottle (which no doubt helped), he tried to get his head around all that had happened in such a short space of time. He wondered whether Steve would find his note to him explaining what had happened. Probably not, he surmised.

There was no going back now: he had lost his job, probably his friendship with Steve, and at times felt as if he was losing his mind. But there was no use in maudlin! He had to get himself to Karachi or some other place before he was discovered.

Karachi - also known as the City of Lights - is a huge sprawling seaport city with a dense population of over 20 million citizens. So, you'd have thought it would be easy for him to blend in with all the other Western tourists and become invisible. The only trouble is, very few tourists go there, and being a Westerner always draws attention - which is okay if you like that sort of thing, but not when you are trying to lie low.

One of the reasons few foreign travellers go there is because of the high murder rate. Indeed, Karachi until recent times, was considered the fifth most dangerous city in the world. And it wasn't until the Pakistani Rangers moved in to clean up the troubled areas that it became relatively safe to go there. Especially in Lyari, which had rival crime syndicate gangs battling each other over territory every day on the blood-ridden streets. At the height of the gang wars, more than eight hundred people were killed each year!

John was very aware of the gangs of Lyari, but he planned to slip quietly into the city, get a forged passport, and go straight to the airport to get a direct flight to the UK.

To reach Karachi, travelling at approximately 10 knots to save fuel, it would take Stokes approximately three days. To ensure that there was enough fuel, he would also use the sails. Stokes was a keen sailor, so that wouldn't be a problem.

His badly bruised and weary body was desperate to sleep, but his mind was determined to stay awake. And now instead of fighting police assailants, he was fighting fatigue. What if he fell asleep and accidentally drifted off course and ended up on the shores of the UAE and in the hands of the police? Or collided with a much larger ship? But no matter how hard he resisted falling asleep, his body had other plans, and slowly but surely, he drifted, not off course, but off to sleep.

On dry land, Steve and his girlfriend, Helga, finally reached the marina three hours later. Despite Helga having to get up early for a charter cruise booked the next morning, Steve talked her into having a nightcap with him on her yacht. This also had a lot to do with him not wanting to face any problems he may encounter upon his arrival at his villa. He knew John wouldn't be taken into custody without a fight and was dreading to find out what damage there might be to his property. The full shocking extent of the damage and the dreadful loss of life, he wouldn't find out about for another couple of hours or so.

It was now the fag end of the day. They parked the car in the nearby marina car park and walked hand in hand along the waterfront towards the marina security entrance. When they arrived, it was the same Indian guard that had been on duty earlier. As soon as he saw Steve and Helga approaching, he staggered backwards slightly in disbelief.

'Mr R-R-Reynolds?' he stuttered, wide-eyed. Thinking that maybe he had a twin. 'Is that really you?'

'Well, who else would I be ya daft cu—' Helga squeezed his hand tightly to warn him against using the 'C' word. Swearing is a criminal offence in the UAE.

'How are you, Sam,' she asked, cutting in, smiling.

'Oh, I am doing fine, thank you, miss,' he answered quickly before saying, 'But – but how is it possible? I saw you, Mr Reynolds, sir, pass by here and sail the Slow Motion out of the marina only a couple of hours or so ago?' He sounded very confused.

Steve looked at him as if he was demented or something. 'What the hell is he talking about?'

'Shh! Be quiet!' ordered Helga. 'Excuse me. What was that?' she asked the guard, thinking she must have heard it wrong.

'It was you! I'm sure of it!' said the guard as he continued staring at Steve, convinced. 'You were driving your motorbike. And I saw your security pass!'

'Wait a moment,' said Helga, now deeply concerned. 'You saw *my* yacht leaving the marina, you say?'

Sam turned his head towards the long-legged blonde and nodded.

Helga immediately barged past him, dragging Steve along with her. *'Quick!* We need to check if it's still here!' she said panicking. Thinking, it can't be true.

Even with the effects of being coked-up to the eyeballs, it didn't take Steve long to figure out who the culprit was that stole his bike and Helga's yacht.

Both started running quickly along the quayside towards her yacht's berth.

'Oh, bloody hell!' said the Indian guard to himself.

They passed one superyacht after another.

'For fucks sake, slow down, will ya,' Steve spluttered, worn out. He pulled his hand away from hers. 'You go on ahead – I'll catch you up!'

He wasn't as fit as he used to be – all that smoking, drinking, and drug use over the last several years had caught up with him. By contrast, the younger, much fitter, leggy Helga, speeded on in front of him.

After a short while, Steve, who had decided to walk the rest of the way, heard Helga screaming.

Steve finally got there, having to stop to puke his guts up a couple of times before he did. He immediately opened his arms out towards her to offer her a hug. But the sight of sick all down his designer suit quickly changed her mind, and she sat down on the hard concrete quayside instead.

'Someone's stolen her!' she stated angrily, crestfallen as she stared into the void.

'No shit!' thought Steve but didn't say it - not while she was so upset. He just smiled uncomfortably.

'We need to call the police!' she then said determinedly as she fumbled for her phone inside her handbag.

'No! Wait! Wait!' quickly said Steve. 'Let's not be too hasty!'

'Too hasty!' she repeated with a surprised look on her face.

'We can't call the cops!' There was a pause. 'I stashed 100 kilos of coke onboard!' Arms dealing wasn't the only thing Steve traded in.

'You did *what?!* Are you out of your *fucking* mind? Oh, *shit!'* she said. 'So, now what are we gonna do?'

'I haven't got a *fuckin'* clue!' he replied as he contemplated the possible torturous outcomes that he might suffer at the hands of the drug barons if he didn't deliver the goods on time. *'Fuck! Fuck! Fuck!'* he repeated out loud, panicking as the sobering reality started to sink in. 'I'm a *dead* man! They're gonna *fucking* kill me, I know it!' Her stolen yacht was the least of his worries now.

'Calm down! Calm down!' she said as she got up from her uncomfortable sedentary position and went and put her arm around him, being careful to avoid the sick. 'Keep your voice down – you're drawing too much attention!' She noticed people looking at them from their cabin windows.

She knew about his drug dealing, but what he hadn't told her was that when he borrowed her yacht to go on the occasional 'fishing trip', he also bought drugs from the Lyari gangs to sell across the UAE. The same drugs which were originally supplied by the Taliban and smuggled out of Afghanistan and across the border into Pakistan.

'Yeah, yeah, sorry. I'll figure something out – I always do,' he then said more quietly, starting to calm down a bit.

'But where will I live now?' she then moaned.

'Don't worry, Blondie,' answered Steve reassuringly (Blondie was his pet name for her), 'I'll book you into a nice hotel for the time being – so that we can continue to meet up and … You know!'

coyly continued Steve, nodding. He was being unusually bashful for a change.

There was an awkward pause while she looked blankly at him, waiting for him to spit it out – making him squirm a bit. '… *Fuck?*' finally suggested Helga, speaking for him, knowing all along what he had in mind.

Steve nodded again and managed half a smile.

'*My God!* Is sex all you ever think of?' she asked him rather indignantly.

Er, yeah, pretty much! thought Steve honestly as his smile decreased.

'You seem more concerned about getting your end away than you do about my yacht. Well, you can *forget* about that for a while!' she told him straight as she slapped him with her handbag and quickly strutted off back along the quayside. 'I'll find my *own* accommodation, *thank you!*' she then called out as he stood there dumbstruck. 'And *don't* contact me unless you have news about my yacht!'

Steve was too knackered still to chase after her (and he wouldn't be able to perform the act even if he had the chance), and so instead, bowed to all the amused people now staring out of their portholes at him. And as he slowly walked away, he gave them the finger.

Steve stared at his taped-off shell of a villa in despair as he stood on the pavement outside while someone in a police uniform propped him up and tried to explain what had happened. And, as the police forensics team went busily about their business moving in and out of the doorless villa at dizzying speed and red and blue lights bounced off the whitewashed walls from police vehicles parked outside, Steve could stand no longer. His knees buckled, and he collapsed to the ground in a state of shock before blacking out.

When Steve opened his eyes a few days later, he found himself early one morning in an ICU, lying in a private hospital bed surrounded by a male UAE doctor and two attractive female nurses. On the night he collapsed, he had suffered a cardiac arrest. The medics managed to resuscitate him, but he quickly fell into a coma. There was a high dose of drugs and alcohol found in his system, and what with all the stress and shock upon discovering that his girlfriend, Suzie, was dead, probably caused it.

And by the time Steve was coming out of his coma, John was arriving at the port of Karachi - but not in the way he had anticipated it, and certainly not in the way he had wanted it.

'Good morning!' said the doctor cheerfully to Steve as he and his nurses fussed around their patient.

Steve didn't speak, just stared at a boring picture on the wall in front of him as the nurses pulled tubes and whatnot off him.

'... You are lucky to be alive, Mr Reynolds,' said

the doctor while checking the heart monitor.

'Why, what happened?' Steve managed to ask, feeling in a slight daze still.

'You had a cardiac arrest and the shock caused you to go into a coma,' the doctor answered in a much less cheerful way. 'You've been spark-out for three days!'

'So what?! That's the length of time I usually sleep when I've been on a bender!' quipped Steve, somewhat garbled – ever the joker.

The doctor in charge looked bemused.

'We very nearly *lost* you!' chirped a female nurse.

'Why? Did I sleepwalk?' continued to joke Steve with a wry smile and a wink, causing a slight chuckle from one of the nurses. Even recovering from a cardiac arrest didn't stop him from flirting.

'I think we can reduce his morphine level now nurse,' said the doctor matter-of-factly.

'Oh, you're no fun, Doc!' retorted the hyperactive patient.

The doctor cracked a smile. Then addressing his patient and speaking rather soberly, he said, 'Fortunately for you, Mr Reynolds, there were a team of medics already tending to the injured SWAT team at your villa on the night of the killings.' There was a pause. 'You do still remember that dreadful night, don't you, Mr Reynolds?'

The patient nodded slowly. Then a tear rolled down each of his eyes as the enormity of what had happened suddenly came flooding back to him. He quickly shoved those horrid thoughts out of his mind. He certainly didn't want to have another heart attack. He needed to get better, sharpish – he had a lot of shit to deal with! Though the thought did cross his mind that he might be better off dead.

Still blurry-eyed, Steve noticed a lone figure sitting patiently in the corner of the room, notepad in hand. He was wearing a suit and tie – looking slightly dishevelled with his shirt collar undone and his tie skewed over to one side, as well as being unshaven and his hair in need of a comb. Steve immediately thought, *copper.*

He could spot one a mile off: he was miserable-looking, scruffy, and yet wore highly polished shoes! He'd been in police custody enough times over the years to know.

'Oh, shit! They've probably discovered my cache of arms, he thought, *and they've now come to arrest me!*

Steve immediately closed his eyes again and pretended to fall back into a coma. However, the doctor in charge wasn't buying it and gently shook his arm back and forth to get his attention.

'Wakey, wakey, Mr Reynolds,' said the doctor. 'A very nice police officer would like to ask you some questions – don't worry, it won't take very long, will it, Detective?' The copper smiled and shook his head, then got up from his seat and approached the bed. 'Then you can get some much-needed rest.'

Fuck me, don't I even get offered a cooked breakfast first? thought Steve. *What sort of a crap establishment is this?!*

'Well, we'll leave you to your job then, Detective,' said the doctor as he made his way towards the door, followed by his nursing staff. 'If you need us, we'll just be outside.'

'Thank you,' said the detective before giving the patient his full attention.

'Don't tell me,' Steve quickly said before the detective had a chance to speak, 'you've come to arrest me for speeding?' The detective chuckled and shook his head. 'I know! Taking a slash in a public place? No wait! *Swearing* in a public place?' Steve's eyebrows then raised, thinking, *as a matter of fact, I did both!*

The detective's smile widened, saying: 'No. *Why?* Are you admitting to those crimes, Mr Reynolds?'

Blimey, a copper smiling. Now there's a surprise! thought Steve. He then cracked a smile back in response.

'Good morning, Mr Reynolds. I am Detective Sergeant Kashif. I'm glad to see that you are making a good recovery!' said the deeply spoken detective.

The local detective spoke perfect English – indeed, his grasp of English grammar was probably greater than Steve's (which wasn't difficult!).

'It must be all that healthy stuff they've been

pumping into me!' responded Steve.

'I expect it is, I expect it is. You obviously haven't lost your sense of humour,' said the detective still smiling as he removed his notepad and pen from his hip pocket. 'Let's hope that you haven't lost your memory either!' Then dropping his smile, 'Now, on a serious note, Mr Reynolds, there are some important and personal questions I need to ask you.' Steve's smile dropped also. The frivolity was over.

There was a moment of tense silence as the detective collected his thoughts. He then spoke.

'I am leading the investigation into the brutal murders of Suzie Wang and the Frenchman, Andre Boucher, who were both gunned down on your poolside terrace during the early evening of July 15th.' Steve listened intently. 'I am terribly sorry to hear that, as I understand you knew them personally.

Steve slowly nodded.

'Am I correct also in saying that you and Miss Wang were romantically attached and that she lived with you at your villa?'

'If you mean by *'romantically attached'*, were we screwing? Then, yeah, we were,' answered Steve bluntly while nodding. 'And, yes, we lived together. But what's that got to do with the price of fish?'

'Price of *fish?'* repeated the detective, confused.

English idioms, he was less familiar with.

'Nevermind. Carry on!'

'And erm, how close would you say you were with each other?'

Steve paused for thought, frowning. 'Very close ... I mean, we had our arguments, but don't all couples?' Steve's eyes started welling up again.

'Yes, yes, of course, of course. But I was wondering if you both had more of a ... shall we say, open sexual relationship?'

'No, definitely not!' quickly answered Steve, shaking his head immediately. 'And Suzie would never sleep around behind my back. She could be flirty, and lots of guys fancied her. I mean, who wouldn't - she is *gorgeous! Was* gorgeous!' Steve wiped his glazed eyes, 'but she would never do anything like that and betray me.'

'I see!' The detective cleared his throat. 'So, how long have you both known each other?'

'... I guess about three months. Suzie was working as a cocktail waitress here in Dubai.' Steve suddenly broke out into a smile. 'She made the *best* Singapore Slings ever! That's where she was from - *Singapore!*'

The detective interjected. 'Well, actually, our records show that Miss Wang was from Hong Kong!'

Steve's smile soon dropped again as he began to think that maybe he didn't know her as well as he thought. His eyebrows raised, muttering just, 'Oh!' There was an awkward pause. Steve then started to get agitated and annoyed. *'Look!* Where's all these questions leading to?'

'I am sorry, Mr Reynolds, I didn't mean to upset you any more than you already are! It's just that … it's just that her autopsy revealed that on the day she died, there were two different specimens of semen found inside her uterus and fallopian tube,' delicately said the detective. 'One matched your DNA.' There was a pause. 'And the other matched the Frenchman's DNA' – *I bleedin' knew that her and that French fucker were at it!* thought Steve, whose blood pressure and heart rate immediately started to show rising on the monitor – 'and there is evidence to suggest that shortly before the murders took place, Mr Stokes may have attempted to rape her!' The detective briefly explained that forensics discovered a text message on Mr Boucher's mobile phone from Miss Wang, telling him to hurry back to the villa because Mr Stokes had tried to force himself upon her. Steve immediately scoffed, raising his eyebrows as if to say, I'd take that with a pinch of salt. He then showed Steve a photo of the deceased's body, pointing out the bruises on her wrists, suggesting a struggle – being careful to hide the gaping bullet hole in her head with his thumb. There was an even longer pause before saying worrisomely: 'One similarity between this case and that of the murdered Filipino hotel worker was that the perpetrator of this crime also went to the trouble of covering the victim's semi-naked body before fleeing the scene – which leads me to suspect that Mr Stokes may have committed these crimes also.' Then as though deep in thought, 'It's almost as if the killer felt remorse directly afterwards.'

Outwardly, Steve tried to project calmness while his mind absorbed the complexities of what he had just heard – but inwardly, he was quickly becoming filled with mixed emotions, including rage. A rage he had not experienced since he fought in Afghanistan. He clenched his fists so tightly under the bedcovers that he could not tighten them anymore.

'... Mr Reynolds! Mr Reynolds! Are you alright?' said the detective, suddenly. Steve had been staring absently into space. He was in shock.

'... Yeah, yeah,' he finally answered as he turned his gaze back towards him. 'It's all come as a big shock, that's all!'

'It is completely understandable, Mr Reynolds. And I am sorry to have to break it to you like this. But the sooner I get answers and can piece everything together, the sooner we can catch the culprit of these heinous crimes.'

Steve nodded, expressing that he too wanted to find out the truth and see the culprit brought to justice.

'... Oh, you mark my words, we'll find the culprit – don't you worry!'

'Well, surely the CCTV footage would've picked up what happened?' suddenly said Steve, sounding surprised that the detective would need to ask these questions when all the proof surely would've been captured on video.

'Alas, I am afraid whoever it was that committed these crimes knew how to deactivate the security cameras as we have no video evidence of the crimes taking place!' stated the detective, making that clear.

'Well, now I know what I know about Suzie, it wouldn't surprise me if she turned off the cameras so that I wouldn't be able to discover her dirty little secret with lover boy!'

'But what you are saying is only supposition, Mr Reynolds – please leave the detective work to me!' then said the detective, less patient.

Steve scowled at him and acted a little put out by the detective's remark – like a naughty child after he'd just been told off – and went silent for a moment.

'Now, I understand that you employed Mr Stokes as an oil and gas engineer?' continued the detective.

'Yeah, that's right,' affirmed Steve.

'And am I also right in saying that he started his employment with your firm about a year ago?'

'Yeah, that sounds about right.'

'Would you say that you know him well?'

'Yeah, reasonably well,' offered Steve, nodding.

'Obviously well enough to let him stay at your villa, Mr Reynolds.'

'Yeah, but at the time, I didn't know that he was wanted in connection with those dreadful crimes,' then quickly protested Steve.

'Both victims were shot in the head from a distance of at least 20 metres, Mr Reynolds. *Twenty metres! And* there were only two bullets fired – both hitting their targets with extreme accuracy!' Steve cringed as he listened. The detective then added, 'The 9x19mm bullets recovered at the scene we believe were fired from a British Armed Forces standard issue Glock 17 pistol.' There was a slight pause. 'I understand that you and Mr Stokes are both ex-Royal Marines!'

Steve confirmed with another nod, saying: *'So!'*

'So, you both know a thing or two about guns,' further probed the detective with his loaded questions, waiting for the interviewee's reactions and responses to see if he could catch him out.

Steve weakly clapped his hands together, saying sarcastically: *'Wow! Great* detective work, Sherlock!'

The detective remained solemn, as this was no laughing matter, and continued with his questioning undeterred.

'As you well know, on the day of the murders, John Stokes escaped from your villa and continues to be at large. Do you know –'

Steve interrupted. 'No, I don't know of his whereabouts!' he stated categorically, putting a stop to that line of questioning.

'Okay. Now tell me what you know about Andre Boucher, please,' then asked the detective with his pen poised ready above his notepad.

'Well, I hired him as a pool attendant a couple of months or so ago. But he spent more time ogling at my girlfriend than he did at doing his job. So, I fired him, only to discover that she – Suzie that is – had re-hired him.' Steve laughed cynically. 'Now I know why!'

There was a pause.

'Go on,' said the detective, keen to know more about the Frenchman.

'Well, apart from him being French, that's all I know. I think he said he was from Paris. To be honest – we never spoke much. I never really liked the cocky bastard.'

The detective ignored Steve's occasional expletives – he had far more important matters on his mind. *'I see!'* he said. 'So, would you say that you were jealous of him then?'

Steve scoffed. *'Jealous!* No, I bleedin' wasn't. *What,* of that skinny blee—'

'Well, a young, good-looking virile man getting the attention of your girlfriend on your property,' pointed out the detective, interrupting him.

'What are you trying to say – that I did it now? Cause I have an alibi. I was at the Dubai World Cup, mingling with several of your cronies. Which they can testify!'

'I am not accusing anybody of anything at this stage, Mr Reynolds. But having an alibi does not rule you out of the enquiry either – maybe you knew that they were having an affair and arranged the two lover's murders – and *maybe* you hired Mr Stokes to do your dirty work for you?!'

'Listen, I've had enough of this! I was very fond of Suzie!' stated Steve angrily. He then started calling for the doctor. *'Doctor! Doctor!'*

'Only – one detail I haven't mentioned,' continued the detective, now speaking rapidly and in an even more solemn tone, 'is that the killer also cut poor Mr Boucher's penis off!' adding, 'Which, so far, has not been found!'

Steve gulped and immediately looked down towards his groin area, cringing at the thought, and just said, *'Blimey!'*

'It *certainly* appears to be an act of jealousy to me!'

'Well, I had nothin' to do with it!'

'Just answer me this one question before I go, please,' insisted the zealous detective.

Steve looked at the detective ready to listen.

'Do you think that John Stokes is capable of rape and murder?'

Steve took a moment to answer. Then: 'Do I think

he is capable of killing? Yes! That was what Her – or I should now say, His Majesty's Armed Forces trained him to do. Do I think he is capable of the rape and murder of women? No!'

Just then, the doctor and his entourage came into the room.

'I think that will be enough questioning for today, Detective,' assertively said the doctor in charge.

'Well, thank you for answering my questions, Mr Reynolds. My time with you has been enlightening! No doubt I will be speaking to you again soon.' Steve just looked at him without emotion. The detective then smiled and added before turning to leave, 'Don't leave the country for the time being!'

After the detective left, it occurred to Steve that he didn't once mention anything about the large stash of firearms he had on his premises. Steve could only assume that the corrupt officials he had dealings with secretly disposed of it, and the detective was either in the dark about it or turning a blind eye. He could only hope that the bent coppers first on the scene did get rid of it before someone with more scruples found it. Otherwise, it could mean a lengthy jail sentence for him.

CHAPTER SEVEN

When John Stokes first opened his eyes the morning after he'd set sail in a bid for freedom, he immediately closed them again and turned his head to one side to avoid the bright sunlight. When his eyes had adjusted, he found himself surrounded only by blue with no land in sight. Or life, other than the occasional sea birds flying by. Oh, how he wished he could fly! Then he would fly well away from these parts to somewhere safe where no one could find him and start a new life. He would even substitute the lovely, hot weather for somewhere cold - anywhere but there. He felt relieved, though, not to have been smashed to smithereens by a much larger ocean-going vessel or capsized in rough seas. Fortunately, the seas had remained calm.

He sat for a moment watching with simple pleasure as the rays of sunlight danced a jig upon the sea and sparkled like pirate's treasure. The ex-Royal Marine then got up from his rather uncomfortable position on the aft deck – he was so tired that it wouldn't have mattered where he slept – and checked that he was still on course for the Strait of Hormuz, and to see how much fuel there was left. He calculated that there would be just enough fuel left to reach Karachi if he kept at the slow speed of knots he was currently travelling.

Once the important stuff was checked, he made himself some breakfast, consisting of a bowl of muesli and a banana, and began eating it while he waited for the kettle to boil to make some coffee. Strong and Black, how he liked it – which was just as well, as there was no milk anyway.

He hadn't even ventured into the living quarters yet. So, after breakfast on deck, he headed down the steep stairs to the cabins. There was a total of three double cabins. Two of them were clearly for the paying guests: everything was spotlessly clean and tidy; the beds were neatly made using crisp, fresh-smelling linen, and displayed at the foot of the beds, using the same meticulous attention to detail, were neatly folded towels with a small bar of soap laid on top in the centre. The other cabin, by contrast, was very untidy: the bed was only half-made, and there were clothes left strewn around the room and underwear hanging out of the chest of drawers, trapped by the drawers. This was obviously Helga's cabin. She was far too busy running the ship to have time to keep her quarters spic and span as well.

He also discovered some expensive-looking jewellery inside an ornate trinket box on top of the dressing cabinet: designer watches, gold necklaces and bracelets, and diamond earrings and fingerings. *That must be worth a few bob!* he thought.

There was proof that Steve spent time onboard: a men's designer wash bag on the dressing table and a pair of men's sized twelve shoes tucked partially under the bed. John looked inside the wardrobe, noticing that Steve also kept some of his clobber there, which he thought would come in handy. One unusual item of clothing he saw hanging up at the end of the rail was a maid's uniform. But not the usual sort of maid's uniform. This all-in-one outfit was very short and had a lot of frills attached. There was also a pair of fur-lined handcuffs hanging from the rail next to it. *Kinky bastard!* thought John as he closed the wardrobe doors and continued searching around for any useful stuff.

He decided that he would sleep in Helga's cabin as Steve's personal belongings were kept there. It was when he was searching around in her cabin that he discovered the large stash of cocaine. It was all neatly laid out in single rows under the double mattress. And the only reason he came upon it was that he decided to turn the mattress over as he didn't like the thought of Steve and Helga shagging on it.

And there it was staring him in the face! *'Oh, fuck!'* audibly said, John. He knew that Steve took drugs, but he didn't know that he was the bleedin' supplier. By his quick estimation, there must have been at least two dozen bricks of the stuff. He hurriedly turned the mattress over as if someone might see it. Then remembered that he was alone in the middle of the fucking Persian Gulf and stopped panicking.

He sat down on the edge of the bed and contemplated what he should do with it. *Throw the damn lot of it into the sea!* he told himself adamantly. Not wanting to be any part of it. *No, that would only cause Steve even more pain and anguish – and I've caused enough trouble for him as it is! I'll leave it where it is for the time being.* After only a moment, a different, much less kind voice then sparked up. *Hold on a minute, knobhead! Why don't you sell the cocaine? Just think of what you could do with all that money! Buy a big house and a fancy new car! There would be lots of beautiful women attracted to ya then!*

John chuckled slightly at the absurdity of him being a drug dealer, immediately dismissing the idea. He then quickly got up and headed out of the cabin and up to the cockpit. On his way there, that stern, pushy inner voice, which he sometimes struggled to control, spoke to him again: *Okay, don't sell the drugs then, Pussy! But don't be a damn idiot, at least sell the fucking yacht and the bike!*

Looking out at sea, there was very little change of scenery, apart from a couple of large shipping vessels that had appeared on the horizon; the sea continued to remain calm, and there was very little wind - certainly not enough to bother with the sails.

He had intended to phone Steve and tell him where he'd left the yacht as well as explain what happened at the villa once he'd reached where he was going. But now he was starting to have second thoughts, thinking that maybe he *should* sell the yacht and the bike and not say anything. His bank account and credit cards would no doubt be frozen by now, denying him access to money, and he only had a small amount of cash on him, which probably wouldn't be enough to get a passport forged and a flight home. ,

After a short while of arguing with himself as he steered the vessel towards the mouth of the Strait of Hormuz, the temporary captain of the Slow Motion finally decided that he would stick to his original plan of telling Steve the whereabouts of the yacht. And only sell the bike - hoping that Steve doesn't mention it! He would wait till he was at the airport and about to board the plane before doing so, though. Just in case his friend had turned informant on him. It's amazing what people will divulge under pressure – torture – to save their own skin. Anyway, by that time he would already be on the plane home with a new identity.

He never liked beards, but as he felt the stubble on his classic square jawline from two days of remaining unshaven, he decided to grow one to help conceal his identity – besides, he didn't have a razor. He had already planned on changing his job title to an independent travel journalist, which would give him a good reason for being in Karachi. Even though, he knew very little about journalism.

As the Slow Motion sailed ever closer towards its destination, the same niggling thought, which had been bothering him ever since yesterday morning, started to niggle at him again. It was his regret for not insisting that he personally – and not Steve – would destroy the incriminating evidence against him in the case of the murdered Filipino hotel worker that caused his angst.

Why the fuck didn't you insist on disposing of the evidence yourself, you twat! screamed the nasty inner voice at him.

'But-but I was tired and injured, and-and I wasn't thinking straight!' John answered out loud, terrified, cowering.

You're weak and pathetic! Don't you realise that if that evidence ever were to turn up, it wouldn't just be you given a life sentence – or worse still, executed, it would be me as well!

'I know! I know! I'm sorry!' bleated John, 'please forgive me, please forgive, father!'

What did you just say? I've warned you never to call me that!

'Sorry, I meant, *sir!*'

Stop snivelling you ugly, stupid bastard, and get down on your hands and knees now and give me one hundred press-ups. *That's an order!*

'Yes, *sir!*' answered the ex-Bootneck.

I CAN'T HEAR YOU, SOLDIER! screamed the commanding inner voice.

'YES, *SIR!*' he screamed back, immediately throwing himself down on the deck to begin his punishment.

By the time he'd finished the gruelling one hundred press-ups, he could no longer hear the terrifying voice from his past. It was as if that person had left the room. John then got up, brushed himself down, and continued as if nothing had happened.

By midday, the winds had picked up. So, John thought now would be a good time to let wind power do its thing and conserve the limited diesel fuel left. Without delay, he quickly set about unfurling the sails. Keeping busy also helped him keep his inner demons at bay.

The Slow Motion had two masts with booms for the main and mizzen genoa jib sails, which were on roller furlers making it easier for John to manage by himself.

The unfurled sails immediately caught the wind as John steered her masterfully onward. He felt a huge sense of relief that his mariner's knowledge and experience had not failed him. He was also aware, though, that if a powerful storm should happen upon him, the traditionally low keel on a gulet yacht would cause her to struggle to keep sufficiently stable and could prove disastrous!

A few hours later, as John sailed into the Strait of Hormuz and crossed the invisible line from the Persian Gulf into the Gulf of Oman, it began to rain. Only lightly at first. But then it started to become heavier, and the sea became choppier. And, judging by the dark clouds in the distance, he was heading into a storm – a big one. Such storms or squalls at sea can start up with very little warning. He thought about switching on the VHF radio and tuning in to the BBC World Service channel for an updated weather report. And although it would be nice to hear a calm and soothing British voice over the airwaves at such a troubling time, he didn't need to be told what his eyes could see was inevitable, so, didn't bother.

The Strait of Hormuz lies between Iran to the northeast and the Arabian Peninsula to the southwest. But neither of these destinations held much appeal under the circumstances. And so, with little choice, he set about reefing the sails for better stability and to avoid damage, secured everything he could in place, then switched the engine back on to give the vessel more power against the increasingly high waves, keeping her at a steady and controllable speed, and continued onwards undeterred.

Steve received his cooked breakfast at last. His first solid meal in a while.

''bout bleedin' time – I'm starving!' Steve announced jocularly as the attractive nurse laid the tray of food on his lap.

'Less cheek from you,' replied the nurse, originally from the northeast of England, 'or you'll get your bottom slapped!'

'D'ya promise?' he retorted, grinning.

She giggled at his corny remark as she left the room.

He never paid much attention to political correctness bollocks, but he did resist patting her on the backside as she bent over.

As he munched away ravenously at his breakfast, his mind switched over to more serious matters – like getting the fuck outta there! He felt very vulnerable, stuck in a hospital bed where anybody could find him (and by 'anybody', he was thinking primarily about the drug dealers who still hadn't received the goods they had paid for and wouldn't think twice about putting a bullet through your skull).

You see, in the world of narcotics, Steve was only a small fish in a very big pond – a middleman, a go-between, and the bigger fish used his services because of the connections he had to corrupt UAE officials and the overseas drug manufacturers. They would pay him vast sums of cash dollars to buy the drugs from the Pakistani gangs on their behalf (which was less risky to them). But lately, they were becoming more and more impatient of his tardiness – because they, in turn, answered to even bigger fish in Europe and elsewhere.

And so, the thought of spending any more time in the hospital made him fear even more for his life. Indeed, every time the door to his private room opened, he anxiously wondered if it might be a gunman entering to kill him.

But despite him wanting to leave the hospital right away, they would not allow it until he'd made a complete recovery. Telling him that he must remain there for at least another week to give himself chance to rest properly and so they could make further tests and check his progress.

Lying in bed, bored out of his skull, Steve's thoughts returned once more to what the detective had told him, which immediately made him feel depressed. What he found the hardest to comprehend was that his friend, John, may have been the culprit. He hardly thought that likely, though. Not *John!* He was far too respectable for a start! Listening to the detective hint John might have attempted to rape her before murdering her made him think back to what John was saying about being set up - believing that there was a cover-up among the Dubai elite. His friend sounded sincere when he spoke about it. But what if John had been lying to him? He had to admit that it was one mighty big coincidence - though, he tended to believe his mate. He had seen first-hand how corrupt some of the UAE officials were. And what if this detective was involved - making this stuff up to try and pin the blame on John? However, the more he listened to the detective, the more genuine and believable he came across. And, of course, not everyone in authority here is corrupt. Steve could only but wonder!

Later that day, Steve tried giving his girlfriend, Helga - or now possibly ex-girlfriend - a call on her mobile. But despite ringing her several times throughout the rest of the day, she didn't answer his calls. Which really added to his anxiety and frustrations, because he needed to ask her a favour - a big one, and quick! He wanted her to sneak his Glock 17 pistol onto the premises so that he could protect himself. He was relieved to notice an armed guard stationed outside his room, though. But even then, his paranoid mind wondered if he might be the hitman.

The trouble was Steve wasn't sure if Helga was even aware of him being in the hospital and all the other stuff that had happened. *I'm sure Blondie would've already been to visit me if she knew,* Steve thought despondently. *She's probably in a huff because I haven't contacted her to apologize for all the trouble I've caused her! Maybe she doesn't want anything more to do with me? …*

Apart from his long-suffering wife in England, Steve's affair with Helga had probably been going on longer than with any other woman. But their relationship had always been patchy, though. And it wasn't unusual for them to regularly split up and then get back together again soon afterwards. Often, it would be her splitting up with him because of her, often correct, suspicions of him having dalliances with other women. Which he always denied, of course. But he did admit to forming a sexual relationship with Suzie and inviting her to move in with him. Something that Helga had never entertained in the past, as she preferred her independence, living and working on her yacht. And, although she was jealous and deeply resented sharing him with another woman, she didn't want to lose him and carried on still seeing him behind Suzie's back, which, in a way, felt empowered her – as she had one over on Suzie.

The truth is, Helga was probably the only person left in Dubai who Steve felt he trusted. So, he really needed to talk to her.

The next morning after breakfast, feeling a lot better and much relieved to still be alive and breathing, Steve telephoned Helga again. The phone rang for a while, and then, '... I don't want to speak to you!' snapped Helga's voice. 'Don't ring me again!''

'But Blondie, I need to speak to ya, babe –' The line suddenly went dead. *'Shit!'* He quickly rang her again. 'Hear me out, please – don't cut me off!'

There was a pause. 'Go on then. Speak!' she finally said, clearly still angry with him. Then just when he was about to speak, she continued speaking at rapid speed. 'Why didn't you call me? I've been worried sick about you these last three days – I thought the worst might have happened!'

'Ah, *babe* – you thought that I might be dead?' said Steve, managing finally to get a word in.

'No! I thought you might have left me for that whore, Suzie!' bluntly answered Helga before continuing incessantly with her diatribe. 'I don't know what you saw in her! Honestly, I don't!' There was a short pause. 'She's not even that pretty – she's short and bow-legged, and I bet they aren't even her *real* tits!'

Steve interrupted her, shocked by her unkind remarks *'Helga!* You shouldn't talk about the dead in that way!'

'Dead?!' she exclaimed, suddenly sounding

shocked herself.

'Yeah, she was shot and killed!' explained Steve. 'What, you didn't know?'

'No, I had no idea. Poor thing!'

'I just heard you speak of her in the past tense, that's all.'

'Really? It must have been a slip of the tongue! *Anyway,* where have you been all this time?'

'Well, if you'd let me speak, I would have explained!' said Steve, agitated.

There was a silence.

'Helga – are you still there?' he asked, unsure, surprised by her unusual silence.

'Yes! Go on – get on with it!' she said a bit impatiently.

'I'm in the intensive care unit at the Emirates Hospital. I had a cardiac arrest,' he began to tell her.

'Cardiac Arrest did you say?!' she asked him to clarify, sounding even more shocked than a moment ago.

'You heard me – I nearly died!'

'Oh my *God!'* she then expressed. 'Somebody must have been looking down upon you!'

'Yeah, the bleedin' paramedic bloke, giving me the kiss of life! I'm sure it was seeing his big hairy moustache looming over my face as I regained consciousness that sent me into a coma!'

'A coma!' she shrieked out loud.

'Alright! Less of the dramatics!' he told her, grimacing as he quickly put the phone to his other ear to soothe the affronted one. 'Yes! A *coma!* Will you lower your voice and stop repeating everything I say!'

'Sorry! Carry on!'

He then went on to tell Helga as briefly as he could about what he heard had happened at his villa that dreadful evening.

'... Oh, that is just awful!' Helga said woefully into her phone.

'Anyway, there's an important favour I need to ask you,' interjected Steve, speaking quietly, just in case anyone was listening outside the door.

Oh, no, she thought, *what now?!*

'You know that shooter I asked you to hide in your handbag?'

'Shooter?'

'Yeah, you know, pistol! Gun!'

'Yeah?'

'Well, I need you to sneak it into the hospital for me.' There was an awkward silence. 'I'm worried someone might try to kill me while I'm here!'

'... Okay,' she finally said, reluctantly agreeing.

'Oh, you're an angel!' he said, pleased.

'I must be to put up with you!' she retorted.

'It's just a precaution, that's all,' he reassured her, adding, 'Bring it in during lunchtime when it's busier!' His forefinger then ended the call.

CHAPTER EIGHT

As the rain began to lash down, John closed himself into the dry cockpit, then grabbed the ship's wheel, gripping it firmly between both hands on either side and steered her upwind towards the eye of the storm. He knew there was no going back now as he braced himself for what was to come.

The skies dramatically turned black, as if the house lights in a theatre auditorium were suddenly switched off at once, indicating the show's performance was about to start - and Stokes had the best seat in the house! And what a show it was! Torrential rain, thunder and lightning, and, before long, the howling winds reached fifty knots and the waves ten metres high.

He kept the bow at a forty-five-degree angle as each wave relentlessly crashed against her - which he'd learnt at his sailing club in Ramsgate many years ago as a boy would help mitigate the impact.

But this wasn't sailing gently around the harbour - far from it. Visibility was dreadful, and she was taking a lot of water onboard - fortunately, most of which washed overboard. And as he rode the crest of one giant wave after another, he could hear plates, bottles and God knows what else smash below deck, thinking, *I hope that's not the wine bottles!* He didn't have time to secure everything! At more than one point, he thought she was about to capsize. But for a thrill-seeker such as John, it was the best roller coaster ride in the world! It was this sort of high-octane adrenalin rush that got him up in the mornings - and why he probably joined the Marines.

He couldn't be sure how long he'd been gripping the ship's wheel, but it was at least two hours - and he was still battling the waves! He felt exhausted, and his hands were cramped, but he was determined to keep holding on and not let the seas take him as they have so many other poor seafaring souls.

Each mighty thunderclap gave him a start, and he would grip the ship's wheel even tighter as he fought the monstrous waves. It was as if the Gods were applauding his mariner skills and encouraging him onwards.

It was now late in the afternoon - though, judging by the colour of the skies, one might easily assume it was midnight - and it seemed like the storm would never cease. Then John was knocked out unconscious! In a brief lapse of concentration, he lost control, leaving the vessel's starboard beam exposed to the wind and the waves. And that was all it took for a giant, powerful wave to crash against her broadside. The force was so great, that it snatched him away from the wheel, lifting him right off his feet, and dumped him over on the other side of the wheelhouse, where he smashed his head against the edge of the charts table.

As previously arranged; after parking her old red Chevrolet Traverse in the open-air hospital car park, Helga came to visit Steve at around midday. As expected, it was a very hectic scene with people coming and going left right and centre. She entered the main entrance, feeling extremely nervous, carrying her heavier-than-usual handbag over her forearm for support.

As she entered the large reception area, she noticed a shop selling, amongst other things, flowers. So, she went and bought the largest bouquet of carnations she could. Then before visiting Steve, she paid a visit to the toilet. She had an idea. Hidden inside a cubicle, she quickly removed the loaded pistol from her handbag, which John had asked her to bring, and hid it among the foliage of the bouquet. She reasoned that if a security guard should stop and search her, they would probably only search her handbag and not the bouquet. And because of the tight-fitting skimpy outfit she wore, it was obvious that she couldn't be concealing any weapons about her person.

She flushed the toilet, even though she hadn't used it, and exited. Then taking the lift to the fourth floor, she made her way along the many long corridors leading to the private care wing where Steve was staying - turning many male doctors' heads and raising eyebrows as she did with her sexy outfit and long platinum blonde hair (and eyebrows wasn't the only thing she raised!).

When she arrived, she asked one of the nurses, which was Steve Reynolds's room, who then pointed it out to her, saying that he was expecting her. A large Indian-looking security guard was sitting outside his room. He looked bored stiff and was probably eager to search her, she surmised - which panicked her even more.

As she approached him, she undid the top button of her blouse to show more of her braless cleavage, hoping it would distract him. It seemed to do the job; he immediately turned his head towards her and spoke to her chest.

'Can I help you, miss?' he asked with a broad cheesy smile.

'Hi, I've come to visit my boyfriend,' she replied with a slightly nervous smile, desperately hoping he didn't want to pat her down and put his hands everywhere.

'I will need to search your handbag first,' he told her in a more serious-minded tone, dropping his smile a little as he got up from his chair and gestured to her to pass it to him.

He had a good rummage inside her handbag, wishing it wasn't the only place he was rummaging around. Then she saw him turn his gaze towards the flowers.

'Okay, you can go in,' he suddenly said, much to her relief, as his eyes flittered back and forth from her eyes to her chest. He then opened the door for her, and she walked briskly in, immediately closing the door behind herself.

'*Blondie!* You came!' Steve called out to her from his bed over on the right, very pleased to see her. His half-eaten lunch was left abandoned on a tray at the end of his bed.

'I don't know why after all the trouble you've caused me!' she expressed as she approached him, stopping short of the left side of the bed, refraining from smiling at him.

He looked directly into her eyes. 'Yeah, I know – I've been a right idiot! I'm sorry, babe!'

'How are you?' she asked him, succumbing to a partial smile. Then not giving him a chance to answer: 'Why haven't you eaten all your food?'

'Cos it tastes like *shit,* that's why!' he answered

frankly, sounding more like his usual self. 'Anyway, did you bring what I asked for?'

She nodded and pointed towards the bouquet of flowers, not wanting to speak in case the guard outside could hear her. He lowered his eyebrows, giving her a quizzical look. 'Yeah, they're lovely,' he said, sounding somewhat ungrateful. She pointed again. There was a pause. His face suddenly lit up and his eyebrows then went the other way, finally realising. A big smile followed as he said, *'Gotcha!'*

'I'm glad you like them!' she said sarcastically. 'I'll put them in the vase.'

Suiting the action to the words, she strutted her way round to the other side of the bed in her short skirt, black stockings, and high heels and put them in the empty vase. Steve watched her goggle-eyed as she did, thinking how fuckable she looked.

'It's so great to see you!' he said, smiling widely. 'You look *amazing!* Come and give us a hug!'

Helga hesitated at first, then leaned down and did so. 'I'm glad you are alright,' she told him, falling for his charms as always.

'I'm not ready to meet St. Peter yet - he'll have to wait!' he said chuckling.

They both then began to kiss. First on the cheek and then on the lips. She suddenly felt his right hand move up the back of her seemingly never-ending left thigh and then up her skirt, where his large hand cupped around her left arse cheek, and his middle finger began to find its way past her skimpy moist panties to her neatly trimmed pussy. She immediately giggled as if it tickled her, saying, 'Hey, stop that!' slapping his right arm and stepping backwards away from him. 'Somebody might come in!'

'Oh, come on, babe, my dick is rock hard now – and I've not cum for three days!' He quickly pulled the covers away and lifted his gown to prove it.

'Ah! Poor you!' she responded by saying, finding it amusing.

'Climb on the bed and ride me!' he said quietly.

'No, I'm *not!'* she quickly replied. Hesitated, and then said, 'I'll wank you off instead if you like!'

He nodded quickly, accepting the compromise.

She pulled the sheets back over his privates with her left hand while her right hand simultaneously grasped his large shaft and began wanking him.

'Faster!' he groaned.

'I'm going as fast as I can!' she replied as the bedcovers bobbed quickly up and down.

He could see her hard nipples projecting through her thin white cotton blouse. 'Let me see ya tits,' he then said, needing extra stimulation.

She tutted, then with her free hand, deftly undid the rest of her buttons, unleashing her boobs, which now bounced freely about, immediately exciting him as she continued with the task at hand (pun intended!).

'Oh, fuck!' he yelped at the glorious sight as his right hand readopted its previous position up her skirt.

'Shh! Somebody will hear!' she told him.

'Faster! Faster! I'm gonna cum!' he groaned, pulling a contorted facial expression.

'Well, hurry up! My arm's aching!' she moaned, pulling a contorted facial expression of her own.

Suddenly, the tray of food at the end of his bed went flying into the air after he accidentally kicked it in his excitement. It landed with an almighty crash, and there was food, broken porcelain and glass everywhere.

'Oh shit!' he cried.

If the moaning and groaning hadn't alerted the hospital staff by now, this certainly would've.

Three things now happened simultaneously: the security guard, followed by the ward matron, burst into the room; Helga swiftly turned to face the window while she hastily did up the buttons on her blouse; and Steve, now looking very red in the face with embarrassment, quickly grabbed the newspaper from his bedside table and pretended to read while covering the slowly decreasing protrusion under the bed covers.

'Is everything thing alright?!' called out the security guard.

'What on *earth* happened?' asked the bewildered-looking matron.

As soon as Helga finished fastening the last button, she quickly spun around and, looking flushed, said, 'Oh, it was just an accident, that's all!' Then thinking on her toes (or in her case, high heels), explained: 'He leaned over to fetch his newspaper and accidentally kicked the tray off the bed!'

Focussing again on Helga's chest, the guard noticed the buttons on her blouse were misaligned, bringing a slight grin to his face, knowing full well what must have been going on.

Steve by now had lowered the newspaper and nodded in agreement.

'Well, you have been a clumsy boy, haven't you, Mr Reynolds?' then said the stern-looking matron patronisingly to him.

Steve nodded again, smiling coyly at her, though inwardly feeling frustrated and pissed off that he didn't reach a climax.

'Don't worry, I'll clear up the mess!' said Steve's embarrassed girlfriend, offering to help.

'No, that's quite alright,' the matron replied curtly. 'I'll call somebody in to do that very shortly.' Then added, 'Visiting time will be over in five minutes!'

Shit it! Steve thought as he continued to smile. Despite his displeasure at hearing this, he didn't want to get on the wrong side of the matron – the food was bad enough as it was.

The security guard and the matron then left, leaving them to their privacy.

'Quick!' said Steve quietly, discarding his newspaper. 'Finish me off!'

Helga sat on the bed beside him and pulled back the bedcovers. Then laughed, exclaiming, 'But it's all shrivelled up!'

Steve quickly pulled back the covers in a huff. Then after remaining silent and sulking for a bit, he said, 'I've gotta get out of here as soon as poss – it's driving me fucking nuts! The longer I stay here, the more chance of danger I will be in!'

'Why? You're not thinking of topping yourself, are you?!' said Helga, worried.

'No, ya *daft* cow!'

'From what then – the matron? She does seem a bit mean!'

Steve laughed. 'No, from the drug barons – *and* the matron.'

Both dissolved into laughter and held each other's hands.

He then spoke with a worried look on his face. 'I need to escape before it's too late. Things aren't what they used to be living in Dubai, and as I've already told you, there are people out there who want me dead!' Helga cringed at the thought. Smiling, he then said, 'How do you fancy getting away from Dubai – living somewhere completely different together, and putting all this crap behind us and starting afresh? I've got enough money stashed away for us to live on for a while – and there's probably enough change to buy another boat!' immediately thinking *A much smaller boat!*

'Sounds exciting!' she replied, albeit apprehensive.

The truth was, Steve had no real reason to stay in Dubai anymore: apart from now having no contraband to trade with, his petroleum engineering business – which was mainly a front to wash his ill-gotten gains through – was about to go into liquidation – poor investment deals (including highly volatile cryptocurrencies) and heavy gambling losses to blame. Something he had kept to himself.

Speaking quietly, he told her of his plan: 'Before you visit me this evening, nip along to the communal toilet just along the corridor' – he pointed – 'and hide a change of clothes for me inside the used paper bin. Then after spending some time in here with me, I'll go to the toilet and get changed, and then while you distract the guard, I'll quietly sneak out and escape down the fire exit staircase and meet you in the car park.

Helga nodded in agreement, once again feeling like a bag of nerves.

After she left and a nurse had been in and cleaned away the mess, Steve reached over and pulled the powerful Glock 17 pistol from the bouquet, pleased to be reacquainted with it again. He quickly checked the clip to make sure it was fully loaded, then hid it under his pillow so it would be handy in case there was a need for it.

John Stokes woke suddenly and immediately began coughing and spluttering as seawater slushed around him. He could taste the salty seawater in his mouth, his eyes stung badly. He found himself lying on his side in the cockpit surrounded by a few inches of seawater. He didn't know exactly how long he'd been lying there, but as he slowly got up, he could see the sun beginning to rise, giving him a good indication. Thankfully the storm had broken, and the sea was now relatively calm. But it also quickly became evident that the vessel was slowly sinking. The cockpit was not as watertight as he had first thought, and she had taken on a lot of water. And to make matters worse, the bilge pumps had seized to work - for how long, he knew not. The engine had kept going though, and there were no immediate signs of other damage. He was amazed that despite the storm, Steve's motorbike had still managed to remain onboard.

The left side of his head felt sore, and he could feel a lump where he hit it. There was no blood evident. The small amount of blood loss had long since dissipated in the salty seawater, which would've helped to heal his wound. But he had much more important matters to deal with now than tending to his wound: preventing the Slow Motion from sinking!

Soaked from head to toe, he swiftly made his way down the sodden teak stairs and waded along to the small engine room. It smelt like a pub after closing time, and he could feel pieces of broken glass and ceramics under his shoes, which crunched under his weight. Once inside the engine room, he immediately set about trying to restart the bilge pumps. Judging by the badly corroded wires connecting the main bilge pump to the battery, he quickly discovered that it had not been maintained and was irreparable. And the backup pump, which should have automatically started when the other one failed, had blown a fuse. So, having located and fitted a spare fuse, at least he was able to get one of the pumps working. And while that was doing its job, he frantically went about bailing the vessel out the old-traditional way.

John had been so busy doing that, what he had failed to realise, though, was that during the time he was unconscious and unable to man the vessel, she had drifted in a north-westerly direction, dangerously close to Iranian waters.

'Fuck!' screamed John, now realising how much time he had lost – and how little fuel he had left. *Call yourself a Marine?* A bad-tempered voice in his

head said, strongly criticising him. *You useless piece of shit!*

In the wake of the storm, the wind had changed in his favour to a downwind easterly direction, and there remained a strong breeze, making it ideal sailing conditions. So, skipping breakfast, he immediately set about attaching the spinnaker sail to gain more speed and to conserve the little fuel he had left, then steered her back on course for Karachi.

He calculated that it would be one more day of sailing before he reached the port of Karachi, possibly less with good fortune. Surely, he had now gained the respect of the sea gods, who would now allow him safe passage.

There were no other vessels in sight. *They must've had the sense to seek shelter,* he thought shaking his head. But he did survive the storm and hoped now that it would be plain sailing - to quote a nautical expression.

During hospital visiting hours later in the evening, as planned, Helga came to see Steve after first paying a visit to the toilet to hide his change of clothes. Once again turning heads and raising eyebrows at what she was wearing. This time she wore an even more revealing short and sexy black cocktail dress and a pair of black knee-length 'fuck-me' boots. She certainly knew how to get a man's attention!

'Did you remember to hide my clothes like we discussed?' asked Steve quietly.

Helga nodded, saying, 'Yeah – I just hope that one of the cleaners doesn't remove the rubbish sack before you get there.'

'Good point. I never thought of that,' he replied. 'We better not leave it too long then before we enact our plan!'

Steve was now more desperate than ever to escape. Helga wasn't the only person who visited him that day: earlier, a representative for the minister of happiness along with two of his heavies came to speak to him about business matters.

The minister's representative advised him that they had seized his cache of weapons and refused to pay him any remuneration, and had decided no longer to do business with him, stating that he was too much of a liability. And warned him that if he tried to cause trouble for them, they – the organisation – would arrest him on gun and drug trafficking charges, and he would spend a very long time in prison – starkly adding, 'if you make it to prison, that is!'. They did, however, tell him that they would continue to turn a blind eye to his drug-dealing escapades, provided he continued to line their pockets, so to speak. Little compensation considering this line of business was also on a slippery downhill slope.

Of course, Steve had no choice but to comply.

'We better give it another ten or so minutes, though,' Steve advised Helga, who was already out of bed with his slippers on, clutching his wash bag with the Glock 17 pistol secreted inside as well as a towel over his arm, 'otherwise the guard might think it a little odd.'

Helga nodded in agreement, feeling as nervous as hell – they both were.

As they waited anxiously, talking about everything and nothing for what seemed like an eternity, she squeezed and played with her nipples to make them as hard as she could for the unsuspecting guard outside. Steve watched on, immediately feeling turned on. He could resist no longer, and after dropping his wash bag and towel, he put his strong manly hands on her shoulders and moved her up against the wall adjacent to the corridor outside, then began kissing her passionately on the lips. He simultaneously placed his right hand up her skirt and started rubbing her already wet pussy. Using both her hands, she pulled her sodden skimpy black lace panties halfway down her thighs, allowing gravity to do the rest as they fell to the floor. Then lifting her silky-smooth right thigh as high as he could with his left hand, he raised his gown with his right and, using the same hand, guided his fully erect penis right up inside her and began fucking her like there was no tomorrow.

It didn't take either of them long to orgasm together, each holding the other's mouth so as not to make a noise.

Both smiling and panting heavily, Steve picked up his wash bag and towel while she quickly picked up her panties and slipped them back on again.

His smile then began to wane, 'Are you ready?' he said as the nerves kicked in again.

She nodded, her smile mirroring his. He then kissed her once more on the lips before heading for the door.

He opened the door to his private room and stepped outside.

'Nature calls!' he said with a smile and raised eyebrows to the guard sitting outside, who looked at him blankly, unfamiliar with the expression. But seeing Steve holding a wash bag and towel, the guard soon realised where he was going.

Steve walked very slowly towards the toilet, looking as if he was struggling to walk, breathing heavily (this time only pretending), and stopped halfway to supposedly take a rest. All so that the guard would think he was still unwell and incapable of making a quick escape.

'Do you need my help, Mr Reynolds', called out the guard as he got up from his seat and began walking towards Steve. The nurses were busy elsewhere.

Steve shook his head, saying, 'No, thanks – I'll be okay!' wishing that he'd not overdone the acting.

'Let me help you!' insisted the guard.

'No, it's alright, I can manage, mate, thanks!' immediately responded the patient with slight panic in his voice, followed by, 'Why? D'ya wanna come in there and hold my hand?' as he looked over his shoulder at the guard.

The guard laughed. Then Steve joined in, relieved to see the guard turn around to go and sit back down. Steve then dropped the facade and carried on to the toilet much faster than before.

Once inside the toilet, he hurriedly searched inside the waste bin, hoping to find his change of clothes. And there they were at the bottom amongst discarded tissues and used tampons inside a tied-up plastic bag. He immediately ripped the bag open and pulled out the contents, shocked at first to see a fuchsia pink polo shirt. *Fuckin' hell, it's pink!* Steve said to himself, feeling a bit peeved. Then sarcastically, *Oh yeah, I'm really gonna blend in unnoticed wearing this, aren't I?* But this wasn't the time to be picky – this wasn't a changing room inside a men's clothing store where he could simply just change it for another colour – and seeing the funny side, he quickly removed his gown and got dressed.

When he was fully dressed, he slowly opened the

door, just enough to peep through, and there Helga was, already chatting to the guard, positioned with his back towards the toilet. *That's my girl!* thought Steve.

Seizing the moment, Steve quietly exited the toilet, then made haste in the opposite direction towards the emergency staircase, trying to be as inconspicuous as he could in a bright pink shirt. Helga caught sight of the toilet door opening as she prised her eyes away from the guard's tenacious gaze for just a split second, then immediately back again at the ogling brown eyes which had now moved southward to her hunched-up breasts.

'… Is it hot in here, or is it just me?' she remarked, pulling her lowcut dress forward and shaking it to it to get more air – much to his pleasure.

Seeing that Steve had made it through the emergency door leading to the staircase, she looked at her Cartier watch (a gift from Steve), then made her excuses to leave, explaining that Steve has awful constipation – cringing as she said it – and she couldn't wait for him any longer.

Helga quickly made her way out of the building to the car park, and as she went to open the driver's door to her car, Steve's head suddenly popped up from inside, scaring the living daylights out of her. She instantly let out a scream.

'*Shh!*' he said, putting his forefinger to his lips, now sat fully upright in the front passenger seat.

She got in, still in shock. 'How did you get into my car?!' she demanded, amazed.

'You left the doors unlocked,' he answered.

'Oh, did I!'

'Yeah.'

They both then laughed and hugged one another.

'Come on! Let's get the fuck outta here – I need a drink!' said Steve after a brief kiss on the lips.

Helga put the gears into first and drove off. Steve immediately lit up a cigarette.

'I think you may have got out just in the nick of time,' suddenly remarked Helga as if she had only just remembered.

'Why?' said Steve, curious.

'Well, as I was walking out of the ward, I passed by two odd-looking guys speaking to a nurse – Eastern European, I think –'

'Oh, yeah!' interjected Steve, now more alarmed than curious. The criminal gang with whom he failed to deliver the drugs were from Russia.

'Yeah! And one of them was asking which room you were in,' she continued to say. 'They looked very … *dodgy!'* The word 'dodgy' she'd picked up from Steve.

'Well, if they were out to get me, they're gonna be pretty pissed off now then!' said Steve, forcing a laugh.

Helga smiled and nodded uneasily.

'… By the way! What the hell were you thinking

buying me a pink shirt?' he asked, shaking his head with a grin, adding, 'It was hardly inconspicuous.'

'That's all they had in your size, big boy!' she answered, grinning back. 'Besides, it suits you! Pink to make the girls wink!' Her grin turned into a giggle. 'And the boys!' she then added, winking at him.

'Piss off!' he quickly responded by saying. Both laughed.

CHAPTER NINE

Thanks to the change in wind direction, the Slow Motion made good speed as she sailed downwind through the Strait of Hormuz and finally crossed into the Arabian Sea.

John had since patched up his head, carried out minor repairs on the yacht, and managed to get a couple of hours of much-needed rest during the afternoon. The weather reports were good for the rest of his journey, and after everything he'd been through, he couldn't wait to get back to dry land. He would be in Karachi in less than twenty-four hours, he cheerily told himself.

It was now nightfall, and John could see the lights from other larger vessels illuminating the horizon. For the first time on his arduous journey, he felt upbeat and wanted to party!

He switched on the radio and tuned in to the first radio station he could find playing anything remotely up-tempo. The tune playing was a cross between Western rock music and Pakistani traditional music. And although it wasn't usually his taste in music, he didn't care! He turned the volume up and immediately began dancing wildly to it. He then found a switch to turn the ambient, multi-coloured outside deck lighting on, and in an instant, the Slow Motion turned into a disco. But it isn't a party without alcohol, so John danced his way down the stairs towards the galley in search of it.

He found one bottle of Courvoisier that was still intact, opened it, and joyfully took a big swig out of it as he headed back up to the wheelhouse. There, he continued partying whilst holding the bottle by the neck and taking swigs out of it every now and again; not daring to let go of it in case that too smashed.

He was soon making loud incoherent noises as if he were there with a large bunch of other noisy partygoers enjoying themselves. John was having a whale of a time. All his troubles seemed to vanish, at least for now. He felt invincible - he had survived the storm, and, managed to evade capture.

What the hell is going on here, soldier?! screamed a terrifying all too familiar voice in his head. *Stop this at once, I command you! Call yourself a soldier!* continued the draconian voice. *You are a disgrace!*

Upon hearing his late father's haunting voice,

Corporal John Stokes dropped the half-empty bottle of Courvoisier out of his hand, which smashed upon impact on the deck. He immediately stopped dancing and went and turned the music off, then stood still with his arms held directly by his sides as if standing to attention. It was as if his father was there with him, inspecting him like an officer on parade would. The once again eighteen-year-old Marine recruit imagined spittle sprayed upon his face as his brute of a father, dressed in full uniform, leaned over to within an inch of him and spoke. His foul-smelling nicotine breath overpowering his son's nostrils.

John wobbled. *Stand still when I am talking to you, you pathetic excuse for a soldier!* came the venomous spitting voice again. John then suddenly crouched forward as if he had been punched hard in the guts – possibly a reflex from some past punishment inflicted upon him by his cruel father. Before petering out, the invasive voice then commanded, *Now get this vessel shipshape, d'ya hear me!* To which, John mouthed, 'Yes, *sir!*' and immediately did as commanded.

John hated his late father, Captain William Stokes, and never made peace with him before he died, nor went to his funeral – very few did. His father had also been a Bootneck and fought in the Falklands and Iraq wars. And because of his overly harsh disciplinarian ways, especially his cruel treatment of enemy prisoners, including women and children, he did not find many compatriots in the Marines.

As an only child growing up in Tunbridge Wells, John often witnessed his father's cruelty and brutality first-hand as he watched him mentally and physically abuse both his mother and him – usually communicating with his fists. His father's opinion of women was very low – bordering on hatred – and his misogynistic ways clearly showed that. He was an unremorseful philanderer and, when he was home on leave, would blatantly have affairs with other women or visit brothels, not caring how hurtful and disrespectful that was to his wife. She had always been too frightened of him to object and dared not try to leave him. It is what John believed ultimately led to her untimely death by taking her own life. And after his mother died, when John was in his mid-teens and his father had left the forces, the spiteful bullying towards him only got worse. And although the physical wounds would heal themselves, the years of mental abuse he endured at the hands of his controlling father, had not healed in his mind. He still greatly feared his father, even after his death.

His father would always harshly criticise and undermine his son, and when John told him that he wanted to be a Marine like him, his father scoffed, telling him, he would never make it into the Marines – of course, time proved his father wrong.

And the day John finally got to adorn the coveted green beret at his passing out parade ceremony, his cold and heartless father never came. A couple of years later, his father died of lung cancer.

Though John detested his father and vowed never to see or speak to him again once he'd finally left home, in some way, he regretted not confronting his father about his abusive past before his passing. Then he could've perhaps found some form of closure. Maybe this explains why he still felt haunted by his father.

Late the following morning, John woke up in Helga's bunk with a sore head - too much brandy the night before. He'd had a terrible night's sleep, and his worn and battered body - and mind - needed the extra rest. When he was finally vertical and had filled his belly with whatever provisions were left, he got on with the necessary shipboard tasks.

As he looked out from the wheelhouse, still feeling slightly bleary-eyed, already on his fourth cup of black coffee that day, he could see the shipping lanes in the distance were a lot busier. With good fortune on his side, he hoped to be docked in port by 18:00 at the latest. Increasingly troubling him, though, were several tiny blips flashing on his radar screen, suggesting that small, motorised boats were heading his way at speed from a north-easterly direction.

The authorities were his first thoughts. Had they finally tracked him down and were coming for him in gunboats?

I warned you about not disclosing where you were going to your so-called friend! smugly said his late father's invasive voice, interrupting his train of thought. *He's ratted on you – that's what he's gone and done, you fool!'*

The disruptive and negative invasive thoughts were becoming more and more frequent, and it was getting harder for John to control them – all the stress and broken sleep of the last few days at sea hadn't helped as he didn't have the mental strength to fight off his inner demons.

Shit! What if it's heavily armed Somali pirates?! John then thought to himself.

Whether it was the authorities or pirates, either outcome was bad news. His Glock 17 pistol would be no match against their weaponry! Still, he kept it close by him.

John stood staring at the radar screen, listening to his thoughts, contemplating what he should do next for the best. To avoid capture, the only thing he could do would be to outrun them. And that would mean lightening the weight load on board.

So, with no time to waste, he immediately put the vessel into full throttle, then began jettisoning any non-essential items not bolted down: tables, chairs, crockery etc., saving Steve's motorbike until very last on the off chance he could avoid disposing of it. He also thought about getting rid of all the cocaine, but then thought against it, as it might yet prove to be a good bargaining chip after all.

Despite the Slow Motion now carrying a lighter load and moving speedily along at full capacity, the radar showed that the flotilla of speedboats was gaining on him. And it wasn't long before they were speeding towards his port side less than two hundred metres away, firing shots in the air. A glance through his binoculars revealed that they weren't the authorities: they were pirates – or maybe drug runners from one of the many Pakistani criminal gangs, Stokes thought.

'FUCK!' screamed Stokes as he frustratingly dashed over to the motorbike and began quickly untying it from the railings in a desperate last-ditch effort to outrun his tenacious pursuers.

As soon as the beast of a bike was freed, to the sound of continued gunfire, he wheeled it the short distance to the stern, opened the gangway section of railing, and after a moment of reluctance and hesitation, rolled it overboard. *What a waste!* he thought as he watched it splash into the sea, but then quickly headed back into the cockpit without further delay and took control of the wheel.

Though the Slow Motion's speed did appear to improve somewhat, as the chase continued, it soon became clear to him that despite his best efforts, he wasn't going to win this race – after all, she was hardly a racing yacht! And it didn't look like his pursuers were going to give up the chase!

By now, they had spread out and soon surrounded the Slow Motion; and it wasn't long before they were tightening their nets, so to speak, to haul in their prize catch.

John decided it was futile to try to avoid the inevitable. And so, with much regret, amid further gunfire and hostile shouts and screams from the fast-approaching speedboats, he switched off the engine and lowered the sails, allowing the vessel to drift and be at the mercy of his captors. The phrase, 'So near and yet so far!' came to mind.

One by one, John felt the speedboats knock against the sides of the yacht as it helplessly bobbed up and down. Then, following orders from who he presumed was the leader – a tall, skinny Pakistani man whose muscles were ripped to the bone, wearing, as were most, just a grubby vest and shorts – John came out of the wheelhouse with both his arms held high in the air in a gesture of surrender.

'ON YOUR KNEES!' the tall skinny man then shouted in clear English as he and several others clambered effortlessly aboard with their guns trained at the imposing occidental-looking captain. Some of them looked young enough to be children still, carrying assault rifles almost bigger than they were. Nonetheless, they were a scary-looking bunch.

John complied again, dropping down to his knees, acutely aware that any wrong decision he made could mean his life. To say he wasn't nervous or scared would be a lie – but he tried to remain calm just as the Marines had taught him to be in these situations.

One of the scallywags then hurried over and frisked John for weapons and valuables, finding none.

John could feel the heat of the midday sun burning into the back of his neck. Looking around, he wondered how many of them were ex-Taliban fighters – maybe he'd even fought a gun battle with some of them in the past?

'Where is the rest of your crew?' demanded to know the gang leader.

'I'm alone,' John answered matter-of-factly.

'Alone?!' repeated the leader, surprised.

John nodded, casually lowering his arms to no objection (he could hardly make a run for it!).

As John was answering the question, he noticed that three of the armed men had gone below deck to search around.

'What is your name?' asked the self-imposed pirate captain, who smiled for the first time, revealing a menacing-looking collection of gold teeth.

'John Stokes,' he answered candidly, inwardly annoyed that he hadn't given a false name as planned. He was so used to saying his real name, it just came out. But he would have to be wiser than this, if he were to survive, he told himself. He could picture his overly critical father now shaking his head but was quickly distracted by the next question.

'Where are you from, Mr Stokes?' the golden-toothed captain asked next, still pointing his Uzi at him.

'England,' just offered John, with a forced smile.

'Ah, England!' repeated the excited leader. Then reeled off several famous English football teams in quick succession: 'Manchester United', 'Liverpool', 'Tottenham Hotspur', …' leaving John slightly miffed that he hadn't mentioned his beloved team. But kept smiling back to appease him. The tall, skinny man then asked, 'What part of England are you from?'

'London!' John gave as his answer, thinking, *he's probably gonna ask me what bleedin' part of London next!*

'Really! I have relatives that live in London – Newham!' the leader then stated, still smiling widely with child-like excitement – and no doubt high on something!

It then dawned on John that the friendly and chatty gang leader was probably just practising his

English and warned himself not to be led into a false sense of security, and to be on his guard – not that he would be able to do much against a large group of unpredictable armed men.

'Anyway! My name is Captain Nelson,' said the leader, puffing his skinny chest out, 'but you can call me, Horatio!' The other gang members around him all laughed mightily. Even John found that funny and joined in with the laughter.

As they'd been talking, John could hear lots of noise below deck, as various items were moved and tossed about in search of loot. The racket then suddenly stopped and up came the three stooges empty-handed and looking fed up. Despite a thorough search, including under the mattresses, they found nothing of real value. However, John noticed that one of the men did have his Glock 17 pistol wedged down the front of his shorts. And he could only wonder if one of them had also taken his cash.

Not wanting to take any chances by being boarded by the authorities and caught in possession of drugs, John had had the foresight to hide all the cocaine, as well as Helga's expensive jewellery, inside a large airtight refuse sack and secured it with ropes to the underside of the hull.

The gang then started speaking angrily in their mother tongue – which John reckoned was a strong dialect of either Urdu or Punjabi – and the laughter stopped. Captain Nelson – or whoever he was – then looked back towards his kneeling captive with a face like thunder and immediately withdrew his machete from its sheath hung around his waist. Stepping closer to Stokes, he put the razor-sharp blade close to his throat.

'Tell me where you keep your valuables now – and don't fucking lie to me!' threatened the now much less friendly captain.

'If I tell you, how do I know that you won't kill me anyway?' asked John, suggesting that there were valuables onboard.

The leader smiled again and withdrew the blade from his throat. 'Oh, so you admit that you have hidden valuables onboard then, English?' 'English' was the new name the gang leader gave to the English captain.

'Yes, a large quantity of cocaine and –'

'Cocaine!' exclaimed the leader, interrupting him and sounding surprised. *'What?* Are you a drug dealer?!' He then laughed along with his fellow gang members.

'No! No! I stole – I mean borrowed my friend's yacht – well, actually, it wasn't his yacht,' quickly tried to explain, John, confusingly, 'it belonged to his girlfriend –'

The leader interrupted him again. *'Slower!'* he said, gesturing.

'Sorry!' John then slowed down his speech.

'Basically, I discovered a large stash of cocaine onboard. And I've hidden it along with jewellery - probably worth an extra few thousand dollars - or more! But before I disclose its whereabouts, I need reassurances from you that I will be kept safe and unharmed and be allowed to keep this vessel!'

John thought it was unlikely that they would want to steal the yacht anyway, as it would be too much of a liability, but he wanted to make it clear to them before he agreed to do a deal - not that he trusted criminals to uphold their end of the bargain, of course. After all, it wasn't his yacht, and he felt responsible for it and hoped that it would one day be returned to its rightful owner. Besides, drugs and expensive jewellery would be much more appealing to them, given the street value of such commodities. He was also mindful that they wouldn't want to hang about much longer, as the Pakistani navy would be on the lookout for criminal activity operating in its territorial waters. So, with any luck, he hoped they would take what plunder there was and leave as quickly as they arrived. Of course, John wasn't born yesterday and knew that he was pissing against the wind, as they could just as easily slit his throat and steal all the booty anyway! But what choice did he have?

As soon as John made his demands, first the leader, then, all the other gang members erupted into laughter. Then as soon as the laughter subsided, the leader, suddenly acting all serious, held out his bent little finger and said: 'Okay, pinkie promise!' causing all the others to burst out laughing again. John continued going along with their childlike antics and joined in with the laughter.

'Well, come on then, English! *Where* have you hidden it?' suddenly said the leader, now less patient.

John then confessed where he'd hidden the bounty: 'It's in a refuse sack strapped under the centre of the hull!' he told them.

'Clever!' commented the gang leader. Then speaking in his native language and gesturing, he ordered a few of his men to go and recover it, which they did immediately, diving overboard with daggers wedged between their teeth.

Ten or so minutes later, two of them popped their heads over the railings and threw the bag of loot onto the deck in front of their leader.

The wired leader wasted no time and immediately started ripping open the refuse sack, revealing the bricks of tightly packed cocaine and the ornate trinket box poking out amongst them. He then swiftly withdrew his machete and, without hesitation, pierced open one of the packages with the tip of the blade and removed it along with a small amount of the white powdery stuff balanced upon it as a sample. Then, bringing the tip of the blade up to his left nostril, he snorted it all in one go. There was a dramatic pause. Then he threw his machete into the beautiful, varnished deck, which wobbled from side to side, smiled widely, and put his thumb up, suggesting he was pleased.

John also smiled, thinking, thank goodness! Then, after a pause, he asked Captain Nelson if he could have a cigarette.

'Sure!' said the gang leader, now seemingly very happy. He nodded his approval to one of his men, who then promptly took one out of his wrinkled cigarette packet, lit it, and gave it to John.

John took a long drag. It had been a long time since he'd smoked a cigarette, and it helped to calm his nerves.

Next, the excited leader pulled out the trinket box and hastily opened it, revealing treasure inside as John had stated. John was hoping that that would be that, and the gang would then take their plunder and go. But oh no, the leader then pulled out one of those eyepieces that jewellers use to check whether precious stones are fake and wedged it over his right eye.

'FAKE!' the captain-cum-jewellery-expert suddenly called out after closely examining a large diamond through the magnifying lens and biting into the gold. Then casually tossed it overboard! '... FAKE!' he called out again, throwing another piece of jewellery overboard after it proved to be phoney.

'… FAKE!' Another piece of jewellery joined the other two with a splash. John looked on, flabbergasted, thinking what a cheap bastard his friend Steve was, as one piece of jewellery after another became discarded. The word 'Fake!' was all John kept hearing until the trinket box was empty, and then that also was tossed overboard. Captain Nelson did not look like a happy man.

'YOU TRICKED ME, ENGLISH!' shouted the irate leader, very displeased. 'NOW I AM GOING TO HAVE TO KILL YOU!'

The gang leader then yanked his machete out of the decking, leaving splinters behind, and walked aggressively towards John, who, after all this time, was still in a kneeling position.

'I didn't realise the jewellery was fake – honest I didn't!' responded John, glancing down at his almost extinguished cigarette.

'And just when I was getting to like you, English!' continued to rant the leader.

'STOP!' shouted John emphatically. 'OR I'LL BLOW US ALL TO SMITHEREENS! ALL I HAVE TO DO IS DROP THE CIGARETTE DOWN THIS FUEL TANK VENT …' As if to emphasise it, John quickly took a big puff on the cigarette, making the ambers light up brightly, and gestured as if going to do so. '… AND BOOM! WE'LL ALL GO UP IN FUCKING SMOKE!'

'Now let's not be foolish, English!' said the leader

much more calmly, '*Calm* down! Don't do anything rash! Let's negotiate.'

'The negotiating is over!' came the Englishman's curt response. 'So, take the cocaine and your sorry-asses and leave now while you still can! OR I'M WARNING YOU I WILL FUCKING DO IT!'

'OKAY, OKAY, ENGLISH, you win! We'll go!' confirmed the leader. He then started grinning for some reason. '*Too late!*' He was looking at John's cigarette stub, which had just gone out. Realising this, John quickly put it to his lips and tried to reignite it. But it wouldn't relight! *Oh, Fuck!* he thought. The angry leader then continued toward John with his machete raised above his head, about to kill him.

'KAEPTUHN!' suddenly called out one of his men, stopping him just in time. The man hurried towards his leader, holding up his mobile phone. He then began explaining something very quickly in his native language as he pointed excitedly at the screen.

The fickle gang leader then grinned again. 'Looks like you are worth more to me alive, English!' he announced.

He'd seen a picture of John Stokes, wanted in connection with the sexual assaults and murders of victims in the UAE, including the most recent high-profile case of the deceased Andre Boucher and Suzie Wang, murdered by the poolside of a luxury villa in Dubai, and read that there was a considerable ransom for his capture and arrest. What made the latest case so prominent was that the murdered Andre Boucher was the son of the French Ambassador to Dubai.

Moments later, one of the men forced a cloth bag over John's head before escorting him to one of the speedboats at gunpoint.

CHAPTER TEN

On the way from the hospital to Helga's hotel, she noticed two motorcyclists in her rear-view mirror that had remained behind her vehicle the whole time. It crossed her mind that they were following her, but then dismissed the idea as her being paranoid, having just been talking about the two Eastern European guys back at the hospital.

'The South of France!' Helga suddenly said excitedly.

'Do what?' said Steve, thinking, *random!*

'The South of France!' she repeated. 'That's where I want to go and live!'

'Oh, yeah?'

'Yeah, I've always wanted to go there. Somewhere like Nice – with sprawling promenades, beautiful spacious beaches, and vibrant café culture. Or Cannes, where one can hang out with movie stars and celebrities! Well, at least during the film festival.'

Steve chuckled. 'We'll see,' he said, reaching over and rubbing her thigh tenderly. 'It's a nice dream!'

'Well, why ever not?' she asked him, already sold on the idea. 'You said you wanted to get out of this place – so, let's do it – get on a plane to the South of France!'

She had already consoled herself in the belief that she was probably not going to get her yacht back and was now ready to move onto the next phase of her life – and who knows, maybe settle down, get married and have kids (she hadn't discussed those plans with Steve yet – one step at a time)!

'It's not as simple as that, my love. I've got a few loose ends to clear up first,' remarked Steve, dropping his smile a little as his thoughts turned to far less pleasant things. Which was how the hell is he going to make things right with his disgruntled drug-dealing clients and get them off his back. He now had no drugs to supply them, nor weapons, and he had no capital to purchase a new supply. And, even if he did have the money to buy more supplies, it would take far too long for him to acquire them and meet his client's exacting demands. These aren't the sort of people one can reason with – trying to explain that he lost their entire order of cocaine just wouldn't cut it (pun intended). His job was to supply them with drugs, plain and simple, and he messed up – big time.

Basically, he was fucked! *Maybe the two of us should escape to the South of France?* he thought.

'Take the underpass – it will be quicker!' he told Helga, pointing to where to turn off.

Helga indicated and took the turn-off for the underpass as instructed. But a glance at her rear-view mirror revealed that the two motorcyclists were still behind them. At this time of night, there weren't many other vehicles on the road, so she put her foot down on the accelerator, but the motorcyclists sped up also.

Then, any suspicions she had of being followed proved to be correct. Both leather-clad motorcyclists revved their throttles and began overtaking her vehicle on either side. Inside the brightly lit tunnel, the noise from the bike's engines were amplified, startling Helga and Steve. Helga put her foot down even further on the accelerator, but the bikers kept up with her. She looked over to her right and saw one of them reach into his jacket and pull out a pistol and aim it at Steve, who at the time was effing and blinding, looking this way and that, wondering what the hell was going on (these definitely weren't pizza delivery drivers!). Acting spontaneously, Helga turned her car sharply towards the biker on her right, knocking him off his bike. But not before painfully sandwiching him between her vehicle and the harsh concrete wall of the tunnel and dragging him for several metres.

When she finally released him, his bike wobbled pathetically before falling over.

By this time, the other biker had sped ahead of their vehicle and pointed an Uzi at their windscreen.

Meanwhile, Steve – useless as ever – fumbled desperately on the floor, searching for his pistol, which must've slipped off his seat in the panic. 'DUCK!' Steve and Helga both screamed in unison as the attacker aimed. The pair did so just in time before their vehicle was sprayed with bullets, obliterating the windscreen. The word 'FUCK!' quickly followed 'DUCK!' Then, spotting the Glock 17, with one hand still firmly on the wheel, she quickly reached down with the other hand, grabbed the weapon, and then bravely came up firing at the remaining motorcyclist for dear life. The first bullet she fired hit the target, sending him crashing spectacularly off his bike. She tried to swerve around him but judging by the way the car juddered and the sickening sounds they heard, she hadn't been successful.

'Keep going!' said Steve as he took the smoking pistol out of her hand and stashed it in the glove compartment, thinking, what a waste of two good bikes!

Despite no longer having a windscreen, Helga continued through the underpass, leaving a trail of carnage and destruction in her wake.

If Steve wasn't sure about leaving Dubai before, after the clear attempt on his life, he certainly was now!

'How'd you learn to shoot like that?' asked Steve, still amazed by her actions and shooting ability.

Seeming unfazed, Helga replied: 'My father taught me – he used to take me hunting as a child.'

'Well, he taught you well!'

'Any enemy of yours is an enemy of mine, sweetie-pie!'

Steve looked across at her and just smiled.

'What are we going to do now?' Helga then asked as they exited the tunnel.

'We need to lose this car – and quick!' replied Steve. Indicating, he said: 'Take this next street!' Which, Helga did. Steve knew the backstreets a lot better than she did.

After a short while, Steve told her to pull over and park up. They were on a quiet abandoned construction site. 'Have you got any spare petrol in the boot?' he then asked.

She nodded. 'I think so. Why?'

'Don't ask questions. Grab your handbag and anything else you want to keep and get out of the car.' Steve promptly got out after having removed his pistol from the glove compartment, and headed for the rear of the car, looking cautiously all around him as he did. Helga did as she was told, grabbing her Abba Greatest Hits CD as well as her handbag, and followed him out.

Steve opened the car boot and spotted a small plastic Jerry can in the far left-hand corner. He picked it up and gave it a quick shake, pleased that it was full. Then without hesitating, removed the lid and started pouring the petrol all over the car's interior.

He threw the empty can inside, then with urgency in his voice, said: 'Quick! Toss me your lighter!'

Helga quickly began searching inside her voluminous handbag for it, resting it on the boot for support.

'… Hurry up!' he said impatiently.

'Give me a chance!' she replied, still searching for it. 'A women's handbag contains a lot of …' She lost concentration.

'Junk!' said Steve sarcastically, filling in the blank.

'Here it is!' she exclaimed, ignoring him, and tossed it over to him as requested.

'Now get back, Helga!' he told her sharply.

Steve struck the flint and tossed the flaming lighter into the car, which immediately caught fire.

'Come on, quick! Let's get outta here!' he said as he caught up with her and grabbed her hand to lead her away.

Helga knew that there was no other choice – not unless she wanted the vehicle traced back to her – but she couldn't help but feel pissed off because now not only had she no yacht but no car either (or a lighter)!

They hadn't got very far when, 'BOOM!', they heard the car exploding!

'Quick! Hurry!' ordered Steve as he quick-marched her along the unfinished, uneven pavement.

'I'm going as fast as I can – you try walking fast in six-inch heels!' she complained, struggling to keep up for a change.

'Well, take them off then,' he suggested to her disapproval.

'No, I am *not!'* she exclaimed unhappily.

'This way!' he then said, leading her down another street and out of sight of the car.

'Yes, sir, Sergeant Major, sir!' she replied sarcastically. Suddenly, no sooner than she spoke, she started to fall over until Steve quickly grabbed her and prevented her from doing so. One of the heels on her boots had snapped off completely. 'FUCK!' she screamed, now having to take them off anyway. Steve managed to hold his laughter in as they continued to walk, listening to her incessant cussing and moaning.

Halfway along, Steve stopped so they could have a little rest – much to Helga's relief. She immediately gave her feet a soothing massage while he removed his crinkled packet of cigarettes from his pocket, took two out, put one between his lips and offered Helga the other, which she refused, shaking her head with a face like a smacked ass.

'Have ya got a light?' he then asked absentmindedly.

'No, *stupid,* you threw it in my car if you remember!' she reminded him, followed by a tut, clearly showing her annoyance at him.

'Oh yeah! Shit!' he remarked. She didn't comment, just carried on looking agitated and annoyed, this time shaking her head.

'Look, cheer up, will ya, Blondie,' said Steve, forcing a smile. 'Look on the bright side – we're both still alive!' '

'Yeah! No thanks to you, we are!' she replied, reminding him who it was that saved their asses. Steve went silent, slightly embarrassed by his inept inaction.

Then upon reflection, Steve commented: 'Yeah, I'm sorry. I know what it feels like to kill someone for the first time.' This time, she remained silent.

Right by them were three cars parked closely together: an old mid-90s Merc, an even slightly older BMW, and a brand-new, shiny Ford. Seeing that Helga was in some discomfort and wasn't very happy, after putting one of the cigarettes back in the packet and the other behind his ear, he said to her, gesturing towards the cars, 'Which one d'ya like best?'

She looked at him and, cracking a smile, pointed to the Merc.

'My first choice as well!' he concurred.

Wasting no time at all, Steve broke into the silver Mercedes-Benz E-Class Coupé using the quickest and easiest method he knew how - smashing the butt of his heavy Glock 17 through the front nearside window. Well, on this occasion it took more than one attempt. But after his fourth attempt, he finally gained entry, much to his relief (it was almost the same feeling of elation he got when his cock finally found its way into a woman's snatch for the first time)! Then after conveniently finding a toolkit in the boot and hotwiring the vehicle, which any self-respecting criminal knows how to do, the pair drove off at speed in the direction of Helga's hotel.

This time Steve drove while Helga rode shotgun (quite literally), both puffing away on cigarettes, which they lit using the car cigarette lighter, hoping there wouldn't be any more nasty surprises that evening.

While driving, Steve told Helga that he agreed they should leave Dubai and book the next flight to the South of France. Which she was delighted to hear, immediately filling her with a frisson of excitement and cheering her up. Though, as he said it, it did cross his mind that there would be lots of other bleedin' Andre's there, which excited him much less, but then he thought, anywhere would be better than here!

‘Where are you going?’ suddenly said Helga, noticing that Steve had taken the road leading to Palm Jumeirah instead of continuing to her hotel.

‘While it’s still dark, I need to pick up a few things from my villa first,’ he said with an uneasy smile.

Once on his street, so as not to draw too much attention to themselves, Steve parked the Merc outside his neighbour’s villa rather than his own; and immediately switched off the headlights and disconnected the battery and ignition wires to turn off the engine.

‘You wait here,’ he said, ‘and ring me if you see any cops come by.’

Helga nodded, looking worried. ‘Take care!’

He then got out of the car and walked the short distance to his villa, keeping a constant eye out for any sign of trouble. He tried to be as quiet as he could, but in the stillness of the night, every step seemed amplified. Thankfully, by this time of night, though, most people were tucked up asleep in bed.

As he approached his villa, he saw Suzie’s Jeep Renegade parked exactly where he’d left it. It brought back painful memories of the last time he was there. He tried to shut them out of his mind and focus on the job at hand, but it was hard not to think about.

There was no longer a police presence there, but as a stark reminder of what took place back then, the property was still cordoned off with police 'Keep Out' tape, and the front entrance was now all boarded up.

Mind you, even if there had been a front door, he didn't have any house keys to get in with, anyway, because they were still at the hospital along with most of his other personal belongings, stored away under lock and key, which left him with no choice but to break into his own home.

Steve pulled the police tape over his head as he bent down and went under it. Then cut across the overgrown lawn towards the side gate as quickly and as quietly as he could. He tried the gate handle, and it was unlocked - exactly how Suzie had left it to allow Andre to secretly enter and join her by the swimming pool that murderous afternoon.

Thank fuck for that! he muttered to himself, saving him the trouble of trying to climb over the high fence. He went through the gate and walked down the paved pathway towards the pool area, constantly on guard in case anyone should jump out at him. He was still feeling jittery from what happened earlier. And to make matters worse, it was then that he realised that he hadn't brought his pistol. There was no time to go back for it now, though.

The pathway led onto the spacious pool terrace - all lit up by the moonlight. Steve stopped at the entrance, immediately noticing that everything was still more or less in the same position as he last saw it. There were two sun loungers close together on the other side of the pool with the side table in between, the pink inflatable Lilo was floating in the pool, and the barbecue was where he'd left it over on the patio area.

He strolled around to the other side of the pool, which activated the security lights, immediately flooding the whole area in bright light, and stood by the sun loungers for a moment to try and make sense of it all. Two half-filled cocktail glasses left abandoned on the table first caught his attention. Then as he moved his gaze across to one of the sun loungers, he grimaced at the sight of blood stains soaked into the fabric. There were also noticeable blood stains on the paving stones by the poolside.

Not wishing to hang around any longer, he quickly moved out of the bright light and over to the patio area which was partially shielded by an awning. As he passed by the barbecue, he noticed a blackened shrivelled-up sausage still on the grill.

The security lights soon went out, making him feel less vulnerable as he tried to force the locked patio door open with a barbecue utensil to no avail. It was weird – he felt like a burglar breaking into his own home. He then remembered he hid a spare key under one of the large heavy plant pots on either side the door. So, with some effort, he levered one of the pots over onto its edge, enough for him to put his free hand under it and feel around for the key. Then, after a little bit of fumbling around, he found what he was searching for and proceeded to open the door.

Sliding the door open, he stepped inside his home, which strangely, no longer felt so. Then, in the pitch blackness, removed his mobile phone from his rear pocket, located his torchlight app, and switched it on. The torch instantly illuminated the white leather sofa, which, only days prior, he was happily chatting upon with his friend John while watching Suzie in the pool. How so much can change in such a short space of time! Steve lamented. The torchlight also revealed the bookcase void of books, now scattered all about the floor, where careless investigators' hands had been.

The first place he wanted to check was the garage. He wanted to see with his own eyes whether the weapons he had stored there were indeed now missing. And so, shone the torchlight in that direction and followed the path of light towards it.

His path took him past the kitchen, where he noticed piles of dirty kitchenware waiting to be put in the dishwasher still. Once at the internal garage door, he discovered it was unlocked, and walked through into the garage.

The first thing he caught sight of was his beaten-up Ferrari. He shone the torchlight towards the area where he had stored the boxes of weaponry, finding as expected just an empty space. And rotating the torchlight to where he usually parked his superbike, he discovered that that too was gone. And even though he knew that was likely to be the case, he still felt disappointed and angry about it. Not that his bike would have been much use to him now, anyway, that he was planning on leaving the country the next day. And the fact that one is not allowed to remove state-registered vehicles from the UAE.

Steve left the garage and made his way hastily past the dining area, then along the corridor to his bedroom. The bedroom door was wide open. Inside, he immediately noticed the bedsheet was strewn in an untidy mess on the floor, and the pillows still had the indentations where heads once lay - and not only his and Suzie's heads from what he understood. Immediately shutting such bitter thoughts out of his mind, he quickly grabbed his large leather designer bag and started shoving as many clothes and pairs of shoes as he could inside.

Looking inside his bedside table drawer, he noticed that things were missing. His marina security pass, for one thing. Which he suspected John probably took to gain access to the marina. Also missing was the big wad of cash he swore he'd left there.

It was while he was searching in the drawer that he discovered the pocket map with the note to him from John. It was smeared with blood. *The forensics team must have missed this!* he thought. He quickly read it:

> *Hi, mate. I'm sorry not to say goodbye to you in person. Unfortunately, I had to make a quick getaway for my life's sake! Three armed assassins entered the property, sadly killing Suzie and the Frenchman before I could neutralise the situation. I immediately fetched her out of the pool, hoping I could still save her, but it was too late. I'm sorry for your loss! ...*

The note then went into more detail about how he took out the assassins one by one. John also reiterated his belief that it was the UAE hierarchy who were to blame. He then ended the note with:

> *Bye, for now, Bro!*
>
> *Yours sincerely,*
>
> *John*

Steve quickly realised that John must've discovered his cache of contraband weapons, admitting to himself that it wasn't very well hidden and, therefore, not surprising – but then again, he didn't expect that John would be staying at his villa. Nevertheless, he was annoyed at himself for not shifting it all sooner. However, besides this, some troubling unanswered questions crossed his mind – not least that maybe the 'assassins' were sent by the Russian Mafia to kill him. But with no time to fully contemplate what John had written, he shoved the map in his trouser pocket, then went and opened the safe, located at the bottom of the wardrobe. Crouched down awkwardly, he removed everything inside and deposited it into his bag: cash, credit cards, two Rolex watches, gold jewellery – including Suzie's, and, most importantly, his passport.

Then, after zipping up his bag, he headed straight out of the property the same way he entered, his mind a blur. On the way out, his phone vibrated. It was Helga warning him to hurry-the-fuck-up and get out of there as she had just seen a police patrol car pull up outside with two police officers inside, and one of them had just gotten out with a great big fucking guard dog! Helga quickly ducked down in her seat to avoid being seen.

'Shit!' said Steve under his breath and quickly turned his torchlight off. Feeling slightly panicked, he hurried outside with his bulging duffle bag over his shoulder and slid the patio door shut behind him. The last thing he wanted now was to be arrested and scupper his plans of leaving Dubai.

He then heard the dog barking and the sound of its nails scratching against the paving stones as it came bounding down the side entrance pathway. Thinking quickly, he grabbed the old rancid sausage from the barbecue and made a dash for the bushes, keeping as close to the rear side of the building as possible to avoid triggering the security lights.

Then just as the big Alsatian dog came skidding out of the pathway and onto the pool terrace, Steve quickly dived behind a large bush about halfway along (he was used to navigating his way around bushes!). The security lights immediately came on, once again illuminating the whole area. Then, to Steve's horror, the trained guard dog came sniffing around the bushes near where he hid. And the next thing he knew was the guard dog was right opposite him, baring its sharp fangs and growling ferociously at him as saliva dripped out of its huge mouth.

Steve covered his mouth and let out a muffled scream. Not because of the scary dog, but because of the sudden realisation that it wasn't a sausage he was holding; it was Andre's severed penis.

Steve then went, *'Urgh!'* and, acting spontaneously, threw the penis as far away as he could over on the other side of the terrace. The dog barked excitedly and then immediately turned and chased around the pool after it, not wanting to miss the chance of a meal.

Then, just as Steve was about to come out from

the bush and head closer to the exit, the dog handler came running out onto the terrace and, seeing his dog scoffing away at something, began shouting at it in Arabic. Which, basically translated as: 'What have you got there, boy?!'

Meanwhile, realising that Steve would probably need her help, Helga opened the glove box, picked up the pistol, and quietly got out of the car. Then shielding behind the parked car in front, she furtively made her way barefooted along to the police car parked outside Steve's villa.

Sat in the driver's seat, the policeman had his head lowered, watching porn on his mobile phone, totally oblivious to the tall blonde version of Wonder Woman creeping up on him.

'Get out of the *fucking* car without making a sound and do *exactly* as I say, or I'll blow your *fucking* head off!' quietly but aggressively threatened Helga, pointing the Glock at his head through the open window. 'And don't think of trying anything *stupid* either!'

As she leaned over the window frame, it looked as though her tits were about fall out of her lowcut dress. And if it hadn't been for the gun pointing at his head, it would have been a pleasant surprise.

Now they say that one can always tell by someone's eyes if they mean business or not. And looking into her cold, steely-blue eyes, he certainly wasn't going to take any chances trying to find out (not that he spent much of the time looking at her eyes). He immediately tossed his phone onto the passenger seat, and with a scowl stuck to his face as if superglued on, he did as he was ordered and got quietly out of the vehicle.

'*Slowly!*' she demanded him. 'Now put your hands on your fucking head and turn the fuck around.'

As soon as he turned around, she quickly removed his SIG Sauer pistol from out of its holster, then ordered the squatty policeman to walk with her to the Merc. She was about twice his height – even without her high heels. And now, brandishing two guns, he most definitely wasn't going to try and take her on.

'Please don't shoot me!' he pleaded in broken English, 'I have a wife and two small children!'

'Well, shut the fuck up and do as I say, and you'll get to see them again!' she told him, pushing him in the right direction.

Once they were at the rear of the Merc, continually pointing both pistols at him, she ordered him to open the boot and get inside.

'Oh, no, please not that! I'm–I'm scared of the dark!' he pleaded in basic level 1 English, sounding genuinely frightened.

She then put the gun closer to his head, saying: 'Well, feel the fear and do it fucking anyway!' quoting from the bestselling book with the added expletive for enthesis. Then irritated, she snarled and said, 'Just get the *fuck* in!'

Reluctantly, he got inside, and she closed the boot.

Back at the rear of Steve's villa, Steve had waited for the policeman to pass by. Then, while the policeman had his back towards him, he slipped quietly away, leaving the distracted dog handler to pull the remains of Andre's cock out of the dog's mouth.

Heart thumping, Steve walked hurriedly down the pathway towards the gate, stopping there briefly to make sure the coast was clear, then briskly cut across the front lawn towards the Merc. He noticed that the other copper wasn't in his car or anywhere else in sight but didn't give it much thought as his only concern was not getting caught.

As he approached the get-away car (it certainly felt like that), he saw Helga now in the driver's seat, waving frantically to him to hurry up.

What the fuck is she panicking for? thought Steve, keeping to the same pace.

Helga hurriedly reconnected the necessary bare wires back together, then touched the live starter wire to them, creating a spark, which restarted the engine. Then immediately pumping the accelerator, she gave it a few revs to ensure it didn't stall.

As soon as Steve got there, he quickly opened the rear passenger door and threw his bag onto the backseat, saying, 'What's the panic for?'

She didn't answer.

'Don't tell me – your father taught you how to hotwire a car as well!' said Steve, impressed, as he got into the front passenger seat.

She nodded, saying, 'Yep!' and slammed her foot down on the accelerator, then made a sharp U-turn, mounting the pavement on the other side, and drove speedily back the way they came.

Shortly afterwards, on their way to the hotel, Steve suddenly said: 'What's that banging noise I keep hearing?'

'What banging noise?' replied Helga, acting all innocent.

Steve heard it again. *'That* fuckin' banging noise!' he said, surprised that she couldn't hear it as well. 'Surely you can hear it?'

There was an awkward pause. 'Don't be mad at me, but ...' started to explain Helga amid the continual banging, 'he's in the boot!'

'Who's in the fuckin' boot?'

'The other policeman – I thought you might need my help, so I locked him in there at gunpoint!'

'You did *what?!'* he spurted out, raising his eyebrows while shaking his head in sheer disbelief. He didn't wait for her to answer. 'Oh, I don't fuckin' believe this!'

'I'm sorry, Steve, but I thought that was the best thing to do at the time. I was *worried* for you!' she said very rapidly as she reached under her seat, picked up his gun, and then gingerly handed it back to him.

'Yeah, but not in our bleedin' boot!' said Steve, now panicking. 'Now we're in fuckin' trouble!'

Helga went silent, looking worried.

'You've been watching too many fucking gangster movies!' he added, raising his eyebrows and shaking his head again while secretly finding the whole thing amusing. Then after a short moment, he suddenly asked: 'Anyway, why didn't you use your gun? Where's *your* gun?'

There was another awkward silence; then, 'I lost it,' she told him embarrassingly.

'Lost it!' exclaimed Steve. 'How the fuck did ya do that?!'

'I don't know – but don't worry,' she quickly said as she reached under her seat again and, this time, produced the policeman's pistol, 'I've now gained this one instead!'

Steve looked dumbstruck and just shook his head again.

'… So, what are we going to do?' asked Helga, clueless. She then turned the radio on to shut out the noise from the boot.

'Oh, yeah! That'll solve the problem, won't it?!' Steve remarked sarcastically.

'There's no need to get funny with me – I was only trying to help!'

'... Yeah, you're right – I'm sorry, Blondie!' he said more calmly.

After driving for a bit longer, they could see the hotel lit up farther along the road.

'Pull up over there in the layby,' he said, pointing to it, 'and we'll leave the car abandoned for the cops to find.'

Helga nodded and parked the stolen vehicle as instructed. The pair then quickly jumped out, grabbing the few possessions they had left in the world and made haste for the hotel, leaving the policeman still locked in the boot, shouting and screaming for help.

CHAPTER ELEVEN

When the door to Helga's hotel room closed behind them, both sensed a huge amount of relief. Even though there was only a thin door between them and the outside world, for a moment at least, they both felt safe.

The first thing Helga did was to book return flights to Nice, France. Return flights because it would be less likely to attract suspicion and appear as if they were going on holiday.

In the meantime, feeling exhausted after having such a tiring and traumatic day, Steve got straight into bed, pistol under his pillow, to try and get a few hours kip before they headed off to the Al Maktoum International Airport at 06:00 for an 08:15 Air France flight.

After Helga's home sailed away with all her possessions, she bought a suitcase and packed it full of new clothes, shoes, and other ladies' needs, which she'd been living out of, quite literally, ever since. So, apart from a few toiletries and make-up, she didn't need to pack.

After taking a soothing bath, Helga joined him. No sex for them that night! Apart from both feeling knackered, they needed to get as much sleep as possible to deal with whatever problems they might be faced with at the airport. For all they knew the authorities could be there waiting for them.

Helga was asleep almost as soon as her head touched the pillow. Steve, on the other hand, couldn't sleep. He kept thinking about the note he found from John. There was something Steve could not quite get his head around - something that didn't stack up. For instance, the patio doors were still intact, and there was no proof of any bullet damage or blood found in the rear lounge where John claimed - almost to the point of bragging - to have killed at least two assassins. He supposed the authorities could have had the patio doors replaced and removed any such evidence of them ever being there. After all, they had several days in which to do it. But if the firefight had been as ferocious as John claimed it was, then there would have been some evidence to back him up, which called into question whether John was telling the truth or not. And if he was lying about that, what other untruths had he woven? Steve had to admit, though, that it was dark, and he only had a weak torchlight.

After going round and round in circles for a while, it suddenly occurred to him that maybe the reason why John would make up a story like that was simply that he no longer had the stomach to fight and was embarrassed that, as an ex-Marine, he acted cowardly and fled. He recalled John's reluctance to pick up the pistol and fire back at the guy firing the submachine gun at them during the car chase from his hotel to Palm Jumeirah.

Steve concluded that he still hadn't the foggiest about what went on. And just as he was getting sleepier and about to drift off, Helga started snoring.

A few hours later, the alarms on their mobile phones rang almost simultaneously, instantly waking them up. The sleepy pair got straight out of bed, and after quickly getting washed and dressed, skipping breakfast, they set off to the airport in a taxi. But not before wiping their pistols thoroughly clean of fingerprints and ditching them and the spare ammo in one of the hotel lobby waste bins, discreetly hidden inside a plastic bag.

On the way out, both noticed that the stolen Merc was no longer where they had left it, which in some ways was a relief because they wouldn't want cop killers also added to their growing list of misdemeanours. On the other hand, the kidnapped cop would now be able to identify Helga; and there was probably already a search party out looking for them, making their chances of leaving the country now even more difficult.

As expected at an international airport, it was teeming with passengers milling about everywhere. Which, of course, was to their advantage, making the pair of them harder to spot (and I wasn't referring to Helga's tits! They were unmissable!).

This time, Helga wore much more sensible footwear and much less revealing attire. And even tied her long platinum blonde hair up in a bun and covered it with a hijab – which she hated.

They decided it would be wise to pretend not to know each other so that if one of them should get caught, the other could hopefully still escape. And so they entered the airport and checked in separately as single passengers.

Once they'd both checked in and made it through security control, feeling a great sense of relief, they casually went and stood next to each other in the middle of the busy concourse and checked their boarding gate number on one of the overhead monitors.

'... I'm just going to do a bit of shopping,' said Helga, discreetly under her breath, as she continued looking at the monitor screen. 'After all this stress, I need a bit of shop therapy!'

'Well, don't be too long – our flight leaves in less than an hour!' quietly said Steve as he stared down at his shoes. Usually, he would have given her the cynical raised eyebrows look but, on this occasion, he did it to his shoes instead. He knew very well from previous experience that her definition of a 'bit of shopping' was often the complete opposite.

'Don't worry – I won't,' she replied, smiling, feeling a lot more relaxed and happier that no one had arrested them at security control, and they would soon be leaving the UAE.

'Well, make sure you're not,' he reiterated grumpily due to lack of sleep. 'I'll meet you back here in half an hour at the latest!'

'Okay, I promise!' she assured him. Excitedly, she quickly turned on her heels and made a beeline for the perfume section of one of the many duty-free shops.

And while Helga eagerly went off shopping, Steve headed for the nearest foreign exchange bureau.

Half an hour later, as Helga was sampling yet another new fragrance, she heard an unfamiliar voice behind her.

'Ms Hellström?' said the deep, heavily accented voice.

'Yes,' innocently answered Helga, turning around smiling.

Her smile soon dropped when she saw the man whose voice it belonged to was wearing a police uniform. Accompanying him were two other unsmiling uniformed armed officers – one of whom was female. The female officer had her hand poised, hovering above her hip, ready to remove her handcuffs.

'Please don't be alarmed, but we need you to come with us now for questioning,' said the officer in charge.

'Buy *why?'* questioned Helga. 'I haven't done anything!'

'All will be explained to you once we can talk more privately in the airport custody suite, madam,' he then assured her in a calmly spoken voice.

'Are you arresting me?!' Helga asked to no response. She felt her knees buckle slightly as the sudden realisation of what was happening hit her: they were about to arrest her for kidnapping a police officer and possessing an illegal firearm! She tried to calm down by telling herself that the authorities won't have any proof.

Helga then heard a further announcement for passengers travelling to Nice to go to their departure gate.

'But I'll *miss* my flight!' she pointlessly tried to reason, panic-stricken. 'The *plane's* about to *leave!'*

'You won't be getting on a plane today, Ms Hellström,' said the police officer, shaking his head.

She looked across the bustling concourse to where she had arranged to meet Steve, but he was not there. He was watching, though.

'Were you trying to look for someone just then, madam?' asked the officer, seeing her appear to do so. 'Are you travelling with someone?'

'No, no,' she quickly replied, immediately keeping her gaze fixed on her captor. Then in a stance of defiance, she stamped her foot down and said irately, 'I'm *not* going anywhere until you *tell* me what you are arresting me for?'

A man dressed in plain clothes, whom she hadn't noticed before, then stepped closer towards her showing her his badge and spoke less amiably: 'I am Detective Sergeant Kashif. You need to come with us now or you'll give me no choice but to arrest you here!'

'But *why?* On what grounds?' asked Helga again.

'I am arresting you on suspicion of the murders of Suzie Wang and Andre Boucher and the kidnapping of a police officer!' he answered, straight-talking, patience run out.

'Murder!' she exclaimed, shocked and angry. 'But that's absurd!'

'Cuff her!' he then ordered the female officer.

Passersby stopped and stared at the scene, all agog, wondering what was happening.

He then read Helga her rights before escorting her with the help of his fellow officers unceremoniously away. 'I didn't do it!' she protested.

The final announcement then came for passengers

to board the Air France flight to Nice - and Steve was gone.

Inside the airport's police detention centre's interrogation room, the arresting officer, Detective Sergeant Kashif, was sitting opposite his distraught suspect, whose eye makeup had run down her cheeks, carried by her tears. Helga wasn't crying because of the murdered victims - she really couldn't give a rat's ass about them - she was upset that her dream of escaping to the South of France to start a new life with Steve was now over.

'Here - have a tissue,' said DS Kashif, as he offered her one from the box on the table.

Helga snatched it out of his hand, saying: 'Fuck you!'

'Now, now,' said the interrogator, 'calm down - this sort of attitude is not going to help you.'

Helga crunched her face up like the tissue, full of rage.

'We have video evidence of yourself entering Steve Reynolds's property at Palm Jumeirah shortly before the CCTV cameras ceased to operate and the murders took place,' he then informed her, speaking to her tits. '*And* we have witness accounts stating that you and Suzie Wang had a brief fling together before she dumped you for Mr Reynolds! Which leads us to believe that out of a fit of jealousy and rage, it was you who cold-bloodedly cut short the lives of two innocent young people merely enjoying themselves by the poolside!' DS Kashif paused to take a breath, then looked her directly in the eyes and spoke more heatedly. 'So, I'll ask you once again, Ms Hellström. Did you murder Ms Wang and Mr Boucher?'

There was a defiant pause. 'No comment!' then came the same response for the umpteenth time. Then demandingly, 'I want to see a lawyer!'

DS Kashif and the other two officers present in the room - one sat next to him controlling the interview recording device and the other stood directly behind the suspect - all grinned at each other.

'This is the Middle East, Ms Hellström, not Europe!' then said the lead detective somewhat sarcastically, now smirking and clearly showing his annoyance that his suspect was not cooperating. 'Things tend to take a little longer out here - damn red tape and bureaucracy!' He then calmed down a bit. 'But rest assured, we will get you a defence lawyer as soon as possible. He sighed and wiped the sweat from his brow. 'The thing you need to understand, Ms Hellström, is that whichever way you cut it, you are looking at a very long prison sentence. And, even if you are not found guilty of murder, you will still be convicted of kidnapping, which the UAE judiciary system takes a very dim view of - especially kidnapping police officers. And before you also try and plead your innocence to this crime, you should know that we have video evidence to prove otherwise, caught on the kidnapped policeman's bodycam showing everything that took place!'

I bet he didn't have it switched on when he was watching underage porn! thought Helga, annoyed at herself for not noticing his camera.

Watching intently through the one-way mirror directly opposite her was Colonel Ahmad Fayed. He was keen to convict at least someone for the murders on UAE soil.

'So, you see, Ms Hellström,' continued the detective as he spoke to her generously proportioned tits again, 'you don't have a proverbial leg to stand on. And life in a UAE prison can be extremely harsh – especially for an attractive European lady like yourself!' He gave her a momentary smile. 'So, you would be well advised to cooperate with us!'

Helga just kept quiet, listening to his threats, shaking her head slightly. She still couldn't believe what was happening to her. It was like a bad dream that she couldn't wake herself up from.

As soon as we saw the CCTV footage of you at Mr Reynolds's villa, we came looking for you at the marina, Ms Hellström, only to discover your yacht wasn't there! We thought you'd sailed away into the sunset somewhere; perhaps to avoid questioning, but then saw video footage of you again, this time, visiting Mr Reynolds at the hospital shortly before he did a disappearing act! And we've been trying to track the pair of you down ever since.'

Helga half-listened – she had her head miles away in the South of France.

'What I want to know, my dear,' probed the detective, 'is what were you and Mr Reynolds both doing at his property at 2.30 am last night?'

Slimy, patronizing bastard! she thought, and the only thing she gave him in response was a cynical smile and stubbornly remained stum.

'It was Mr Reynolds that was with you, wasn't it, Ms Hellström?' he then asked without waiting for an answer. 'And it was you that helped him escape from the hospital!'

'No comment!' she nonchalantly replied now, staring at the clock above the detective's head, smiling inwardly at the thought of Steve now thousands of feet in the sky on his way to the South of France. She could imagine him sipping on a Jack Daniels – and probably chatting up one of the attractive young air stewardesses. Her eyes began to water again, and a teardrop ran down each of her cheeks. She quickly wiped them away.

'So, what is your involvement with Steve Reynolds then?' the detective quizzed her. There was a silent pause. 'Oh, don't tell me that you were romantically involved with him as well!' There was another pause while he studied her body language. 'You *were, weren't* you?! How intriguing! *A love triangle!''* he then commented almost excitedly before muttering to himself, 'A *deadly* love triangle!' He then pulled himself together and asked her directly, 'So, were you both involved in the murders then?'

'... Look, you're wasting your breath! I am not saying another word until I can speak to a lawyer, and you inform the Swedish Embassy where I am being held in custody!'

'Don't worry, that is being taken care of,' quickly answered the detective, almost dismissively. He then stated directly, 'The pair of you were at his property to remove any last traces of evidence, and for Mr Reynolds to collect his passport and belongings so the two of you could fly away together and make your escape, isn't that correct, Ms Hellström?'

Helga remained defiantly quiet as usual.

'Look, it's *no use* denying it!' he then said, becoming heated again. 'We have your so-called boyfriend detained in another interview room right now, and he has admitted to it!'

'Admitted to *what? Where* is he? I *want* to see him!' she demanded, breaking her silence. At first, she wanted to smile widely at the news, part of her selfishly hoping that it was true so that she could at least see him one more time but refrained – she was too aware that this could be a ploy to get her to talk. And her assumptions were correct – it was only a ploy. By the time the police had reached her gate to look for him, the plane had taken off. And as far as the UAE top brass were concerned, they were glad to see the back of the known criminal – indeed they would have gladly paid for his plane ticket out of the country and let France deal with him.

'I am afraid that won't be possible,' quickly came the curt response. The detective then added, 'Not unless you cooperate and help us with our murder investigation.'

She reluctantly succumbed to his relentless pressure and spoke about what she knew. 'Well, there is not much to tell really –'

'Well, just tell us what you know,' he said more calmly, quickly turning his gaze away from her to look at the recording device and make sure it was still recording.

'I admit I went to Steve's shortly before the murders were carried out, but it was only to meet him,' she explained. 'We had originally arranged to meet at the Meydan racecourse to watch the Dubai World Cup together, but instead, I decided to get a taxi to his villa – to surprise him, you see. And to make that *bitch* Suzie jealous. Sorry! I know you shouldn't talk of the dead in that way – but she was a bitch – she was just out for his money!' She paused.

DS Kashif nodded, saying, 'Go on.'

'Well, when I got there, I saw that the side gate was open, so, decided to enter the property that way. I could hear the two of them laughing - Suzie and the pool attendant I mean - and when I reached the end of the path, that's when I heard the gunshots and saw they had been killed. I immediately turned around and ran, fearing for my own life.'

'But - but didn't you see who fired the shots?' the intrigued detective quickly asked, hoping for some form of a description.

'No, I'm afraid not,' she answered thoughtfully. She then admitted, 'I didn't tell anyone I was there that evening, not even Steve, as I was scared that I might get blamed for it - which is what is happening now.' She then began to rant on, 'I mean, sure, I hated the woman for stealing my man and betraying me, but I didn't hate her enough to kill her - otherwise, trust me, she would have been dead long before now! And by the way, it was me who dumped her, not the other way arou—'

'Okay, okay, this session is over!' announced the weary detective, interrupting her; at which point, the recording stopped, and he got up from his chair and started to leave the room.

'... But wait!' Helga called out in desperation. 'What about me seeing Steve now?!' But the detective in charge left without saying another word. *'Excuse me! Excuse me …!'*

CHAPTER TWELVE

When one of Stokes's captors yanked the opaque coarse woollen bag off his head, it was still pitch black inside the room. He then suddenly felt a tightly clenched fist land in his abdominal region, winding him and causing him to double over in pain, followed by men laughing. He hadn't had the chance to prepare himself – if he had that wouldn't have happened, he told himself. 'Where am I?' he called out to no answer. Then, a large hand, placed on his forehand, forcefully pushed him backwards against a wall, where he immediately slid down to the cold concrete floor, along with pieces of old broken plaster.

The door to the room then creaked open, allowing light to briefly flood in before it closed sharply shut again with a loud bang. As his eyes gradually adjusted to the light, he could just make out the silhouettes of two large males leaving what he quickly realised was a tiny makeshift prison cell (he hated confined spaces). He then heard a key turning inside the lock, followed by two bolts being slid across the heavy wooden door, confirming his assumptions.

Once again subjected to complete darkness, he immediately rolled himself up into a tight ball, terrified, like he had been as a little boy when his cruel father would lock him in the cupboard under the stairs for hours on end. Tears began to stream down his cheeks as he remembered not only his screams but those of his beloved mother when his father would beat her until there was silence.

Get up! You snivelling little scaredy-cat! grown-up John heard his father's voice telling him. *Don't just sit there! Give them hell!*

Stokes quickly got up – it was as if it was his father yanking him up from out of the cupboard – and, using his hands stretched out in front of him as his eyes, took no more than four steps to the door.

'LET ME OUT, YOU MOTHER-FUCKERS!' screamed Stokes angrily as he banged his fist hard against the door. 'YOU HAVE THE DRUGS – SO LET ME GO!'

'SHUT UP, INFIDEL PIG!' called back one of his captors on guard duty.

John soon realised he was wasting his time trying to reason with them – besides, they were just the foot soldiers. And so, reluctantly, he gave up and felt his way around the damp and dilapidated walls of his stygian cell - kicking over the piss bucket with a clang as he did - until he came to a corner on the opposite side of the room and sat back down on the floor again. This time he didn't get upset, he started planning how he was going to get out of there. Time was of the essence, as he probably only had one or two days at the most to make his escape before being handed over to the UAE authorities in exchange for the reward. Maybe an extra day while the gang tried to negotiate a higher price.

He didn't know what time it was but guessed it was the early evening. He could hear a cacophony of noises outside, so he knew that he must be near a busy road, probably in the heart of the city - but which city? His guess was Karachi.

Shortly after, he heard the call to evening prayer, so now knew it was sunset and that he had guessed right.

Outside in the corridor, someone switched on a light, allowing a tiny amount of light to enter under the door. And even though there wasn't much light, the glow he found comforting.

Casting his eyes around the high-ceiling room, high up on the rear wall, he could roughly make out the small rectangle shape of a blacked-out window. He immediately got up to investigate.

There was no bed or chair to stand on, but being

tall and standing on tiptoes, he could reach up with his arms outstretched and feel around its contours. It certainly wasn't large enough for a man his size to pass through – even in his younger days when he was a lot slimmer. But there was a narrow window ledge he could pull himself up on to see through the window once he'd removed some of the paint. Using his fingernails, he began vigorously scratching it off – just enough to be able to peep through without it being noticeable to his captors.

He could feel wetness at his fingertips where he had bled, but that was a small price to pay to be able to spy on the comings and goings of his kidnappers. And after a bit more painful perseverance, the last piece of paint finally flaked off the glass, allowing some more light into the room, and for him to be able to peep sufficiently through.

Using his upper body strength, Stokes kept his body elevated off the ground long enough to get a reasonable view of what was beyond the external wall of his cell. Immediately adjacent to it was a small floodlit courtyard surrounded by high walls. Several men were standing around chatting and smoking cigarettes together – one of them he recognised as the tall-skinny gang leader, who was preoccupied with speaking on his mobile phone. Probably calling the authorities about the ransom money, he didn't wonder. Parked along both sides were several motorcycles lined up one after another. And, at the far end, he could see a double gate leading onto what he assumed was a main road. Now and again, he could see the tops of tall lorries and buses go past. If he could only get beyond there, he thought, then he could lose himself in the crowd. And with over twenty million people living in the city of Karachi, that shouldn't be too difficult.

He listened very closely to the chitter-chatter outside to try and pick up and understand any words they were saying. But his understanding of Urdu was very limited.

There was no way Stokes could escape with that number of men about, though - especially as they were armed to the teeth. And so, despite his desperation to do so, he thought better of it and decided he would wait till the vast majority of them had left the compound.

Just then, he heard footsteps along the corridor - along with the smell of hot food. He immediately jumped down and went and sat back down in the corner, keeping his head down, pretending to be asleep.

A serving hatch built into the door, which Stokes hadn't noticed before, suddenly slid open, and a large hand deposited a small tray of food and water onto a narrow shelf on the other side.

The guard delivering the meal then screeched, 'FOOD!' startling John slightly even though he was awake. If he had been asleep, he certainly wouldn't have been after hearing that. The hatch then closed with a loud bang. *He will be the first to feel my wrath when I get out!* thought Stokes.

John had no appetite for food but got up and went over to fetch the tray and have a look out of curiosity, anyway.

It was as he expected a very watered-down curry with little or no meat in it. There was also a piece of cold and stale naan bread and a plastic cup of water. John was feeling dehydrated, so, quickly drank the water down in one go, leaving the food on the tray untouched. He could manage to go without it for the short amount of time he intended on being there. And the last thing he wanted right now was to get the shits!

Stokes concluded he would just have to be patient and wait for an opportune moment to make his escape. And so, in the meantime, decided to do some press-ups and sit-ups – this time because he chose to. He needed to be fit and strong if he was to get out of this place. As he was doing the press-ups, he looked at the food again, thinking, maybe I should try and get some of it down me to help boost my energy levels. Then thought, the guard had probably spat in it – or worse – and quickly changed his mind.

Stokes decided to take another look out into the courtyard, which was still crowded with men idly chatting.

Much later in the evening, John could hear a lot of loud and excited voices, this time from inside the compound. He must have dozed off because it woke him up. It sounded like it was coming from a room nearby, a little farther along the corridor. Every so often, men cheered in jubilation as if they had just won a bet at something. *Probably cards,* he thought.

John decided to try and speak to the leader and went over and started banging loudly on the door again to get someone's attention. 'I demand to speak to your leader!' he called out repeatedly to no avail. Then after a moment, the guard opened the hatch and shouted, 'Shut up and go to sleep, infidel!' He liked using that word.

The guard probably wished he hadn't opened the hatch because Stokes had had enough of him by now and jabbed two fingers into his eyes, causing him to scream in pain. 'I can't see!' he hollowed, or words to that effect in Urdu.

John lost his temper, and he, too, soon regretted his actions: almost immediately, he heard the sound of several footsteps dashing along the corridor, followed by the door key turning inside the lock and the bolts sliding sharply across; then, the door burst open, knocking Stokes backwards, as four angry gang members came rushing inside (the tiny cell couldn't fit any more inside than that) carrying wooden batons and started severely battering their prisoner with them.

One of the baton-wielding captors shoved the end of his baton sharply into Stokes's stomach – only, this time, he was prepared for it and didn't even bat an eyelid; he just grinned at his surprised enemy.

'Oh, so you think you're a hardman, do ya?' asked another of the gang as he grabbed Stokes by the front of his shirt with one hand and raised the other, ready to punch him in the face. Stokes responded by nutting him in the face first instead. He felt the blood from the gang member's busted nose splatter all over his face.

'Does that answer your question, fuckface?!' snarled Stokes.

Infuriated, the gang members forced him to the ground and continued beating him with even more severity. John just took the punishment – there was nothing else he could do.

'This is what we do to scum like you!' screeched one of his attackers, lambasting him while he thrashed him repeatedly.

'I didn't commit those crimes! They're lying – it was a setup!' proclaimed Stokes.

Moments later, the gang leader, Captain Nelson, or whatever his name really was, stood at the doorway. 'STOP!' he yelled in Urdu. 'You imbeciles! If you kill him, we shan't get any reward!'

The gang members left the makeshift cell, leaving Stokes battered and bruised lying on the floor, but not before the one he'd poked in the eyes lent down and spat at him.

As soon as the door was locked, John heard the gang members arguing heatedly with each other – the leader doing most of the yelling.

John got straight up, brushed himself down and went and had another look out of the window. Some of the men had taken the argument outside – which he perceived was about whether they should kill him or not. The beating was a cold sobering reminder that if it hadn't been for the ransom money, he would probably be dead by now.

He would have to wait till the morrow before he attempted his escape. Until then, he would try and get some much-needed rest.

The excitement and noise soon quietened down. John figured most of them had probably retired to their quarters within the compound. And, as he lay uncomfortably on his side in one of the corners of the room with only his large muscular bicep as a pillow, he finished hatching his escape plan, which involved his uneaten meal.

In the morning, John woke up with a start: he heard several motorcycle engines revving – he knew that sound well. He had slept through the call to morning prayer and the early morning rush hour traffic, but was now wide awake and alert, ready to put his plan into motion. He quickly rubbed the sleep from his eyes, stretched his neck, which clicked slightly, and then got up quietly and went over and stood below the window, ready to pull himself up and look outside, looking over his shoulder towards the door first before he did. Then with little exertion, his head rose above the window ledge, enabling him to peer through the small area of exposed glass.

Sure enough, most of the gang members were leaving the compound on their motorcycles, including the leader, who was on his phone again. He was unmistakable at his lofty height – and looked quite comical on the back of the tiny bike someone else was driving.

John watched as the last motorcyclist left through the double gates and onto the busy road. He counted at least a dozen of them, which by his reckoning left only three or four to guard him. And two of them were still out in the courtyard closing the gates together.

There was no time to waste; it was now or never! John jumped down and immediately started screaming for help as he quickly went over to the tray of food left from the night before. He picked up the bowl of curry and poured a large amount of it into his mouth, allowing some of it to trickle out onto his chin and down his shirt. Then resisting the urge to gag, he curled up into a ball in the centre of the cell and pretended to be in awful pain.

After a moment or two, he heard a guard running down the corridor and then the hatch opening. Stokes's body then began to convulse as if he was having a fit, and he started spewing the disgusting stuff out of his mouth (the smell alone made him feel genuinely sick, which helped!).

Stokes knew that the last thing the guard wanted was for him to die in there without receiving the reward money. And it would be on his head if that happened.

Panicking, the guard hastily unlocked the door. Then speedily came into the room calling out to a colleague to come and help. As he got down on one knee and leaned towards his weak and seriously ill-looking prisoner to try and prevent him from choking, Stokes grabbed him by his baggy tunic and pulled him sharply down to the floor, wrapping his right leg around his skinny body and rolling on top of him as he did. The guard – the one who gave him the most grief – started to scream before Stokes swiftly placed his large hand over his mouth. Stokes was back in Afghanistan. He grabbed the guard's dagger from its leather sheath, and in one quick motion, slit his throat from ear to ear, spraying blood everywhere. Gurgling sounds replaced the guard's muffled screams. Then another guard suddenly came running in screaming 'Allahu Akbar', looking bewildered, before falling to his knees with the knife firmly wedged into his chest, which Stokes had unhesitatingly thrown as he entered the cell. More blood!

There were still two armed men in the courtyard which he needed to take care of. Stokes reached down and grabbed the pistol from the waistbelt of his last kill, quickly realising it was his stolen Glock 17, and, stepping over his body, entered the corridor with caution. 'All clear!' he mouthed to himself as he moved swiftly along with the pistol held out in front of him between both hands, turning his body sharply to the left and right as he passed several doorways, leaving a trail of bloodied footprints with each step.

At the end of the corridor was the communal kitchen. It was a filthy mess, with empty or near-empty bottles of beer and spirits left lying all over the place – some still upright, while others were on their sides – ashtrays overfilled with fag ends, and untouched lines of cocaine as a reminder of the celebration the night before. *They won't have much to celebrate when they discover I'm gone!* Stokes mumbled to himself.

Soon after Stokes entered the kitchen, the door to the courtyard suddenly burst open and a guard came rushing through brandishing an AK47. He took a bullet to the head straight away, instantly redecorating the white walls a crimson red.

Standing directly behind him in the doorway, no more than a metre away, was another guard armed with another AK47: a mere boy, who looked about fourteen. He just stood there, staring downwards at the lifeless body now at his feet, shaking uncontrollably at the gory sight of blood, splintered skull bone and bits of brain splayed over his sandals as his oversized weapon bobbed up and down. Stokes paused momentarily with his pistol aimed at the terrified greenhorn soldier's head. The boy suddenly looked up, meeting the veteran soldier's gaze. Then, bang! there were now two dead guards lying one on top of the other in the doorway.

Unflinching, Stokes quickly robbed the guards of their cash, then stripped the adult guard of his traditional clothing and got changed so he would look less conspicuous - this was survival!

Before he left, though, there was still one more thing he had to do. Earlier, when he passed by one of the rooms in the corridor, he spotted all the bundles of cocaine piled up inside. So, without a second thought, he grabbed a large saucepan of cooking fat from the antiquated stove and a box of matches nearby and proceeded to set light to the cocaine - wishing he'd got rid of it in the first place.

He watched for a moment as the blaze took effect. Then rushed back to the stove and switched on the gas. He was adamant that no other prisoners would have to endure what he went through there – at least not for a while.

Then, just as he was about to leave, he spotted the guard, whom he threw the knife at and thought was dead, crawling slowly towards the kitchen entrance. Stokes hastily picked up his pistol from the nearby table and pointed it towards the injured man. He was trying to say something to Stokes in English, spitting blood as he did. Stokes moved closer to him and crouched down to listen. 'Captain Nelson will want his revenge – that was his youngest brother you just killed!' he garbled breathlessly. Bizarrely, Stokes's immediate thought was, *maybe Captain Nelson is his real name after all?!* The guard's eyes then closed. Stokes felt his pulse – he was dead this time.

The smell of gas was now palpable in the air. Stokes sprung up and hurriedly made his way out of the building and into the brightly sunlit courtyard. The reflection of sunlight bouncing off the whitewashed walls dazzled him at first. He shut the door behind him and dashed over to the last two remaining motorcycles.

He needed to cut loose fast before the place exploded, not to mention the other gang members came back. Or the rangers came to investigate –

someone was bound to have heard the gunshots and alerted them. He needn't have worried about them, though, because in the part of the city he was in, even the rangers dared not go. As he would soon discover, he was in the troubled gangland slums of Lyari, Karachi, where gunshots and murders are commonplace.

One of the motorcycles had the key left in the ignition - *probably for a quick getaway,* thought Stokes, which was precisely his intention. Without hesitation, Stokes quickly wheeled the bike over to the large double gates, thinking, *those guards won't be needing this anymore!* It was nowhere near as powerful as Steve's bike, but it would have to do.

Once there, he lifted the latch and opened one of the doors just enough for him to get through. Then jumped on the bike, turned the key, and off he went out onto the bustling road amidst engines backfiring, horns blowing, and angry people yelling and shaking their fists as vehicles cut in front of each other with seemingly no concern for road safety. And Stokes thought the traffic in London was bad!

Not long after he'd set off, he heard a loud explosion coming from the direction he'd just left. *Mission accomplished!* he thought.

CHAPTER THIRTEEN

Stokes got as far from the compound as he could before the fuel ran out – which ended up being only two miles away. He should've taken the other bike, he told himself, slightly miffed. Then, quickly dismissed the thought from his mind. He had more pressing things to concern himself with, like finding somewhere to get a fake passport for one thing, which shouldn't be too difficult in a city infamous for its piracy of copyrighted printed matter, including passports and visas. But first, he needed to find a base while he arranged that. And so, after abandoning the bike on some roadside somewhere, he continued along the same road on foot in search of a cheap hotel.

There certainly didn't appear to be many foreign tourists about. And despite dressing up in traditional Pakistani clothing and now sporting a beard, Stokes felt as if the locals were staring at him from all directions, and his attempt to blend in with them wasn't kidding anyone. Or maybe he was just too self-conscious and paranoid? Most of the locals seemed very polite and friendly, though, he thought - even to the point where they would cross the busy road to greet him and shake his hand (even if it was ultimately to try and persuade him to come and visit their families' shop to sell him something he didn't want). Stokes was probably more frightened of crossing the horrendously busy roads than he was of the Lyari gangs!

The streets were filthy and cluttered with rubbish and rubble left lying around. A stark contrast to where he had recently come from in Dubai. He noted the architecture was very British and reminiscent of Pakistan's colonial past.

The bad odours competed with the delightful smells of fresh aromatic spices wafting by from street food vendors' stalls. Karachi certainly is an overwhelming shock to the senses!

John was starving, so he stopped to buy some street food and quickly ate it while he carried on walking.

After weaving his way through hordes of people and being bumped into numerous times, he decided to turn off the busy road he was on and walk down yet another busy road instead. He was lost in an unfamiliar city but was reluctant to stop and ask someone where he was - just in case that very someone turned out to be one of Captain

Nelson's gang. He didn't know who to trust, so he trusted no one. It was best to be cautious.

He noticed several hotels a little farther up the road and, having walked in the searing heat for a while, relished the thought of a cold beer and decided to take the risk and venture inside one of them. And, while there, he could ask someone he deemed to be trustworthy for the information required. And if it turns out to be full of gang members, then so be it.

It was around midday when Stokes entered one of the international hotels. As suspected, the bar was very crowded. There was thumping European dance music playing (or Eurodance as they call it), which he didn't recognise – nor cared to. Making his way farther inside, he noticed that many of the occupants were young foreign backpackers. Some had probably only just arrived or were perhaps leaving as they still had their backpacks with them.

His entrance immediately turned heads and drew odd looks; his sheer size was enough to do that, but it was more than likely because he had the kaftan on back to front, and it was far too small for him. The dark bloodstains showing up against the light beige material probably had a lot to do with it as well.

Stokes ordered a beer, paid the bartender the money, and then drank the whole bottle down in one go. 'Another!' he called out against the din around him, slapping the bar. Suddenly he heard somebody directly behind him say, *'English?'* Stokes's immediate reaction was to go for his gun but stopped himself as he quickly realised it was an Australian accent, and it was probably one of the backpackers just being friendly to a fellow traveller.

Stokes turned round, and sure enough, standing before him with a big welcoming smile was a tall, slim-built, handsome young man - probably in his mid-twenties - with short dyed-blonde hair.

'Yeah!' said Stokes, answering his question with a faint smile. It was good to see a friendly fellow westerner - even though he was Australian!

'Just arrived?' then asked the ebullient Aussie, continuing to smile.

John nodded, mumbling something before downing almost the entire contents of another bottle of beer.

'You must be thirsty, mate! Can I get ya another one?' offered the Aussie.

'Sure, thanks!'

'It's not Castlemaine four-ex, but it ain't too bad for the price!'

John chuckled, then reminded himself where he was and casually glanced around the place.

'Six more beers, please mate!' the Aussie called out to the bartender. Then turning his head back towards the stranger, said, 'Come and join us if ya like,' as he pointed to the table where he was sat with five noisy companions.

John hesitated at first. 'Sure, why not!' he answered smiling again – grateful.

'I'm Roger, by the way!' then said the Aussie, offering his hand out to be shaken.

John obliged. 'I'm …' There was a slight hesitation again. 'Mark – Mark Simpson'. He remembered his pseudonym this time.

'Pleased to meet ya, Mark!'

'Likewise,' replied Stokes with a more pronounced smile.

'If ya don't mind me saying, you don't look all that great, mate!' said the Australian concerningly, now in a more serious tone. 'Is everything alright? You look like you've been in a fight – is that blood on your kaftan?'

John, or Mark as he now called himself, looked at him blankly at first, then answered, 'Oh, yeah. I took a wrong turn and got mugged. One of the bastards hit me on the nose, causing it to bleed.' For effect, he touched his nose to check if it was still bleeding. 'And before I knew it, they'd run off with my wallet, phone and camera.'

Roger looked at the musclebound guy in front of him somewhat incredulously and then commented, 'There must've been a lot of them!'

John just nodded and replied, 'Yeah!'

Changing the subject, the guy asked what John was doing in Karachi.

'I'm an independent travel journalist,' Stokes answered as planned. 'Well – I was – I should say. Until my phone and camera got nicked, that is.'

'You ought to report it to the police,' advised Roger whilst paying for the beers.

John didn't answer.

Roger then handed the newcomer one of the bottles, saying, 'Anyway, at least you're okay – that's the main thing! Cheers, Mark!'

'Cheers!' repeated John as they clinked bottles together. John then asked Roger the same question. 'So, what are you doing out here?'

'Well, I finished Uni, and like most postgraduates, went off travelling and loved it so much here that I decided to stay. And here I am two years later still!' he explained. 'I now mainly help fellow backpackers find accommodation and show them around the place. Karachi can be quite a culture shock and extremely overwhelming when you first arrive and don't know anyone.'

John half-listened as he scanned the room for the umpteenth time and supped his beer.

Roger bunched the other beer bottles together in readiness to lift them, saying, 'Come on, let's go and join the others!

John just smiled and then followed him to the table.

John soon became acquainted with the other foreign backpackers and patiently answered the same tedious questions that Roger had already asked him. Among the cheery bunch was a loved-up couple from Germany, a guy from England, another guy from Belgium, and a girl from Spain. All young and eager and fresh out of Uni. He felt relaxed in their company and even found himself laughing and joking, which he hadn't done in a long while. All the while, keeping a cautious eye on the door in case any gang members should suddenly show up.

A few rounds later, all but John and Roger remained at the table.

'... If you are only planning on staying for a few days, you can stay with me if you like,' offered Roger, slurring his words slightly.

'... Well,' responded John, a little unsure.

'It's really no bother – you can kip in the spare room for free. My apartment is only five minutes away!'

'Okay, that would be great!' said John, clinking his beer bottle against Roger's. He could certainly do with a shower, he thought, not to mention a good night's kip.

'No worries, mate!'

A little later, the pair left the bar together and headed over to Roger's apartment. On the way, they nipped into an indoor market so John could buy some Western-style clothes (he'd given up on the traditional look) and some other essentials, constantly mindful that by now the criminal gang would know of his escape and be out searching for him.

While most of the people inside the market were friendly and hospitable, the pair did encounter one individual who made his dislike for Westerners clear. One of the shop owners, a large, bearded, middle-aged man wearing a kaftan and a turban, called out to them as they passed by his shop, 'The Western powers are the *worst* terrorists in the world!' He paused for only the briefest of moments. 'They bomb innocent women and children!' he vocalised angrily to them, full of hatred. All the while swinging his amber prayer or worry beads back and forth around his forefinger.

I'll give him something to worry about in a minute! thought Stokes, starting to feel his blood boil. But not wanting any trouble or undue attention, John and Roger ignored his insulting remarks and carried on walking straight past him without giving him the satisfaction of an argument - though, John would've dearly liked to have given him a piece of his mind - and a punch on the nose - arguing, at least the west doesn't coerce woman and children into wearing suicide vets and go round chopping people's heads off in the name of religion! There was no doubt the outspoken man had a beef with the West; and being so close to the border with Afghanistan, for all they knew, he could've been a

Taliban sympathiser, or maybe connected to the criminal gang he was evading. He was still ranting and raving as they left the market.

John and Roger decided it was best not to hang around and find out and, instead, risked their lives crossing the dangerously busy road and then continued the short distance to Roger's fifth-storey apartment.

As Stokes had by now found out, he was still in the district of Lyari; so, while his ears listened to Roger waffling on, his eyes kept a constant lookout for anyone who may be following them.

The apartment was very basic, as John expected it would be in this poor part of the city, but it was clean and self-contained with a kitchen-diner, lounge, two bedrooms, and a bathroom. Any cracks on the old, dilapidated plastered walls were concealed by potted plants everywhere – some huge. John also noticed rather strange-looking framed pictures of mythological Greek gods with huge erect penises hanging on the walls. 'That's Pan – the Greek god of the wild!' exclaimed Roger excitedly, noticing John looking at it. 'He looks it!' remarked John, somewhat bemused. The apartment also had a tiny balcony where Roger had put a couple of plastic chairs and a small table to relax and watch the serene beauty of the Asian sun go down while, paradoxically, listening to the constant humdrum of Karachi life on the busy and chaotic streets below.

It was late afternoon. John took that overdue shower, then went straight to bed, foregoing the cooked meal Roger had offered to cook for him. He was completely spent and couldn't keep his eyes open even if he tried.

Despite the constant racket outside, including the occasional gunfire, John slept soundly and didn't wake up until about eleven the following morning. When he finally got out of bed and cut across the hallway to the bathroom, dressed in only his tight-fitting boxer shorts, he caught sight of Roger slouching over the dining table with a cup of herbal tea in his hand, looking much the worse for wear. While John was fast asleep, he was out partying most of the night and now paying the price.

'Morning,' Roger managed to say as he watched John cross the hall, admiring his Herculean body and the large lump in his boxers. John didn't hear him or chose not to answer – he wasn't quite awake yet and was never usually very friendly in the mornings anyway.

Once John was washed and dressed in his new Western-style clothes, he joined Roger at the dining table. He was already on his fourth cup of herbal tea by then.

'Good night, was it?' John half-joked upon seeing the state of his new flatmate.

Roger only managed half a smile, saying, 'I think

so?' Then pausing to think, '… To be honest, I can't remember!'

John chuckled, then helped himself to some unopened cereal still on the table. No sooner had John started eating when Roger quickly got up and made a mad dash for the bathroom to puke his guts up.

A little later, he returned, mumbling, 'Never again!'

'Yeah, right?!' thought John, smiling to himself – he knew the feeling well.

'Chai?' offered Roger.

'No, ta. Coffee, if ya have it, please.'

'It's only instant!'

'That's fine!'

'… By the way!' suddenly said Roger as he scooped out a teaspoon of coffee granules from the jar. 'You were talking loudly in your sleep last night – you sounded like you were having a nightmare. Occasionally screaming out … *medic,* I think it was?' There was a pause while Roger began pouring boiling water into a mug. 'D'ya remember?'

John remembered every single detail about his reoccurring nightmare but didn't respond – he just carried on munching his cereal loudly to try and quieten the battle noises, which had now returned inside his head. He'd been having the same vivid nightmare repeatedly for the last five years since the traumatic incident in Sangin - but like many veterans of military conflict, he preferred not to talk about it. The trauma of what happened that day, and on many other occasions whilst serving his country in Afghanistan, don't just go away. And even though he had physically left the battlefield, the battle had never left him. He would often hear the haunting melody of The Last Post playing inside his head and picture himself standing with his head bowed alongside his fellow serviceman while others less fortunate lie horizontal at their funerals.

Roger sensed by John's silence that he didn't want to talk about it, so, quickly changed the subject and started talking about his fondness for plants instead. He had noticed the horrendous scarring on John's back and the bald patch at the back of his head where hair could no longer grow, as well as the military tattoo on his forearm, and so figured he might be suffering from PTSD.

After hearing about the wonders of plants for a while and his passion for ancient history, from fear of going back to sleep again, John decided he would broach the subject of acquiring a counterfeit passport.

He told Roger that the muggers had also stolen his passport and that he needed a replacement in a hurry to get back to the UK and deal with urgent family matters, explaining that it would take too long to get one from the British Embassy.

'... I do know somebody who may be able to help you in that matter,' Roger informed him, 'but he won't be cheap!'

'Excellent! Please take me to him!' requested John, pleased, as he set his mug of coffee down on the table and quickly stood up.

'What, *now?!'* said Roger, slightly taken aback.

'Yes, come on, let's go now! There's no time to waste!'

'But – but – I need to get changed!' exclaimed Roger, suddenly all a fluster. He was still wearing the same lairy, tight-fitting Lycra outfit he had on while out partying into the early hours. And if John had any doubts about Roger's sexuality beforehand, he certainly didn't any longer. 'And besides,' continued Roger, 'I'll miss my yoga class!'

'Don't worry about that,' said John, hurrying him along, 'you're fine as you are!'

CHAPTER FOURTEEN

'It's just down here,' said Roger, pointing ahead. 'I told ya it wasn't far.'

John would now find out whether he was right to trust the Aussie.

Roger led the big guy down yet another narrow back street amid the noise and clamour of everyday life in an overpopulated city. John wasn't sure if the strange looks and stares they were getting from within the shadows were because of his tour guide's flamboyant clothing or because they had entered a no-go zone for tourists – probably both.

Roger had a reasonable understanding of the local slang and used it to converse with people, which seemed to help with any tensions there might have been.

'... Are you sure you can trust this guy – what's his name ... Mustafa?' said John, wiping the beads of sweat from his brow.

Roger murmured a 'yeah', and the pair continued

to the forger's small antique bookshop: a front for the man's criminal enterprise which lay hidden away in the basement.

As they approached the old bookshop, Roger then spoke matter-of-factly.

'Leave all the talking to me, alright, Mark!'

'Sure!' John replied, nodding.

'And if he offers you chai, don't refuse or he'll be offended.'

'Got ya.'

It felt like stepping back in time to a bygone era. The shop was cast ominously in shadow by the tall European-style building opposite. Outside were rows of dusty dog-eared books, all neatly lined up on shelving on either side of the entrance. And, inside, the window displays contained many more books - some with English titles whose sleeves were either badly torn or, like many of the old books, long since discarded.

As they entered, the old rusty bell above the door rang a tired and worn-out sound. Even the shop owner, sitting reading a newspaper at the far end of the shop, looked antiquated. Apart from him, the only other person in the shop was a boy standing on steps struggling to slot a weighty tome in place high up on a shelf. Expectedly, it was dark inside and smelt musty.

'Salaam alaikum!' said Roger with a big smile as he greeted the old man.

'Salaam alaikum!' repeated the old man with a more guttural sound, lowering his newspaper to reveal an equally broad smile - and several teeth missing.

Stokes half-smiled as the other two continued conversing politely in Urdu. Still unsure. Senses on full alert. Half-expecting someone to suddenly burst through the curtain at the back of the shop and start shooting at him at any moment.

Nobody did, though the sudden loud bang of the cumbersome book the boy was holding hitting the floor caused Stokes to turn his head sharply in that direction and go for his gun - which, much to his relief, he didn't have to withdraw.

Smile abandoned, the shop owner shot up from his chair enraged, shouting abuse and wagging his finger at the poor frightened boy. Anybody would think he had committed a serious crime. *Strike him, and I will do the same to you!* thought Stokes, remembering how his cruel father treated him.

'Go and fetch us some chai!' the shop owner then ordered the little red-faced boy in Urdu.

Roger and John just stood there, smiling awkwardly.

The shopkeeper's smile then returned as if nothing had happened. 'Who is this, Roger?' he asked sweetly, now in well-spoken English, eyeing up the stranger.

'Allow me to introduce my friend, Mark!'

announced Roger. 'Mark – this is Mustafa!'

As both men shook hands and greeted one another politely, Roger glanced nervously towards the open door, then returning his gaze, said, 'He urgently needs a passport to fly back to the UK.

There was a pause. 'I'm sure we can sort that out for you, Mark,' said Mustafa, now with an even bigger smile, 'but first, we drink chai!' He then looked past the two tall men in front of him, towards the door, muttering frustratingly, 'Oh, where has my incompetent little shit of a nephew got to!' Then making small talk while they waited, Mustafa commented on Roger's sporty attire. 'Did you come here on a bicycle?' John felt the urge to laugh but resisted.

Just then, his nephew came briskly through the doorway, deftly balancing a tray of hot teas with one hand, saving Roger the trouble of answering.

'Hurry!' Mustafa called out to the boy, followed by, 'Please!' as he gestured to his customers to join him sitting around a small table. He then boasted, 'This is the best tea in the whole of Pakistan!' John would sooner drink coffee but kowtowed to diplomacy and pretended to like it.

Once the glasses of chai were empty, the shop owner told his nephew to lock the door and turn the door sign around to display 'closed'. Then got up and instructed Roger and John to follow him. He led them through the ornate curtain, then partway along a corridor until they came to a doorway where a small flight of steps led down to the basement.

The large basement area was a hive of activity, with several industrial-sized printing machines all being operated at once. Mustafa continued to lead the Westerners to his small office down at the far rear end of the room.

On the way there, Stokes spotted an emergency exit door over on the other side, which led directly outside to a set of wrought iron stairs leading up to an alleyway – useful to know if he needed to make a quick escape.

'Please, take a seat,' said Mustafa as he sat behind his highly polished Sheesham wood desk. 'There is a lot of risk attached to what I do, you understand. And so, my fee must reflect this!' He then went on to boast about him being the best forger in Pakistan and that Stokes made the right choice coming to him.

Alright, less of the waffle – get on with it! thought Stokes, wondering how much it'll cost.

'… If I get caught doing this, I could get a lengthy custodial sen—'

Becoming more and more impatient, 'How much?' Stokes asked outright.

After being interrupted, the forger chuckled. Picked up a pen and paper and wrote down his fee, sliding it across the desk towards his potential customer, saying, 'This is my fee.' It read: 1,182,903.00 PKR Rs. He then added, 'And I will require fifty per cent up front!'

Stokes quickly tried to work out how much that was in British Pounds, thinking it seemed excessive. He couldn't help feeling that the widely smiling forger was taking him for a ride. Seeing the befuddled look on the foreigner's face, Mustafa converted the amount for him. 'Five thousand pounds sterling!'

Bloody hell! thought Stokes. He knew it wouldn't be cheap but didn't expect it to be that much. Though, he didn't let his face betray what he was thinking – Stokes was good at that! With the money he stole from Steve's villa and the criminal gang members, he would have enough to cover it, with just about enough left over to buy a one-way plane ticket. It was a lot more than he wanted to pay but wasn't about to waste time trying to haggle; his priority was getting the job done as quickly as possible so he could be on his way. And the fact of the matter was, he hadn't a clue what the going rate for a forged passport was, anyway. So, he nodded his approval, saying, 'Okay!' and proceeded to count out the equivalent of £2,500.00 in cash and hand it over to the expensive forger.

After shaking hands, Mustafa reached into his desk drawer and pulled out two large handfuls of foreign passports: some Australian, some US, some

German, some French, some Spanish, some Norwegian, and some British - and there was a lot more than that stashed away. He tossed them onto the table, quickly separating the red British passports from the rest, and slid them towards Stokes, saying with a big grin, 'Take your pick!'

Stokes leaned over the table and slid one of them nearer to him and picked it up. Inside was a photo of a young lady - probably in her early twenties - with the name Ms Sarah Bernadette Williamson. Picking up another, more used-looking passport, revealed the once owner was called David Tomkins - also youngish looking. Probably both tourists who had their passports stolen.

Observing the guy's photo more closely, John was convinced that he was one of the backpackers in saw in the bar the day before - though, he couldn't be certain. Regardless of whether it was him or not, the thought of using someone else's stolen passport did not sit right with Stokes - indeed, he thought the whole process stank. But what choice did he have?

Stokes gently tossed the passport towards the forger, so that it landed just in front of him on the table, saying, 'This one will do!'

As well as being well-worn, the passport also had the stamp marks of numerous countries within its pages, which would appear more realistic for a travel journalist.

The forger picked up a pen, asking Stokes for his full name.

'Mark Simpson,' John replied, straight-faced.

'Occupation?'

'Journalist.'

... Then after jotting down all the other details required, the forger got up, saying, 'I now need to take your photograph - please go and stand over there by the wall.'

The forger never once asked why his customer needed a fake passport - he didn't give a shit! For him, it was purely business, which suited Stokes.

Stokes went and stood over by the wall as instructed while the forger picked up his digital camera from the top of a filing cabinet and made his way around to the other side of the table to join him.

Meanwhile, Roger remained sitting, uncharacteristically silent for most of the time - no doubt still feeling the ill effects of a hangover.

As the fugitive stood briefly having his photo taken, he thought about all the poor backpackers robbed of their passports - and probably other valuables - and the anguish that that must have caused. He felt somewhat reconciled that they would at least get a new passport once their embassies had been informed. He also felt angry that if the corrupt UAE officials hadn't stitched him up in the first place, none of his misdemeanours since would have happened!

When the snapping had finished, Stokes asked: 'When will it be ready?'

'Come back in two weeks!' the forger replied somewhat dismissively as he opened the door for them to leave

'What?! You've got to be kidding, I can't wait that long!' replied Stokes, sounding a little panic-stricken and annoyed. 'No, no, Mustafa – I need the passport within the next couple of *days!'*

'I am afraid this is not possible, Mr Simpson,' said the forger, sinking his head slightly into his neck – sensing the big man's annoyance.

'Well, make it possible then!' demanded Stokes with no more time for niceties. 'Look, this is *urgent!'*

'If you want it done within forty-eight hours, that will cost you an extra two thousand pounds!' the greedy businessman argued.

Stokes scoffed and shook his head. 'You must take me for a fool!' Now angry, he held Mustafa up against the door, demanding his money back and threatening to take his business somewhere else. There was a moment of uncomfortable silence, when suddenly his father's hateful voice popped into his head, saying, 'Oh, just *kill* the bastard and get it over with, why don't you?' Then Roger, seeing the need to step in, spoke to Mustafa in Urdu. Whatever it was, he said, seemed to have worked. Smiling widely again, the forger instantly agreed to have the passport ready for him to pick up in a couple of days for the same price he originally quoted, explaining that there must have been a simple misunderstanding.

'Good,' said Stokes, letting go of him, but still thinking that he'd been ripped off.

Mustafa shook hands with John again and said: 'See you in two days!' adding, 'Come at 11 pm when the shop is closed,' instructed the forger. 'Use the basement side entrance. I will leave the door unlocked and wait for you in my office.' There was a slight pause. 'And see that you bring the rest of the cash, Mr Simpson – no cash, no passport! Understood?'

Stokes nodded briefly, saying, 'Don't worry, I'll bring the cash.'

Stokes then left with Roger following closely behind him.

Walking back towards Roger's apartment, curious, John had to ask: '… What on earth did you say to the guy to make him change his mind so rapidly?'

'I told him that you were a crazed killer!' replied Roger. John burst out laughing.

Both decided to stop at a restaurant for lunch. Roger was so hungry he was past caring about what people thought of his choice of clothes. Besides, most locals knew him and were used to seeing him in outlandish garb anyway – just not usually in the middle of the day!

Roger offered to pay for the meal, which John thought was kind of him and accepted gracefully. They sat at a small table in the centre of the restaurant: John sat facing the door, on constant alert, with Roger sat opposite.

While in the restaurant, John noticed Roger's attention suddenly become diverted towards a group of men that had just entered and sat down over to Roger's right. Roger then did that thing one does when one wants to avoid someone's attention: he slowly slid lower down in his seat and brought his outstretched right hand up to the side of his head so it could rest on it. Which only did the opposite of what he was trying to achieve and was an immediate giveaway – at least to Stokes sat opposite him. The sudden look of dread on Roger's face also did little to conceal his attempt at being inconspicuous. The men, however, appeared not to notice him and continued chatting noisily with one another.

'Is something the matter?' asked John, slightly concerned.

'No, no,' just answered Roger, who was becoming more and more agitated.

John didn't believe Roger for one moment. Especially when he said he'd lost his appetite and wanted to leave before he'd finished eating.

And, while Roger quickly paid the waiter, John scoffed down his remaining food and followed his new companion hastily out of the restaurant. John didn't press Roger as to why he wanted to leave so suddenly, but he had a good idea it had something to do with the four guys who had just walked in. They looked an unsavoury bunch at best.

Back at Roger's apartment, Roger went straight to bed while John did a tough physio workout. Maintaining a fighting fit body requires hard work and dedication. A warrior's weapon also needs to be maintained, so, straight after the workout, he stripped his pistol apart and gave it a good clean. So far, he had managed to keep his gun hidden from Roger – he didn't want to alarm him and cause him to phone the police. Checking the mag, he discovered that there were only six bullets left. He had no spare mags – so if he did run into trouble again, he would need to make every bullet count.

John decided to remain inside the apartment for the rest of the day, thinking it was best to lie low. As did Roger, it would appear (quite literally), remaining in bed for most of the day!

Later that evening, when Roger finally resurfaced, he cooked a meal for them both: a delicious vegetable curry – as Roger was vegan. And although John usually hated vegetarian food (or the thought of it), he found himself enjoying it –

though he would have much preferred a big juicy sirloin steak, cooked rare with blood oozing out the sides.

During dinner, they talked about all manner of topics, including John's time in the British armed forces, which he mostly skirted over, not wishing to bring back bad memories. John felt that Roger was also holding back on some personal issues. No mention was made of his quick exit from the restaurant. But Roger did open up about being gay, telling Mark/John how difficult it was for the LGBT community to live in a religious state. As, apart from the stigma attached, it was a criminal offence.

'... Aren't you worried about getting caught then?' asked John making polite conversation.

'Of course, but one just has to be discreet!'

Discreet?! Blimey, you could've fooled me! John thought to himself.

'Anyway,' continued Roger as he opened yet another can of lager, 'it's much easier being gay if you're a Westerner living out here.'

Roger then lit up his favourite recreational drug of choice: weed, offering John a drag from his joint, which he declined. He didn't need any hallucinogenic drugs to feel that way!

'You're all tensed up,' said Roger, exhaling a thick cloud of the pungent-smelling stuff, which lingered in the still air. 'Go on – it will help you feel relaxed!'

'No, ta,' John repeated, slightly wary, thinking, *I*

know your game, mate! 'I'll just stick with beer.'

Moving ever closer, the inebriated Aussie began to tell his dinner guest about his failed love life, making John even more uneasy. John had already made it clear to Roger that he was one hundred per cent heterosexual – just in case he got the wrong idea. John noticed how Roger looked at him sometimes and quickly turned the subject around to his failed relationships with women – emphasising the word 'women'. He could hear his deceased father's laughter in his head.

But Roger was either too off his head or didn't care and started to make his affections towards John known by placing his hand on John's large muscular thigh and attempting to kiss him. John immediately pulled his hand away, protesting, 'Hey! What the fuck d'ya think you're doin'?!' Turning square on to Roger, he then held up both his fists and, first looking at his left one, said angrily, 'This one is called *"Fuck"*' then looking at his right fist, 'and this one is called *"Off"* – which one d'ya wanna meet first?!'

Roger looked terrified (not as terrified as John looked when Roger tried to kiss him, but still terrified), immediately moving backwards with his palms flapping in the air, saying, 'Please don't hit me!' and began apologising profusely.

Suffice to say, and much to John's relief, Roger didn't try it on with him again. But despite showing his anger, John found the whole episode quite amusing.

The next day, the pair hardly said a word to each other all morning. Roger was in a bad mood and having a right hissy fit - purposely banging pots and pans about while doing last night's washing up, making it clear to his guest that he had overstayed his welcome. John got the implicit message loud and clear and just ignored Roger's immature behaviour, which he put down to embarrassment. Once he got his passport, he wasn't intending on staying around, anyway.

While Roger went out shopping in the afternoon, John had a nose around the apartment. It was mostly out of boredom - he hated being cooped up anywhere with nothing to do. But he was also curious as to *why* an intelligent young man such as Roger, who appeared to have no job and just hung around backpackers drinking beer and smoking pot all day, would involve himself with a shark such as Mustafa. What was their connection? Was there more to it than Roger merely happening to know someone who forged passports and visas?

When snooping around Roger's bedroom, John found out, and it both surprised and angered him. Hidden underneath the lowermost drawer of an old set of wooden chest of drawers were several passports of various nationalities, bundles of cash, and gold jewellery (he only discovered it because he inadvertently pulled the handle too hard, causing the drawer to come all the way out onto the floor). And rummaging around further, he found approximately two kilos of weed and one kilo of cocaine stashed away there. Which certainly wouldn't have been only for Roger's consumption. The amiable Aussie wasn't as innocent as he appeared.

Fuck! thought Stokes. *I bet he's been selling the foreign backpackers' drugs while also stealing from them.* It then suddenly dawned on him: *he probably supplies the passports to his chum, the forger, and takes a share of the cut! The slimy bastard!*

It immediately got him thinking about what he should do for the best. What if the same criminal gang supplying the drugs to Roger were the same ones that had kidnapped him?! Roger could lead them straight to him!

After first pocketing a couple of wads of cash, John quickly shoved everything else back where he found them and put the drawer back in place. He wasn't going to wait around the apartment any longer to find out if his assumptions were correct and quickly dashed into his bedroom and started packing his rucksack.

CHAPTER FIFTEEN

Stokes left the apartment as discreetly as he could – first checking to make sure there was no one suspicious-looking hanging about outside. John never liked departing without saying goodbye – which he seemed to be making a habit of recently – but considering what he now knew about Roger, he couldn't take the risk. He had been glad of Roger's hospitality (except when he tried to kiss him), but he no longer trusted the guy, and it was time to go. Plus, he was really starting to get on his tits.

Once on the main road, Stokes flagged down a rickshaw and took a twenty-minute ride to the famous Burnes Road (named after the 19th-century British spy doctor, James Burnes) to get something substantial to eat. He fancied trying the chicken biryani, which he'd heard so much about. It is so busy and chaotic there, with a great many restaurants and cafés, that he felt it would be a good place to remain incognito. He certainly felt it would be safer than staying where he was. Besides, it was always a place he wanted to visit. He could hang around there until it was time to head back over to the bookshop and collect his passport. Fingers crossed it would be ready in time so he could quickly pay the balance and be on his merry way.

While John was there, enjoying the flavoursome food before him, he also took great delight in seeing the faces of astonished local children light up as he performed simple magic tricks for them. Then before leaving, he pulled a Rupee from behind each of their ears for them to keep.

The time seemed to have passed quite quickly. Now feeling as stuffed as a keema naan, Stokes climbed into a rickshaw and gave the driver the directions to the bookshop in Lyari. At first, the driver refused to take him, shaking his head, saying, 'It's too dangerous!', but he offered him twice the money, and off they went.

Stokes preferred taking a rickshaw; it's much easier to get out of than a taxicab should he run into bother and need to make a quick exit. Though, judging by how rickety this one was, it was debatable whether it was safer. And in hindsight, it probably wasn't a good idea after eating all that rich food! Feeling slightly queasy, he thought, *This is the last time I ride in one of these damn contraptions!*

The streets were just as busy as earlier. Though to Stokes's advantage, it was now dark outside, and the chances of being spotted by Captain Nelson's gang were a lot less.

And after winding their way through the god-forsaken bumpy, narrow streets, the driver stopped abruptly outside the bookshop. Relieved to have got there in one piece, Stokes alighted the death trap and quickly paid the man, who wasted no time in speeding off, glad not to be stationary for any longer than necessary.

The sign on the bookshop read 'closed', and the interior was in complete darkness. Having checked the coast was clear, Stokes walked past the shop and then down the tiny alleyway towards the steps to the side entrance. The alley was quiet, except for some homeless people taking refuge there. He paused momentarily to look over his broad shoulder. Then proceeded down the rusting wrought iron stairs – even the stairs were rickety.

Peering through a small and narrow barred window about halfway down the stairs, Stokes noticed the basement was in complete darkness except for a tiny glow of light, which he assumed emanated from Mustafa's office at the far end.

When he reached the landing, he slowly and somewhat awkwardly turned the door handle and pulled the door open with his left hand instead of his right. His gun hand was firmly clasping the handle of his Glock 17, poised and ready to extract it from its holstered position at the front of his trousers if need be.

He cautiously entered the basement, and headed for the dimly lit office, trying not to bump into printing equipment on the way. As he approached the office, the office door opened, allowing a little extra light to escape, and out stepped Mustafa, clutching what Stokes hoped was his duly finished forged passport. Only this time, the forger wasn't smiling. Beads of sweat rolled off his brow, and he looked terrified.

I'm not that frightening, am I? thought Stokes, before quickly sensing something was awry.

Stokes broke the awkward silence between them. 'Is everything okay?' he asked, unsure.

The forger nodded, still without a smile.

'I have the rest of the money,' said Stokes, reaching into his pocket and removing a large bundle of cash, adding, 'It's all there!'

He handed it over to the old forger, who, in return, nervously handed him the forged passport, his hand visibly shaking, quietly saying, *'Shukria.'* The forger immediately shoved the money straight into a pocket in his kaftan without even counting it, which Stokes thought was a bit strange.

Then, as Stokes began checking his passport, he heard a groan coming from the other end of the room. The bright overhead florescent lighting then suddenly came on, completely illuminating the room. Stokes then heard a familiar voice he'd hoped never to hear again.

'ENGLISH!'

'Fuck!' Stokes mumbled under his breath, thinking, *Captain-bleedin'-Nelson!*

Stokes casually placed the passport into his jacket pocket and began to slowly turn around, knowing it was pointless going for his gun – it would be suicide. And his judgement call was right: positioned at the opposite end of the room was indeed Captain Nelson and his motley crew pointing a shitload of weaponry directly at him!

'PUT YOUR HANDS ON YOUR HEAD!' screamed one of the gang members, gesturing with his Kalashnikov irately at him.

What is this, Simple Simon Says? thought Stokes.

'Jolly good to see you!' remarked Captain Nelson sarcastically while toying with his machete. He looked like he was high on drugs.

The gangly, gold-toothed gang leader was standing behind a man kneeling petrified on the floor with his hands secured behind his back, whose identity was concealed by a hood but whose naked upper body clearly showed signs of brutal torture.

Captain Nelson gesticulated with his machete, and without hesitation, the old forger hastily fled via the fire exit – his footsteps heard quite clearly as he dashed up the iron stairs for dear life – causing laughter among the gang members.

Then with a flourish, Golden-Teeth whisked the hood off his prisoner's head to reveal it was Roger.

Stokes didn't recognise him at first: his face was severely cut and bruised, matching his body; his right eye was swollen and remained closed, and his mouth had been Gaffer-taped. He looked in a terrible state!

The gang leader then ripped off the Gaffer tape revealing Roger's swollen and bloodied mouth had teeth missing.

'I'm sorry, mate! Please forgive me!' rapidly cried out the young Aussie, spitting blood as he spoke. 'They followed me home and made me talk!'

'It's okay, Roger!' Stokes called back to him, understanding his predicament.

Stokes had witnessed torture all too often and understood that even the most hardened of soldiers could eventually succumb to torture.

Then, addressing the smug-looking gang leader directly. 'I will be worth a lot more to you alive than dead!' stated Stokes. 'If you kill me, you won't receive the full reward for my capture!'

Captain Nelson sniggered. 'Have you not heard the latest news about the poolside murders, English?'

John shook his head.

'The UAE authorities now have a new prime suspect, and consequently, the bounty on your head has halved. So, I would much sooner kill you than collect the miserly reward offered!' said the leader, adding angrily, 'Especially since you *killed* some of my men, including my *little brother,* and *destroyed* my compound!'

Now although the news of him no longer being a prime suspect in the above case may have offered Stokes some momentary relief, he still firmly believed, despite having insufficient evidence against him, that the authorities would want to pin the other sexual assault and murder case on him - well, if they didn't have him assassinated first, that is! And he still had the slight problem of escaping from a room full of drugged-up maniacs pointing guns at him.

'Well, before you kill me, at least tell me the name of the new prime suspect!' said Stokes, stalling for time.

'I can't remember *what the fuck* her name was - some *crazy* Scandinavian woman!' the even crazier gang leader informed him, filled with rage.

Stokes knew who that most likely was.

Then speaking a little calmer, Captain Nelson said: 'Apparently, the prosecution can place her directly at the crime scene, and she had a powerful motive to kill the couple. So, it looks like an open and shut case which you would most likely get off, as you British like to say, scot-free.' The gang leader sniggered again (he did that a lot), saying, 'Too bad, I'm going to kill you anyway!' Then drew his attention again to the helpless victim kneeling before him. 'I shall enjoy killing you very shortly, English, but first, I will show you what happens to people who cross me!'

'Let him go!' pleaded Stokes. 'It's me who you want, so let him go!'

Stokes knew it was futile pleading with a tyrant, but out of sheer desperation, he did so anyway. For he knew what was coming, and there was nothing he could do about it except continue watching the horror show.

Grabbing what he could of the Australian's short hair, the ruthless gang leader placed the blade of his machete against his throat and carved into it like he was just serving the Sunday roast. The room suddenly went silent as blood sprayed in all directions! Then before his victim's dying body had even hit the floor and was yet cold, he began hacking it to pieces. The carnage was too much for some of the young, newly recruited gang members, who began to grimace and flinch. Some chose to look away completely.

'YOU SADISTIC BASTARD!' screamed Stokes as he stood firm and watched on unflinchingly. Teeth gritted, nostrils flared, now angry as hell!

'... I want you to witness what I'm about to do to

you too, English!' breathlessly announced the moronic killer, frothing at the mouth, finally stopping the slaughter. Excitedly, he then reached down and picked up Roger's bloody severed lower right leg and raised it in the air for everyone to see; the foot, still slightly attached, flapped about as he did. Then with blood dripping down his arm, he sickeningly joked, 'Leg, anyone?!' as he pretended to bite into it. Which immediately elicited nervous laughter among the gang members – more so when he nearly slipped over in the pool of blood in which he stood. Not stopping there, he then jokingly threw the body part to one of the squeamish younger ones to catch, causing more mayhem and laughter.

While everyone was distracted, Stokes saw this as his opportunity to act. Money wasn't the only thing he took from Roger's apartment: before entering the premises, he'd crudely Gaffer-taped a large kitchen knife to his upper back, so the handle was in easy reach at the back of his collar.

Then, without hesitation, Stokes reached inside his collar and grabbed the handle of the kitchen utensil/weapon and, in one swift action, brought it straight out and threw it with almighty speed and power at the gang leader. And, with no time to check if it had reached its target, he immediately turned and dived into the office, quickly crouching behind the doorway for cover. Almost immediately, angry shouts of 'Allahu Akbar' and bullets came at him, shattering the office windows and fluorescent lighting. Any screams of agony went completely unheard due to the sheer ferocity of firepower.

Shaking off pieces of broken glass, Stokes pulled out his Glock but refrained from firing, mindful that he only had a few bullets left. He spotted the forger's camera on the edge of the table nearest him. Taking a risk, he leaned over and quickly grabbed it, then shoved it in his rucksack. If he did ever manage to get to the airport, he would need a camera to back up his claim of being a travel journalist, he thought. Then he immediately admonished himself for being so stupid, as, if he did make it out of there, he could easily have bought one at the duty-free shop anyway.

A few stray bullets then hit the fluorescent lighting above the work floor, instantly turning the rest of the basement into darkness, apart from a tiny amount of street lighting coming through the small sidewall window.

Shortly after, the gang's tirade of bullets stopped, and Stokes heard Captain English's voice. 'You missed me, English!' he called out. However, his voice now sounded less energetic – more strained and wearier.

Stokes didn't respond, remaining silent.

'… *English* – are you still alive?' he then asked,

unsure.

Stokes answered with two gunshots, instantly killing two of the soldiers ushered forward by their leader. Their lifeless bodies fell near the doorway, enabling Stokes to daringly lean out and quickly grab one of their Kalashnikovs before retreating inside to take cover again. There were more angry shouts in Arabic and Urdu, quickly followed by more rapid gunfire from the other end of the room, peppering the office walls inside and out.

Then, with his finger on the Kalashnikov's trigger, just as he was about to return fire, he faintly heard the sound of breaking glass coming from the window over by the sidewall, shortly followed by a loud explosion. It was a stun grenade, which quickly filled the basement area with thick acrid smoke.

Ears ringing, Stokes quickly pulled his scarf up over his mouth and nose, then peered out of the doorway. He could vaguely make out what looked like a SWAT team of Pakistani Rangers, fully kitted out with night vision goggles and laser beams attached to their assault rifles, come bursting in through the doorways on either side of the room, firing towards the gunfire. Flashes of gunfire illuminated the room everywhere.

Stokes never thought he'd be glad to see the authorities but, on this occasion, he was!

Rather than attempting to shoot his way out,

Stokes opted for a more stealthy way to exit the premises: crawl out instead. Now was not the time to be a hero. So, abandoning the cumbersome assault rifle in favour of his pistol, he lowered himself onto his belly and did just that, trying desperately not to cough too loud from smoke inhalation. And amid the chaos; hiding behind one large printer after another, he furtively made it to the exit door without being seen, ready to shoot anyone that got in his way.

It was just as well he left the office when he did, as a few of the rangers took cover there only moments later. But his troubles were not over yet; crouched down, he peered out of the doorway, spotting more armed rangers rapidly descending the stairs. *Fuck!* he screamed to himself. Thinking quickly, he shoved the barrel of his pistol down the back of his trousers and came out with his hands in the air, yelling repeatedly, 'DON'T SHOOT! I'M A HOSTAGE!

The ranger leading the others stopped and barked something to one of his men, who, following orders, quickly escorted him by the arm up the stairs to safety.

As with all hostage situations, that meant being debriefed by the authorities, which Stokes knew would inevitably lead to his arrest. He was, of course, glad to have made it out of there alive and in one piece – he thought it was a bleedin' miracle –

but to avoid capture, he had to act fast!

As Stokes was briskly led away towards the flashing lights of the many police vehicles stationed at the end of the alleyway, suddenly, at lightning speed, he elbowed the ranger in the face, dazing him before bundling him out of sight behind a large dumpster. Then forcing him to the ground, one well-targeted punch knocked him out cold.

The ex-Bootneck quickly checked both directions, then hurried back down the alleyway, past the bookshop staircase, and onwards in search of another way out of the maze of narrow passageways to join a main road and flag down a taxi to the airport. By now, there were very few people about due to the time of night and the police presence.

The gunfire soon stopped, and Stokes could only guess, judging by the number of rangers present, that the criminal gang were now either all deceased or wounded and captured.

Continuing at a brisk pace, Stokes spotted a man up ahead, crouched over, struggling to walk. It was Captain Nelson.

At first, he wasn't sure: being bent over as he was, it was hard to tell. But when he stood momentarily to rest, Stokes was in no doubt that this tall, lanky man was him.

The shitbag must have fought his way out of the other exit and made it out through the rear of the shop!

thought Stokes, cursing.

Bent on revenge, Stokes withdrew his Glock 17 and quickly caught up with him. 'Stop right there, you sick fuck!'

The sick fuck stopped and began to laugh, recognising whose voice it was. Stokes wheeled around him, continually pointing his gun at his head, snarling the whole time. Lit only by the moonlight, the pair's eyes then met.

'Looks like you now have the upper hand, English,' painfully remarked Captain Nelson, sounding raspy. He was clutching a deep wound to the stomach. It looked like Stokes's knife had hit the target after all.

Stokes pushed him against the nearby wall, about to shoot him, saying, 'Shut the fuck up!'

The tall man could stand no longer, collapsing to the ground. Then ignoring Stokes, struggling to speak, he uttered, 'Roger was a weak, betraying, low-life piece of shit, and deser—'

'He didn't deserve that!' interjected Stokes angrily, pointing his weapon at the gang leader's head again.

'Don't shoot! Don't Shoot!' pleaded the dying man as blood continued to flow from between his fingers. 'Help me to a hospital, and I will give you riches you've only ever dreamed of!'

Stokes spontaneously let out a cynical laugh.

'… We are not that different, you and I, English!'

continued the gang leader, now gurgling blood. 'You have killer eyes!'

Snarling, Stokes began to squeeze the trigger.

'Wait! Don't you at least want to watch me suffer a little longer?' the gang leader asked quizzically.

'No, I don't have the time,' was the blunt answer.

Then, knowing his time was up, with a wry smile, Captain Nelson said, 'Kiss me, Hardy.'

'Kiss this!' answered Stokes as he wedged the muzzle of his pistol into the tyrant's mouth and fired. *'Scum!'*

Wiping the Glock clean with his scarf, he then placed it into the dead man's right hand - dithering ever so slightly as he tried to remember whether the guy was right or left-handed - then hurried from the scene.

Finally, out of the labyrinth and desperate to get to the airport, Stokes flagged down the nearest mode of transport: a rickshaw.

PART TWO

CHAPTER SIXTEEN

Two years later.

Drinking fancy coffees, sat outside a trendy café in the upmarket Pantiles area of Royal Tunbridge Wells, were best friends, Ruth Winters and Mary Reynolds. The pair often met there for a catch-up. It was a Saturday morning in the height of summer, and both were appropriately dressed in stylish loose-fitting summer dresses, befitting wealthy ladies of leisure. They were discussing both their favourite topics: men.

'All the dating sites I've tried have been a waste of time,' said Mary, an attractive, medium-height brunette pushing forty, as she switched off her app disappointedly.

'Oh, you'll find someone soon enough,' remarked her friend, a less attractive, slightly dumpy blonde around the same age, putting her tall latte glass back down on the table. 'You just need to be patient, that's all!'

'Patient!' Mary exclaimed. 'I've not had sex in over a year!'

Ruth burst out laughing. *'Shh!* Keep your voice down!' she begged, quickly looking left and right to check if anyone heard.

'Well, not if you don't count my Rabbit,' continued Mary with a big salacious grin.

Her friend was now in stitches. 'Oh, *stop* it!' she said, covering Mary's mouth. 'You're too much!'

'Well, every date I've been on has turned out to be a disaster. The men either look nothing like their photos or have turned out to be as boring as hell!'

More laughter.

'The trouble with you, sweetie, is that you always go for the wrong type,' stated Ruth.

'No, I do not. What *do* you mean?' asked Mary, slightly indignant, frowning.

'You know very well the type I mean … bad boy's. Sound familiar?'

There was a slightly awkward pause.

'Well, if you're referring to my ex-husband, then, yeah, you have a point. Getting married to that sociopath was the biggest mistake in my life!'

'You used the word, "ex". Are the pair of you finally divorced then?' asked Ruth, curious and keen to discover any new gossip.

'No, I now refer to him as my ex because our marriage has been well and truly over for a long time. *He'd* like me to agree to a quick divorce so he

could get his money-grabbing hands upon half my estate if he could. But I'd see him in court first!' Ruth nodded along with what her friend was saying. 'Besides, he's doing alright for himself in Dubai, or wherever the fuck he is right now.'

'Haven't you heard from him lately, then?'

'I haven't heard from him in ages!' answered Mary. 'Nor do I care to – he can go to hell as far as I'm concerned!'

'I know he treated you very badly, what with him being a womaniser and the rest of it, but the two of you must have loved one another once upon a time –'

'The only person that Steve has ever loved is himself!' Mary interrupted by saying. 'We married far too young – anyway, let's not talk about him; it always depresses me when I think about that git and the way he treated me.'

'Yeah, sorry, Mary, I shouldn't have brought him up – the bastard!' said Ruth, placing her hand caringly on her friend's arm. 'Let's face it, all men are deceitful, cheating bastards!'

Mary laughed. 'D'ya wanna another coffee?'

'Oh, no thanks, I've got to go. I've got an appointment at the hairdresser's shortly,' answered Ruth, quickly checking the time on her mobile phone.

'Okay, Ruth. Well, let's meet up for a coffee again soon!'

'Yes, let's! And keep positive,' said Ruth, getting up to leave, 'Mr right could walk in that door any moment – you've just got to have more faith.'

Mary smiled and nodded. 'Bye, darling!'

'By sweetie!'

Mary finished her coffee, paid the bill, and after gathering her things, headed straight home to her 2.5-million-pound, six-bedroom property in the affluent area of Calverley Park.

She didn't live very far from The Pantiles, and as it was a beautiful sunny morning, decided to walk home. Her stunning Georgian home, with its white-washed, Decimus Burton architecture, overlooks the magnificent park. She'd lived in the property ever since her marriage to Steve Reynolds almost twenty years ago.

Her husband inherited the property from his late father, whom he'd rarely seen as a child and knew very little about, let alone that he owned such a large property. His mother, who died from a tragic accident when he was very young, he now believed was probably never really married to his father; and, after being taken into foster care, Steve never saw his father again.

Mary's wealthy parents, who were now both retired, had had high hopes of the newlyweds having a large family and living happily ever after in the spacious property, but that wasn't to be.

On her way through the park, Mary watched with

envy as loved-up couples affectionately held hands and kissed in the glorious sunshine, wishing it were her. Some had small children with them. A desire long now sadly given up on since her separation from Steve several years ago.

As she continued her walk, the warmth of the midday sun was replaced by a sudden chill down her spine. The thought that someone could be following her began playing on her mind. Glancing cautiously over her shoulder every so often, though, reassured her otherwise. A young woman had been raped and murdered in the area recently, so it was not surprising that she felt uneasy.

She could see her house on the crescent just up ahead but stepped up her pace anyway. Once at her front door, she glanced cautiously over her shoulder once more before entering.

Apart from her beloved fourteen-year-old Sphynx cat, Cleo (short for Cleopatra), Mary lived alone in her capacious six-bedroom house. But she had friendly neighbours and often had family and friends over to keep her company. She also liked going out a lot, so was very seldom lonely. She just missed being in a loving relationship to share her beautiful home and life with.

Like always, the friendly feline greeted its owner at the door, meowing and purring affectionately. Though not as quickly as she used to as she was now getting on a bit.

'Hi, Cleo!' said Mary excitedly as she bent down to stroke her pet's chamois-like hairless body and kiss its bald little head. 'Look what mummy's bought you for your lunch, my darling!' She removed a tin of her pet's favourite gourmet cat food from her handbag to show her. 'Your favourite treat!' she announced, spoken in a way a mother would speak to her child. In some ways, Cleo was a substitute for a childless marriage, which gave her comfort. Mary then stood up again, saying, 'Come on, let's get you your lunch, then!' and headed for the kitchen at the end of the hall with her purring cat following her.

Mary didn't need to work but chose to help part-time in a local charity shop on the High Street. Besides the fulfilment of helping those less fortunate, it also gave her something to fill her time with. Socialising with the upper echelons of society in fancy restaurants and bars, not to mention the numerous private house parties she attended, could be quite tiresome. And more often than not these days, she substituted a wine glass for a paintbrush in her hand (she'd tried holding a glass in one hand and a paintbrush in the other, but that didn't work).

She was a talented portrait artist and had exhibited her work in a few high-profile art exhibitions and galleries – though she did it for pure pleasure and enjoyment rather than as a means to make money. She converted one of the master bedrooms on the second floor into her art studio. It had two large Georgian sash windows facing the park, allowing plenty of light through.

Later that afternoon, Mary was in her art studio working on finishing touches to her most recent piece when her mobile phone rang.

'Oh, blast!' Why does it always ring when I'm busy painting!' she mumbled, tutting.

It woke Cleo up, who had been sleeping on her favourite windowsill. All that fine dining had made her feel tired.

Mary thought about letting it ring, but then saw it was her friend Sasha's name on the screen and decided to take the call, knowing how annoyingly persistent she could be.

'Hi, Sasha!' she said, pressing the speakerphone button as she walked over to one of the windows.

'Hi, Mary!' Sasha replied excitedly. 'I'm not disturbing you, am I?'

'No, not at all!' Mary answered, lying.

'Oh, good. I thought you might be painting or something.'

Mary didn't respond but thought, well, why is she ringing me now for then?

'I just phoned to check if you are still coming to my 40th in a couple of weeks?' continued her friend.

'The answer is the same as I told you last week *and* the week before –'

'Well, it's just that I need to know for numbers, that's all, sweetie. The Italian restaurant can only accommodate sixty covers, and I've had so many people ask if they can come ...' boasted Mary's friend, pausing to take in some air.

Mary felt like saying, she'd be happy to let someone else take her place, but knew it would upset her, so said: 'Yes, *of course,* I wouldn't miss it for the world, darling!'

'Oh, I'm so excited, I can't wait. I've already decided what dress I'm wearing …'

As Mary half-listened and gazed aimlessly out of the window towards the park, she noticed a man seemingly staring up at her, taking photographs. It immediately made her feel uncomfortable and exposed, especially in light of the recent sex attack and murder. He suddenly stopped as if aware she was watching him and immediately began jogging in the opposite direction – which she thought was a bit suspicious and odd. Aside from his black tracksuit and baseball cap, he was too far away for her to get a good look at him. She quickly reasoned it was probably just some tourist interested in the architecture.

Twenty minutes later. '… so don't forget, we're all meeting at 7 pm – Mary, are you listening?' suddenly asked Sasha, unsure.

'Yeah, *sorry!* What was that again?'

'I said, don't forget everyone's meeting at the

wine bar first for pre-dinner drinks.'

'I shan't forget!' answered Mary, thinking, *there's no chance of that!*

'Is everything alright?' then asked Sasha. 'Only, you seem a bit subdued.'

'Yeah, I'm fine – just a bit tired, that's all.'

'They'll be a few single guys there from my office!' then announced Sasha excitedly, meaning well.

Oh, great! cynically thought Mary, knowing the men she was probably referring to – dull as hell. 'Sasha, I must go,' she suddenly announced, desperately searching for an excuse to end the call, '... there's someone at the door! Thanks for your call!'

'Oh, okay, sweetie. Well, see you in two weeks, then!'

'Yeah, bye!'

Relieved, Mary ended the call feeling slightly miffed, thinking, *Why do my friends always feel the need to remind me I'm single – as if I don't already know that*?! All her friends were either married or in solid relationships – and most had children. She continued ranting about it to herself for a while: *And why do they automatically take on the role of matchmakers as if I am incapable of finding a man myself? ...*

After Mary had calmed down, she made herself a mug of coffee and went and stood by the window again, curious to see if anyone might be acting suspiciously as before. But all she saw were people going about their everyday business, enjoying themselves in the afternoon sun. Nonetheless, even though she tried not to let the news of the local rape and murder case trouble her too much, living in a large house on her own did make her feel even more vulnerable and edgy.

No longer in the mood for painting, moving downstairs to the ground floor lounge, Mary curled up on her comfy leather sofa, with Cleo nestled on her lap, and began reading a Jackie Collins novel, which Mary soon abandoned, frustrated that all the women in the story were having sex and she wasn't!

Now feeling horny, Mary stopped stroking the cat in favour of caressing a different kind of pussy – which like her cat, was equally bald (Mary regularly underwent the Hollywood wax treatment).

She made her way up to her bedroom on the first floor – which also looked out onto the park – stepped inside, closed the door, shutting her meowing cat out, kicked off her sandals, and threw herself onto her king-size bed, not caring that she'd left the curtains wide open. The thought that someone could be secretly watching her playing with herself, perversely, turned her on even more. She then chuckled to herself, thinking, they'd have to be extremely tall!

As she lay on her back, sexually fantasising with her eyes closed, her right hand hitched up her skimpy dress, then began gently rubbing her already wet pussy through the cotton of her white panties. Soon they were off, giving her long slender fingers more freedom of movement as she spread her legs farther apart and caressed her clitoris with circular motions. Slowly at first before speeding up as the pleasure increased and her orgasm drew ever closer.

Mary soon began to moan loudly with unreserved pleasure, oblivious to her cat scratching rampantly at the door and now meowing even louder. Wriggling her hips and thrusting them back and forth, she imagined a stranger's big cock was wedged deep inside her instead of two fingers slipping vigorously in and out.

Not completely satisfied, while one hand continued frigging herself, her other hand hurriedly pulled open her bedside drawer, reached in and grabbed her monster of a vibrator. Which, she deftly switched on with the same hand - so as not to lose momentum - and put to immediate use, screaming out in ecstasy as she inserted it deep inside her.

Sensing she was close to orgasm, with sweat now pouring out of her, she continued to slip all nine inches of it in and out of her soaking wet vag at an ever-increasing speed, trying desperately not to let the sound of the noisy vibrator or her cat put her off. Perish the thought: she was so close to climaxing now – it was never usually this intense or quick to reach her climax! Then, supported by her legs and shoulders, with her feet planted firmly on the bed, toes curled inwards, she thrust her hips upwards one last time, arching her back fully as she screamed at the top of her voice and climaxed.

As if on cue, her doorbell rang. *'Shit!'* she muttered. She just remembered that her mother and father had said they would call round in the afternoon.

CHAPTER SEVENTEEN

As soon as she heard the doorbell ring, Mary sprung off the bed, sped into her ensuite bathroom for a quick wash, put on some fresh knickers, and then hurriedly made her way down the stairs to open the front door. She knew it was her mum and dad because the letterbox was wide open, and she could hear her mum's voice calling out her name.

'Hello dear!' first said her mum, Susan, followed by her dad, Rupert, as she opened the door to greet them.

'Hello!' replied Mary, somewhat in a fluster with her dress partially trapped between her knickers before she spotted it and quickly sorted it out.

'You look a bit flushed, sweetheart - are you alright?' asked her father.

'Yes, fine - I've just been doing a bit of housework upstairs,' answered their daughter.

'Your mother said she thought she could hear the

vacuum cleaner!'

Mary just smiled coyly, now with an even more rubicund complexion.

There was a pause. 'Well, are we just going to stand here talking all day or are you going to invite us in?' said the father jovially.

'Yes, of course, sorry, come in – I was miles away!' Mary was wondering if her parents had heard her tumultuous screams as well. 'I'll put the kettle on.'

'Oh, these are for you, dear!' said Mary's father, handing her a large bouquet of flowers he'd forgotten he still had in his hand.

'Ah, thank you – they're beautiful!' expressed Mary, taking them from him and giving them a quick sniff.

'What a beautiful day it is!' commented her mum.

'Yes, it's gorgeous!' Mary replied, closing the door behind them.

'Living in this big house all on your own must take a lot of hard work to clean –' her mum then said.

'I'm not alone – I've got Cleo to keep me company, haven't I darling,' she instantly replied, picking up her cat and cradling it in her arms.

'Well, our daughter doesn't have a job, so she has plenty of time to get on with the household chores!' remarked her father insensitively.

Mary cleared her throat. *'Excuse me!* I work three

days a week in a charity shop, I'll have you know.'

'So, you do! Sorry, please forgive me, my darling, I forgot!' said her father with a regretful look. 'And very commendable that is too!'

'Take no notice of him, Mary,' said her mum, shaking her head and tutting. Then jokingly adding, 'He's going a bit senile in his old age, that's all, dear!'

'Being senile has its advantages!' he retorted. 'There're no more repeat programmes on the TV! And you keep meeting new people all the time!' There was a pause, and then he repeated what he just said for comic effect. Mary laughed, but his wife just rolled her eyes, saying, 'That awful joke is like him ... as old as the hills!' This time they all laughed together.

'What are you two like?! You should both go on Britain's Got Talent!' said their daughter, smiling. 'Now, why don't you go and sit down in the lounge, and I'll bring your drinks through to you?'

'Okay, dear,' they both answered smiling, doing just that while Mary went to find a vase to put the flowers in and boil the kettle.

'What did you have to go and say that for?!' said Susan discreetly to her husband, scolding him as they went and sat down.

'Say, what?' he replied rather sheepishly.

'You know very well what! About her not having a job,' she replied, reminding him, 'you know how sensitive she after everything's she's been through!'

'Oh, yes, that! Look, Mary's doing okay now. We can't keep smothering her in cotton wool – she's a …' He had to think a moment. '… thirty-eight-year-old woman, for Christ's sake!'

'Well, the medication is helping, but I fear her mind is still very fragile!' responded Susan with a worried look, continuing to speak in hushed tones.

There was a moment of silence, and then the mother spoke again.

'… I blame our daughter's depression on that no-good husband of hers after all the pain and suffering he put her through!' she said bitterly as the mere mention of him churned up bad memories.

'If I ever see him again, I'll ring his bloody –' angrily said the dad, also feeling bitterness towards the husband.

'*Shh!* Here she comes!' said the mum, interrupting her husband while putting her finger to her lips and tapping his arm.

Even before Mary and Steve finally separated, it was Mary's parents who took the brunt of her mood swings and bouts of deep depression, leading to more than one attempt at taking her own life. She often found life very difficult to cope with and was forced to give up her promising medical career (ironically, as a busy NHS doctor, she overlooked caring for herself). Indeed, it got so bad at one time – especially after her second miscarriage – that her parents abandoned their home in Sevenoaks to move in with her so they could keep a close watchful eye on her. And even though time proved to be a great healer, and mentally, Mary was now in a much better place than in the past, they continued to be very worried and concerned for her well-being – albeit sometimes overly so.

'Are you two talking about me?' asked Mary as she entered the room with a tray of hot drinks and biscuits. 'My ears are burning.'

'No, no, no dear,' said her mother, 'your father and I were just saying how well you are looking!'

'Oh, thanks!' Mary replied with a cynical smile, not totally convinced.

'So, what have you been doing with yourself since we last saw you?' asked Mary's father …

Late that evening, alone in her big house once more with only her cat for company, Mary drank the last drop of red wine from a whole bottle she'd downed, and after double-checking the doors and windows were all locked, she drunkenly climbed the stairs to her bedroom.

Once inside, Mary crossed the expansive floor space from the door to the large sash window and peered out. It was past midnight, and the park opposite was now quiet and still.

While still in full view of the window, she began to disrobe, her curvaceous body backlit by her bedside table lamp. First off came her dress, pulled straight up over her head and tossed towards a chair, missing it completely; then fumbling, she began removing her bra.

Watching her from within the wooded area of the park with a pair of powerful binoculars was the same man taking photographs of her property earlier.

As her bra came off, revealing her petite but beautifully formed breasts, he felt instantly aroused. She then turned around and, sliding her thumbs into her white laced panties, much to his delight, slowly slipped them off. Her cute pale ass was also a sight to behold.

The pervert continued watching his prey for as long as he could before she slunk out of view. He kept watching in the hope that she would reappear. She did shortly afterwards - now dressed in her sexy negligée - to close the curtains and end the peep show - not that she was aware anyone was watching. Disappointed, he allowed his binoculars to rest against his chest, turned, and left.

A few days later, Mary was out socialising with a few of her girlfriends, all sitting around a table drinking cocktails in a trendy bar in the centre of Tunbridge Wells late in the evening.

The dimly lit bar was quite busy for a weeknight. There was a group of about ten celebrating someone's birthday in one area, which helped swell the numbers, a few smaller groups dotted about here and there - including Mary and her friends, and one lone guy sat drinking beer at the bar. He was of large muscular build, cleanly shaven, with short black hair, dressed in a pair of smart black trousers and a tight-fitting white short-sleeved shirt left untucked, which showed off his dark tan as well as his big muscles.

It was a fun atmosphere and the music playing seemed to be to everyone's taste.

''ere, don't look, Mary, but there's a sexy-looking guy at the bar who keeps looking across at you!' said Angelica after giving her friend a nudge.

Now, whenever someone says not to look, it's almost impossible not to. And that's what Mary did. Just a quick casual look, but it was long enough for them to catch each other's eye. Both smiled warmly.

Mary looked gorgeous, elegantly dressed in a short, slinky black dress, black stockings and suspenders - she never wore tights on a night out - and matching black patent stilettos.

Mary and Angelica immediately looked at each other and giggled like they were pubescent schoolgirls once again.

'You're right, he is rather sexy!' said Mary,

blushing ever-so-slightly.

'What are you two smiling and giggling about?' suddenly asked Ruth, who had been busy chatting with Debbie, sat next to her, before her ears pricked.

'Mary has an admirer,' answered Angelica, raising her eyebrows.

'Where?' demanded Ruth excitedly, who was probably the most pissed out of all of them.

'Over by the bar in the white shirt!'

Unhesitating, she glanced over her shoulder at him. He was now in profile ordering another bottle of beer (they don't have beer pumps in this sort of place) from the barman. Then turning back to face her friends, 'Phwore! I wouldn't kick him out of bed!'

Her three wide-eyed friends laughed in unison.

'Ruth!' exclaimed at least two of her friends.

'You're a married woman!' then stated one of them jokingly.

Everyone at the table laughed.

'Get me my divorce papers, and I'll sign 'em right now!' drunkenly responded Ruth to more raucous laughter.

'Here's to hunky men!' said Angelica, raising her glass. 'Cheers!'

Everyone clinked glasses, saying, 'Cheers!' with big lustful grins before necking the contents.

'It's your turn to get the next round, Mary!'

announced Ruth, placing her empty cocktail glass onto the table heavily. 'Mine's a Creamy Pussy,' she reminded her, adding, 'I wish!'

More laughter ensued; then the others told Mary what they'd like to drink also.

'It'll give you the chance to make acquaintances with your new admirer!' said Angelica with a saucy look.

'He'll probably be glad of someone to talk to – look at him, he looks all sad and lonely, sat there by himself!' said Debbie, grinning mischievously.

Mary ignored her friend's further attempts to get her hooked up and headed for the bar. She had to admit to herself, though, based on looks, he was her type.

'Hiya!' said the barman. 'You ladies seem to be having a good time!'

'Yeah, we always like to have a good laugh,' she replied, suddenly feeling self-conscious and a tad nervous as she glanced towards the tall, dark stranger sitting only a few feet away from her. She was very aware of her friends all staring at her in anticipation.

'What can I get ya?' then asked the barman, chirpily.

Mary reeled off the order of drinks, slightly embarrassed by the crude names she gave.

She then heard a deep, husky voice, which wasn't the barman's. 'Which one of those drinks is yours!'

he asked with an alluring grin.

She turned to him, grinning back, and answered coyly, 'That would be telling!'

The guy chuckled. 'Sorry, I didn't mean to be too forward.' He then leaned towards Mary and held out his hand awkwardly for shaking, casually saying, 'I'm Mark, by the way.'

'Oh, I'm Mary,' she replied, obliging him with a lingering handshake.

'They're shaking hands!' announced Angelica excitedly, stating what the others could already clearly see.

'Celebrating something, are you?' the stranger asked.

'No, we're always this noisy!' Mary replied, chuckling.

He chuckled with her, then took a swig out of his bottle.

'I've not seen you in here before,' she said, sitting on the barstool next to him while she waited for the barman to finish making the cocktails.

He caught a flash of her bare milky-white thighs above her stocking tops as she adjusted herself comfortably into position. His eyes quickly reverted to hers, not wanting her to think he was anything but a gentleman.

'I've only just moved into the area,' he replied. 'So, I'm still getting acquainted with it.

'Oh, right ... So, where do you come from, then?'

'Ramsgate. Have you ever been?'

'No, I've been to Margate! That's nearby, isn't it?'

'Yeah, very close.'

'My ex and I used to go there occasionally.'

'Are you still single?'

Mary hesitated at first, then answered, 'Yeah.'

'Me too,' he responded with a growing smile.

Quickly changing the subject, thinking the conversation was moving a little too fast, she asked: 'So, what made you want to move here then - was it work?'

No, not especially. I work as a freelance travel writer - so it doesn't really matter where I live,' he gave as his answer.

'That must be interesting!' remarked Mary, now feeling a lot more relaxed.

'Yeah, it can be,' began to answer the stranger.

Mary kept hearing her tipsy friends giggling and making lewd remarks about them, which she found off-putting. And when she casually looked over her shoulder, she saw all three gawking at them. She pulled a face at them as if to say, shut up and stop staring, she quickly turned her head back towards Mark again, saying, 'Sorry, my friends can be very annoying at times - carry on!'

He laughed. 'That's alright,' he said, smiling and giving Mary's friends a quick wave. 'I was only going to say the travelling can be very tedious, that's all. Anyway, what about you?

'What do I do for a living?' she asked, unclear.

'Yeah?'

'Nothing as exotic as what you do!' she answered. 'I work in a charity shop just up the road.'

'Oh, yeah? And how long have you worked for Oxfam, then?'

Mary started to tell him, then paused. '… Wait a minute. How did you know I worked for Oxfam?'

'Well, I saw it on the way here, and I suppose I just guessed,' he told her, quickly adding, 'D'ya like working there?'

'Yeah, I love it! I get a lot of self-satisfaction out of helping those in need!'

'I can believe it,' he said, thinking what a lovely kind person she was. 'Have you always lived here?' he then enquired, seeming genuinely interested.

'No, I was born in Sevenoaks, but moved here when I was in my twenties.'

Mark moved his head sharply backwards, acting surprised. 'What, you mean to tell me that you're not still in your twenties?!'

Mary laughed, jokingly slapping him on his thigh, 'Stop it!' she said. 'I'm two years shy of forty, I'll have you know!'

'Well, you certainly don't look it!' he remarked, smiling while continuing to look into her eyes. She looked at him doubtfully. *'I'm serious!'*

'Yeah, right! That old cliche. I bet you say that to all the girls you meet!'

'You look *stunning!* Honestly! I noticed you the moment I stepped in here.'

'Really?!'

'Yeah, you're beautiful!

'Ah, thanks!' she replied, flattered.

Just then, the bartender served Mary the drinks. 'Thirty-two pounds, please madam.'

'I'll get those!' said Mark, having already removed his wallet.

'No, that's alright. That's very kind of you bu—'

'Please! Let me buy them for you,' he said insistently, offering the barman two crisp twenty-pound notes.

'Well, alright. Thank you very much – you're too kind!'

The barman took his money. 'Keep the change!' Mark told him. He then quickly downed the remainder of his beer and said, 'Well, I'm gonna get going now.'

'Oh!' she just muttered, sounding a little disappointed while thinking, *I bet it was my annoying friends putting him off! Or maybe he found me boring?*

'It was lovely meeting you, Mary!' he said getting off his stool.

'It was lovely meeting you too, Mark!'

Both smiled widely. It was obvious that they had enjoyed each other's company – albeit briefly.

Hesitating, he suddenly said: '… I would love to

go out for a coffee with you sometime.' Which instantly brought a smile back to her face. 'And perhaps you wouldn't mind showing me around the area?'

'Yeah,' she said, pleased. *'Sure!* I'd love to!'

'Great!' he replied happily.

The pair then quickly exchanged phone numbers.

'I'll give you a ring sometime soon then!' said Mark, after logging her number into his phone.

'Yeah, please do,' she replied, trying not to sound too eager or desperate.

He offered his hand out for shaking again, and as they did, he leant towards her and kissed her on the cheek. She reciprocated.

They said goodbye to each other, then he turned one way to leave, and after picking up the tray of drinks, she turned the other way to rejoin her curious and now even more excitable friends with a smile so incandescent it lit up the entire room.

Mary placed the tray of drinks onto the table, still smiling her head off, her cheeks red as the cherry floating on top of her Slippery Nipple, and without saying a word, sat down.

'*... Well?*' said Ruth, eager as the rest of them were to find out how it all went.

Mary calmly took a sip of her drink.

'Come on, don't keep us in suspense – you know we're all dying to know!' said Angelica, excitedly. '*What's* he like?'

'Mark is very nice!' she answered coolly.

'Oh, the pair of them are on first-name terms already!' wryly interjected Ruth.

'*Just* very nice?!' asked Debbie with a dirty grin and a twinkle in her eye.

'He's very, very ... *very nice!*' was Mary's response, full of excitement. 'He came across as a *real* gentleman!'

'They all do, to begin with, sweetie!' then said Ruth cynically.

'Oh, trust you to be a killjoy!' remarked Angelica. 'Take no notice of her – she's only jealous!'

'*Of course,* I'm bloody jealous!' Ruth retorted, laughing.

'... So, did you exchange numbers, and have you arranged to see each other again?' then excitedly asked Angelica, bursting to know.

There was a dramatic pause, then, 'YES!' Mary screamed with delight to both questions.

CHAPTER EIGHTEEN

After an unexpectedly enjoyable evening, John Stokes closed the door to his cramped, damp-ridden, one-bed rented flat in Tunbridge Wells and went and sat down on the edge of the bed; his head, full of emotions.

He wasn't supposed to enjoy himself! And certainly not allow himself to become romantically attached to Mrs Mary Reynolds. He was only supposed to get acquainted with her; and gain her confidence and trust before killing her.

'I *won't* do it!' he kept repeating to himself.

Yes, you fucking will! bellowed his irate father's voice inside his fucked-up head.

'You never allow me to enjoy myself!' John yelled defiantly at his father.

For the last week, since he moved into the area, he'd been stalking her; watching her every move; where she lived, where she worked, where her favourite hangouts were, who her friends and family were, whether she was dating anyone or not – watching her undress. And now having met her – as briefly as it was – he felt an instant attraction towards her. He hadn't felt this way about the others.

His mood quickly changed from being happy to downright depressed. He felt very lonely in his shithole of a flat with only the living mould on the walls for company. He hated being lonely and longed for a stable relationship.

Only one week before, John was living a quiet life by the sea in Ramsgate, Kent, staying at his elderly aunt's (on his father's side) very modest but nicely kept three-bedroom house on the East Cliff. It was just her now: all his other relatives were either deceased or with whom he had long since broken ties – and were as good as dead to him anyway.

Aunt Mary was tall and wiry and had long, lank, and thinning ash-coloured hair – and despite being in her seventies, she kept herself fit. It was his dear old aunt he would often stay with at times of trouble when he was a boy – especially when his drunken father would mistreat him.

He'd taken refuge there once again, since escaping from the UAE and then Pakistan about two years prior. She seemed to understand him like no one else ever did. Since her husband passed away a few years ago, she was glad of the company.

He'd taken up sailing again, which he enjoyed immensely and helped him relax and take his mind off things. Anything to help him forget his troubled past! Otherwise, he very seldom went out or saw anybody. He was still a wanted man and, therefore, continued to maintain a low profile – indeed, he had started to get used to living a quieter life. But he did still keep abreast of the news in the UAE.

But a phone call one week ago to the day would change all that.

It was about one o'clock on a Wednesday afternoon. He was in his childhood bedroom when his mobile phone rang. At first, he just stared at it, wondering who on earth it could be. *Nobody ever rings me!* he thought. He let the persistent ringing continue a little longer, then picked up his mobile phone from his desk – the same old tatty desk he did his school homework on as a child – and answered it.

'Hello?' said John cautiously.

'Whatcha, mate! D'ya recognise my voice?' said the caller. There was a deathly silence. 'It's Steve – Steve Reynolds!'

John knew who it was. '… Hi, Steve!' he responded less enthusiastically. He wondered how Steve knew his new phone number. 'Well, this is a surprise! How the devil are you?' He then remembered telling him about his aunt. *He probably knows where I'm now staying,* he suddenly thought. *It wouldn't have been difficult to find out her home address and telephone number.*

'I've been better –' Steve began to answer.

'Steve, first of all, I wanna say, I'm sorry that I haven't been in touch with you before now – it's just that –'

'Don't worry, mate,' said Steve now interrupting him. 'You don't need to explain.'

'I honestly had every intention of returning what I took from you, but –'

'It's alright, mate – all that's now in the past and forgotten about. Anyway, my ex-girlfriend, Helga, won't be needing her yacht for a long while now that she's banged up in a UAE prison. She was done for kidnapping a police officer, the silly girl!'

'Yeah, I read about that,' said John, sounding concerned. 'So, she wasn't charged for murder, then?'

'No, they didn't have enough evidence to convict her in the end. You are now once again the number one suspect! But even if you did commit those murders – and I'm not saying that I think you did – I couldn't give a fuck, to be honest!'

There was an uncomfortable silence again while John contemplated what Steve had just said before reiterating what he told him two years ago, 'I didn't do it!'

'I believe ya, mate, I believe ya,' Steve told

him. 'As long as your conscious is clear, then, that's all that matters!'

John thought that was a bit rich coming from him.

Then moving away from the grim topic of conversation they'd started, Steve said, 'It's good to talk with ya, John!'

'Yeah, you too,' he replied.

'We have a lot of catching up to do.'

'Yeah, not 'alf!'

'How's your dear old aunt?' Steve then asked him out of the blue.

He knows where I live! immediately thought John, briefly answering, 'Fine, thanks – she's fine!'

'So, you managed to escape to England, then …?'

John paused again '… Yeah!' he just said, not wishing to elaborate on it. He wasn't sure that he could trust him – especially after what he discovered about the man in the UAE. But as Steve just said, all that's now in the past. And as far as John was concerned, it was best to keep it that way!

'The cops haven't caught up with you yet, then?' Steve then half-joked.

'No – they came sniffing around once about a year or so ago, but I've managed to keep one step ahead of 'em,' quickly answered John, refraining from saying any more.

'Good!' Sensing that John didn't want to talk about it (over the phone, at least), Steve said: 'You'll have

to tell me all about your escapades over a few pints the next time we meet!'

'You betcha!'

'Perhaps go and see a football match together!'

'Yeah, that would be great!'

John kept wondering what the real reason was he called. That soon became clear.

'So, where are you living now - are you still in Dubai?' asked John, starting to wonder.

'Never mind that right now,' Steve replied somewhat abruptly in a more serious tone. 'Listen, d'ya remember when I saved your ass back in Dubai, and you told me that you would return the favour someday -- whatever asked of you?'

Steve's mood had changed, and he now sounded agitated as if something was bothering him.

'Yeah?' replied John, slightly hesitantly, already beginning to regret ever saying it.

'Well, I now need you to honour that favour. I'm in a dire situation, mate! My business went into liquidation! I am now bankrupt and completely broke, and I owe some bad people an awful lot of money!' explained Steve, sounding desperate.

'I don't have any spare cash, Steve!' quickly interjected John. 'I'm pretty brassic myself if that's what you are asking for?'

'I don't want cha money. I want you to do something for me,' said Steve, gravely serious. There was a pause. 'I want you to kill my wife!'

'What?! No fuckin' way! You're joking, right – you can't be serious?!'

'I'm not joking – I mean it! I want her dead within the next few weeks so that I can get the ball rolling, claiming on our joint life insurance policy and her half of the estate – what's mine is hers, and what's hers is mine, and all that shit!'

John listened in stunned silence, not quite believing what he was hearing, as Steve spoke coldly about having his wife bumped off purely for money. Then argued, 'Well, if you want her dead so badly, why the fuck don't you do it then?!'

'Because, if I do it, it will be too bleedin' obvious. That's why I'm asking *you* to do it!' explained Steve, now sounding a little angry and sarcastic. 'Look! You said that you would do any *fuckin'* thing for me I asked, did you not?' continued ranting Steve, getting more and more worked-up.

'Yeah, but –' started to say John.

'Yeah, but nothin'!' interrupted Steve, now even angrier. 'What's a matter – have ya lost ya balls!'

'Fuck off!' John angrily responded.

'Listen, I saved your fuckin' life and you owe me this! Listen, If I don't pay back the money I owe very soon, I'll be a dead man! Do you understand?!'

'Alright, alright! Calm down!'

'We'll don't *fuckin'* argue with me then and *listen* to what I want you to do!'

There was an ugly and prolonged silence.

'… Do this one big favour for me, and I'll never ask another favour from you again!' stated Steve, now a little calmer, quickly adding, 'There'll also be a good whack of dosh in it for you!'

'… Go on!' finally said John, reluctantly. He didn't want any money - not blood money. He just wanted a peaceful life.

'... She lives in Tunbridge Wells,' started to explain Steve. 'So, you'll need to rent a place there. Follow her and get to know her every move - where she hangs out and so on. Then become acquainted with her - you accidentally, on purpose, bump into her in a café or a bar or someplace else and get chatty and friendly with her - you know what I mean, gain her confidence so that she feels safe and comfortable with you, trusts you. Then one day, suggest going on a nice little day trip together - somewhere picturesque but remote where there are high cliffs overlooking the sea. Then when you go for a walk, push her off the edge and make it look like it was an accident - drag the bitch screaming if need be!' He then reminded Steve about his wife's previous attempts to commit suicide and reassured him that no one would think any different this time!

As John listened to Steve's nefarious plan, his head was in a whirlwind of despair. Steve was right: he probably had saved his life; and in return, he had foolishly promised to do any favour Steve asked – but he just hadn't anticipated this! John had killed many times before, so how difficult could it be to kill again? It's not like he knew the woman – he's never even met her before. Just a quick sharp shove over the cliff edge, that was all, and he could move on with living a peaceful life!

'... Seduce my wife, if you must,' continued Steve, 'but whatever ya do, don't get romantically involved or emotionally attached to her! Don't be taken in by her sensuality and beauty!' He then added sinisterly, '... Or I'll have to put a hit out on both of you!' Though it was always hard to tell whether Steve was serious or not – John took him seriously on this occasion, however.

There was another long silence.

'So, are we good?' asked Steve.

'Yeah, I'll do it,' affirmed John.

Steve then gave John his wife's home address.

When the call ended, John angrily threw his phone at the pillows on his bed, shouting, 'Arghhh!' followed by several expletives.

His auntie quickly came and called to him from the other side of the door, 'Are you alright in there, Johnny-boy?!' she asked, checking to make sure – she knew only too well about his sudden angry outbursts and uncontrollable temper.

'Yeah!' he called back. He wasn't alright – far from it!

Shortly afterwards, he came out of his room

carrying a large sports bag.

'I've gotta go!' he told his aunt solemnly.

'Go? But, where?' asked his aunt.

Her nephew didn't answer.

'But I've cooked you your favourite steak and kidney pudding for lunch!' she said, disappointed. 'Can't it wait?'

'No, I'm sorry, Aunt. I don't have time.'

'... But when will I see you again?' she asked, now worried and concerned.

'I should be back in a few weeks!'

Saying this, he kissed her forehead, then made his way through to the internal garage, jumped into his uncle's uninsured, old Ford Fiesta, and drove off.

John paced up and down his tiny Tunbridge Wells flat, thinking - he was always *thinking* - completely unaware his arms were swinging back and forth. It was as if he were on parade once more. He was also oblivious to the angry shouts from the flat below, who had been awakened by the loud sound of floorboards being constantly pounded, and the occasional shrill of military drill orders being made. His psychosis was getting much worse!

After a while, the noise stopped, and his sweat-drenched, exhausted body flopped onto the bed where, much to the relief of his fellow tenants, he quickly fell asleep.

He woke up about ten hours later. For the rest of

the morning, he kept thinking of Mary, and little else; he couldn't get her out of his mind. She wasn't the bitch Steve had portrayed her to be – far from it, she was lovely! He wanted to phone her there and then and arrange to meet up as discussed but stopped himself – it was too soon! He'll ring her in a few days he decided. He didn't want to appear too keen, or it might put her off. And so, for the next few days at least, he would have to continue admiring her from afar.

CHAPTER NINETEEN

It was Saturday morning, and after three anguishing days lying in wait, John Stokes finally plucked up the courage to ring Mrs Reynolds.

He always felt awkward and uncomfortable around women. It was funny: he had fought bravely in war zones, and yet, when it came to arranging a date with a woman, he was terrified.

'… Hello,' answered Mary's sweet voice.

There was a slight hesitation, and then John spoke. 'Hi, Mary. It's Mark – we met the other night,' he said, slightly nervously. He'd had quite a lot to drink the last time he spoke with her and had built up some Dutch courage.

'Hi, Mark!' she said excitedly, happy he'd rung. 'It's lovely to hear from you! I had a great night – when was it …? *Wednesday!*'

'Yeah, I could see that,' he replied with a slight chuckle.

'All the more pleasurable for meeting you!'

'Likewise!'

'I thought perhaps you wouldn't ring,' she admitted.

'Are you kidding me!' he said, much more animated than usual, while at the same time thinking, *I knew I should have rung her sooner!* 'I'm looking forward to having you escort me on a sightseeing tour of Tunbridge Wells.'

'I wouldn't get too excited!' she joked. 'There's not that much to see!' Both laughed.

'How about this afternoon?' John then asked.

'Yeah, sure, why not!' she answered upbeat. 'Do you know where The Pantiles is?'

'The Pan-tiles?' he responded vaguely. He knew very well where The Pantiles was. He'd followed her there several times already. 'Oh, yeah, I know where it is!'

'Well, let's meet at the bandstand – that's easy to find,' suggested Mary.

'Okay, what time?'

'Say, one o'clock – we could have a spot of lunch there if you like?'

'Sounds good to me,' he replied chirpily. 'I mean, who wouldn't want to have lunch with a beautiful woman like you!' As with when he first met her in the bar, he could hear himself using the same sweet-talking (corny) chat-up lines he'd heard Steve Reynolds say to women back in Dubai.

… The call ended, and John quickly got washed and changed into something more presentable. He couldn't remember the last time he went on a proper date with someone - or at least that's how he liked to think of it.

He combed his hair in front of the cracked bathroom mirror - the same mirror he'd punched a couple of days ago. This time, however, his reflection showed a happy smiling face. His smile soon dropped, though, when the sobering thought of why he was there came flooding back to him.

John quickly turned away from the mirror. His image had been replaced by his father's! He thought about not meeting Mary and driving back home to Ramsgate, but a part of him wanted to see her again. He should have been more assertive with Steve and not agreed to his evil request, he told himself.

He went and sat down on the grubby sofa to collect his thoughts: he reasoned that if he didn't kill her, then Steve would have someone else do it instead - someone much less sympathetic, that wouldn't spare her the pain of death. Whereas he would be quick, and she would hardly feel a thing. He would break into her home when she was fast asleep, he told himself.

His dark thoughts were suddenly interrupted by a loud banging on his front door.

John got up and cautiously answered the door. It

was the skinny little guy and his grossly overweight wife from downstairs – the ones he'd been keeping up half the night with his incessant marching and screeching.

'Excuse me, but we need to have a little talk with you!' said the husband, looking up at John, arms crossed, annoyed.

John just scowled at them.

'What's the meaning of you waking us up in the middle of the night with that awful racket of yours!' he demanded, repositioning himself behind his wife.

Again, Stokes didn't answer.

'Well … what have you got to say for yourself?' the equally annoyed woman then asked, adding, 'It used to be nice and quiet before you showed up!'

'… It's the giant rats!' John finally answered straight-faced.

'Giant rats?!' the woman exclaimed, shocked.

'Yeah, huge, great big things! I have to whack them sharply on the head to kill them!' John explained. 'I have a whole wastebin full of 'em – d'ya wanna see?'

'No, I *don't!'* shrieked the terrified woman, grabbing her husband by the arm and dragging him away. 'Come on!' she said to him, 'we need to go and call pest control!'

John grinned as the couple hurried back down the stairs, then slammed his door shut, making them audibly jump. Then, shortly afterwards, he left the flat and made his way to The Pantiles to meet his date.

Mary arrived at the bandstand about ten minutes early and waited patiently for her date's arrival, hoping that he would show up and not let her down – it wouldn't be the first time this had happened. She reminded herself that he had phoned her, so she had no reason to think he wouldn't come. She felt a little nervous; it had been a while since she'd been on a date with a man. And she'd only met this guy once – she didn't even know his surname; what if he turned out to be just like the others?

John could see Mary up ahead as he made his way through the bustling crowd towards her. She was pretty hard to miss, looking divine in a flowery summer dress, dominated by yellows.

As well as the busy cafés, bars, and restaurants dotted about The Pantiles, there was a market lining the main thoroughfare.

Both caught each other's gaze and immediately smiled and waved. Any dark thoughts had left him, and he was determined to enjoy himself – at least for the time being anyway.

'Hi, Mark!' said Mary, looking radiant.

'Hi, Mary!' replied John, quickly adding, 'You look gorgeous!'

'Oh, thank you!' she said, blushing slightly.

He quickly glanced at his watch. 'I'm not late, am I?'

'No, I got here early.'

'Oh, good!'

A little belatedly, both then kissed each other on the cheeks and hugged. Mary glanced over his large frame as they did to check if anyone she knew might have noticed them.

'Are you hungry?' asked Mary continuing to smile.

'Yeah, not 'alf!'

'Well, there's a good restaurant just along here' – she pointed – 'which I like to go to.'

'Please lead the way!' he said, gesturing …

In the restaurant, Mary and John had an enjoyable time getting to know each other better – at least so Mary thought. John continued to spin his deceitful web of lies about being a travel journalist. Being an ex-Royal Marine, he'd travelled the world extensively, so he could quickly reel off a list of countries he'd already been to – mostly war zones – and talk about them quite convincingly. Though, he was careful not to mention Dubai. By contrast, Mary was most open about her life, telling Mark all about her acrimonious split from her husband and her bouts of depression. She believed it was best to be open and honest from the start, should the date go any further and develop into a relationship. John acted as if it was the first time he'd heard it.

She had noticed the tattoo of a dagger on John's arm, and when quizzed, he did admit to being a Royal Marine in his younger days - which is how the conversation about her husband also being an ex-Royal Marine came about. She told him how her controlling ex, Steve, badly treated her and made her life a misery: blatantly having affairs with other women and disrespecting her. As John listened, although he wasn't usually an emotional sort of guy, part of him couldn't help but feel her pain - the same pain he felt when his dear mother suffered the same fate at the hands of his abusive father. That caring side of him also felt a sharp pang of guilt, remembering when he, too, had mistreated women.

They quickly dropped that topic of conversation - it wasn't exactly the most pleasant or cheerful way to spend their first date - in favour of a much more light-hearted one.

As promised, for the rest of the afternoon, Mary took John on an express tour of Tunbridge Wells. First, they visited the famous Chalybeate Spring of which the town is named, situated very near where they were in The Pantiles, discovered back in the 1600s, and where Royalty often came to bathe, hence, its Royal status. They then visited several other landmarks - including High Rocks and Groombridge Place Gardens, which they travelled to on the scenic Heritage Railway Line.

High Rocks is a 3.2-hectare ancient geological site of giant sandstone rocks or boulders surrounded by magical woodland and lakes. As the name implies, some rocks are as high as 40ft; and some have gulls big enough for people to pass through, interlinked with bridges for the benefit of tourists.

Standing very close to the edge of one of these giant rocks, John suddenly had the urge to push Mary to her death. They were all alone and shielded by bushy trees. It was his chance to kill her. But he held her securely by the arm instead, telling her to be careful. And in that moment of embrace, the two spontaneously turned to face each other and kissed.

It was only a brief kiss on the lips, and both felt a little bit embarrassed immediately afterwards, but there was no denying the spark they had between them. The rosy-cheeked pair then continued exploring the rest of area as well as each other.

Having spent a very enjoyable afternoon together, John and Mary arrived back in the centre of town around sixish. John offered to escort Mary home, and walking hand in hand, the beaming couple cut through Calverley Park. The sun was still shining, and there were lots of people milling about, determined to make the most of the fine weather.

'What a lovely park!' commented John, acting like it was his first time there.

'Isn't it just!' Mary replied. 'I feel very fortunate

waking up to this glorious view every morning!'

'You mean to say that you live in one of those grand houses?' he said, pointing up ahead, knowing full well where she lived.

'Yeah, the white-ish one directly ahead is mine.' She paused. 'And technically speaking, half my husband's, I suppose.' She then laughed.

'It looks magnificent!' John wasn't sure how long he could keep up this charade. He hated living a lie.

Then on a more serious note, Mary said: 'That ratbag wants me to sell it, but I would loathe doing that … I've become very attached to this property – the trouble is I can't afford to buy him out.'

There were far fewer people near where Mary lived. But a group of rowdy teenagers on mountain bikes, wearing the customary menacing-looking black hoodies, did catch their eye. They were showing off to each other, doing wheelies as frighteningly close to people as they dared. One elderly couple told one of them off, only to get a tirade of vile verbal abuse from him, shortly followed by his friends joining in.

'Oh, those poor people!' exclaimed Mary, concerned. 'That gang of hooligans often hang about here causing trouble!'

John could feel his blood rise, thinking, they better not bother us.

'… The trouble is – kids of today know they can

get away with it!' continued Mary.

John just nodded his head in agreement.

One of the yobbos then noticed John and Mary walking their way. And full of bravado, brazenly decided he would try and intimidate them too with his fancy bicycle tricks. Well, Stokes was having none of it. And as the youth's bike sped directly towards them with its front wheel raised high in the air, Mary recoiled in trepidation while Stokes coolly held his ground. Then as the front wheel moved predictably to the side of him, having only narrowly missed his face, he nudged the delinquent's shoulder, sending him and his bike flying. There was a loud thud, and the yobbo screamed in pain, '*Arghhh,* my leg's broken!'. Mary missed what happened because she had her eyes closed. John let go of her hand and went straight over to seemingly assist the snivelling cry-baby, who was now lying on the ground still straddling his bike, and purposely stepped on the spokes of the spinning rear wheel as he did, snapping and bending several of them out of shape. Stokes then leaned down next to the youth's ear and whispered threateningly, 'If I see you or your mates hanging around here again, I'll break your other fuckin' leg! Got me?!' Terrified, the teenager nodded.

Stokes calmly got up and went and held Mary's hand again. 'I offered him my help, but he didn't want it,' said Stokes shrugging his shoulders.

'Has he broken his leg, d'ya think?' asked Mary, concerned.

'Nah!' he replied with a cynical grin.

Just then, the other yobbos came tearing towards their injured friend.

'He fell off!' Stokes told them with a smirk.

'It serves him right!' said Mary as the two continued up to her house.

Standing at the top of the steps to Mary's grand house, John and Mary spoke briefly before saying their goodbyes.

'Can I see you again, Mary?' John asked tentatively, hoping but not one hundred per cent convinced she would.

'Sure, I'd *love* to, Mark,' she replied feeling somewhat tired, 'but can we make it just a trip to the pub next time?!' Both laughed.

'Yeah, good idea!' he said, adding, 'By the way. What *was* the name of the cocktail you were drinking the other night?'

Mary blushed slightly, then chuckled, '… Slippery Nipple.'

John grinned, saying, 'Ah! That explains the cherry on top!'

Both laughed again, then reverting to what they were talking about, Mary told him, 'I'm seeing my folks tomorrow, and I shall be working Monday and Tuesday, but I'm free Wednesday if you like.'

'Wednesday it is then!' said John bright-eyed and

smiling broadly. 'I'll give you a call to arrange a time.'

Mary's smile matched his. 'Super!'

Both then went silent for a moment; then gave each other a lingering hug which developed into a passionate kiss.

'Bye!' they both said joyfully.

CHAPTER TWENTY

After saying goodbye to Mary, John Stokes walked happily back the way he came through the park. There were no signs of the yobbos, only the tyre tracks they'd left behind on the damaged lawn.

Mary had gone straight up to her bedroom where she could watch her new love interest as he sauntered away. She had thought of inviting him in but knew one thing would probably lead to another and didn't want to give him the wrong impression of her. Mary certainly desired him but decided it was too early. Besides, she hardly knew him. Wait till you've been on at least one more date, she told herself. Her cat came to join her on the warm windowsill.

On his way back to his flat, John's happiness quickly faded as his head became dominated by the heinous crime to had agreed to commit.

I'm not gonna do it! John told himself. *As soon as I*

get back to the flat, I shall ring Steve and tell him I've changed my mind – and sod the bleedin' consequences!

John closed the door to his pokey flat, sweat pouring off of him, feeling slightly nervous and apprehensive.

You're making a big mistake, nagged his father's voice inside his head.

John ignored him and began removing his phone from his pocket. No sooner had he done so when his phone began to ring. It was Steve.

John took a deep breath, thinking, *Fuck!* still unsure how to put it to him.

'Hello, Steve,' he said matter-of-factly, 'I was about to call ya …'

'I hope it was to tell me that it's sorted!' said Steve, business-like, sensing something was up. There was a long pause. 'Oh, don't fucking tell me that you've chickened out again?'

'Look, Steve,' said John, 'I appreciate what you did for me in Dubai, but – but what you're asking me to do is wrong, and I won't be any part of it.'

'You've *fucked* her, haven't ya?!' Steve said aggressively. 'You've gone and bleedin' fucked her!'

'No!' John answered adamantly.

'Well, you've bleedin' fallen for her, then!' he snapped. 'I *knew* it! You *cunt!'*

'Fuck off!' quickly responded John. 'And if you do send anyone to kill us, I'll be the one doin' the

killing!'

'You've just made a big *fuckin'* mistake!' said Steve angrily through gritted teeth.

'Listen, I don't want any more to do with ya, so you can go and do one!'

'If you don't do what I asked, I will go straight to the fuckin' cops and tell them of your whereabouts - I'm sure the UAE authorities will be very pleased to finally meet cha!'

'Blackmail, eh?'

'Somethin' like that.'

John let out a nervous laugh. 'Do ya worst - even if I was arrested on suspicion of murder, they have nothing to go on! You disposed of the evidence, *remember!'*

'Well, that's what I wanted ya to think,' smugly spoke Steve, now less heatedly. 'I *lied!* I kept your blood-stained clothing and the murder weapon.'

'Yeah, *right!* You're bluffing!'

'No, I'm not *fuckin'* bluffing, mate - I'll ping you the photo if ya like, then you can see for ya bleedin' self!'

'No, *don't* do that!' Stokes quickly told him, while cursing himself for not disposing of the evidence in person at the time. He was worried the photo might get into the wrong hands. He of course knew Steve was playing him but couldn't take the risk.

I warned you that you should have disposed of the evidence yourself, you numbskull! chirped in his father's aggravating critical voice.

'Well, I'm glad you are now starting to see sense,' said Steve, more relaxed.

After a pause.

'So, you planned this all along then – getting me to do your dirty work?' questioned Stokes.

'Well, I was hoping it wouldn't come to this – but as you know, I'm a gambling man, and I always like to hedge my bets.'

Asshole! thought Stokes. *I should never have trusted him in the first place!* Seething, Stokes said morosely: 'I'll get it done!' and quickly ended the call.

That same evening, Mary busied herself phoning around her girlfriends to tell them how her date with Mark went.

'... Really! What a proper snog?' asked Ruth, sounding almost in awe.

'Yeah, it was as we were about to say goodbye – it was a long one, as well!'

'What, his todger?!'

'Ruth!' exclaimed Mary, jovially feigning shock. 'Honestly, what are you like?!'

Both laughed.

'Well, it's usually the other way round!'

'True!' admitted Mary, laughing.

'We had a brief kiss at High Rocks, too.'

'Oh yeah?!' said Ruth, continuing to rib her friend. 'I've heard about what goes on up there!' Mary

continued to listen, puzzled. 'Did ya know, it's now become a very popular dogging site – in fact, they're thinking of renaming it to *"High Cocks"!*'

Both burst into hysterics.

'Now *stop,* or I'm gonna piss myself!' Mary insisted to her friend, crying with laughter.

Then after the laughter subsided, Mary continued.

'... Yeah, Mark just grabbed me by the arm, pulled me towards him, and we snogged!' she said, full of excitement, adding, 'It all happened spontaneously!'

'*Wow,* I'm definitely jealous now!' responded Ruth, jokingly. Then said earnestly, ' ... Well, I'm pleased you had a lovely time – you deserve it!'

'Thanks,' said Mary happily. '... I know we've only just met, but I really like him – he seems like such a great guy – plus he's really hot!' Both chuckled. '... Come to think of it, I don't even know his last name.'

'Oh, Mary, honestly!' expressed Ruth. 'Sounds like you're smitten.' There was a pause. 'So, will you bring Mark along to Sacha's party? You know that if you do, Simon and Claude will be jealous!' she said, referring to Sacha's male friends, who have both shown a keen interest towards Mary. Both worked in the City of London. Both flashy and arrogant bankers (you read that correctly – though, they were also a pair of wankers!).

Mary chuckled. 'I did think of asking him, but I'm not sure if he'd want to go?' she answered. '… He's rather shy.'

Ruth snorted, 'Well, you could have fooled me! He's clearly not when it comes to being amorous!'

'Well, I meant reserved,' Mary clarified, explaining, 'He doesn't like crowds or loud noises – as soon as we had lunch, he was eager to get away from the hustle and bustle of The Pantiles and go somewhere more peaceful.'

'So, he could get you all alone at *"High Cocks"* and have his wicked way with you,' said Ruth with her typical sardonic wit. 'You've got to watch the quiet ones, ya know!'

'But that's what I like about Mark: he's not like most other men I've met, who only want to talk about themselves all the time – telling me how great they are and the rest of it! Mark told me he enjoys listening to me – which I thought was sweet – and even encourages me to talk about myself. He hardly ever talks about himself ...'

Ruth couldn't help wondering why not but didn't interrupt her friend and express her slight concerns: she didn't want to burst her bubble and spoil her newfound happiness. Indeed, she couldn't remember the last time Mary was this happy.

'Anyway, Ruth, I'd better go and feed the cat,' said Mary. 'The poor thing must be hungry by now.'

'Okay, sweetie. Did you want to meet up for a coffee in the week?'

'Erm, well, I've arranged to meet up with Mark sometime next week – so I'm not sure when I'll have time, what with work and –'

'Oh, *I* see. Now that you've got a *boyfriend,* you don't have time for your girlfriends!' said Ruth, teasing.

'No, that's *not* true – and he's not my boyfriend,' responded Mary, taking the bait.

Mary had a certain sweet innocence about her and could easily be gullible at times.

'It's just that,' continued Mary, 'as Mark and I are still in the early stages of getting to know each other, I want to see him as much as I can –'

'Don't worry, I fully understand – I was only kidding with you. I'll see you at the party next Saturday!' said her friend, chuckling.

'Yeah,' confirmed Mary, hoping she hadn't upset her friend, even though it would appear not.

'And invite Mark to come along with you – I'm sure everyone will want to meet him!' said Ruth, knowing she certainly would.

'Yes, I will. Alright then, bye for now Ruth!'

'Bye, sweetie!'

It was getting late, and after finishing a large glass of Rioja, Mary decided to call it a night. It had been a long day, and after talking to her long list of friends about her date with Mark, she felt exhausted and headed up to bed.

It was a balmy night, and as she closed her eyes and lay naked with only a thin white cotton sheet covering her, she fantasised about Mark penetrating deep inside her. She began pleasuring herself but soon drifted off into a deep sleep. By now, her cat was also asleep, curled up in its usual position at the end of the bed.

An old rusty key entered the lock in the rear kitchen door of Mary's house. The door creaked open, and, dressed in his old military combat uniform and wearing gloves and a balaclava, in walked Corporal John Stokes.

His phone torchlight led the way, through the kitchen, then along the hall corridor to the bottom of the stairs. As he did, he couldn't help noticing the cupboard under the stairs – it immediately brought back bad memories. He quickly shut those stark thoughts out of his head to concentrate on his mission.

The old staircase creaked under his weight, but the intruder continued regardless. Confronted by several doors, he paused at the top of the stairs. Some were closed, and others were left ajar. Before entering Mary's room, which he'd secretly seen her undressing inside enough times to know was hers, he first wanted to check if any visitors were staying over. Starting with the floor above, having snooped about, finding rooms only used for storage and an art studio, he descended the stairs and continued with the rest of the rooms on Mary's level. Pushing one door open revealed a double bed, still with a winter duvet over it. Another bedroom had an empty baby's cot inside, and scanning the torchlight around the walls revealed a fairy-tale-like scene filled with cute animal characters beautifully painted. The door to the next room was open wide enough to see it was the bathroom. So, without stopping, he crept along the landing to the last room, quietly opened the door and stepped inside.

He could hear Mary breathing heavily as she slept, her nakedness now fully on display, having kicked the sheet off herself during her deep slumber and leaving it in a crumpled mess at the foot of the bed.

As John moved closer, he noticed a bottle of sleeping pills and a half-drunken glass of water on her bedside table. He moved slowly around her bed with his torchlight and glaring eyes fixed upon her, then settled at the end of the bed, staring at his prey's beautiful lithe shape as she lay vulnerable on her side. Her long hair splayed partially across her face. He willed her to move onto her back so he could get a good look at her breasts and genitalia. But frustratingly, she remained in position with only her chest moving as she breathed in and out.

The voyeur watched with warped fascination as it did so. Up and down. Up and down. The power was within his grasp to stop that. As he had on many occasions – to end life.

The cat suddenly stirred and meowed to the stranger, immediately snapping John out of his trance. He spotted a pair of dumbbells lying on the floor but bludgeoning her to death would be too messy. Far simpler would be to smother her using the spare pillow, then empty the bottle of sleeping pills down her throat and make it seem like a suicide.

With the pillow tenaciously gripped between both hands, he leaned over the bed towards Mary's sweet face and …

CHAPTER TWENTY-ONE

The morning had long broken. The Sun's powerful rays penetrated the curtains into Mary's bedroom, illuminating the room. And a beam of light shone through a gap in the curtains directly onto her bed where she still lay, dead to the world. The way the sunlight kissed her naked body appeared angelical-like.

Her nose twitched, her eyes partially opened, and simultaneously, she stretched out her arms and legs. Her head ached, and she felt hungover. She had overslept. But it was Sunday, so who cares! She reached over and grabbed her half-filled glass of water and quickly drank it, not bothered it was stale - it was too strenuous for her to get out of bed and go and get a fresh one.

She flopped her head back onto the pillow, which now felt like a slab of rock; then immediately twisted her head towards the door. It was open. She never leaves her bedroom door open. It puzzled her for a moment. Her cat wasn't in her bedroom either. She remembered she'd had quite a bit to drink, though. *I must have just left it open,* she surmised.

Ten minutes later, her head was still throbbing. Dragging herself out of bed, she slipped into her silk dressing gown and furry slippers and slowly descended the stairs, one hand on the bannister rail, heading for the kitchen where she kept the paracetamol. She immediately felt a cold chill in the air.

'*Cleo!*' Mary called out. '*Cleo,* darling, where are you!' But there was no sign of her pet anyway. She was starting to get worried. '*Cleo* – come to mummy!'

The moment she stepped into the kitchen and discovered the door wide open, the alarming realisation of what might have happened suddenly hit her: a burglary!

'Oh, Christ!' she said out loud. She was sure she had locked it.

Mary immediately panicked and phoned the police. She also thought of contacting her mum and dad but changed her mind, not wishing to worry them any more than they already do about her.

Surprisingly, when she searched her house, she found nothing missing: no expensive jewellery, designer gear, electrical devices, or cash, even.

Something must have disturbed them, she thought. *I*

bet it was those hooligans messing about in the park yesterday – they probably saw me entering my property alone … She then suddenly thought, *'Oh my God, what if they came into my bedroom when I was asleep? And what if there's still somebody hiding in the house? It's a big house! It's possible! They could be hidden in one of the many wardrobes … or the attic!* She'd watched a thriller recently where the killer did just that: waiting for the right moment to pounce. *Oh, where the hell are the police!* she mumbled to herself, now even more frightened. *They could be about to pounce on me at any moment!*

Nerves jangling, she went straight over to the kitchen island and grabbed the largest knife from the wooden knife block holder. *What am I doing?!* she asked herself admonishingly. *Calm down, calm down. If anybody had wanted to cause me harm, they would have done it by now!* she reasoned, putting the knife back in its place.

To her relief, Cleo casually breezed in through the open door, meowing.

'Oh, Cleo, *there* you are! Mummy was getting worried about you!' Mary picked her up in her arms and cuddled her – comforting herself as much as the cat.

The doorbell then rang loudly, making Mary jump out of her skin and causing her cat to spring out of her arms onto the kitchen floor, and she quickly went to answer the front door. *That'll be the police,* she thought.

Feeling distraught, she quickly opened the door. Standing there smiling with a bunch of flowers was Mark, AKA John.

'Oh, Mark! I'm so glad you're here!' she told him, sounding relieved before throwing herself into his powerful protective arms.

'Why? What on earth's the matter?!' he asked, showing concern.

'My house was broken into!'

He just looked at her, shocked.

Mary unravelled herself from him and stepped back into her house. '*Please* come inside,' she said, gesturing. 'I woke up this morning to discover the kitchen door was wide open – and I know damn well I locked it.'

She held her hand out for him to hold and quickly led him through the hall to the kitchen where he laid the flowers on the kitchen top. Mary was too preoccupied to pay any attention to them.

'Did they steal much?' he asked, already knowing the answer.

'That's the strange thing – nothing was taken!' she answered, frowning and shrugging her shoulders.

'Really? Oh well, that's good!'

'I think they must have been disturbed and left abruptly,' suggested Mary, still visibly shaken up despite the brave face.

'Yeah, you're probably right,' agreed John, examining the door. 'There doesn't appear to be any signs of a break-in, though!'

'I know – it's all very odd!'

'Are you sure you didn't just forget to close it?' suggested John. 'I remember you saying how tired you were!'

Mary shrugged her shoulders, no longer sure anymore.

'Have you called the police?' he next asked, looking straight at her.

'Yes, that's who I thought was at the door – they should be here any minute.'

John listened without commenting while he checked around for any evidence he may have unwittingly left behind.

You damn fool! John suddenly heard his father's voice say again for the umpteenth time. *Fancy not locking the fuckin' door behind you!*

'Shut up – not now,' mumbled John.

Had he purposely left the door open to frighten her and make her feel she needed his protection – to control her? Well, if he had, it worked.

'What was that?' asked Mary.

'Oh, nothing,' he replied, smiling awkwardly. 'That's a nice painting,' he then commented, quickly diverting Mary's attention as he pointed to it. It was a serene scene of children playing happily in a meadow. 'Did you paint it?'

'Yes, I did,' she answered a bit more cheerily.

'It's wonderful!'

'Oh, thank you,' she replied, pleased. 'Would you like a coffee?'

Just then, the doorbell rang again.

'Oh, that must be the police now!' she announced, further relieved. 'I'll just go and let them in.'

John smiled reassuringly at her before she headed for the door.

A few minutes later, she returned to the kitchen with two uniformed police officers. But Mark was gone.

'… Mrs Simpson … Mrs Simpson!' repeated one of the police officers. Mary was staring vacantly at the spot Mark had stood only a moment before, wondering where he was – and why he had left.

'Yes, sorry. I was miles away. What was the question again?'

'At what time were you first aware that a burglary had taken place …?'

After conducting a brief investigation and making their report, the police merely advised her to update her home security by adding an alarm system.

As soon as the police had gone, Mary tried calling Mark to find out why he'd left so suddenly, but there was no answer. So, she decided to call her parents after all instead, who, upon hearing the news, came over straight away to support her. They consoled their daughter as any good parents would but remained unconvinced that an intruder had been inside the property, believing she most likely forgot to close one of the exterior doors. Her father also reiterated what the police had advised her about updating her home security, offering to help. And her mother told her to sell the damn property and buy a smaller one. 'This property is nothing but bad luck for you!' she claimed.

Mary reassured her parents that she would be perfectly alright on her own, and after finally convincing them, they left late that evening.

She did try ringing Mark once more before retiring. But again, no response.

The following morning while working in the charity shop, Mary was busy serving behind the counter when Mark/John walked in. At first, she didn't notice it was him. He picked up a few items he was only mildly interested in looking at while waiting for the customer to leave.

'Thank you. Bye!' Mary said to the elderly lady. Then casting her gaze over in his direction, she realised who it was and immediately began fluffing up her hair.

'Mark!' she said smiling widely, pleasantly surprised. 'What are you doing here?'

'Hi, good morning!' he replied, smiling back as he strode over to her. 'I wanted to apologise for leaving without saying goodbye yesterday. It's just that I didn't want to get in the way – and at the time, I thought it was probably best I just left discreetly. So, I left via the side gate. Of course, I realise now that was the wrong thing to do.'

'No need to apologise. It's quite alright,' Mary assured him. 'I just wondered why you left so suddenly – that's all. I tried ringing you. Didn't you get my calls?'

'No,' lied John. 'My battery was dead!'

'Oh,' she responded, putting cash in the till and closing it. 'Thank you for the lovely flowers, by the way!'

'You're welcome,' he replied with a brief smile before asking, 'Hey, did the police find any vital evidence at the scene?' quickly moving the conversation on.

'No … Well, not as far as I'm aware,' was her answer. 'I told them about the hooligans in the park that afternoon ...'

'And?'

'They didn't really comment.'

'The police won't do anything about it – they rarely ever do!' remarked John.

'The police recommended I update my home security.'

'Oh, yeah!' was all that came out of his mouth.

You idiot! You should've snuffed her out when you had the chance! said the woman-hater's voice inside his head.

Ignoring his inner demons, John perked up and said, 'Hey, d'ya fancy joining me for that pub lunch we talked about?'

Mary Smiled. 'Yeah, why not – I don't usually go to the pub on my lunch break, but one glass of wine won't hurt! My lunch break is between 1-2 pm.'

'Great! Any pubs you recommend?'

'The Ragged Trousers – just up the road in The Pantiles is good!'

'Shall I meet you there?'

'Yeah, I'll see you there just after one.'

'I'll order you a glass of wine – what would you like?'

'Oh, erm, a glass of Chardonnay, please. That would be lovely! Thank you!'

'Are you sure you wouldn't prefer a … what was it … a *Slippery Nipple?!'*

Just as he was saying the rudely named cocktail, a couple of rather conservative-looking old ladies walked in and walked straight back out again.

Mary and John both burst out laughing. 'You'll get me into trouble, you will!' said Mary trying hard to control herself.

After leaving Mary to her work, John found the pub she suggested, ordered a pint of Guinness and found a quiet spot in the far corner.

As John supped on his pint of the Black Stuff while waiting for Mary, he pictured her lying asleep naked in her bed and how beautiful she looked. But he was angry at himself for breaking into Mary's home – indeed disgusted. And although he wasn't there to rob her of her physical possessions, in a way, he did steal something even more precious of hers – something he could never return: her privacy. And if he'd carried out what he set out to do, he would have taken her most precious possession of all: her life!

He couldn't go through with it. For the first time in his sad and lonely life, he felt love – or something he imagined closely resembled it. Whatever it was, it felt good anyway. He could see himself spending the rest of his life with her! *Fuck Steve!* he thought. *I won't let him or anyone else hurt my Mary – I'll kill the fucking lot of 'em!*

Slightly late, Mary walked into the Ragged Trousers and almost immediately saw John waving to her. Being a Monday afternoon, the pub was quiet – just a few other people sat around tables.

As promised, John had a glass of Chardonnay waiting for her on the table.

'*Wow!* You scrub up well!' he told her as he got up to greet her, noticing her freshly applied make-up.

'Oh, thanks!' she replied, hoping that she hadn't overdone it.

'Cheers!' they both said as they clinked glass.

They ordered some pub grub, and after spending a short but lovely time together, Mary asked him if he would like to come to her friend Sasha's 40th Birthday party on Saturday night with her.

At first, John seemed a little reticent but then acknowledged he would. '… Sure, I'd love to!' he said, smiling.

'Oh, good! It'll be a blast, I promise you!' she said, excited. 'My friends are all dying to meet you!'

'So, will I need to get all dressed up?' John asked, looking slightly concerned.

'No, you don't have to wear a jacket and tie if that's what mean - not unless you want to?'

John jokingly pulled a horrified face and shook his head causing Mary to laugh. 'Oh, that's a relief - I don't do dressing up anymore - I had enough of that in the Marines!'

'Just an open-neck shirt and a pair of smart trousers will suffice!' she said, placing her hand on his muscular thigh.

'I can manage that,' he replied as he looked into her eyes, smiling broadly.

'We're all meeting at the Lush Vine wine bar at the top of the high Street for seven. And then going for a meal at Luigi's restaurant across the road - I hope you like Italian?'

'I *love* Italian!' answered John happily, nodding.

'I'll tell Sasha to arrange another space.'

The pair then leaned towards each other and kissed on the lips.

'John?' a man's voice called out from the bar. John hadn't noticed him enter the pub.

John ignored him.

'Corporal John Stokes – is that you?' the stranger persisted in asking him as he came closer, walking with a slight limp.

John and Mary looked up at him with a blank look, followed by John immediately putting his arm around Mary, purposely to conceal his military tattoo.

'It is you, isn't it!' said the man, convinced. 'I'm Lance Corporal Paul Setterington. Remember me?'

John shook his head, thinking, *Fuck!* He did know him, albeit for a short time. They both served in the same regiment in Afghanistan about ten years ago.

'We served in Helmand together – until I got my bastard leg blown off and became discharged!' the veteran continued without pause.

Mary linked her arm around John, smiling awkwardly towards the stranger.

'You must have me mistaken for someone else, mate,' John told him straight-faced. 'My name is Mark Simpson.'

There was a moment of silence while the veteran stared intently at John's face.

'… I'm sorry mate. I was convinced I knew you,' he said shaking his head in disbelief. 'Well then, you must have a double, cos he looked just like you!'

'No worries!' said John, forcing a smile.

Then after apologising again for disturbing them, the man turned and limped back towards the bar –

the prosthetic leg more noticeable now.

'Poor guy!' said Mary, mildly shaking her head. 'He must be confused.'

'Yeah,' replied John. Then sounding slightly agitated said, 'Shall we get going?'

'But you haven't finished your Ploughman's ...'

'It feels a bit stuffy in here,' explained John, 'and I could do with getting some fresh air.'

Mary looked at her watch. 'Oh crikey, is that the time?! I better be getting back to work now anyway.'

Hand in hand, both then got up and left while the veteran, double whiskey in hand, looked over his shoulder at John, still convinced it was Corporal John Stokes.

John Stokes escorted Mary back to her place of work, where they briefly kissed and said their goodbyes. As John walked away, he felt relieved his cover hadn't been blown - at least not in Mary's eyes.

CHAPTER TWENTY-TWO

John and Mary met a few times during the week leading up to the party. On one occasion, the pair were enjoying a midmorning cup of coffee, sitting outside a café in town, when they heard Ruth's loud voice.

'Hi! Fancy seeing you two here!' said Ruth, rather animated, holding two bags filled with shopping in each hand. 'May I join you?'

Do we have a choice? Mary thought to herself, preferring she didn't but not showing it, greeting her with a friendly smile instead.

'Yes, of course!' straight away said John, smiling also. He got up and pulled a chair out for her to sit. 'I'm John, pleased to meet you!'

'Pleased to meet you too!' said Ruth, holding her hand out to be shaken (or kissed) while admiring his physique. John's big right hand shook Ruth's chubby little hand. 'Mary's been telling me all about you. Mark, isn't it?'

'Yeah – Mark Simpson.'

'I expect you know who I am. Mary's probably told you all about me!' said Ruth unabashedly.

John hesitated (Mary hadn't mentioned her once).

'Been shopping I see, Ruth!' commented Mary, quickly changing the subject while subtly informing Mark of her name.

'Yes, just some new clobber to wear to the party Saturday,' she replied. 'I couldn't decide whether to wear the red or black number, so I bought both – of course, then I also needed to buy two matching pairs of shoes!' She laughed and snorted at the same time.

Both John and Mary glanced at each other with a wry smile.

'So, which colour have you decided to wear?' asked Mary out of curiosity.

'Oh, I don't know, darling – I'll make my mind up on the day!'

A busy young waiter then appeared.

'Could I get two slices of Carrot Cake and a Cappuccino,' said Ruth. 'And don't forget to sprinkle plenty of chocolate on top!' she called out demandingly as he started to leave as quickly as he arrived. Then speaking to Mary and Mark confidentially, 'They can be quite stingy with their chocolate here!'

Mary and John both grinned at each other, finding the whole episode amusing.

'Ah, isn't it a gorgeous day!' commented Ruth. To which the other two just smiled and nodded. 'Mind you – my geraniums could do with a good spot of rain ...!'

John couldn't help but notice her huge boobs – with an appetite to match. *They must be fake,* he said to himself.

Then after a pause for a gulp of air. 'Mary tells me you're a travel journalist Mark' said Ruth, intrigued to discover more about her friend's new love interest.

'Yeah, that's right,' he answered, unsure whether it was a question or not.

'*And* that you used to be in the Royal Marines!'

John nodded and cracked a smile, beginning to feel on edge.

Going nowhere with that question, Ruth then asked, 'I understand that you're not from around here?'

John shook his head, already bored with her tiresome questioning, saying, 'No, I'm from Ramsgate,' and wishing the waiter would hurry up and bring her carrot cake so her mouth would have something else to do other than asking him annoying bloody questions.

'Never been,' she said, adding snootily, 'Never had the desire to either! Give me the warmth of the Costa del Sol any day!'

Oh yeah, it's really classy there, isn't it?! he said

sarcastically to himself.

'So, what brings you to Royal Tunbridge Wells, then?'

'Well, I'm thinking of moving here so I'll be closer to London,' he answered without flinching. Even he was starting to believe his own bullshit.

Mary glared at her friend willing her to shut up, but she continued with her incessant questioning.

'Oh, is that where you work?'

John nodded. 'Yes, mostly. A lot of my work is for Reuters International.'

'Reuters, eh? Impressive!'

'Yeah, I go on a lot of their assignments.'

'Do you!'

'Oh, look!' suddenly said Mary, 'here comes the waiter with your coffee and cake!'

Mary and John saw this as their chance to escape. And quickly finished their coffees in unison.

'Ruth, it was lovely seeing you,' said Mary as she and John got up, 'but we need to get going.'

'Oh, going somewhere nice?' inquired Ruth, being her usual nosy self.

Neither answered – just smiled uncomfortably.

'... What a shame,' continued Ruth, disappointed. 'Just when I was enjoying getting to know Mark.'

'Yes, sorry, Ruth!' said Mary (not really). 'Anyway, you'll get the chance to see Mark again on Saturday.'

'Oh, you've persuaded him to come then?'

Mary smiled and nodded.

'Bye, Ruth,' said John with a forced smile. 'It was nice to meet you.'

'See you Saturday!' Mary said as she linked her arm around John's and the pair promptly left.

'Bye!' said Ruth. Then chuckling, she embarrassingly called out, 'Don't get up to anything I wouldn't do!'

As they were leaving, they could hear Ruth's bombastic voice telling the waiter to take the Cappuccino back to sprinkle more chocolate on it.

Mary didn't mean to be unkind to her friend; it's just that sometimes Ruth could be interfering, which she found irritating at times, even though she knew she only meant well. Men had tried to take advantage of Mary before - especially her wealth.

'Wow!' exclaimed John, raising his eyebrows. 'Doe's Ruth always give the blokes you meet the "third degree"?'

Mary laughed. 'Oh, just ignore it. She can be a nosy so-and-so sometimes, but she's quite harmless really. Though I must admit, it is annoying.'

'Well, I hope your other friends aren't going to bombard me with dull questions at the party!' said John, grinning.

'No, don't worry - they'll be too busy getting drunk and enjoying themselves!' stated Mary, adding, 'And if they do, they'll have me to deal with!'

John's grin morphed into a smile.

'Don't you dare now change your mind about going, or I will be very disappointed!' she told him, half-jokingly.

'I'll be there! Any chance I get to spend more time with you will make me happy!' he expressed as they continued walking.

'Ahh, that's very sweet of you!' she replied, putting her head tenderly against his shoulder.

'I feel very fond of you, Mary!' he said, turning his head towards her.

She looked up at him. 'I feel the same way about you too, Mark!' she said as their eyes met.'

'I've never met a woman as wonderful as you!'

'Oh, stop it - now you're making me blush.'

The two continued being lovey-dovey on their way to the train station, where they stopped to embrace each other and kiss. Earlier, John had told her he needed to attend an afternoon meeting at Reuters International in Canary Wharf, London. A lie, of course.

'Would you like to come to my house for dinner this evening?' Mary asked him before he left to get his train.

'I would love to!' he replied, delighted.

'8 pm, okay?'

'Yes, that will be fine - I'll be back from London by 6 pm!' he said, smiling broadly.

'Salmon, okay with you?'

'Perfect! See you later!' he replied as he started to leave, blowing her a kiss.

'Bye!' she called out to him as he made haste for the station entrance.

Mary felt truly happy. So much so that when she got home, she immediately sent her estranged husband an email telling him that she had met someone else and would willingly give him a divorce and agree to sell their house.

John waited until she'd left the station – he watched her through a window in the waiting room – then promptly left.

Walking back to his flat, John anxiously rehearsed what he'd say to Mary about his trip when he saw her later that evening. But it wasn't long before his mildly troubling thoughts were shoved aside by his father's scolding voice, telling him off for saying he worked for Reuters: *What if that gobby bitch, Ruth, checks up on you? Then what?* His son didn't respond – he just listened obediently as usual. *I say kill her! And after you've run her through, kill Mary, too! Neither of those whores is good news for you, and you know it!*

John ran the rest of the way to his flat, hoping this would help clear his head of such malign thoughts. But his hate-filled father's voice just scoffed and told him: *You can't run from me, Son! You are no different than me!*

'Yes, I *fucking* am!' angrily shouted John as he violently slapped his head several times to try and rid himself of his father's menacing voice, caught up with emotion as passers-by hurriedly crossed the road to avoid him. 'Go away and leave me *be!'*

John continued audibly arguing with himself for a little longer – *Like father, like son!* the annoying and aggravating inner voice kept saying – but he eventually won the argument by staying positive, thinking of his blossoming relationship with Mary. He was so looking forward to seeing her later.

Back inside the flat, his mobile phone rang. It was Steve calling again. Feeling drained, resting on his sofa, John ignored it like he had several times that week. Of course, Steve never left messages: he didn't want to incriminate himself. But John knew it was probably to tell him it was his final warning.

At 8 pm on the dot, John rang Mary's doorbell. She opened the front door to reveal him smiling from ear to ear, holding a bunch of red roses in one hand and a bottle of red wine in the other.

'Hi, Mark!' said Mary, beaming straight back at him.

'Hi, these are for you!' John said as he presented her with the flowers. He was wearing the same clothes as the first time they met: all in black.

'Ahh, my favourite!' she remarked, immediately taking the flowers from him this time and smelling them. 'Thank you, they're gorgeous, but you didn't need to go to the trouble – you bought me some lovely flowers only a few days ago! Ah, you're so kind!' They kissed each other on the cheeks. 'Come on through, Mark. I shall be dishing up very shortly.'

She still had on her plain-looking apron, which completely hid her scintillating sexy little black number. Indeed, her dress was so tiny that when John first saw her, he thought she didn't have anything on underneath – which immediately got his heart racing; and it wasn't until she turned to lead him through the hall and into the kitchen that he noticed the dress. She also wore a beautiful pearl necklace and matching earrings and had her hair and make-up done.

'You look beautiful!' he told her.

She laughed. 'What – with this piny, on?'

John nodded. 'Especially with that piny, on!' Both laughed.

Music played in the kitchen: a 90's R&B Slow Jam, to which Mary seductively moved her hips. 'Oh, I love this one!' she said, twisting her head towards him. John's hips remained in the same position.

'How did your afternoon go?' she then asked him as they entered the kitchen.

John hesitated.

'London. How did your meeting go in London?' she reminded him.

'Oh, yes, *London!* It went well, thanks. Boring as

hell, but meetings usually are.'

Moving the topic of conversation away from his bogus trip, John stiffed the air and said: 'Hmm! Smells good!'

'Hopefully, it tastes as good!' she said – though John wasn't quite sure if she was joking.

'I'm sure it'll be delightful!'

'You haven't tried my cooking!' Both laughed. 'Help yourself to wine – there's a bottle of red already open somewhere.'

'Thanks!'

'Ah, there it is!' she said, quickly fetching the bottle and a highly polished empty glass. As she handed them to Mark/John, her hands tenderly caressed his.

John could see the dining table at the far end of the room had already been laid, including lit candles. *Very romantic!* he thought.

'Cheers!' said John.

Mary picked up her almost empty glass, saying cheers as the pair moved closer to clink glasses.

'Very smooth!' commented John, having tasted the wine.

'Yes, I like it.'

'Here, let me top that up for you,' he said, which he did.

'Would you like to take a seat, John? I'll serve the starters,' she told him, moving over to the fridge to fetch them.

'Sure,' he replied, taking his glass and the bottle of wine with him.

'ALEXA!' Mary suddenly called out. 'PLAY A MOTOWN COMPILATION!'

'Playing a Motown compilation,' answered the automated voice.

Before opening the fridge, Mary removed her apron, tossing it to one side. Then after using the open fridge door as cover to quickly preen herself, she took out the already plated starters, which were two different varieties of melon wrapped in Parma ham.

Wide-eyed and smiling, John watched her approach him, carrying a plate in each hand, her little black number now fully on display.

'Here we are!' she said as she leaned forward to put his plate down in front of him as a Marvin Gaye song played in the background. 'I hope you like melons!' she continued saying to which John grinned widely, replying thank you.

He could smell her sweet perfume. He wasn't up on the names of perfumes. But whatever it was, it smelt expensive. It wasn't some cheap copy like other women he previously dated wore. It was a classy smell, like the lady herself.

He also noticed she wasn't wearing a bra – you could tell by how the dress fabric moved so freely and easily. Maybe she wasn't wearing any knickers either, he pondered for a second, excited at the thought. His appetite for food was quickly replaced by an appetite for sex. He imagined ripping off her dress and sucking her tits before bending her over the table and fucking her hard from behind. All the signs that she wanted it were there. But for now, he must show some decorum, he told himself, and be content sucking on the melons on his plate instead.

'Bon appetite!' she said as she sat opposite him, causing a ripple effect upon her loose-fitting dress as her breasts bounced freely underneath.

She noticed him staring momentarily at her chest but didn't appear to mind. She, too, wanted desperately to cement their relationship with a good fuck. The sexual tension between them was palpable but neither one wanted to make the first move.

Once the first course was done, Mary quickly cleared the plates and then served the mains, which had been kept hot in the oven. Her cat looked up at her licking its lips. 'This is not for you, Cleo,' she told her.

'This is delicious!' John said as he tasted his first mouthful of salmon.

'Oh, I'm glad that you like it,' she replied, pleased to hear it. Both clinked wine glasses again. 'One can't go wrong with salmon!'

The evening was going swimmingly well, and the chat flowed as smoothly as the wine.

The weather, by now, had taken a turn for the

worse: the sky quickly darkened, rain lashed down, and they could hear thunder in the distance – the result of all the humidity from the recent summer heatwave.

'My garden could do with a spot of rain,' commented Mary as she started to clear the mains plates.

'Here, let me help you with those!' He got out of his chair and followed her to the sink with his empty dirty plate and cutlery.

He watched with pleasure as her arse wriggled about to the music while she rinsed her plate. Then, standing directly behind her, trapping her there, he handed her his.

'I really enjoyed that,' he said (now whether he was referring to her arse wriggling or her cooking, one cannot be sure. Probably the former!).

'Thanks!' she said as she looked over her shoulder at him, smiling sweetly.

'So, what delights have you in store for dessert?' he asked, catching another pleasant whiff of her seductive perfume.

She immediately swivelled around, planting her perfectly rounded backside against the cold porcelain sink, and looking directly up at him, boldly stated: 'I'm your desert!' Then pulled him towards her and planted her luscious lips squarely on his. Well, somebody had to make the first move she figured. And John certainly wasn't complaining.

Both began kissing each other passionately. John then moved his lips across her left cheek, down to the part of the neck just below her ear, taking a trail of her rouge lipstick along the way, and continued kissing her. Mary tilted her head back as he did. She could feel her nipples harden at the mere thought of what was to come. It was the moment they had both longed for and anticipated.

Almost frenetically, John then released the ultra-thin dress straps off her dainty shoulders and, in one motion, pulled her dress straight down, revealing her ripe melons, which he then began to lick and suck (much better than cheesecake). Both his hands cupped around their naked form for support as the tip of his tongue got to work. Then, grabbing her ass cheeks - one in each hand - he lifted her onto the edge of the sink. She splayed her arms out on either side for support, sending the plates she had just cleaned crashing to the floor. The cat hissed loudly as one nearly hit her. Then leaning back against the taps, Mary opened her legs wider apart (not the most comfortable of positions to have sex, but she was in the zone and didn't care. She just wanted to feel his big cock inside her!). *'Fuck me!'* she called out.

Both his hands now free, his left hand fondled her right tit, tweaking her hard nipple with his first and second fingers as he did, while his right hand pulled her wet panties over to one side exposing her glistening snatch. His right-hand fingertips began rubbing her slit up and down. Should he fingerfuck her or lick her out? He opted for the latter. And, bending down, put his tongue once again to work. There was no danger of him getting a renegade pube in his mouth, as Mary didn't have any. Mary soon began wriggling and writhing about in ecstasy. 'Fuck me!' she told him again. She then went to put her right hand on his crutch, but John quickly stopped her, grabbing her wrist firmly with his left hand and moving it away. For a split second, she wondered why he'd done that but was too busy enjoying herself to give it any more thought. The more he resisted, the more it turned her on.

When his jaw began to ache, he then inserted his first two fingers inside her instead, moving them rapidly in and out to the sound of another Motown classic and her screams of pleasure.

Suddenly the screams of pleasure turned into screams of agony: with all that movement, she had accidentally switched on the cold tap and freezing-cold water gushed down her back, soaking her. She jerked forwards, head butting John, who then spontaneously moved backwards, tripping over the screeching cat, and landed on the marble floor with a thud.

Both John and Mary burst into uncontrollable

laughter. And that was the end of their first sexual encounter.

After the laughter subsided, and Mary had quickly changed into something much less sexy, she offered to make him a coffee.

His mood seemed to have quickly changed. 'No, thanks. I think I'll make a move,' he told her with hardly a smile.

She looked surprised and disappointed. 'But don't you want to stay the night and finish what we started?' she asked, giving him a dirty grin.

He shook his head. 'No, sorry, Mary. It's been a long day and I'm gonna get going. Thanks for the lovely meal.' He leaned over and kissed her briefly on the cheek.

'But it's no trouble. We don't have to have ... sex if you don't want to – but please stay the night, won't you?' she said, almost pleading with him to stay.

'I can see myself out. Goodnight, Mary.' He then turned and headed for the front door.

'But it's pouring with rain outside – you'll get soaked!' she called out to him to no avail.

She heard the door shut and immediately burst into a flood of tears.

CHAPTER TWENTY-THREE

This time, John didn't need his late father's critical voice telling him what a fool he'd been; this time, he criticised himself for believing he could fully please Mary sexually – or any other woman. Having c-PTSD was the main cause of his impotence and inability to get or maintain an erection for penetrative sex. It made him feel like he was only half a man. And for an alpha male like Stokes, it was very embarrassing and depressing, which often resulted in all that frustration turning into extreme anger – especially when he heard his father's voice mocking him inside his head.

Soaked to the bone, Stokes entered his flat, exhausted. The blood on his hands and clothing had been washed away by the torrential rain.

An hour or so earlier, right after Stokes left Mary's house, Mary felt upset and needed to speak to someone. She phoned her friend, Ruth, using the landline phone in the hall because her mobile was still charging. While dialling, Mary noticed her address book was skew-whiff on the table. *Strange,* she mused as she straightened it with her free hand. *I expect that the cat did it.*

As Ruth picked up her mobile phone, she could hear Mary sobbing.

'Mary, whatever's the matter?' she asked, concerned.

'It was a disaster!' exclaimed Mary tearfully.

'What was a disaster?'

'Me and Mark having sex!' said Mary. 'I'm such a clumsy idiot!'

'*Why?* What happened?'

'Well, I invited him round for a romantic dinner. Everything was going well. Then after the main course, we kissed, and one thing led to another …'

'… Yeah? And?'

'I accidentally head-butted him during foreplay!'

Ruth began to laugh.

'It's not funny, Ruth,' Mary told her. 'Talk about embarrassing! I'm sure that's what caused him to leave early. Even though, at the time, we both saw the funny side of it. Or at least, so I *thought.* Because, shortly after, his mood completely changed, and it seemed like he couldn't wait to get out the door!'

'*Oh my god!* How on earth did you manage to head-butt him?' asked Ruth, trying not to laugh again.

Mary didn't answer her question, she just started sobbing again and said, 'I've gone and ruined it, I know I have!'

'Listen, sweetie. Don't let yourself get upset over something as trivial as that!' said Ruth, trying to make her see reason. 'Especially over a man!'

'I know it's silly. It's just that I wanted everything to be perfect!' explained Mary, wiping her tears away.

There was a pause; then Ruth spoke in a more serious tone.

'Mary, I know it's not what you want to hear,' said Ruth, trying to be as diplomatic as possible – knowing how sensitive her friend could be, 'but I don't think this new bloke's right for you –'

'Sorry?!' immediately responded Mary, now annoyed. Then without waiting for Ruth to repeat it, she said, 'There you go again, criticising my judgement in men. You can't help yourself, can you?! I knew it was a mistake calling you! You're just jealous!'

'I knew you would react like this!' then argued Ruth.

'So why did you say it then?'

'Listen, Mary, I know you're upset, but there's something I need to tell you.'

There was an awkward pause. Both then tried to speak at the same time '… Go on!' said Mary, wondering what crap her friend was going to say next.

'I was about to send you an email explaining what I've discovered about him when you rang,' said Ruth sounding concerned.

'About *what?'*

'... I don't think Mark Simpson is who he says he is –'

'Oh, don't be so ridiculous!' quickly interjected Mary again.

'Well, for one thing, he doesn't work for Reuters!' There was a moment of silence as Ruth expected Mary to interrupt her again. 'I phoned the headquarters, and they told me they've never heard of him, confirming my suspicions!' Mary continued to listen without interruption. 'So, knowing he'd lied about that, I then began digging around his military records –'

Suddenly the doorbell rang.

'Oh, sorry, Mary,' said Ruth, 'that'll be my husband coming back from the boozer – the knobhead's probably forgotten his keys again!'

The doorbell rang again.

'I better go!' continued Ruth, speaking quicker. 'He didn't take a coat with him, and I expect the poor thing's soaked! I'll ping the email over to you later. Take my advice and keep away from him! See you Saturday, *Bye!'*

The call ended before Mary had a chance to finish

saying goodbye.

Mary couldn't believe what she had just heard and was furious at her friend for interfering. *There must be a simple explanation,* she told herself, not wanting to believe it. *Maybe the person Ruth spoke to simply made a mistake and got it wrong. Or perhaps Mark said Reuters to try and impress me? That'll most likely be it!* she then reasoned, starting to feel slightly cheerier. Nonetheless, her friend had sowed the seeds of doubt into her head. *But if that is true, he still lied to me, though.* She wondered what else Ruth had discovered about her mysterious new man. Mary had to admit that she knew very little about him.

As Mary made her way back to the kitchen, she caught a glimpse of herself in the hall mirror. She looked terrible: she had smudged eye makeup where she had wiped away her tears, and her neatly styled hair now looked a mess.

While waiting for her friend's email, she made herself a coffee and finished clearing up the kitchen. *That's strange,* suddenly thought Mary: one of her kitchen knives was missing from the knife holder block. She searched around for it but couldn't find it anyway. And, another cup of coffee later, she still hadn't received an email from Ruth, so decided to call it a night – double-checking she had locked the kitchen door this time.

The following morning, Mary rang Mark several

times, but as per the night before, he didn't answer. She had some important questions for him she needed answering.

Mary still hadn't received the email from Ruth. And every time she rang her, it went straight to voice mail. She expected Ruth was probably busy and just hadn't gotten around to sending it yet, or she was still trying to find out more background information about Mark. Or perhaps she just forgot? It wouldn't be unlike her, Mary thought.

Today was Friday – the day before the party – and Mary had arranged to pick up her party dress from a local high-end boutique at 11 am.

It was while she was in the boutique that her phone rang. It was Mark.

'Hi, Mary, it's Mark! How are you?' He spoke as if nothing was the matter.

Mary hesitated to speak at first, unsure quite how to respond. 'Okay,' she said, clearly not.

'Where are you now?' he asked, already knowing exactly where she was. He had followed her and was now leaning against the corner of an adjoining street, gazing right at her.

'Erm' she said hesitating again. 'I'm out shopping on the High Street – I've just picked up my new dress to wear to the party tomorrow. You are still coming tomorrow aren't you?'

'Yes, of course,' he replied. 'Why wouldn't I?'

'Oh, no reason. I just wanted to double-check,

that's all,' she answered, feeling pleased.

Maybe she *had* overreacted about his unusual behaviour the previous evening? And those nagging questions she wanted answers to seemed a lot less urgent now that she was finally speaking to him.

She did ask him why he hadn't answered her calls, though. He could sense that she was a bit miffed, and after the briefest of pauses, explained: 'Yeah, I'm sorry, babe' – *'Babe!'* she thought, breaking into a smile. *He's never called me that before.* Then she thought, *That's funny, that's what Steve used to call me* – 'but I had some business calls I had to attend to earlier.'

'I thought that was probably the reason,' she told him, now feeling slightly silly and annoyed with herself for over-worrying as she had.

'Reuters have offered me an overseas assignment,' he continued to say. 'I told them I would need a little time to think it over.' He was watching her reaction while trying to remain out of sight.

Mary's face dropped, and she looked sad. 'Where?' she asked.

'Brazil!' he answered off the top of his head. Then, as if anticipating her next question, he told her, 'Probably for a couple of months.'

'A couple of months!' was her initial surprised response.

'Yeah, I know, it's a bummer.'

'Well, I don't know what to say,' she mumbled. 'Obviously, I will miss you - especially as we've only just started getting to know each other. But of course, I understand.'

John remained silent.

'Would you like to meet up today sometime?' she then asked him, hoping he would say yes.

'Unfortunately, I can't meet up today, Mary - there's something I've got to deal with. I'll see you tomorrow, though. 7 pm at the Lush Vine, right?'

'Yeah, that's right,' she confirmed, sounding somewhat down.

'See you tomorrow then!'

'Yeah, see you tomo—'

'Hey, has your friend Ruth been sticking her big nose in about me again?' he suddenly asked light-heartedly.

Mary chuckled. 'No - well ...' Mary hesitated.

'Go on, you can tell me.'

'The interfering cow has been checking up on you and told me that you didn't work for Reuters!'

John laughed. 'She's lying!' There was a pause. 'You don't believe her do ya?' He was angry but didn't show it.

'No! *Of course not!* I told her that I didn't believe it and that she was a jealous liar!' answered Mary, thinking, why did she have to go and say that to him?

'Good for you!' he said, careful not to give away his true feelings.

There was a pregnant pause.

'... I mean, you can always ring Reuters to find out if I work for them or not if ya like!' he said confidently, knowing by saying that she probably wouldn't.

'No, no, don't worry! I trust you – I wouldn't do that!'

'Good! Because, if there is no trust in a relationship, it is better to end it!' he told her in a more serious tone.

'Yeah, yeah. I agree,' said Mary, feeling a little taken aback by what he'd just said, uncertain how to take it.

'Did she say anything else?' he then asked her.

'No, that was it!'

'All right, bye, gorgeous!' he said chirpily.

'Yeah, bye!' she replied, just managing to squeeze in, 'I can't wait to see you tomorrow!'

Having spoken to Mark, Mary felt a lot more reassured about their relationship and no longer wanted to hear about what her so-called friend, Ruth, had discovered about him, believing more and more that she *was* jealous of her and telling lies.

Before speaking to Mark, Mary had thought of telephoning Reuters to find out if what Ruth was saying was true, but she was now glad she hadn't because it meant going behind his back as if she didn't trust him. And for now, at least, she was prepared to throw caution to the wind and go on living her fairy-tale dream.

Mary left the store smiling and headed home. John watched her exit, though he didn't continue following her as he had some shopping of his own to do.

John entered his flat and plonked his shopping bag down on the table, making a clank and causing the hacksaw he'd just bought from the DIY store to pierce through the bag's flimsy plastic. The spade, he'd left in the boot of the car.

He could hear Ruth's pathetic muffled screams for help from within the dingy bathroom walls. At first, he wanted to rescue her, untie her sore and bloody wrists and ankles and remove the tightly bound Gaffer tape from her mouth, but his father wouldn't let him. And instead of John Stokes entering the bathroom, it was Captain William Stokes, the cruel torturer, rapist, and murderer!

William grabbed the bag of tools and burst into the bathroom angrily shouting, 'SHUT UP! No one can hear you, you *stupid* bitch!' It was true, the people in the flat below were away on holiday. She continued to scream. 'I SAID SHUT THE FUCK UP!' he repeated, slapping her hard across the face as she lay stretched out naked in the bathtub shaking with fear. Her badly cut, scolded, and bruised body, displayed evidence of brutal torture. She began to sob.

The stench from messing herself, unable to clear it up, was awful.

'You've been talking to Mary about us – poisoning her mind – haven't choo?!' William asked her sternly. 'HAVEN'T CHOO?!'

Ruth shook her head. 'No, I haven't!' she cried, hindered by the Gaffer Tape. *'I swear!'*

'Yes, you have, you – nosy – fat – stinky – lying – bitch!' He slapped her again. 'She told us you contacted Reuters and told her Mark was lying about working for them! Now tell us what else you've told her about us!'

'Do as he says, Ruth,' then warned John's contrasting calm and caring voice as he cleared away her excrement with a bunch of toilet paper. 'It will be a lot easier for you if you do.'

'But I've told you everything!' she mumbled, barely coherent.

'Told my *father!'* he corrected her in saying. 'This was his idea, not mine – I would have sooner finished you off at your house rather than wasting all this time and energy bringing you here, but he *insisted* on interrogating you.'

Sitting beside her on the edge of the bath, John gently wiped away her tears with his thumbs. 'There, there now, don't cry!' His softly spoken words didn't console her, however, as she only saw one person in the room with her: a madman (Dr Jekyll and Mr Hyde crossed her mind). John then cupped his hands around her chubby, crunched-up face, leaned over to her right ear, and whispered: 'Tell my father what he wants to know, and I promise I will show you mercy!' He then looked her straight in the eye, smiled, and gave her a knowing wink as if it was their little secret.

There was a brief pause while he removed the blood-matted stray hair away from her face and kissed her tenderly on the forehead.

'Now stop crying and promise me you won't scream, and I'll remove the Gaffer tape from around your mouth,' he told her nicely as he then began stroking her head.

After a moment, she stopped crying and nodded.

'Okay then. I'll remove it. But if you dare scream, my father might –' He paused to correct himself, *'probably!'* he said, nodding, as he picked up the shower hose beside her, 'give you a scolding hot shower again!' Her eyes widened at the terrifying thought. *'Or!'* he continued to say as he next picked up a large, bloodied knife from the floor (the one he stole from Mary's house), 'cut choo to ribbons!'

Ruth lay frozen still with fear as John slowly began to remove the tape. 'I'll try my best not to hurt you,' he said, lending her a tenuous reassuring smile. '… *There!*' he said as he finally removed the tape, 'that wasn't so bad, was it?'

'I don't want to die! Please let me go!' she pleaded. 'I won't tell anyone, I promise!' She started crying again.

'Shh – shh – shh, stop crying and tell me everything you told Mary.'

'You're sick – you need help!'

'SHUT YOUR FUCKING HOLE!' William now screamed back at her.

John tutted and shook his head. 'Aww, why did you have to go and say that? Now you've upset him again!' He then told her to say sorry.

'Sorry,' she mumbled, snivelling.

'Speak up – my father can't hear you!'

'Sorry!'

'That's better!'

'I swear I didn't tell Mary anything more than what you already know! So, *please!* Let me go!'

'It's not up to me,' John told her, pulling a weird, contorted, sad face. He then said, chillingly, 'And besides, I've just been out and bought brand-new tools and a shovel,' adding, 'They're not cheap, ya know!'

Ruth wasn't sure if she was now listening to John or his father.

John suddenly looked over his right shoulder as if being interrupted by his imaginary father standing behind him and started shaking his head. His head then snapped back towards her, looking as mean and angry as hell, screaming, 'YOU FUCKING LYING WHORE!' She knew instantly who she was dealing with then. William picked up the knife and slashed her across the chest, severing her left boob almost off.

Ruth screamed with pain as blood and silicone oozed out of her.

'NO!' shouted John as he firmly grabbed what he believed to be his father's right wrist with his left hand and banged it with force against the edge of the bath until he let go of the knife. Then, reaching inside the flimsy plastic bag of tools by his feet, John quickly pulled out a hammer and chisel and, while Ruth continued to scream, leant over her and placed the point of the chisel onto the centre of her head; then, without a second thought, raised the hammer and, with one almighty blow, delivered the coup de grâce, forcing it deep into her skull. For a moment, in a surreal sort of way, it was quite beautiful the way the blood gushed and sprayed out of the top of her head like an erupting volcano!

You fool! shouted his father's voice inside his head. *I was just about to get the truth out of her!*

John hurried out of the bathroom, slamming the door shut behind him. And leaning firmly against it (as if to trap his father inside and keep him away from him), he closed his tired eyes and took a deep breath. He then went and made himself a cup of tea.

Once he'd had a break, John spent the rest of the day dismembering Ruth's body and clearing up the mess he'd created for himself in the bathroom. His previous female victims had all been unpremeditated attacks – mainly through sexual frustration - whereas this one, he had planned - albeit a spur-of-the-moment decision - which, like the other killings, he believed his evil father was responsible for. There was no sexual attraction towards his latest victim, though – he just needed to get it done, and quick, so that she didn't blab her mouth off and blow his cover.

He'd seen the sight of blood on many occasions before, which didn't bother him too much, but the sound bone makes when sawn into was the worst part for him to stomach – this and the horrendous smell made him physically sick more than once.

He put Ruth's body parts into two heavy-duty refuse sacks so it would be less noticeable when he loaded them into the boot of his car later that evening for disposal.

CHAPTER TWENTY-FOUR

It was Saturday, the day of the party, and by 7 pm, the Lush Vine was already bustling with guests celebrating Sasha's 40th Birthday.

The party invitation card read: Dress Code – Glamourous. And judging by the way most guests dressed, they had adhered to that.

Mary arrived a little after seven, dressed in a beautiful, full-length, sparkly, black, sleeveless gown, her hair tied up in a bun, bright red lipstick, and wearing diamonds and pearls, looking like the glamourous archetypal Hollywood star.

As she made her way through the crowd to greet the Birthday Girl, carrying her clutch bag in one hand and Sasha's gift bag in the other, her eyes wandered about the room, looking for Mark.

'Hi, Mary!' called out Sasha as soon as their eyes met.

'Happy Birthday, Sasha!' said Mary with a big smile.

Both moved their cheeks towards each other for kisses, 'Mwah! Mwah!'

'You look beautiful!' remarked Mary, admiring Sasha's designer gold lamé knee-length dress.

'So do you!' replied Sasha – though it was always hard to tell with her whether she was being sincere. God forbid any woman that dared to upstage her – especially on her birthday! However, if the organisers were handing out an Oscar for best costume design, Mary would have won it.

'This is for you,' said Mary, giving Sasha her present, glad to rid herself of it so she could replace it with a glass of complimentary Prosecco instead, which she immediately grabbed from the passing waiter's drinks tray.

'Thank you, Mary!' said Sasha handing her gift immediately to her husband, who was nearby, to put with the rest of her mountain of pressies.

Looking over Sasha's right shoulder, she spotted her friends Angelica and Debbie sitting together at the far end of the room, but no sign of Mark, or Ruth for that matter, anywhere. *Oh, I hope he turns up!* she thought.

'Cheers!' said Mary and Sasha as they clinked glasses.

'I met your new boyfriend earlier,' said Sasha, which immediately got Mary's full attention. 'He seems like a great guy!'

Mary smiled, relieved he was there after all.

'Yeah, he is!' she answered with a smile.

'Well, it's great to see you, Mary,' said Sasha somewhat abruptly, spotting some more friends bearing gifts at the entrance.

'Yeah, you too!'

'See you in a bit!'

Both quickly hugged, then went off in opposite directions. Mary then spotted Mark chatting with her girlfriends, smiling, and looking like he was having a good time – a bit too much for her liking. Having struggled to find a good catch, she didn't want this one to slip through the proverbial net. *He must have been in the toilet,* she thought to herself.

'Hiya!' said Mary as she approached them smiling, which they all reciprocated, immediately pausing their conversation.

'Well, you're all looking nice 'n' cosy together!' remarked Mary over the din from all the other partygoers.

Mark/John stood and kissed her on both cheeks. 'Hi, babe! You look gorgeous!' he said in her ear.

'You look very nice yourself!' she replied, squeezing his biceps reassuringly. He was wearing a new cream linen suit and a black silk open-neck shirt. The jacket conveniently concealed his badly bruised right forearm.

'Did you manage to get everything sorted out you needed to yesterday?' Mary asked him.

He nodded and flashed her a smile. 'Yes, thanks.'

'Oh, good!' she said while swaying her hips slightly to the upbeat music.

If she knew what that had entailed, she most certainly wouldn't have said that. She hooked her arm around his and the pair clinked glasses as others stared at them, some disapprovingly – namely the two love hopefuls, Simon and Claude, who were stood at the bar together, dressed in their expensive designer suits, drinking Champagne and not the cheap equivalent on offer.

'Did you walk through the park?' suddenly said Mary with a chuckle, noticing Mark's muddy shoes. It was the only pair of shoes he had, and although he'd scrubbed and cleaned everything else after disposing of Ruth's body in nearby woodland, he'd forgotten about his damn shoes.

'Sorry?' said John, unclear what she meant.

She indicated towards his shoes. 'Your shoes – they're muddy.'

Inwardly, John felt annoyed with himself and could hear his father's voice telling him what a disgrace he was to the Marines. He chuckled back, quickly dismissing the unwanted intrusion in his head. 'Oh, yeah. I walked through the park – I was hoping I might see you on the way here.'

After standing and chatting for a little while, both sat down to join the others.

'I was just saying to Debbie,' said Angelica, 'I wonder where Ruth has got to – it's unlike her to be this late?'

Mary nodded, saying, 'I was wondering that myself,' which, in truth, wasn't the case until Angelica mentioned it - she had been too busy staring into her new man's dark and mysterious eyes.

John just listened without comment.

'I expect she'll turn up soon,' said Debbie. 'You know what she's like - she'll probably make a grand entrance any moment!'

All three ladies laughed. John just managed to crack a smile. He knew otherwise.

'Another drink, ladies?' offered John, getting up.

'That was a silly question,' answered Angelica, laughing. 'A medium white wine, please,'

'Same for me, please, Mark,' said Debbie, twinkling her eyes at him.

'I'll have a glass of Merlot please, darling,' said Mary, suddenly realising that she'd called him 'darling' for the first time. *Crikey, our relationship must be getting serious!* she thought.

John squeezed his way through the crowd to the bar.

'Hi, how ya doin'?' he said to the two single guys, Simon and Claude to be polite. But they completely ignored him and carried on talking.

Fuckin' toffs! John thought to himself. He recognised the pair of them from earlier, getting out of a new Lamborghini, parked illegally out front.

He also noticed them giving him the daggers while he was sitting holding hands with Mary.

John ordered the drinks, and while waiting to be served, he felt one of the assholes brushing their hand harshly against his left shoulder.

'You've got dandruff on your jacket, my man,' he said with an insidious smile as he continued trying to cause John discomfort.

John immediately made his presence felt: he reached up with his right hand, grabbed the guy's fingers and squeezed them tightly as he removed his hand, saying, 'Don't worry about it!' with a false smile to match.

Noses in the air, Simon and Claude promptly moved away from the bar to join Sasha, who was still greeting late arrivals. But still no sign of Ruth, Mary and her friends noticed.

'Do you think something might have happened to Ruth?' commented Debbie, looking concerned.

'Like what?' asked Mary.

'I don't know - something bad - an accident maybe?' answered Debbie.

'I'll give her a call,' said Angelica, removing her phone from her handbag.

Maybe I upset her the other night? Mary suddenly thought to herself, feeling a pang of guilt. *And now she's ghosting me – but if that were true, why would she ignore all her other friends too?* It didn't make sense.

'... No answer!' said Angelica, shrugging her

shoulders.

'Maybe she's got stuck in traffic – you know what the traffic's like around here,' said Debbie, shooting in the dark. They all nodded in agreement to that. The traffic in Tunbridge Wells is dreadful.

'Well, hopefully, she'll make it to the restaurant,' said Mary optimistically.

John came back with the tray of drinks, and after more clinking of glassware, John and Mary got around to talking on a more intimate level.

'Have you made up your mind yet as to whether you will take on the assignment to Brazil?' she asked him directly.

'Yes,' said John straight-faced. He kept her in suspense for a little while.

'... Well?' responded Mary, looking concerned.

John then grinned. 'I've decided not to take the job.' To which Mary's face lit up, full of delight. Then looking most sincere, he said: 'I would rather forgo the lucrative contract so I can spend more time with you!'

'Oh, Mark, that is so sweet!' Using his chunky thigh to prop herself up, she squeezed it firmly, then leaned over and kissed him lovingly on the cheek. Both looked into each other's eyes and smiled, resisting the desire to rip each other's clothes off right there and then. They settled for a cheeky snog instead.

Dianne and Angelica simultaneously looked at

each other with raised eyebrows and smiled.

'Oh, I'm so pleased to hear that!' expressed Mary full of joy.

John then put his arm around her. 'Here's to us!' he said, raising his glass.

Mary repeated what he said, and both clinked glasses.

'I may even look for a new job,' he uttered.

'Really? What would you do?' she asked him, interested to know.

'I dunno,' promptly came his answer with a titter and a shrug. 'I'm tired of travelling – so anything that doesn't involve that. Ideally, I'd like to settle down and start a family.'

Mary's face lit up again. Having a child was something she wanted more than anything in the world. Her biological clock was ticking away, but there was still time!

'The problem is – I'm running out of money fast and it's becoming too expensive to stay at my hotel!' he confessed to her quietly.

Mary looked at him and smiled reassuringly. 'Don't worry! You can come and stay at my house,' she said, adding, 'It's not as if there isn't much space!'

John smiled widely. 'Really?! Are you sure you don't mind?'

'Course not!'

'Well, that's very kind of you!'

Just then, the noise levels in the room increased as people started to leave and head over to the restaurant. Sasha had announced it was time to go, but John and Mary had been so wrapped up in each other that they hadn't heard it.

'Come on!' said Mary, dragging Mark up. 'The others are going!'

It could all work out fine, thought John. *Now that that nosy so and so Ruth is out of the way and can no longer interfere. Mind – I will still have to deal with Mary's husband,* he suddenly remembered while he half-listened to what Mary was talking about as the pair held hands on their way out.

If they were to be an item, though, he knew it meant telling her about his impotence, which ran the risk of her not wanting to be in an intimate relationship with him. It had been the case with other women when they found out – some even mocked him. However, they didn't survive to tell the tale! But unlike the others, he had strong feelings for Mary and was prepared to take the risk and tell her. Exactly when, though, he wasn't sure.

'… Mark – Mark!'

'Yeah?' he said as they crossed the street towards the restaurant.

'I was asking if you've ever been to Italy before?'

'Sorry. Yes, I have!'

'Ah, it's so good not to have to wear those horrid face masks anymore,' Mary then commented as they entered the premises,' John just smiled …

John and Mary sat beside each other towards the far end of a very long table, which stretched to almost the entire length of the restaurant. And for the most part, John found himself enjoying the occasion, apart from when he would hear the odd snide remarks from Claude and Simon, who, fortunately for John and Mary, were sat at the other end. Said on purpose to rile him, of which he was very aware. Mostly derogatory, childish remarks along the lines of 'all brawn and no brain' – which John could take. But it was later on, during the desert when their alcohol-infused rants became increasingly louder and more and more spiteful, that started to get Stokes back really up – especially when they began deriding Mary. He quickly began to see red and knew that if he stayed there listening to their foul mouths any longer … well, who knows what he might do! Sticking the asshole's heads down the toilet and drowning them soon came to mind. But instead, he wisely chose to make an excuse and leave. Sometimes it's best to remove oneself from the situation. Think of the bigger picture! He'd thought about asking Mary if she wanted to abandon the party, but he could see she was having a good time and didn't think that would be fair.

Removing his phone from his pocket, he pretended to check his text messages. He then leaned over and spoke into Mary's ear.

'I'm sorry, babe, but I've got to go!' he said with urgency, explaining, 'My dear old auntie's had an accident!'

Precariously suspending the spoonful of gelato en route to her mouth, with a look of dismay, Mary turned her head towards him, saying, 'Of course! Of course! What happened?!'

'She had a fall and has broken her hip!' he answered. Then quickly kissed her on the cheek, discreetly saying, 'Bye!' followed, as an afterthought, by, 'I'll call you,' and left.

Another reason John wanted out of there was he was getting cold feet about telling Mary of his erectile dysfunction problem and didn't want to let her down (pun intended!).

John hurriedly left the restaurant and crossed the road, delivering a *Mai Geri* (front kick) to one of the Lamborghini's wing mirrors, knocking it off its mounting as he passed it. A part of him was hoping that the two flash bastards would follow him and try and beat him up - he could tell they hated him. Then he could inflict excruciating pain upon them. But he knew that wouldn't happen. Cowards like that are all mouth - no balls.

Even though John had lied about his aunt's injury, he decided to visit her anyway. It had been a few weeks since he last saw her. And apart from getting away from the foul stench of bleach in his flat, not to mention the rats – which he hadn't lied about – there was another good reason why John wanted to visit Ramsgate. John wasn't lying about running out of money, either. As a fugitive, he couldn't work – in fear of being discovered, of course – and the little money he had left, he'd either borrowed or stolen from his auntie.

John quickly packed his bag, tossed it onto the back seat of his Ford Fiesta, and was off. 'The landlord can keep his damn deposit!' he muttered as his car screeched away.

When the restaurant closed, Mary chose not to continue partying: she, too, by then, had had enough of people's furtive glances and hushed conversations about her and the new mystery man in her life circulating the room and, instead, got a taxi home. If Mark or her best friend Ruth had been there, maybe she would have continued partying long into the night, but she was no longer in the mood.

Earlier in the restaurant, she had tried to ring Ruth again, but as before, she didn't answer. And when Ruth didn't show up for the meal, as with her other friends, she just assumed Ruth had decided not to come after all – and gave up trying to contact her, thinking, no news is good news.

It wouldn't be until the next day that she would find out why her best friend couldn't come to the party!

CHAPTER TWENTY-FIVE

Mary first heard about Ruth's disappearance when she switched on the telly Sunday morning. The young female news reporter said that police investigators were now treating the woman's disappearance as a potential crime and were deeply concerned for her safety. And, according to her husband, he had returned home late from a night out to discover the front door wide open, upturned furniture and pools of blood in the hallway, and his wife missing. The husband, who is currently still in police custody for questioning, is believed to be the only suspect in the case. When the police arrived at the couple's place of residence, the husband was said to be in an extreme state of intoxication. The suspect vehemently denies any wrongdoing and claims the blood found on his clothing, believed to be that of his wife, was caused by him slipping over when he entered the property.

Mary couldn't believe what she was hearing at first. She sat almost the entire time holding her head between her hands glued to the screen in shock.

The news report then showed a blown-up photograph of Ruth and the cordoned-off property where she was suspected of being abducted, with the request for witnesses or anyone with information that might shed any light on the case to contact the investigation team at the Tunbridge Wells police station.

Though Mary didn't know Ruth's husband well, she couldn't imagine he would have done anything to hurt her, even though they argued a lot together. *But then,* she thought, *who knows what goes on behind closed doors? Maybe he finally snapped!*

Switching on her phone revealed several missed calls, including two on Friday from an unknown caller, who hadn't left a message. She listened to her friends' long-drawn-out recorded messages from earlier on, hoping they might have an update on Ruth, only to hear what she'd already just heard on the news.

When the messages had ended, it dawned on her that maybe those missed calls on Friday could have been her husband checking if she knew where his wife was. It was not uncommon for Ruth to have sleepovers with her friends, especially when her husband was on an alcohol bender.

Mary suddenly felt awful and immediately began dialling the number. Though doubted, even if it were his number, he would answer it, assuming he was probably still in police custody.

'Hello?' said the tired, croaky voice.

Slightly surprised, Mary recognised it was Ruth's husband.

'Jim?' she said, questioning whether she'd made a mistake.

'Yeah,' Jim answered sharply, immediately followed by, 'Listen! If you're another bleedin' news reporter, you can piss off!'

'It's Mary - Ruth's friend. I've just heard the terrible news!'

There was a slight pause. 'Sorry, I thought you were - it's just that I'm being bombarded by bloody news reporters at the moment and –'

'Don't worry - I just wanted to see if there was anything I could do to help, that's all,' she told him. 'I'm surprised you answered the phone. I thought that you might still be –'

'No,' interjected Jim, 'the cops didn't have any concrete evidence to arrest me, so they had to let me go. I'm on my way home now.'

'Oh, you poor thing!' she said, not really knowing what to say to a man whose wife had just gone missing. 'You must be absolutely distraught and consumed with worry!'

'I'm worried sick!' There was a silent pause. 'I didn't kill her – which everyone seems to assume! I love the woman, for Christ's sake! Someone's taken her – I know they have!' Then more heatedly. 'I bet it was the same sicko who raped and murdered that poor innocent girl near here recently – and whom the useless bleedin' cops *still* haven't caught!'

'You don't know that, Jim!' said Mary, giving him some hope while hoping to God that it wasn't true herself.

'Well, something terrible must have happened to her – otherwise, how do you explain the blood, and the table lying on the hall floor … and the porcelain vase smashed to pieces! There was unquestionably a violent struggle!'

Mary couldn't answer that, so instead asked the obvious, 'Have you checked the local hospital? Maybe there was an accident,' she said rapidly, adding, 'she could have fallen and cut herself on the broken va—'

'Yes, yes, yes,' he said, interrupting her impatiently. 'Look, I appreciate your concern, but I've got to go. I can see a horde of reporters and a TV crew outside my house!'

'Okay, Jim. Well, please let me know if you hear any more news.'

'You, likewise,' he said quickly before abruptly ending the call.

Still dressed in her PJs, Mary made herself a

strong black coffee and, skipping breakfast, next rang Mark to see how his auntie was and if he'd heard the disturbing news about Ruth, to which he briefly replied, his auntie's doing fine and recovering in hospital. And he hadn't heard about Ruth's disappearance. Both, lies, of course. 'Oh, I hope to see you soon,' she told him. 'So that we can live happily together in my house!' Then after the short phone call to him, she began ringing around all her and Ruth's close friends.

It was late in the afternoon when Mary finally finished chatting to everyone - and still, no one was any the wiser about Ruth's mysterious disappearance. It was all just supposition.

It had crossed her mind, had Ruth staged the whole thing so she could escape from her husband and start a new life? Well, it happens! Maybe she was having an affair with someone?

Mary quickly dismissed those cynical and unkind thoughts and finally got around to doing some household chores to help take her mind off things - which she quit shortly after starting in favour of painting instead.

When he wasn't sailing, John spent most of his time at his aunt's house, assiduously checking the news channels to find out if the police search parties were getting any warmer in their efforts to find the missing person, Ruth Winters. But as John observed, these searches were as cold as Ruth's dismembered body parts.

As the days agonisingly went by, Mary and her friends slowly began coming to terms with the grim realisation that their friend, Ruth, may be a victim of cold-blooded murder and feared the worst. They helped in organised searches, combing local woodlands for clues, including the ancient woodland known as Chase Wood which is only about a mile from Tunbridge Wells town centre and very close to where Ruth lived.

While Mark/John was away pretending to care for his poor aunt, Mary and he kept in touch with one another, which unbeknownst to her, conveniently kept him updated on the latest developments in the search for her missing friend. Not that John was worried anyone would find Ruth's remains buried in woodlands anymore: he had since returned to the shallow grave to dig them up, having concluded it would be much harder to find someone at the bottom of the English Channel!

Despite John's self-assuredness, however, Mary would soon uncover some ugly truths that would lead her to the grim and shocking discovery of what happened to her best friend, Ruth, and the identity of the person who killed her.

The truth started to unravel when she went to see Ruth's husband at his home on Friday morning. Despite him making it clear that he wanted to be left alone - which she respected at this time of grief

– she possibly had some vital evidence which could help clear his name and needed to see him. She had been in such a state of shock and pre-occupied searching for Ruth's whereabouts that it had only just occurred to her, what if the person who rang the doorbell while she was on the phone with her friend wasn't her husband but was, in fact, her abductor and possibly her killer? If her husband was telling the truth and he hadn't killed her in a drunken fit of rage upon his return home – which she believed to be true – then possibly her theory was correct. The police had already made a statement saying it was unlikely to have been an attempted burglary, as even if a burglar had attacked the victim, why would they then leave empty-handed? And why would they have bothered to abduct her? She had phoned Ruth at around 11 pm, and if her husband could prove he was still in the pub at that time, either from eyewitnesses or CCTV footage, he would have an alibi. There must be a record of the call on her mobile phone.

'Are you sure you don't mind me coming to see you?' Mary asked Ruth's husband.

'Not at all. Please come in – I'll stick the kettle on,' he answered, much more amiable than the last time they spoke. 'I'm sorry if I was a bit curt with you the other day. It's just that –'

'No need to explain!' said Mary as she entered the

front door. Once in the hallway, the hairs on the back of her neck immediately stood up as she imagined the horrors that might have taken place there. Thankfully, there were no traces of blood left on the parquet flooring, and the wooden veneer table was now upright and back in its place, albeit minus the vase. The police had taken all the forensic evidence they could, and apart from the police tape still in place outside the property, one wouldn't even know a crime had taken place there.

'… So, what is this important piece of information you have for me?' asked Jim as he handed her a mug of tea and sat next to her on the settee in the front room.

'Earlier the same night Mary went missing, I was talking with her on her mobile when the doorbell rang,' Mary began to explain.

'… I wish you'd have come forward with this information sooner,' said Jim, grateful nonetheless.

Mary nodded, saying, 'I'm sorry Jim – it's just that my mind has been in such a whirlwind since –'

'Well, hopefully, it will help the police with their investigation. Better late than never!' he said, cracking a smile. 'About 11 pm, you say?'

'Yes.'

'Well, I didn't leave the pub until well past eleven, and I have witnesses to collaborate the fact!' said Jim perkily. 'Of course, it still doesn't prove that whoever rang the bell was the perpetrator, but it is a helpful lead, and hopefully, it'll get me off the hook. Thank you.'

'Ruth and I were – sorry – *are* good friends, and I'm glad to help.'

'It's been an awful ordeal. Not only is my wife missing, presumed dead' – Jim's eyes started to well up – 'but I've had to endure being interrogated on suspicion of her murder!'

Mary rubbed his arm to try and comfort him. 'It must be dreadful for you.'

'And I've been informed that our back garden is going to be excavated.'

'Oh, dear, oh dear,' said Mary, sighing. 'Well, we must contact the police now,' she then said, taking control, 'so that I can give my statement.'

Mary then remembered. 'Do you have Ruth's mobile phone?' she asked, half expecting him to say no, presuming the attacker took it along with his victim.

'Yes, it's in the drawer,' he answered, pointing to the sideboard drawer. Mary's eyes lit up. 'I only came across it this morning! I was just about to take it to the police station when you rang – forensics have been badgering me for it ever since …' He started to get upset again. '… I kept telling them I didn't know where it was. They seem to think that I've hidden it.' He then looked at her curiously. 'Why?'

'Well, the phone's data records will show the time

I rang her and collaborate my story.'

'Of course!' He looked at her, impressed.

Mary chuckled slightly. 'I read a lot of crime novels!'

'Oh!' he remarked, smiling a little broader than previously.

'May I take a look at Ruth's phone?'

'Sure!' He got up to fetch it. 'While you're doing that, I'll give the station a ring.'

Mary took the phone from him.

'I found it in one of my old Wellington boots kept behind the front door, ' he quickly explained on his way out to the hall. 'Though, what the devil it was doing in there is anyone's guess!'

When Ruth opened the door, assuming it was her drunken husband that fateful night, John Stokes had barged in, knocking her backwards, where she must've accidentally – or perhaps purposefully – dropped the phone into the boot.

Switching the phone on, Mary searched the app for her number – it was easy to find as hers was the last call made. Bingo! The call log read: 11.05 pm.

While holding her friend's phone in her hand, she recalled the awkward conversation she had with her: Ruth proclaiming that Mark Simpson was not who he claimed to be – which saddened her even more.

With another press of a button, Mary accessed Ruth's email messages. And there it was: the last unfinished draft Ruth had written to her, detailing what she had unearthed about her new lover so far.

The email message read:

Hi, sweetie!

It was fab to see you at the café earlier today. Now please, don't take this the wrong way, as I know you are very fond of Mark Simpson; but as a dear friend, I felt compelled to inform you about some truths I have unearthed about him you need to know.

There was something about the man which aroused my curiosity and suspicion today. So, I contacted Reuter's International, whom he claims to work for, and they told me they had never heard of him! Then I remembered you mentioning a little while back that Mark was mistaken for someone else called Corporal John Stokes by a fellow ex-Marine and decided (with great effort) to dig up Mark's military records.

Firstly, I found nobody listed as Corporal Mark Simpson; however, there was a Lance Corporal with that name. But his photo looked nothing like the Mark Simpson you know – and he died about ten years ago from combat injuries. Then I searched for Corporal John Stokes: and sure enough, there he was – the spitting image (albeit younger) of the guy you are dating! And get this: he received the Military Cross for attempting to save the life of – wait for it – none other than *Lance Corporal Mark Simpson!* Digging further into his medical records, I discovered that the Royal Marines discharged him from the military on medical grounds – not because of the physical injuries he sustained while on tours of duty in Afghanistan, but because of his severe mental state.

He's a loon, Mary! Stay the hell away from

The email abruptly ended there.

Oh my God! Mary mouthed inaudibly. She felt like she'd been kicked in the stomach and wanted to be sick. Switching the phone off, Mary tossed it onto the settee and dashed into the hall where Jim was still speaking on the landline to the police. 'Can I use your toilet!' she quickly managed to blurt out before pushing the downstairs toilet door open and throwing up down the pan without waiting for his answer.

Part of her once again wanted to ignore what Ruth had discovered. But this was something she could no longer do! *What if John Stokes had abducted her and killed her?* she thought. *And what if I'm next?!* She felt frightened!

'Are you alright in there?' Jim called out upon hearing her discomfort.

'Yes – yes, I'm fine, thank you,' she called back to him after wiping away the puke and saliva dangling from her lower lip.

She agreed to go to the police station immediately with Jim and give evidence, not mentioning for now what she had discovered about the man she had believed – and still desperately wanted to believe – was Mark Simpson. She wanted to wait until she got home and investigate this mystery man for herself – in case Ruth had got it all wrong.

CHAPTER TWENTY-SIX

Mary returned home from the police station - having given her evidence - and after making sure she'd locked all the windows and doors, switched on her laptop and immediately began her investigation into the real identity of Mark Simpson.

The glasses she wore to read were no longer rose-tinted, her head now as clear. She recalled his dissociative behaviour, like recently when his mood suddenly changed and he abandoned her at her house, and the ease with which he lied - personality traits often associated with dangerous minds.

By the end of the afternoon, she had found all the information she needed. Ruth was right: his real name was John Stokes; he didn't work for Reuters International, and the military had discharged him on medical grounds for having severe mental issues. Even more shocking, Mary discovered that

John Stokes was a wanted man!

Christ! What do I do? she asked herself as she paced up and down her kitchen while her cat blissfully continued munching away at the treats in her bowl. Though she had no proof it was John Stokes who had abducted and possibly murdered her friend Ruth or had committed the other atrocious crimes she had read about, she no longer trusted him and certainly didn't want to see him again. She couldn't bear the thought of confronting him directly over the phone about what she knew – listening to him tell her one lie after another as he had on so many occasions – so she decided to end their relationship by text instead. Nervously, she hit the send button. Done! Hopefully, she would never have to see him again.

Just then, her doorbell rang. *Oh, fuck! What if it's him?!* Mary at once thought. It was times like this when she wished she'd installed CCTV cameras or one of those new Amazon Ring Video Doorbell devices that everyone except her – and Ruth – seemed to have. She started to panic. The doorbell rang again. When Mary last spoke to Mark/John, he never mentioned anything about him returning to Tunbridge Wells today. Maybe he had wanted to surprise her? She reminded herself of the times he'd done that before. *Ignore it,* she recommended to herself. Then it rang a third time. *'Fuck! Fuck! Fuck!'* she heard herself saying now – and she never usually swore. She thought about calling the police. But she'd need to check who it was first, or she could be wasting valuable police time, not to mention looking foolish. *Stop panicking,* she told herself, *and go and check. I bet it is him!*

She grabbed one of the remaining large kitchen knives and, hiding it behind her back, cautiously headed for the front door.

'Who's there?' she nervously asked behind the safety of her locked and bolted front door.

'It's Steve – your husband!' he called out to her. 'I got the ferry across from France this morning.'

There was a brief silence.

'Are you gonna open the bleedin' door and let me in or not?' he then asked her somewhat impatiently.

'What the fuck are you doing here?!' she asked as she tossed the carbon steel knife behind the door with a clang.

'You know what the fuck I'm doing here! It was you who emailed me last week, remember? … To tell me that you've got a new bloke in your life and that you finally agreed to get a divorce and sell the property!'

'Yeah, but I didn't expect you to come here in person to discuss it!' she responded, sounding annoyed. Then sarcastically, 'I forgot that you find it difficult to spell and form sentences!'

'Ouch! That was a bit harsh.'

'Anyway, I thought you were living in Dubai?'

'Look, it's a long story,' said her husband as they continued talking through the door. 'I haven't lived there for two years. Let's just say I took an extended holiday to the South of France.'

'You went on the run you mean!'

The pair were almost shouting by now.

'Look! Do you wanna talk about getting a divorce and selling the house or not?'

'Yes, I do!' she replied as she reluctantly unbolted the door. Her parents were right: this house had brought her nothing but bad luck, and she would now be glad to sell it and move somewhere safe and remote. 'Just a min—'

Suddenly, Mary let out an almighty scream. She could feel herself being dragged forcibly backwards away from the door, unable to stop it from happening, struggling to breathe as the large muscular tattooed arm locked around her throat.

'MARY!' shouted Steve, concerned, still locked out of his house. 'WHAT'S HAPPENING?!'

'Don't let him in, Mary!' said the well-familiar voice, whose after-shave was equally distinct. 'He wants to kill you!'

It was John Stokes. He had been hiding in wait in the cupboard under the stairs - the very same frightening cupboard his father had put him in as punishment when he was a small boy. The graffiti doodles he had etched into the walls out of sheer boredom using his pocketknife with only the light from a small hand torch to see by still visible – a stark reminder of his dark past – how he had so much wanted to use that knife on his father.

Yes, it was the same house he grew up in with his late mother and father as a child. And the same house of horrors now as it was back then.

'How did you get in?!' she tried to ask, shocked. But her question went unanswered.

'LET ME IN!' Steve commanded while banging his fist repeatedly against the solid oak door.

John continued ranting about how Steve had tried to blackmail him into killing her, and because he refused, Steve had now come to kill her himself. But just as he had claimed that UAE dignitaries had raped and murdered the Filipino hotel worker and assassins had killed Suzie and the Frenchman at Steve's Villa: these were all just fantasies – delusions and hallucinations manifested in his warped and twisted mind. He alone carried out those heinous acts of crime.

Knowing what Mary knew about him now, she didn't believe a single word he uttered but tried to keep calm and go along with what her unhinged captor said.

Steve began kicking against the door. 'WHO'S THAT IN THERE WITH YOU?!' he called out frantically to no response, desperate to gain entrance. 'LET HER GO OR I'LL FUCKING KILL

YOU, D'YA HEAR!'

Along the hall, Mary glided past the cupboard under the stairs, past the severed telephone cable wire, and into the kitchen, where he let go of her onto the cold marble flooring.

Ever since John's father bequeathed his estate to his other son - his illegitimate son and John's half-brother Steve Reynolds - in his will, filled with bitterness and hate, John vowed he would one day reclaim what he believed was rightfully his - by whatever means. And although John knew of his late father's favourite son's existence, Steve, on the other hand, never knew he had a half-brother. Even when they met each other for the first time in Dubai - which John instigated - Steve never imagined John and he were related - even though many similarities might suggest it.

Abruptly changing the subject from Steve's intentions to kill her, while standing straddled over her, he firmly told her that they couldn't sell the property because it wasn't theirs to sell; and then began telling her about his right to the property. Terrified, Mary continued to keep quiet while he spoke - convinced now that he had murdered Ruth and God knows how many other poor souls.

The banging on the front door then stopped.

'... I was happy to share the house with you, Mary,' he confided, 'but no, you had to go and spoil it by snooping on me just like your nosy friend had before I put an end to that!'

Desperately worried about what he might do next, she finally spoke: 'Let's talk about it before you do anything further you might regret,' she said as she continued looking up at him, forcing a smile.

'We could've been happy together, Mary!' John told her with a cold, unsmiling stare.

'We still can be, darling!' she replied to him sweetly in an attempt to conciliate him.

'It's too late,' John told her upon hearing his father's grave voice inside his head tell him *You know what you've got to do now – what you should have done a while ago!*

Daring to allow her eyes to wander as he continued to waffle; looking for a means of escape, she noticed a rusty old key left in the back door she didn't recognise. It was the old backdoor key, kept hidden in the garden under a large rockery stone since John's childhood, and now used once again to gain access to the property whenever he chose.

'… I wish there could've been another way!' he finally said before descending upon her, using his body mass to pin her down. She instinctively screamed before his massive hands wrapped tightly around her tiny throat, putting a stop to that. She pathetically slapped him repeatedly across the head and scratched his face as she futilely writhed around, kicking her legs about, desperately trying to escape.

Then she saw Steve through the kitchen window. He was holding a large piece of rock above his head and about to throw it (she had never been more pleased to see him).

Following the rock smashing through the window, everything that followed happened frenetically. Steve quickly reached inside, undid the lock and burst through the door screaming at John to let go of her. And with no time to contemplate what the fuck John Stokes was doing there, let alone strangling his wife, he pounced on top of him, pulling him off of Mary. Mary quickly gasped for air before scrambling away to crouch in a corner and watch in terror as the two Titans battled it out.

As the half-brothers grappled on the floor amongst the shards of broken glass, John freed himself from Steve's tenacious headlock by pulling a lighter out of his pocket and burning one of his elbows (a trick he'd learnt not in Afghanistan but from the streets where he grew up). 'Argh!' screamed Steve in pain, immediately letting go. John then elbowed his opponent square in the face, dazing him, and, quickly pulling himself up, began kicking him repeatedly in the stomach.

'STOP IT!' Mary screamed to no avail.

John then turned and started to head for the island where Mary kept the kitchen knives, but Steve grabbed his lower right leg firmly with both hands, stopping him.

'Stop this madness!' Steve said, spitting blood. 'What the *fuck's* wrong with you!' It was not the John Stokes he knew in Dubai – or thought he knew.

'D'ya wanna list!' swiftly responded John, twisting around and taking a swipe at Steve's head and missing.

'Call the police!' Steve shouted across to Mary, who was still in shock.

Mary had left her mobile phone on the dining room table at the other end of the kitchen. Coughing, she began crawling along the glass-littered floor on her bare hands and knees to fetch it amidst the grunting and groaning from the other two.

Steve reached up and grabbed John's polo shirt with his right hand, ripping it as he pulled him down towards him and hooked his left arm around his neck before twisting him around and throwing him over his left knee and onto his back.

Without hesitation, Steve threw himself onto his crazed opponent and, sat straddling him, began throwing punches at his head. 'It was *you* who killed Suzie, wasn't it?!'

John didn't answer and seemed to enjoy taking the punishment.

'WASN'T IT?!' Steve then screamed at him angrily, demanding to know. 'FUCKIN' ANSWER ME!'

'... YES! IS THAT WHAT YOU WANNA FUCKIN' HEAR!' John screamed back at him, spotting the piece of jagged rock just about within his reach. 'I did you a favour, you ungrateful bastard – she was sleeping with the young Frenchman!'

Steve ignored what was now old news, asking instead, 'So, killing all those armed assassins at the villa was all bullshit then?'

John, or perhaps it was William, began grinning and nodded.

'And I suppose that story you fed me about how you bravely tried to save the stewardess at the hotel before being clobbered over the head was bullshit, too!' Steve continued to ask, now throwing fewer punches.

John nodded again, seeming to find it amusing – though, about what exactly, it was hard to tell. 'Except I *did* get hit over the head. Before I killed her, the bitch put up a strong fight and, in the struggle, grabbed a nearby empty Champagne bottle and caught me with it!' Then more soberly, '... I didn't intend to kill her – it's just that she wouldn't stop screaming, and she left me with no choice.'

Steve shook his head. '... WHY, JOHN?'

John laughed mockingly as he let his younger half-brother continue bashing him about. 'You have no fuckin' idea, do you?!'

Steve stopped punching him. 'No fuckin' idea about what?' questioned Steve as he stared directly into John's dead eyes, perplexed and feeling exhausted.

'You can blame our evil father!'

'What?!'

John laughed again. 'You are my half-brother – you stupid cunt!' he finally revealed.

Slouched over him while feebly pinning him down still, Steve listened wide-eyed while John continued, glad to take a breather.

Sounding bitter, John next told him: '*I* should have inherited this house and all the rest of the old bastard's assets, *not* you!'

'You're deluded!'

'Not about that I'm fuckin' not!'

'And so, you thought you'd just help yourself to my possessions – women included?!' snarled Steve, even more angrily.

Smirking, John snapped back. 'Listen, their lives became fucked-up the moment they met cha! And I wanted you to feel the same suffering and pain I felt all these years – you low-life piece of shit –'

Steve punched him in the face again, causing his nose to bleed.

'*Argh!* Good punch, brother!' mocked John.

'You're no brother of mine!'

John just laughed.

By now, Mary had her phone in her hand and,

ignoring the fragments of glass embedded deep into her bloody knees and hands, terrified and shaking, began dialling 999.

'Even if you'd succeeded in killing the pair of us,' stated Steve, 'whatever made you think you'd be able to take possession of our house, you deranged psycho?!'

'Ouch!' John quickly responded by saying, acting horrified. 'I prefer emotionally unbalanced.' He purposely let out a maniacal laugh, then calmly gave Steve his answer while at the same time furtively reaching for the rock with his outstretched right hand. '… I no longer intend to reclaim the house. I had hoped to move in with Mary, but she's gone off me – like all the other bitches I meet. No, I intend to burn the house down with the pair of you in it. I've already loaded the kerosene into the shed, ready to complete my mission. If I can't have it, then nobody else will!'

Grabbing the rock firmly between the outstretched fingers of his right hand, John swung it rapidly towards Steve's head, knocking him out instantly – maybe killing him?

Preoccupied, waiting desperately for the operator to hurry-the-fuck-up and answer her bleedin' call, and her view partially blocked by the island, Mary hadn't realised that John was the victor.

Cut, battered, and bruised, John got up and, no longer hindered, went and grabbed one of the kitchen knives.

'Emergency, which service?' asked the irritatingly calmly spoken female operator.

Scared shitless, Mary screamed, dropped the phone, and began to run. John was coming for her with only the island between them!

Brandishing the large kitchen knife in his right hand, John sped around the far end of the island chasing after her with only one intent in mind: to kill her.

Her best chance of escape was out the front door, hoping to God some passers-by could save her – and preferably walking a fucking great big German Shepherd dog – better still, two fucking great big German Shepherd dogs.

She knew it was pointless exiting through the open kitchen door because the side gate was locked with a padlock and Steve had most probably climbed over it, which for her diminutive height would be a struggle.

Now aware of Steve's body lying motionless on the floor, unsure if he was dead or not, she jumped over him and continued running towards the hallway. The sight of blood that now engulfed Steve's head convinced her he probably was dead. But she was no longer screaming; all she wanted to focus on was reaching the front door and getting the fuck out of there.

Mary knew it was hopeless trying to escape, but

she wanted to choose when she died. Not let someone else make that choice if she could help it. The same as in the past when she decided to commit suicide and end her life – it was her choice! So, fuck John Stokes! She wasn't going to make it easy for him!

Not daring to glance over her shoulder, heart pounding, Mary ran straight into the hall. If she had looked over her shoulder, she would have seen that John was no longer running; he was calmly walking her way – but he was long-legged and took long strides.

Then, just as she undid the latch and began opening the door, she felt her head smash against it and then fall to a heap on the doormat. Blood dripped profusely down her face, but she was still conscious, still alive! A sharp shove in the back from John Stokes was all it took.

Grabbing Mary by the hair with his left hand, he dragged her screaming in agony away from the door and released her in the middle of the hall, where he had more space. Then with his back facing toward the kitchen, he knelt beside her and raised the sharp-pointed knife in readiness to stab her.

Except, it wasn't Mary he saw lying there helpless, the same as it hadn't been the other victims he'd seen before he slaughtered them either: it was his father.

Now, if John had been facing the other way, he would've been aware of his half-brother approaching him from behind, carrying the same bloodied rock he had used on him.

Now it was Steve's turn to get his revenge. The talking was over – it was now a matter of kill or be killed! Feeling dazed, with blood still trickling down the side of his head, he raised the rock and swung it towards John's head. But John reacted quickly, moving his upper body swiftly forward and over to the left while tucking his head into his chin, avoiding the full impact of the blow as the rock brushed against the target.

For the moment, anyway, Mary was spared. However, Steve was less fortunate. As John dodged out of the way, he swung the knife behind him, stabbing Steve in his upper right thigh. But with his adrenalin pumping as much as it was, it felt no more painful than a needle prick administered by an overzealous military nurse; and grabbing John firmly by the wrist with his left hand – with the tip of the blade still embedded into his flesh – he kept him held in this position while simultaneously swinging the rock back the other way and, this time, succeeding in swiping it directly against John's head – cracking his skull open.

Meanwhile, while still lying with her back against the floor, using her arms and legs, Mary managed to slide backwards and remove herself from harm's way. Then, slowly standing up, she staggered over to where she earlier dropped the knife and picked it up.

As Steve attempted to hit John with the rock a third time, John rolled onto his back and, tucking his knees tightly into his chest, kicked Steve with such force it knocked him backwards, causing him to release John's wrist and drop the rock.

John scrambled to his feet, leaving Steve bewildered as to how his opponent was still conscious, let alone able to stand. But it was Steve now in possession of the weapon. He grabbed hold of the bloody knife - which due to its size and weight dangled from his meaty thigh - and pulled it sharply out of his leg, releasing even more blood. John quickly removed his ripped and blood-soiled shirt, throwing it to one side before clenching his fists and tensing his pectoral muscles in a show of primal strength.

The two silverback-like combatants then squared off, each waiting for the other to make the first move.

As they partially circled ant-clockwise around the spacious hall, Steve caught sight of Mary, standing in the corner brandishing a knife. 'Keep behind me!' he told her as he stood between John and her, shielding her as best he could.

Steve tossed his knife back and forth between his hands a few times, attempting to confuse his foe, whose eyes watched the glistening blade constantly as the last rays of sunlight caught it through a westerly window. Then Steve made his move, slashing John right across the chest.

Mary took a sharp intake of breath. Despite all the despicable atrocities John had committed, she still hated seeing anyone get hurt.

John attempted to grab the knife but failed, sustaining another laceration to the chest. He was beginning to look like Bruce Lee in the movie Enter the Dragon – only much taller and broader, and he didn't make those weird, funny noises Bruce Lee made! His immediate response was to kick Steve's injured leg, causing him considerable pain, before retreating to avoid being caught by another slash from Steve's carving knife.

Both had lost a lot of blood and were now extremely weak, but each was determined to be the victor and continued fighting.

The stairs were right behind John. Turning, he made haste for them to give himself a height advantage. As he reached the fifth or sixth step, he was suddenly aware that Steve was chasing him. John made his way a little farther up the stairs, then glancing over his shoulder, he suddenly stopped and executed a back kick to Steve's face, sending him flying backwards and landing on his back at the bottom of the stairs with an audible thud.

The front door was ajar – so Mary could've easily

escaped by now. But she hadn't because she was too caught up in the moment to give it a second thought. And besides, when she saw Steve was still alive, her natural caring instincts were to stay and help him. A medic doesn't cowardly flee the battlefield to avoid danger and save only themselves - and they care for the enemy also (except when one is alone with a madman who is trying to kill you!).

John immediately hurried down three or four steps before throwing himself at Steve. 'LOOK OUT, STEVE!' Mary called out to him, but it was too late: before she could even get the words out, John was already on top of him and had begun strangling him. Still gripping the knife, Steve attempted to stab John between the ribs, but John had his arms securely pinned to the ground with his knees. Steve also tried using his legs to free himself, but he wasn't as flexible as he once was, and due to his stab wound he found it impossible.

For a brief moment, Mary just stood there, frozen to the spot in horror, not knowing what to do as she watched her estranged husband slowly and painfully dying. She thought of the disrespectful way he had treated her and the upset and suffering he had caused her. The number of times she'd cursed him and wished him dead even. Why not let him suffer a painful and miserable death? But despite how much she loathed him, he had courageously saved her life. Then she saw Steve's face turn blue.

Now, at this point, if she had charged over to John with the knife raised above her head, screaming her head off, and plunged it straight into his neck, severing his jugular vein, then this whole ordeal would've been over. John would be dead! However, she didn't do that. What she did instead was to charge over to him, knife raised above her head, screaming her head off, and stuck it into his upper right arm (well, as a doctor, she was trained to save lives, not take them!).

But at least she achieved her objective of causing John to immediately let go of Steve, which enabled him to breathe again.

She quickly withdrew the blade before John could grab it and threw it onto the floor behind her (she couldn't face stabbing him again), then moved swiftly behind him and, clasping her hands together as if praying, put them under his chin and, with all her might, yanked him off of Steve.

'What are you doin', Mary?! I was trying to protect you from him!' John told her, almost shocked that she would do such a thing.

Oh yeah, like when you had your hands tightly squeezed around my throat! thought Mary, deeply angry.

It took Steve a moment or two to recover. He'd fallen in and out of consciousness. He could hear

Mary screaming at John, calling him a monster – which he hated – and, turning his head to the left, with blurry vision, he saw him elbow her in the stomach, causing her to double over in pain and let go of him. He then realised he was still holding the knife. And with a sweeping action, using his left hand for support as he moved over onto his left side, he stuck the point of the blade into John's gut.

John stumbled backwards, bumping into Mary, before tripping over himself and falling onto his backside. Spotting where she'd dropped the knife, she quickly went over and picked it up as Steve, with the knife still in his hand, began frantically crawling towards his downed assailant, going for the kill.

'KILL HIM, MARY!' John shouted. But his plea wasn't directed at Mary Reynolds: it was to his aunt Mary, who was now standing in the wide-open front doorway, looking as mean and scary as fuck, with a pump-action shotgun in her hands.

'STOP RIGHT FUCKING THERE!' she screeched. 'AND DROP YA WEAPONS NOW!'

Reluctantly, Steve and Mary did as ordered.

John smirked and immediately went to grab one of the knives.

'Leave it!' she demanded her nephew, less shouty. She then continued talking directly to him. 'I thought this is where you'd be.' Then as if talking to a child, she told him sweetly, 'You've done

enough killing, Johnny-boy!' Then, pointing the gun straight at him, she said without emotion, '... I'm sorry!' and shot him dead!

The End.

Acknowledgements

A big thanks to Steve Wyse for making my visions of the book cover a reality!

Printed in Great Britain
by Amazon

44880958R00239